A Fish Could Love A Bird

Sheila Clarke

iUniverse, Inc.
New York   Bloomington

A Fish Could Love A Bird

iUniverse books may be ordered through booksellers or by contacting:

iUniverse
1663 Liberty Drive
Bloomington, IN 47403
www.iuniverse.com
1-800-Authors (1-800-288-4677)

Because of the dynamic nature of the Internet, any Web addresses or links contained in this book may have changed since publication and may no longer be valid. The views expressed in this work are solely those of the author and do not necessarily reflect the views of the publisher, and the publisher hereby disclaims any responsibility for them.

ISBN: 978-1-4502-6156-2 (sc)
ISBN: 978-1-4502-6157-9 (ebook)

Library of Congress Control Number: 2010914985

Printed in the United States of America

iUniverse rev. date: 10/20/2010

For all the remarkable women who have touched my life

"Wheresoever you go,
Go with all your heart."

—*Confucius*

Chapter 1

FOUR IS AN UNLUCKY number. Poor four. Picked on because Chinese people pronounce it *si* which sounds similar to their word for *death*. There we sat, on Flight 414 in seats 44A and 44B as we left the Vancouver Airport en route to Kuala Lumpur. All those fours did not bode well for our new life together in Malaysia. My clammy white hand was enveloped by the dry darker hand of Wong Lee Chen, my husband of two weeks. In spite of my cosy buttercup-yellow sweater and a blanket stamped *Air Malaysia* wrapped around my knees, I felt cold. Sweat beaded on my forehead and my scalp felt as tight as a shrunken wool toque. Even my red curls felt more tightly sprung than usual.

I had just said goodbye to three of my loves: my mother, my father, and my country. Only minutes ago, my parents and I had stood like valiant soldiers in the Vancouver Airport, bidding farewell. Without any warning, I found myself weeping softly. Just as suddenly, my quiet tears escalated into a noise that resembled an animal headed for slaughter. My mother, though more restrained, followed suit. Dad, with his own tears barely managing not to overflow, put his strong arms around us. Chen stood on the sidelines appearing uneasy. There would be no hugging in public for him. Besides, this was an intense and private time for my family. My leaving would be the second huge loss my parents had been dealt in three months. At departure time, I was inclined not to look back, but I knew my dad would wave until we were completely out of sight. He did. I blew kisses and Chen waved as we walked away backwards. Passing through the security gate screamed of finality. If I wanted to run back to Mom and Dad, now was the time. For a fleeting moment it was tempting. I inched closer to my sweetheart.

With the runway behind us and the safety procedures message droning in the background, we felt a sense of relief from the stress of preparations for our wedding and honeymoon, interspersed with passports, shots, flight arrangements, packing—not for a few weeks, but possibly for a lifetime. Oh yes, and there was Chen's graduation from med school, Class of 2000, at the University of British Columbia the week before our wedding.

"It's time for us to go easy, Lauren. We'll have a seventeen hour gap between our strenuous year in Canada and whatever lies ahead for us in Malaysia. Let's try to relax."

"Yes." I mumbled, "Whatever lies ahead of us in Malaysia. That's the question."

"At least I know I have a job. I feel really lucky about that," Chen said.

"Yeah, I'd say that having a promise of a job four years before you graduate is a slice of Chinese luck."

The only other pre-planned arrangement was that we, arriving penniless, would live with Chen's parents. When I made some mundane remark about the changes he would find after being away for four years, he said, "Changes aren't a concern of mine. The only change that concerns me is my new wife and wondering if I can make her happy. Living with my parents will not be easy for you."

We'd had that discussion before but, maybe naively, I still wasn't anticipating a problem.

"I'm certainly expecting to like *them*," I said.

"They'll probably *like* you, but that doesn't mean they'll be happy about our marriage. I'm sure they'd hoped to have had some involvement in my choice of wife. In the days when marriages were arranged, it meant that two whole families were uniting. I've heard that in China there are over twenty-thousand registered matchmakers. Marriage was far too important to leave to the children. Love was not a factor—in fact, it was a negative."

"Are you serious? Why was that?"

"I suppose the husband's family thought love would weaken the authority of the mother over her daughter-in-law. Of course, traditions tend to be more relaxed in Malaysia than in China, but certainly some issues remain important."

"Your parents *said* they hoped we'd be happy."

"They did, but it might have just been my skilfully written letter to them. That letter might even have left them feeling thankful I was coming home at all. The fact that your father is a doctor will work in our favour. I'm not sure what to expect."

I didn't favour the idea of being more acceptable to the Wongs because of my dad's profession. I didn't like it at all, but decided to stuff it into the hamper with a lot other things that needed washing.

Chen was the *first son* of Wong So Kwok and Tan Soon Siok. That was plain and simply why we were on that airplane. His parents expected him to bring honour to the family and secure their future needs. They had both toiled for years to make it possible for Chen to go to medical school overseas. Wong owned a modest rubber plantation near their home in Taman Damai in the center of Malaysia. His mother, Tan, contributed by running a beauty salon. Chen was expected to work hard as well. Fortunately he was a bright and motivated student who earned stellar marks. With extra support from his father's wealthy brother in Singapore, Chen's opportunity was realized.

"It's tradition," Chen said. "I've always known exactly what my parents expected. I've achieved what was expected. Now I'm going home. Everything is just as they had planned, except for you."

"Whew! That makes me feel like an extra piece in a puzzle—totally redundant."

"Sorry, lah. Let's not get stuck on it. You're the one who taught me to expect the best. Besides, we're supposed to be relaxing, not thrashing out our differences and difficulties."

When the stewardess asked us what we'd like to drink, Chen said, with a chuckle, "I'm going to have orange juice, for old time's sake. I had my first taste of orange juice four years ago on my first flight. It was so sour it made me... what's the word?"

"Pucker?"

"Yeah, pucker. I've missed the tasty juices in Malaysia. People drink a lot because of the heat. You'll see people carrying drinks in plastic bags, tied with plastic strings or you may see bags hanging from a tree branch while the owner is working or playing."

"Sounds like an accident waiting to happen." Then, not wanting to give up a chance to wave the eco flag, I added, "Besides, never-break-down-plastic bags suspended by never-break-down-plastic strings, doesn't impress me."

"Maybe not, but keep in mind that Malaysia is considered a third world country. You won't like everything you see."

"I'm sure you didn't like everything you saw when you came to Canada." I thought of Chen—four years younger and leaving his family as I had just done today.

"How did you *feel* when you left for Canada?"

"Shaky. In fact, when you were saying good-bye to your parents today, I thought of mine when I was leaving for Canada. They were all at the airport—my parents, my brother Lee Fang, and my sister Lee Yee. My brother had been teasing me for weeks about the beautiful Canadian women and Lee Yee kept thinking of more things she would like me to bring back for her from Canada. But as it became time for me to go they were unusually quiet. This was the fulfillment of the plan that had driven my parents for years and actually seeing me leave left them speechless, and as far as I knew, emotionless."

"No Chen. There's no way your family could have felt emotionless. Surely your mother had tears, didn't she?"

"I've never seen my mother cry, but I knew that she would miss me. Often I had lifted my eyes up from my homework and caught her smiling at me with a mixture of love and sadness."

"That makes me happy, Chen. I feel some kinship with your mother already."

Our chatter was interrupted by the arrival of dinner. Lifting the plastic cover exposed white fish, rice, some over-cooked vegetables, a foil package of chilli sauce and canned lychee nuts for dessert. Bland, soft and colourless as it was, it provided some diversion.

Warmed by dinner and Chinese tea, Chen and I felt weary and decided to try to sleep. After putting the seats in the reclining position, we drew both blankets together and tugged them up to our chins, making a feeble tent. With the small pillows behind our necks and the window blind down, we put our bodies as close together as we could, and tried to sleep. Chen beat me to it. I knew he had zonked by his regular breathing and the soft, whispering sounds issuing forth. My sweetie, sleeping so peacefully, had no facial hair. His skin was flawless and his carefully combed, shiny, black hair flipped up at the front, with the help of gel. His body was strong, lean, and long. Even his fingers and toes were long. As usual, he looked scrubbed and unwrinkled. I kissed his forehead gently.

My mind wouldn't stop darting between my home in Vancouver and my future home in Malaysia. I was not at peace. The unknown abounded. Chen was *going* home; I was *leaving* home. He was asleep; I was awake, dwelling on my future. In a critical mood, my brother Richard had once said, "It's easy to love someone, but could you make a life together?" Though part of me was concerned, marrying Chen and going to live in Malaysia had been my choice. I should be fine. After all, I'm an adventurer. I crave the experience of living in Southeast Asia—walking on the beaches, swimming in South China Sea, travelling to neighbouring countries and learning about new cultures. I'm also an artist. In the spirit of an artist, I want to create, to express my feelings and open my heart and soul to all that there is. Most importantly, I love Chen. I love his mind, his body, his calmness and caring. I had dated a variety of guys—from frat-party types to jocks and nerds. Entanglements in the past had left me feeling alone and abandoned. But Chen and I complemented each other. I was excitable, he was calm; I tended to be impetuous, he stayed on an even keel; I thought creatively, and he, logically. We were compatible. Chen had arrived at the same conclusion more easily than I. He was born under the sign of the Monkey and I under the sign of the Dragon. Monkeys and Dragons are compatible. That was that. I recognized that I seized onto Chen for the comfort and security of our relationship, with a challenging adventure thrown in. And yet now, as the time approached, I felt apprehension. I got vibes that I was walking into a culture that would have definite expectations of me—expectations that may curb the freedom I'd grown up with in Canada. Would I have patience and tolerance? This adventure was not mountain biking at Moab or windsurfing at the Gorge. The stakes were high in this one. Some of my parents' friends simply would not, or could not, understand my choice of husband. Actually, some of my own friends were almost as bad—even my brother! That *really* punched me. Now, a matter of hours away from my new life on the other side of the world, I still expected things to be wonderful. Why then, did little doubts and concerns flit around my curls like bees waiting to sting?

The snack cart bulldozed its way down the aisle. I knew it was important to sleep. I tried the visualization process to stop my mind from focussing on my uncertainties. I thought of Jericho Beach in the early morning. The sun was coming up slowly… slowly… reflecting on the water in English Bay. The waves were lapping slowly in… slowly out… slowly in… slowly out… slowly…

I think I slept for several hours. When I awoke the cart was back, clattering and lurching along the aisle with cold, wet terry-towels to refresh the passengers in preparation for breakfast.

Yawning, Chen looked at his watch. "We'll be in Hong Kong in five hours. Won't it be good to get out and stretch?"

"Yes. I just hope I can walk. My legs feel as if I'd run a marathon. Any chance of a Starbucks in Hong Kong? How long will we be there?"

"Haven't a clue about a Starbucks. We'll only be a bit over one hour in Hong Kong. Then we'll be on the last lap. Should get into Kuala Lumpur around three this afternoon."

"Good. Who'll come to meet us?"

"My dad, I guess. My mother will want to prepare the meal. Auntie Tan Soon Lai will probably help her. She'll see it as a ticket to be part of the action. She won't want to miss this opportunity to check you out!"

"Really, Chen? Is she just curious, or is she a real dragon lady?"

"She's definitely curious. I'll leave it to you to decide if she's a dragon lady."

We shuffled along the Hong Kong Airport, me pulling my hand luggage, including my lap top computer which I wouldn't let out of my sight, and Chen's backpack bobbing up and down on his back. Never had I been surrounded by such an international crowd. Seas of people wearing saris, *kabyas, tedungs*, business suits and European and North American tourists looking as if they were at the beach already rather than at the airport in a sophisticated city. I was amazed to see the variety of shops. Besides the large Duty Free shops, there were countless others selling jewellery, silk clothing, books, candy, toys and cheap souvenirs. My heart leaped when we found a Starbucks, but my excitement evaporated when I realized we didn't have any Hong Kong money.

"Let's ask if they'll take Visa," I said.

"Surely not for two cups of coffee… but ask in case."

They did accept my Visa. Chen laced his coffee with sugar

and cream and stirred it briskly. I chose a coffee mocha with whipped cream and a shake or three of nutmeg. I ran my tongue back and forth through the whipped cream, then sipped slowly, savouring every swallow as if it were the last one I'd have for a long time—which it well might be.

We felt almost perky by the time we re-boarded.

"Only six more hours to go, *mon bijou*, my jewel," Chen said.

"*Only* six! That's quite enough! How about if I put my head on your lap and my butt and feet on 44B?"

Chen hesitated before he agreed. I knew he wasn't thrilled with my suggestion, but he also knew I hadn't been able to sleep much and that my patience was nearly spent. I felt myself relax as he stroked my cheek, but from my cheek down, I felt totally uncomfortable. After a lot of wiggling and twisting I gave up. I took out my sketch book, and began drawing the land from my aerial perspective.

"Hey! Look, Chen! Look at the map. We'll soon be flying over Malaysia!"

The latest picture to appear on the screen showed the position of our plane in relation to our destination. We could see Malaysia at last—a long, narrow peninsula, suspended from Thailand and fading into the Andaman Sea on the north, the South China Sea on the east, the Strait of Malacca on the west and Singapore, sitting on the equator, on the southernmost tip of Malaysia. My arms and neck were tingling with a wave of excitement… and just a tinge of apprehension.

"Sit in the window seat, Lauren," said Chen, standing up and changing places with me. "It's good we're arriving on a clear day. I want you to see the beaches and the colours of the water. Nearly the whole eastern side of Malaysia has sandy beaches. Tourists are just beginning to discover them. There are quite a few resorts north of Kuantan. I want to take you there sometime."

"Good. I'll be ready! How far are the beaches from Taman Damai?"

"Four or five hours, I suppose. I haven't been, you know. My family doesn't go away on holidays—except sometimes to visit family. I've just heard about the resorts and seen them from the air."

"It's like we're sitting in an aerie looking down on the world," I said.

"What's an aerie? I've never heard that word."

"It's a high nest for a bird of prey, like an eagle. They have incredible eye sight and can see their next meal from great heights."

"Okay. Sounds like a good word. I'll file it away."

I smiled, imagining the inside of Chen's brilliant mind lined with endless files—all colour-coded. Yes. There it is: *aerie,* right between *aerial* and *aeriferous.* Of course.

The flight attendants had collected our blankets and headphones and were offering a final beverage when we swooped like eagles over Singapore.

Heading north to Kuala Lumpur with my nose on the window, I said, "Those trees look like thousands of shiny stars from here. What kind are they?"

"They're oil palms. Look. We're flying over the state of Johor now. Next it will be Negeri Sembilan. Selangor is Federal Territory and it surrounds KL."

"Hey, enough! I have to learn this stuff a bit at a time."

"Sorry," said Chen, looking apologetic. "You're right."

According to the flight captain we would be landing in Kuala Lumpur in eight minutes. No more time to think about the past or the future. Our hiatus was ending. Time to check in with the present. I took a deep breath and expelled it noisily.

"You'll be alright, Lauren," my husband said as his lips brushed my cheek briefly. "Try to relax and just be the way you are. We're together in this."

Those words comforted me. I felt that *being in something*

together might be a western concept. After all, he had just spent four years in Canada. Would he revert to the ways of his upbringing when he returned to Malaysia?

I took out my mirror, applied my *Brun Moderne* lipstick and gave a few tugs at my untameable curls. My friends were doubly justified in calling me *Buschy*. Not only was my surname Busch, but it well described my hair. I left my sweater on so I wouldn't have to carry it, and we sat silently until the plane gave its little thud announcing our arrival.

Chapter 2

CHEN SWIVELLED HIS HEAD and exclaimed about the architecture and efficiency of the new Kuala Lumpur International Airport. For my part, anything would have looked good at that point. My whole body felt stiff and chilly from being confined in tight, air-conditioned quarters for seventeen hours. I extended my limbs and mobilized my neck with my favourite Pilates exercises. Porters trundled by, pushing snakes of interlocking trolleys. People headed in all directions, pulling and pushing at their bags and boxes and jabbering loudly in languages foreign to me. Kids who weren't sound asleep were celebrating their freedom by bouncing around like hail hitting pavement.

Wong was waiting for us at the airport. Chen saw him as soon as we entered the Arrivals Hall.

"There he is!" Chen said. "In the red shirt. Standing by the pillar over there."

"What do I *call* him?" I asked urgently.

"Call him *Pa*!" Chen replied firmly.

Pa sounded like something from a cowboy movie. But never mind. Pa it would be. Although Pa was not fat, he had a square build and a thick neck that gave the impression of considerable girth and strength. His mop of straight, black hair didn't show a sign of white and his smile revealed a set of very white and even teeth. He spied us quickly, as well. We walked toward each other, our weariness blooming into alertness. Chen was pushing a cart loaded with our suitcases, while I struggled to keep up with my stuffed purse and a large woven bag full of books and the overflow from my suitcases banging against my knees with every step. I hoped I looked a bit less like a bowl of second day mashed potatoes than I felt. Chen, by comparison, looked dapper in spite of the killer trip.

"Chen! Good to see you," his dad said as he shook Chen's hand and clutched his upper arm.

"Good to see you, too, Pa. Meet my wife, Lauren Busch."

"Welcome to Malaysia, Lauren." He said it as if he'd rehearsed it, then lowered his gaze to the floor. "Aiyo! Lots of luggage!"

"More coming next month, too," Chen said.

Wong stared at our paraphernalia as if it reinforced the idea that we were here to stay. *Both* of us.

I broke into his thoughts by giving his hand a hearty shake and saying, "I'm happy to meet you, Pa. It's really nice that you could pick us up." Wong gave me a startled look. I tried to imagine why. Later I learned that only "women of the night" get *picked up*.

Leaving the artificial cool of the airport, the sun felt like heat to chilled bones. The huge cloud of warmth embraced and comforted me. Unfortunately, the good feeling was short-lived. I was not prepared for the sun's intensity. The air was still and heavy. I plonked down my bags and pulled off my sweater. I would simply have to carry it. Arriving at the car, a mid-sized Malaysian-made Proton Saga, I began to better understand Wong's concern for the amount of luggage we carried. Two cases filled the trunk and two smaller ones plus my sizable multi-coloured tote, were pushed in beside me. Chen jumped in the front seat with his dad. I had assumed he would sit with me. I felt reduced to just another piece of luggage. Again, I wondered if Chen would revert to being a macho male form of humanity now that he was back on his native ground. For a minute I was choked, but I decided to concentrate on inhaling the smells, sights, and sounds of my new country. The oil palms we had seen from the air, I now saw from a different perspective. They were much stockier and less graceful than the coconut palms I had seen in Hawaii, but the fronds had an impressive size and glossiness. These handsome trees were all lined up and following the contours of the land. The highways seemed perfect—no damage from months of freezing temperatures and salt for these roads! Flowering trees and shrubs grew on the road dividers, and colourful banners and metallic palm trees swayed in the breeze. At first they seemed garish and out of place to me, but before long I thought of them as festive and welcoming. While I was admiring the sights, Wong lit up a cigarette and held it between nicotine-stained fingers. The window was rolled down a few inches and he flicked ash out the opening. The warm, smoke-filled air floated by my face, down my windpipe and into my lungs.

"How far is it to Kuala Lumpur?" I asked.

"We're going to by-pass KL," Wong replied. "We'll go through the Sungai Besi toll gate and up along the Hulu Kelang highway. Joins with Jalan Sungai Buloh." He was driving on the left-hand side of the road and appeared to be very much in control of the route, the car, and life in general.

I was bummed on two accounts. First, that Wong was a smoker, and second, that we were not going through Kuala Lumpur. I was anxious to see it. Even the name sounded romantic. I refused to shorten it to KL though everyone else seemed to. To me it would be *Kuala Lumpooor.*

"Maybe you can catch a glimpse of the Twin Towers from the toll gate," Wong said.

A glimpse? Big deal! I want to lie on the ground beneath them and look straight up! I want to take pictures.

"Aren't they the highest towers in the world, Chen?"

"The highest *twin* towers. Are they still, Pa?"

13

"Yes. At least for now."

Chen and his dad chatted intermittently about the family and Malaysian business. I felt excluded, but kept up my watch out the window. When we got into the mountains, the foliage thickened.

"Oh, Chen!" I said. "Take in those trees! They're like endless huge heads of broccoli!"

"That's the jungle," Chen chuckled. "Just thick green masses of broccoli, ropes and roots."

Wong finished his cigarette and butted it out in the ashtray. The window was rolled up to encourage the air-con. The roads were impressive; not only their size, but the way they wound like a tapeworm around the mountains. Everything was luscious green. I tried to imagine what kind of critters lived under that dense mass of foliage. Certainly snakes. I thought of my childhood fascination with the gigantic, writhing reptiles coiled up on the pages of the *National Geographic* magazines. I would peek quickly, then slam the magazine closed with a shudder.

"Are there tigers in that jungle, Chen?"

"I guess so. What do you think, Pa?"

"Not so many now. Get sold for skin and body parts for medicine."

Ha! I've read about that. Aphrodisiacs! As if.

"Look at the top of that mountain," Chen said, pointing. "That's the Genting Highlands. The castle at the top is the Casino."

"Casino? It's huge! Why so big?"

"It's a busy place. Full of Chinese people—all ages, from youngsters to grandparents."

"Is it just for Chinese people?"

"No, but Muslims are forbidden to gamble. They're policed by Malay cops, actually, so it's mainly Chinese people who go. A lot of people come from Singapore and some come from the airport when they're going through KL."

"The rich people gamble in private rooms," Pa said in a voice shaded with envy. "Would you like to see it? I could drive up there and show it to you." I sensed that Wong couldn't bear to drive by when he was so close. "No, thanks," I said. "I don't like anything about gambling." Wong's head swivelled around as if he were checking to see if he had heard correctly. No doubt I'd lost a lot of points on that one, but it was okay. That's *me*.

Three hours later we turned north toward Taman Damai, the town where the Wong family lived. In spite of the air-conditioning in the car, my hands began to sweat. My apprehension returned. What was Wong thinking? What would the rest of the family think? Would they look at me in dismay? Disappointment? Even hatred? Would we have dog or blowfish for dinner? My friend, Samantha, the epitome of calm and peace, taught me to breathe deeply to reduce stress. I tried to recall it now. Seeking a feeling of comfort and ease, I tucked my chin in and folded my hands lightly on my lap. As I focused on a small mole on the back of Chen's neck, I consciously tried to make my breathing smooth, deep, and regular. As stressful thoughts fought to enter my mind, I gently picked them up, put them in a blue box and replaced the cover.

"We're nearly at Taman Damai," Chen announced brightly.

I came out of my reverie and started to take notice. We passed fruit trees—large trees with bright red fruit the size of a small kiwi fruit, and sprouting coarse lime green hairs about half an inch long.

"What are they, Chen, the little red fruit with the hairs?"

"Rambutans—a bit like a grape but with a thick skin and a big stone. You'll like them, I think."

Narrow, over-loaded, grubby shops were open to the street. We drove by stores specializing in herbal medicines, magazines, snacks, mangoes, fabrics, dried herring, eyeglasses and guitars. A car repair shop sported a sign above the door—*Woksyop*. At a higher elevation, dominating the surrounding area, I could see a mosque with an impressive gold dome trimmed with royal blue.

"Would I be able to go inside the mosque sometime?"

"Can not. Why do you want to do that?"

"It's beautiful, Pa. I have no idea what it's like inside. I want to know."

"All over the town you'll hear wailing sounds from there five times a day. You'll be tired of it soon. After, you won't even notice it.

Pa Wong reduced his speed and turned onto Jalan Kupas. Row houses, in strips of eight, lined both sides of the road. High wrought iron gates stood proudly at the front of every house and the fences sealed off each family's territory. As well, I couldn't help noticing that the windows had bars. Presumably it was for security, but I couldn't imagine it was necessary. I found it discomfiting to see so many barriers. The roofs of the homes pitched forward, extending about fifteen feet across the courtyard, providing shade from the sun and protection from the rain, I supposed. They seemed to use the space as an extension of the house: as a gathering place, to dry laundry and even to safely park the car and motorcycles.

Pa Wong blew the horn when we arrived at #88. Unlike the numbers of our seats on the airplane, the house numbers were very auspicious. Strangely, I took some comfort in that.

Chapter 3

THE LONG AWAITED MOMENT arrived. My knees knocked together. Would they hold me up? A receiving line formed in the breezeway. They stood like clay warriors, in awkward silence. All eyes rolled back and forth between Chen and me. There was no doubt that they were glad to see Chen, but at the same time they couldn't seem to stop ogling me. Chen turned to his mother and put his arms around her. Their eyes glistened, probably as close to emotional as they were ever likely to be.

Chen led me to his mother and simply said, "This is my wife, Lauren." Tan took my hand in hers and smiled as much with her kind eyes as her lips. She was a slight woman exuding gentleness, luckily inherited by her son. Tan wore beige polyester slacks and a rayon blouse with a brown, green and rust floral pattern. I noticed black satin slippers on her small feet and a narrow gold ring on her worn hand. Gazing into my face she said, "You are welcome, Lauren." Now I was the one with misted eyes. I would never forget those words. "Thank you, Ma."

Chen shook hands limply with his Uncle Wong So Ho, a rigid, grey monochrome of a man with thinning hair dragged over the top of his balding head. One front tooth and one incisor were missing. Like Pa Wong, his brother held a cigarette in his nicotine-stained fingers. He said nothing to me. Auntie Tan Soon Lai, in a traditional Chinese red satin cheongsam with matching satin shoes and dainty gold earrings and bracelets, flashed a smile at Chen. He responded with something about her being as pretty as ever. *Is she Ma's sister? The wren and the peacock! Sisters?*

Just then, as if he had held back to make a stage entrance, Chen's younger brother, Lee Fang leapt in. He was a bit shorter than Chen but equally lean and with very fluid movements. His black hair was streaked with blonde and one earlobe sported a gold earring.

"Aiyo! Isn't this great?" he called out as he walked toward Chen, managing, as the rest of the family had, to keep his eyes on me at the same time. "Hi, big brother! Good to have you back. I like who you brought with you!"

"This is Lauren, Lee Fang,"

"Thought so," Lee Fang said with a grin. "How was the trip?"

"Lo-o-ong," I said, feeling an immediate kinship with Fang. I sensed that of all the family, he was the one not harbouring disappointments or judgments of me.

We all, except Auntie Lai, took off our shoes to go inside. Going through the door, we were face to face with an altar of some sort. We turned right and entered a room featuring a round table and ten chairs with two softer chairs at one end. Auntie Lai's high-heeled shoes made staccato notes on the floor as she came toward Chen and me. She carried two tall glasses of pink guava juice. A slice of lime perched over the edge of the glasses.

"What a beautiful colour—sort of dusty rose with a tint of orange," I said. "It looks very refreshing. Thank you, Auntie Lai."

"Most guava juice is green but I like the pink," she said, analyzing my green eyes and my red, blotchy complexion as she spoke. I am self-conscious about my skin. It wouldn't now, or ever, measure up to the smooth, yellow tones of Chinese complexions. Children's voices in the breezeway distracted me from my feelings of inferiority. The door opened and three more people came into the room. "Lauren, this is my husband, Khoo, and my children, Zi Meng and Zi Qing," Auntie Lai said.

Now there were ten of us. I began to wish we had name tags. Zi Meng was a sweet girl of about nine, looking pretty in a pink and yellow striped top, a pink cotton skirt and a ring with a pink stone on her finger. She looked like a mini version of her fashion-conscious mother. Her eight-year-old brother, like all the males present, wore shorts and a T-shirt.

"Where's Lee Yee?" asked Chen.

"She couldn't come because her mother-in-law's brother is visiting from America—needed her to help with a family reunion they are having," Wong said. "She is disappointed. But can come on the weekend. Good enough."

"I'm disappointed, too. I'm very anxious to see her," Chen said.

"I'm disappointed. And shocked," I whispered to Chen. "What in heck do her in-laws think *this* is, if it's not a reunion!"

"Shh," Chen said quietly. "Lee Yee is part of *their* family now. Not ours. We'll probably see her on the weekend."

Quickly I saw the corollary; I am now part of the Wong Family, not the Busch family! Never!

My jitters were soothed by delicious smells of ginger, coriander and garlic wafting from the back kitchen. Florescent light reflected off the red plastic tablecloth. At each place a small bowl of rice with chopsticks balanced across the top, a small plate, a small cup for tea and two tiny saucers—one with finely chopped garlic, the other with chopped green chilli peppers. Nearer to the middle of the table were several dispensers of soy sauce and a pile of narrow, thin candyfloss-pink paper serviettes.

We flocked to the table and sat on metal chairs with thin red cushions. Auntie Lai brought in a platter of butter prawns the size of Canadian toonies and placed them on a round, revolving lazy-Susan that covered a considerable space in the middle of the table. When we'd devoured that delight, sweet and sour pork and baby kailan appeared. No time was wasted. The third course was steamed chicken smothered with black mushrooms and fried garlic.

"Let's drink a toast to the bride and groom!" Lee Fang said. "We hope they'll be prosperous and have lots of children." *What about happy? And healthy?*

"I'm thankful for Chen returning," Tan said. *Had she doubted he'd return? If she only knew...*

"Let's drink to all of that," Wong said. Lifting their little tea cups, they all (except So Ho) said, "To Chen and Lauren."

Zi Qing sat beside me. He squirmed and wound his legs around the rungs of the chair. "Do you make pretty pictures?" he asked.

"Oh, yes," I said. "I love to make pretty pictures! Do you?"

"Yes, but I can't do it very good," Zi Qing said.

"Let's make some pictures together sometime. I'll tell you some secrets to make it easy."

"I like you," he whispered.

"I like you, too, Zi Qing," I whispered back, thankful to know for sure that one person here really liked me.

Ta Da! The *pièce-de-résistance,* a celebratory patin river fish, arrived complete with head on. I hoped they wouldn't put the ugly thing facing me, but I expected they would—because I'm the guest of honour or something.

Wong lifted a piece of fish from its bed of cilantro and broth, and put it on my plate. Tan kept my rice bowl filled, and Auntie Lai poured endless tea into our small cups.

Nine people surrounded me—slight, shiny, raven-haired Chinese people, and me—a not-so-slight, freckled, paper-white skinned, curly red-haired Canadian who, until an hour ago, had not met any of them—except, of course, Chen. Images of Sesame Street characters singing "one of these things just doesn't belong..." darted into my head. Was I the Sesame Street circle, joining hands with the Wongs and expanding their circle, or the square staying alone in a box? In this morbid frame of mind, I heard Zi Qing asking no one in particular, "Why has Auntie Lauren got a spoon?"

"Auntie Tan gave it to her. It's because she's Canadian," answered his sister, Zi Meng, importantly. "They use a spoon and a fork and sometimes even a knife." Then she added, "*Knifes* can cut your luck right in two!"

I'd had some previous practice with chopsticks and was determined to use them, though sometimes I was more successful than others. The wide ceramic soup spoon was my back-up tool— literally. The food was delicious and I managed acceptably well. I was feeling almost smug, when I realized that a fish bone had lodged in my throat. Instinctively I choked and, with my tongue hanging out, gagged. Add to that my fear-filled eyes and I must have looked like a crazed idiot. I felt truly panicked—not to mention thoroughly embarrassed. Quickly, Chen came to my rescue. First, he led me out of the room, calming and reassuring me. Then with a light in one hand, and a long-nosed, tweezer-like instrument in the other, he retracted the bone. What a relief! He gave me a hug and we returned to the celebration. The plates had been removed which was encouraging, but we were still not finished! Auntie Lai brought in a platter of wonderfully cool and colourful fruit: watermelon, papaya, pineapple, and something like a small pear but with rosy pink skin. I had lost my appetite for food, but the cool fruit did feel soothing on my scratched throat.

As soon as the meal was finished, everyone stood up. There was no relaxing in a state of well-being, or prolonging the pleasure of the meal with chatter at the table. Khoo told the children that it was time to go home.

"But my homework is all done and it's not late," Zi Meng said.

"Don't argue," Auntie Lai said sternly. "You know you have a math test in the morning."

"My homework's done, too, and Auntie Lauren, you said you would tell me some secrets," Zi Qing pleaded.

"No secrets tonight, Zi Qing. But maybe we can make some pictures after school tomorrow." I said.

"Zi Qing, you have your Chinese lessons after school tomorrow," Auntie Lai called out sharply as she took dishes to the kitchen." *Whoa! Guess who's the Sergeant Major in that family. No wonder Khoo is a man of few words!*

"Come on. Time to go, lah," said Khoo as he walked to the door, pushing the children ahead of him. "Nice to meet you, Lauren," he called over his shoulder.

"Nice to meet you, as well, Khoo… you too, Zi Qing and Zi Meng."

The men, Wong, his brother So Ho, Chen, and Fang, took their chairs to the breezeway outside. I took some dishes to the sink and offered to help.

"You must be tired," Tan said. "Not much room here. You can sit at table." Then, as if the thought had just appeared, she said, "or you like to sit with Chen?"

"Thanks, I think I'll do that. That was an amazing meal you two prepared." Tan smiled.

I wondered how welcome I would be in the men's circle, but I'd made my decision and faced them chair in hand. The air was heavy with heat, moisture, and cigarette smoke. Lee Fang jumped up, took the chair from me and put it down between Chen and him. Wong, Uncle So Ho and Chen were drinking cognac and discussing the woes of the rubber industry. Fang had a can of Coke. He asked me if I'd like something to drink, but I declined, saying I was floating in Chinese tea.

"You drink much tea in Canada?"

"Yes, a lot. My favourites are English Breakfast and Earl Grey. Chen taught me to like Oolong tea at a cafeteria on campus when we first met. We had curry puffs with it."

"How do you remember that? How did you meet Chen?"

"I was working part-time at the library at UBC. He spent a lot of time there."

"Yeah, I'm not surprised. He's very smart, lah. Not like me, already. I didn't like school much. I like music and martial arts. Our sister, Yee Lee, she's smart like Chen."

"What instrument do you play?"

"Drums and gongs. It's for Lion Dance. We practice three times a week after work."

"Sounds like fun. I'm looking forward to seeing a Lion Dance. I've only seen one on TV."

"Much better to see one close up with the beat banging in your ears," Fang laughed.

Just as he was talking about the beat banging in your ears, I overheard words banging in mine. Uncle So Ho's tongue must have been loosened by the cognac. He was talking about Canada with disgust in his voice. When he saw me watching him, he looked at me with a despicable glare and continued ranting.

"Canadians very anti to Chinese. Gave them bad jobs. Cook, wash clothes. Put tax for school, jobs, policing. Gave dangerous jobs on railroad. Wouldn't let us be citizenship." Whoa. At least I knew Soho had a voice!

"Okay, So Ho!" Wong said, in a manner of a parent chastising a child.

"Okay… but head tax fifty dollars, then five hundred dollars—each! Then wanted Chinese to fight in war but were afraid if then we want to be citizens."

"Enough, already," Wong said again. "That makes Lauren feel bad and that happened long before she was even born."

I had vaguely heard of head tax and could easily believe the war politics. But Wong was right. It did make me feel bad—more specifically, ashamed.

Wong turned in my direction and gave me a smile that suggested he would care for me and protect me as he did the rest of the family. Maybe I had over-reacted about his smoking and general bossiness. I smiled back.

"How big is your rubber plantation, Pa?" I asked.

"It's about two hundred hectares—not very big," he said, sounding surprised that I was even slightly interested.

"Sounds big to me. How far is it?"

"Takes us about a half hour to get there. We drive together— So Ho, Fang, and me. Other workers stay closer."

"How many workers are there?"

"Usually ten, with three of us.

"Could I see it sometime?"

Wong looked *really* surprised that time. "I guess you can," he said.

"That would brighten our day, Lauren," Fang said.

"Can I come, too?" asked Chen.

"Maybe better not. I'll put you to work."

"You would, too." Chen laughed.

Later, as I made my way up the tightly spiralled stairs with artificial ivy intertwined in the railing, I did a quick assessment of the Wongs. Seemingly, I had Tan to teach me, Wong to protect me, Fang to entertain me, Zi Qing to admire me, and best of all, Chen to love me. So Ho, Auntie Lai, and her little girl, Zi Meng, were unknown quantities. In spite of them, I felt a wave of thankfulness and relief.

Chapter 4

I AWOKE TO THE most complex bird talk I had ever heard. Their conversations seemed in sentences and could in no way be described as chirps, warbles or twitters. Intricate patterns of the tonic sol-fa whistled in a range from pianissimo to forte.

Chen lay motionless beside me on a bed that had a strong inclination to sag in the middle, making snuggling almost imperative. Snuggling I liked. Snuggling in the tropics promised to be another matter. Even lying in bed I felt as if I'd been working in a hayfield in the mid-day sun. Lazing on my back, I looked up at some water stains on the ceiling near the window. The walls were open for about eighteen inches from the top. I imagined it was to encourage any whiff of breeze that might come along to continue on to the other rooms. The downside was the acoustic logistics, the whole gambit of night noises. This morning, someone was snoring loudly. Big honks. So Ho was suspect. Perhaps the others had learnt to sleep through it. I figured at least his snorts might camouflage any sounds from our end. A small fan, attached to the wall opposite the bed, was plugged into an outlet half way up the white walls. The red satin bedspread was alarming. To me it signalled brothels, but I already knew that to the Wongs, it spoke of good luck and fortune. We folded it and carefully laid it on top of a dresser we had concocted using our suitcases. Half a dozen wire hangers hung from three large hooks on the wall, and two well-worn towels were draped over smaller hooks at the side.

Chen snoozed on. I got up quietly and made my way to the bathroom downstairs. I was surprised to find Tan up. She wore a colourful sarong and had started breakfast preparations.

"Good morning, Ma."

"Morning, Lauren. You sleep good?" She looked at me with a trace of a frown, staring directly at my white muslin nightie.

"Quite well. I woke up when I heard the birds talking. I hope they're as pretty as they sound. What kind are they?

"Don't know. Don't see them."

With that topic finished, I commented that she was up early.

"Before six on week days, already. I make congee—that's rice porridge, and coffee. Everyone takes their own when ready. The men leave at six o'clock. Wait. I give something to you."

She shuffled off in fabric slippers and returned with a folded cloth. "It's sarong," she said. "Lai helped me choose—she's good with colours."

I opened it up exposing a swirled pattern of burnt sienna, ivory, and shades of brown.

"Oh, Ma. It's beautiful! Thank you so much."

"We wear them lots at home. Wrap any way you want."

Just wear it! hung in the air. "I'll practice," I said as I turned to go into the bathroom.

Inside, everything was wet. Obviously, Tan had been in to clean. The toilet was a squatter. There was a hose on a hook beside it. To my chagrin there was no toilet tissue. I approached the squatter. The decision was whether to face the wall behind me or the one in front of me. Last night I decided to experiment and declared it a toss-up. I straddled, peed, and hosed. Wet! Wet! I wondered how all the Muslim ladies in the beautiful, long, silk dresses manage. I stepped into the shower, which was circled by a two-inch lip, but no curtain. I turned the button on the instant hot water heater. The water temperature was impressive; the flow was not. Eventually, I stood in the shower dripping and trying to shake some of the water out of my mop of curls. I reached for my towel only to find that it, too, was soaking wet. I wrung it out and tried to wipe the excess water from my body. All that was left was to wrap the sarong around me and hope it would stay together until I got upstairs.

When I returned to our room, Chen was awake and held out his arms for me. "Good morning, my Canadian-Malaysian bride. That's a pretty sarong."

"Your mother just gave it to me. I think she might have been anxious to have me more covered up. You're going to have to help me anticipate when I might offend without meaning to."

"You'll do fine. Come back to bed. Surely it's too early to get up."

I grabbed the invitation. Shedding my new sarong and my offending nightie, I jumped into bed. I loved just lying beside him and feeling surrounded by his perfect body.

With Wong, So Ho, and Fang at work and Tan at the wet market, we were alone in the house eating the congee that Ma had left for our breakfast. Little bowls of chopped onions, peanuts and small dark brown eggs were lined up in a row on the counter.

"What's with the wee dark brown eggs?"

"They're century eggs, sometimes called thousand year eggs."

"Yum."

"Duck or quail eggs are preserved in clay, ash salt, and lime, for about a month I think. They're definitely a delicacy. You probably won't like them right away. They give off a smell of sulphur and ammonia. Do you want just a little taste?"

"Not today, thanks. Chinese people seem to put a huge emphasis on food."

"Absolutely."

The ceiling fan was whirling air laced with spices from our banquet the previous night, shades of tobacco, and something else that reminded me of mothballs.

"How come you didn't tell me that your dad and his brother smoke?"

"Because I knew you would hate it and it's something I can't change. My Auntie Lai smokes, too. Guess she thinks it's classy."

"Do they know how bad it is for them?"

"Probably, but it's a habit."

"Can't you get them to stop?"

"No, it's their house. I can't tell them what they can do. As you'll see, they're not here very much. Sometimes they smoke outside. We just have to ignore it."

"I'll have a hard time ignoring it. In Canada I don't think I know more than three people who smoke. Now I find that three of your family members smoke. Don't they know they're ten years behind the times?"

Chen looked a bit disturbed. "Ten years behind western times, but not Malaysian times," he admitted.

I regretted my comment. I knew that although we can see flaws in our own country, we don't like them pointed out to us by foreigners. I promised myself I'd be more sensitive.

"I'm especially surprised at your Auntie Lai. How can your mother and your Auntie be so different?"

"For one thing, my mother is eighteen years older. She was the eldest girl of a family of six children. She's always had a lot of responsibility and she's always been a slave to what she thinks is her duty. On the other hand, Auntie Lai has the flair and glamour. She owns a jewellery store in the town. She knows a lot about gems, the price of gold and all that stuff. Her shop is in a row of five jewellery stores on the main street."

"Five? How can she be successful with all that competition?"

"Because Chinese people buy a lot of jewellery. They wear a lot, they give it for gifts and they trade it back to the dealer when the price of gold goes up."

"How do the people know what the price of gold is? Look it up on the computer?"

"They don't have to because there's always a sign in the windows… sort of like posting part of the stock market. Very competitive. I think Auntie Lai works hard and does well."

"I'm sure. What does her husband do?"

"He owns the KFC in town."

"KFC? No kidding!"

"No. He bought it just before I left for Canada. He does a big business. You have to understand the people here. The Muslims don't eat pork, the Indians don't eat beef, but everyone eats chicken. And they all eat meals out. A lot."

"I like the idea of eating out a lot. Let's go to Khoo's KFC— some night when we feel like an oily, salty, treat. You know the ropes, let's do these dishes. You wash and I'll dry," I said when we had finished our breakfast.

Chen looked a bit mystified. "It can't be very hard. I think they use this," he said picking up a plastic tub labelled *Axion*. It's for washing dishes in cold water. He dabbed a well-used dishcloth on the Axion paste, rubbed it on the dishes and rinsed them under the water tap.

"Where can I get a dish towel?"

"I think they let them dry on the rack."

"Who's *they*?" I asked, knowing full well it was Tan.

"Okay, okay! This morning I did them. Don't give me a hard time. What would you like to do today?"

"Actually, there's nothing I'd like more than to go for a good long walk, just to see what's what. Should we have coffee first?"

"No, let's have some while we're out."

"Okay. But before we do anything, will you tell me about the altar opposite the front door?"

"Sure I will. Let's go look. The shelf in the upper right is for the General Kuan Kung. He gives good luck for business. To the left is the pot full of sand to hold the joss sticks. There are always two sticks or more—just one is for funerals. At Chinese New Year, there is a special cake to stick pins in. On New Year's Eve, the God of Prosperity is added. Below that, it's the Kitchen God and an offering for him. He is the home guardian. The oranges and the small cakes are for our ancestors to eat."

"Sure. But how do ancestors eat the cakes?"

"Of course they don't. It's symbolic. When the cakes get dirty, my mother replaces them with fresh ones. Superstitions play a big part in the daily lives of Chinese people."

"Thanks. Umm. It's fascinating. Does every house have an altar?"

"No, but many do. You have to believe in that stuff. Most young people have a small altar beside the house. It's not so obvious. The oldest son is supposed to have one. Let's go."

"I'll be ready in five."

As I walked up the stairs, my mind was filled with thoughts about the altar. *Would we have to have one? Probably we would. After all, Chen is the eldest son! It creeps me out! I'll have to think about it later.* I put on a green wrap-around skirt patterned with white seashells and a white T-shirt. After rummaging through my suitcase I found my favourite sandals, multi-coloured woven leather beauties that I had bought on South Granville Street before our wedding in Vancouver. With a skiff of lipstick and a good coating of sunscreen, I drifted down the stairs and past the altar with the mysterious symbolism, to meet Chen.

At the end of our street, he said, "There's Wiwa. I remember him. He makes *roti canai*. Now *that's* a real treat! Come. Let's get some."

"I did not see you for a long time," said Wiwa in a musical voice. "Are you the Wong boy?"

"Yes. I've been studying in Canada. This is my wife, Lauren Busch. I want her to try some *roti canai*."

"Hi, Wiwa. This looks like a very skilful process. Is it a type of pancake?"

"More like thin rubber."

"You said it, not me!" Chen said with a grin. "Give us each two pieces and some dried-pea sauce to dunk it in."

We sat on a couple of wooden crates turned upside down while Chen waited for my response.

"Ummm, it *is* delicious!" I said. I'd wondered how I could eat two pieces twenty minutes after I'd had my breakfast, but it was easy.

Chen paid Wiwa two ringgit and said, "Okay. Let's go."

We walked through the neighbourhood passing maids and grandmothers minding young children. Some of them remembered Chen and called out to him. He introduced me to everyone who spoke. Comments ranged from "So big!" to "So nice, lah!" The most amusing remark was from a happy older lady who laughed and pointing at my red, frizz-ball head said, "So busy hair!"

An outdoor Kopi Shop was our next stop. I sensed a feeling of community as I watched people sitting in small groups, chatting or reading the paper. It was nine-thirty. We sat on generic red plastic chairs at a round table. Most people had a cup of coffee or Milo. Some had a plate of noodles or a bowl of soup. I could smell curry and garlic. In the middle of each table sat a bottle of chilli sauce and a small flask of soy sauce. A tall, lanky man with cloth hat, oblivious to all, was playing a guitar and singing quietly. On the back wall large posters advertised Tiger and Carlsberg beer. An ad for Marlboro cigarettes showed a cowboy on a horse inviting us to "Come into Marlboro country." The doorman was a sleeping cat with a bobbed tail who opened one eye when anyone came in the shop.

"Want noodles? They're really good."

"We just had our breakfast, then Roti Canai. Now you're asking me if I want noodles?"

"Let's share some, then," Chen said, going toward the counter.

He soon returned with two cups of coffee, one plate of noodles and two sets of packaged chopsticks. The dark brown noodles had bits of green onion, squid, chicken and chillies—just sticky and limp enough to cling to the chopsticks, my chin, my lap, or wherever they landed. Looking around, I saw the other noodle-eaters tilting their heads forward and chewing and sucking until the whole wad of noodles was gone.

"I don't think I'll ever be able to slurp my noodles, Chen. In fact, I find it just a bit disgusting. The noodles are delicious, though. I don't like to complain, but I really don't like sugar in my coffee."

"I didn't put sugar in. It's because the milk is sweet. Malaysians like to use sweetened milk in their coffee. I'll dump it and I'll ask for fresh milk."

He came back from the counter with fresh coffee and a small pitcher of heated milk.

"Thanks. This is hot and strong, just how I like it. Aren't these people going to work?"

"Probably. Some may work shifts or they may work in shops which won't be open till ten or ten-thirty—or even eleven. Many people eat their breakfast on their way to work. Others buy it and take it to work with them. It's very cheap."

We dawdled down the street, watching people starting to unlock and open up large metal doors, exposing their shops for the day. Some were busy sweeping or washing the sidewalk in front of their shop or rolling down the awning that would attract and shade the customers. One merchant was pushing huge baskets of dried fish and mushrooms toward the entrance and lifting covers off other large containers.

"Chinese people use quite a lot of dried food. It's efficient and convenient for kitchens with not much refrigeration. Cheaper, too. They have good peanuts. Want to try some?"

"Sure, but please, just a few."

The air had one smell: a combination of spices, dried fish and a bit of dust.

"I'll have one scoop of peanuts," Chen said to the shopkeeper.

We left the shop with a pink plastic bag of nuts swinging from Chen's hand and continued down the street.

"Why are there so many ledges and drop-offs on the sidewalks everywhere?"

"I'm not sure. Maybe the storefront sidewalks used to belong to individuals and they tried to join them up. You're right. The uneven ledges really are everywhere—even inside the houses. If there's one at the front door it could be to trip the evil spirits if they try to go inside. Actually there's one at our front door."

"Do you really *believe* there are evil spirits trying to get into people's houses and that they can be stopped by a *ledge* at the *door*?"

Chen was silent.

"Do you, Chen? Tell me!"

The colour deepened in Chen's face. "I do and I don't."

"That's a weak answer. Yes or no?"

"Intellectually, no. But when you've grown up with these beliefs and customs you don't really question them. It's like you don't want to ignore anything that shouldn't be ignored—just in case…"

"Really? Hmmm. I can't believe it, Chen!"

"I admit there could be an auto-suggestion component. You know—if you think something will work, it might well do so."

I was beginning to feel saturated with this expedition when I saw a place where I could buy some paints and paper for Zi Qing. The large stationery store was crammed with books, maps, equipment for book binding, office supplies, cards, wrapping paper, art papers, tacks, special computer papers, games and toys. The lighting was poor and the quality of some things wasn't what I was used to, but I could feel my excitement rise as I looked around. I found an eighteen by twelve pad of watercolour paper and decided on some pastels.

"These will be a good start for your dear little nephew."

"You might just have to check them out yourself," Chen said, as we walked along.

"Oh, I wouldn't do that! Don't you remember how exciting it was when you were a child to have a new box of perfect crayons?"

"Yes, I guess I do. Oh! Here's the clinic. Dr. Chong's. Let's go in and see if he's busy."

I wanted to resist, selfishly thinking that the sooner Chen met his future boss, the sooner he would be starting work. But I could sense his desire and followed him in.

"Can I help you?" asked a young woman swathed in a vermillion silk sari and a multitude of thin gold bangles on her wrist.

"I'm Wong Lee Chen. I'd like to talk to Dr. Chong, if he has time."

"I'm Padma. Yes, I'm sure Dr. Chong will be pleased to see you. Sit down."

We sat on a bench with at least a dozen other people. The walls were white with black marks and dirty areas around the door handles and light switches. The two long benches were at right angles to each other. Cushioned seats covered with red vinyl had cracked in a few places exposing yellowed foam stuffing. Three brass ashtrays were overflowing with cigarette butts. I felt nonplussed, but did my best to be positive. After all, Dr. Chong would be Chen's mentor. I knew that when Chen was a child with a broken leg, caused by falling through a damaged sewer grate, he was in awe of Dr. Chong.

Within minutes we could hear the tinkling of her narrow gold bangles as Padma returned and ushered us into Dr. Chong's office.

The doctor grabbed the arms of his chair and pushed himself up. His body seemed to hang from his wide, stooped shoulders and his skin was funereal grey. But his eyes reflected what I had seen in my own dad's eyes—intelligence and caring. He grasped Chen's hand and said, "Welcome home. Welcome home indeed."

"Thank you. Dr. Chong, this is my wife, Lauren Busch."

I liked the way Chen introduced me. It rang with pride.

"Welcome to you, too, Lauren," he said as he took my hand in his. "I hope you'll be happy here."

"Thank you, Dr Chong. I'm wide-eyed with interest. Chen and I have been walking around town. We've stopped to eat several times—and it's only eleven o'clock."

"That doesn't surprise me. Malaysians love their food. How would you like to come in on Monday morning, Chen, and we'll make some plans?"

"Certainly, Dr. Chong. Should I come around eight?"

"That's perfect. I'll look forward to it. It's wonderful to have you back. You, too, Lauren. Thanks for stopping by."

We stepped outside. The heat of midday and the thought of Chen starting work in three days were weighty.

"Let's go home, Chen."

"That's not a bad idea. We can come out again later, when it's not so hot."

When we got to the house, Chen asked me if I wanted something to eat.

"No! After congee, coffee, roti canai, noodles and peanuts, food is the last thing I want."

"What's the first?"

"I really don't know." It was the truth. I really didn't know. My system had stalled. Chen was doing his best to help me get oriented, but I had no idea what I was going to do when he started work on Monday. "I just feel so tired. What I really want to do is sleep."

"Then that's what you should do. Jet lag is something that needs to be dealt with. Sometimes you just have to give in to it, regardless of the time. I'll bring you up a glass of water." He was determined to teach me the importance of keeping hydrated in the tropics. In the few minutes before he returned, I asked myself what I could do to prod my body into action. I knew that jet lag was only part of my problem. I felt so disoriented.

"I want a bicycle, Chen. I need exercise—not to mention some way to get around. You should get one, too. Maybe we could ride to see Lee Yee. The price is right."

"Those are valid reasons, but the problems are dealing with the heat and safety. Roads are narrow around here and motorcycles rule in the traffic."

"I wish you wouldn't be so quick to put up road blocks," I said with a touch of exasperation. "I thought I had a good idea that would help me to be a bit more independent."

"I'm the Monkey! I'm the one who should want everything *right now*! Just don't expect everything so quickly. This is your first day here and you're worrying about your independence. For one thing, you have to get used to traffic being on the left hand side of the road. It's not as straightforward as it seems. Even more important, it's not like Canada where the pedestrian is the first consideration. Here, the vehicles have the right of way. Be patient," he said, kissing my cheek gently. "Have a good sleep. You'll be surprised how much better you'll feel."

I hoped he was right.

Chapter 5

SEVERAL DAYS LATER, I met my sister-in-law. Chen had his arm around Lee Yee when I walked into the room. Their smiles were identical. She was slight like Tan, but had her dad's good looks. A round face and glowing skin suggested that she may have swallowed a full moon. Her bluntly cut black hair flowed in sync with every movement of her head. Chen held out his arm to me and with one arm around each of us he said, "The two girls in my life, Lauren and Lee Yee."

Then, to my shock, Lee Yee put her arms around me and said, "I am so happy! Now I have a sister."

"I can say the same. Now I have a sister." *I've never had a sister and I've lost my only brother...*

"Mok Ping Kwai, come and meet Lauren," Lee Yee said to her husband who had come through the door carrying two heavy bags of fruit. He was a handsome young man, with gelled hair scooped back smoothly on his head. He put the plastic bags on the floor and extended a hand to me.

"Hi, Lauren," Mok said.

"Don't forget me. I'm Wong Lee Chen. I feel like Prince Charles must have felt when he was married to Princess Diana."

"I'm glad to meet you too, Chen, but Lauren is a lot prettier and we've been so anxious to meet her. Lee Yee felt very upset when my mother made her stay home last weekend. Ma sent these rambutans. Our tree is loaded."

I fought back the impulse to tell Mok that his mother had no right to *make* Lee Yee do anything, and that she could *stuff* the rambutans. Instead, I said, "I saw some of those fruits when I first drove into town. They look more like a hairy animal than a fruit."

"Look, Lauren. The skin is softer than you'd think. If you can make a small cut with your fingernail, you can open it easily. Here. Try it. Watch for the stone."

I took a nibble and, as Chen had explained, it tasted and looked like a meatier version of a grape.

"They're good," I said. "But the best part is the brilliant red colour and the coarse lime green hairs. They'd look great in a wicker basket."

"Spoken like an artist," Chen said.

Lee Yee said, "Lauren, I want to see some of your work. What's it like?"

"A lot of it is large and bold. I like to use joyful colours and happy subjects. My materials will be arriving from Canada in the crate. It's coming by sea—safely, I hope. The other night I dreamt the box had come apart and all my tubes of paint were bobbing around in the ocean. The tubes had been pierced and the colours were swirling and blending through the waves..."

"That's what I'd call a colourful dream," laughed my new sister. "Do you think maybe the sharks teeth pierced those paint tubes?"

"Mok, I think we have a couple of creative minds here," Chen said. "They'll be good friends, don't you think?"

"You're right. It's good."

"Where is everybody?" asked Lee Yee.

"I don't know where Pa and Uncle So Ho are, but Ma is working at the salon and Lee Fang is off beating the drums and cymbals somewhere."

"I could have guessed all that," Lee Yee said. "Fang has a real passion for drum bands. They practice at Au Chin Boon's. I think his father is their coach. They get hired to work with a Lion dance troupe for celebrations and sometimes funerals."

"He's so agile and quick, I'm surprised that he's not *in* the lion," I said.

"Oh, he often is. It takes lots of practice just to do the ground stunts—even more to do the acrobatics. He's taken Tae Kwon Do lessons since he was a kid," Yee Lee said. "That's what you have to do—anything to make your body strong and flexible, lah."

"Here he is," Chen said. "We've been talking about your talents, Lee Fang. How about showing off for us?"

Not needing any encouragement, Fang flipped his feet up and started walking on his hands. While we were admiring that, he went over to the narrow spiral staircase and proceeded up in the same mode. He topped that by coming down the stairs two at a time! We all cheered.

When Tan walked in, her first words were, "Have you eaten?" We assured her that we had and passed her a bowl of rambutans. Then she said how nice it was that we were all together at last. Fang was beside us, still standing upside down. Tan didn't seem to notice.

"When Wong and So Ho come, we go to *restoran* for dinner tonight," Tan said. "To celebrate us together."

"That will be nice, Ma," I said.

At seven o'clock all eight of us sat at a round table-for-ten at the Zui Yue Lou Restaurant. The two extra chairs were quickly removed, and the eight remaining equally spaced. Business was brisk. Whole families, parents, grandparents, and babies, crowded around the large tables, talking over each other and laughing with glee. As far as I could tell, everyone was speaking Chinese. In the background, soft, plaintive, monotonous music was coming from an instrument that looked like an elaborate xylophone. The table was set very much like Ma's, with round cloth-covered tables and lazy-Susans, small bowls of chillies and garlic, flasks of soy sauce, and flimsy pink serviettes. Our waitress scurried over to our table. With no greeting or smile, she passed heavy menus to each of us—rather futile, since Wong ordered the meal with no consultation. Beer and Chinese tea arrived within minutes, followed by a variety of mushrooms and vegetables in oyster sauce. Tan exuded contentment—happy to have her family together, and no doubt relieved to park her apron for an evening. Wong was in a good space, proud of his expanding family: Lee Yee and Mok, (even though they were no longer *officially* family), and me. So Ho was mute, but Fang and Lee Yee compensated, by asking Chen questions about the big chunk of time they had been apart. The courses arrived efficiently, one at a time—deep fried chicken, scallops, sea cucumber, poached prawns and seafood fried rice wrapped in lotus leaves. I wondered if we would eat the leaves, but no; they lent flavour and provided well deserved presentation points for the cook. Just as the waitress took the serving plate, I felt something run over my foot! With eyes and ears alert, I looked down and saw a *rat* scamper under the next table. I shrieked. Everyone in the crowded room turned to gawk at me, before going on with their meal. I shook.

"Tell somebody, Chen!" I pleaded.

He was reluctant, but finally searched out the manager, who shrugged his shoulders and walked away. I couldn't believe it. Bad enough to endure a rat running around, but even worse that the management didn't care! Chen returned just in time for the arrival of the steamed rock cod lying in a broth with shredded spring onions and cilantro, its wide lips stretching across its face and blank, white-rimmed opaque eyes staring left and right. My appetite was on hold, but Wong put a generous portion on my plate: the dubious honour of being treated as a guest. They expected me to enjoy everything and show my appreciation by eating a lot.

I checked slowly and thoroughly for fish bones, remembering my experience on the first night. Nothing could be left. Luckily, I liked almost everything with the exception of the sea cucumber. One bite was the best I could do. The soft, gelatinous texture made my guts churn. Luckily, I had tasted it *before* Wong said it wasn't a vegetable, but a marine item, sometimes called a sea slug! Tan contributed that sea cucumbers were a tonic, full of good things, hard to cook, have to remove skin and hydrate for four days… very auspicious, very expensive. Then Wong, without so much as a wink, announced that it was an aphrodisiac. What next! How could a restaurant meal be such an adventure?

Chapter 6

MONDAY WAS MY DREADED first day alone. Chen left for work at Dr. Chong's clinic before seven-thirty. I walked down the steep circular staircase, through the main room, past the altar and out the front door of the Wong family's home. No, I must think of it as *our* home, since for now it was the only one we had. I sighed as I sat on a red plastic chair at the entrance to the row house, with a sketchbook on my lap. Emptiness engulfed me. I sat there waiting for something to come to me. Nothing came. Pa Wong's car and Fang's motorcycle had left early in the morning, and were now replaced by a huge folding clothes rack bending under its load. Clearly, Tan had done the washing before she left for work. I must find ways to help her. This was the most comfortable time of the day. It was relatively cool. I must enjoy it. I watched the neighbouring families starting their day. A small rooster pecked at some gravel at the side of the paved road and three dogs looking like identical triplets lay by the storm drain. All of the dogs I had seen since coming to Malaysia appeared to be related, being medium-sized, tan-coloured and short-eared. Only the length of their tails varied, a condition perhaps due to fortune in battle rather than heredity.

A school bus pulled up next door and a dainty young child, with gleaming black locks and a large pink plastic pack on her back, climbed on board. Her younger brother wanted to get on the bus, too, but was restrained by a grandmotherly woman. A man, bent with age and wearing only a white sarong wrapped at his waist and plastic flip-flops, shuffled along the street. He puffed on a cigarette while talking on a handphone. I was fascinated by his image and automatically opened my sketch pad. In a matter of minutes, I had captured his likeness. Perhaps someday it might be the jumping off place for a painting. Next door a woman hung washing on lines strung back and forth at the front of her house and across the lawn. I spotted newly washed canvas shoes perched over the tops of the fence posts. Chinese people seemed to be fanatical about clean clothes. I suppose the issue that keeps the process churning is that everything gets saturated with sweat.

From the mosque, for the second time that morning, the Imam called the Muslims to prayer. I didn't mind the droning sound. I found it quite comforting to be reminded of a higher being five times a day. Putting my hands above my head I stretched lazily. Two large pots of fuchsia bougainvillea, trained to climb up the side posts, formed a narrow canopy along the edge of the roof. The blossoms resembled small three-sided boxes made of brilliant-coloured tissue paper. I wondered how such delicate and brilliant blossoms could flourish in such hard, dry, red soil. Idly, I also wondered if the plants got their water directly from the moisture in the humid air rather than through their roots as they do in Vancouver. In our back yard the purple irises would be in full blossom. My mother might, at this very minute, be planting the annuals—petunias, bacopa, marigolds and snapdragons. Clay pots of Martha Washington geraniums with lobelia trailing over the sides would line the patio. The dogwood blossoms would be dropping…

My mouth felt dry and my forehead wet. Glancing down

the street, I noticed that Wiwa had set up his stall. He would be cooking roti canai. Breakfast for me had been rice porridge, congee, with various condiments. This morning I chose peanuts and diced green onions. It didn't compare with toast and jam, but tasted okay. I wondered if I would ever reach the stage when I'd want to add anchovies and century eggs to the basic soupy rice. Although my breakfast was sitting heavily in my stomach, I found myself drifting down Jalan Kupas toward the odour of hot oil and curry coming from the hawker stall. At least Wiwa would be someone to chat with.

"Hi. Are you back for roti canai? You must like it," Wiwa said in his pitter-patter voice.

"Yes, I do like it. The smell coming from here was irresistible. But I'll have just one, please Wiwa. And a bit of the pea curry to dip it in. Do you mind if I make some sketches of you while you're making the canai?"

Wiwa looked puzzled. "Why do you want to do that? I am only cooking roti canai."

"Don't forget I've been in Malaysia less than a week. Everything's new to me. Anyway it's fun for me to try to capture action. You don't mind, do you?"

"No, I would like to see it," he admitted.

Sitting on an up-turned wooden box, I began making quick sketches of the Indian man as he spread the batter thinly on the grill with a narrow spatula, turning it several times, before grabbing it with his hands and flipping it round and round, high in the air and folding it skilfully. He slid the masterpiece onto a piece of newspaper and handed it to me along with a small plastic bag of sauce tied with a plastic string. The oil quickly wicked into the newspaper. The roti was a bit soggy and rubbery but undeniably delicious. I leaned forward to take a bite, and the pea curry dripped on my toes and sandals. While I ate, Wiwa looked at the sketches.

"You make me look real. How do you do it... and so fast?"

"I'll show you. Watch. I'll sketch that bicycle going by. See,

I don't watch the page much, I watch the action and move my hand."

As a customer got out of his car and walked toward the stall, I left saying, "I have to get out of the sun now. See you tomorrow."

I trudged back to the house with sweat running down my neck and my white cotton blouse sucked to my back. The early morning reprieve from the sun was over. Hopefully it would be cooler in the house. With the fan whirling the air might still have some remnant of early morning freshness.

Back at the house I kicked off my sandals and put them neatly on the four-tier shoe rack outside the front door. I poured myself a glass of water from the tap. It was neither hot nor cold. In this climate, Chen told me, the most refreshing drinks are at room temperature. Ice water may sound appealing but actually, soon after you drank it, you seemed to feel even hotter.

I sat at the kitchen table with the fan pointed directly on me. Air con was turned off during the day because no one was home except me. I was alright with that because I found it very noisy and I knew it was expensive. Canadians pay a lot to heat their homes in the winter, while Malaysians spend a lot to cool their houses all year long. Although Chen and I had been here for nearly a week, I was still struggling to think of this as home. Wasn't Vancouver my home? I felt as if I were just visiting here, on a trip or maybe a student exchange. Chen's family had welcomed me as they had promised, although I wondered if their good intentions would last. I found the Wongs reserved and undemonstrative. No hugs or kisses in this household! On the positive side, they were polite and kind. Chen's mother, Tan, seemed anxious to please me in the food department, and I recognized her efforts by showing appreciation and interest. Wong was more difficult to read. For one thing, he was seldom home. After dinner, he and his brother So Ho just seemed to fade into the night without a word.

I checked out the small, cluttered kitchen. The large round arborite table with a collection of chairs and stools nearly filled the room. Shelves along one wall held dishes, cooking tools, dish towels, empty egg cartons, newspapers, ripening bananas, ginger jars, spices and red, turquoise, and blue plastic containers in a multitude of sizes. Air-tight re-cycled cans were now labelled Rice, Tea, Sugar, or anything else that needed to be protected from the moisture. My in-laws cooked in woks on a gas fire in the outside kitchen at the back of the house. A large gas tank sat on the floor underneath the shelf. The deep sink had one tap. Tan used it for washing vegetables and fruit. My thoughts turned to my mother's large, highly efficient blue and white kitchen—the hub of the house for our family. Our family. Now my mom, my dad, and myself. Had I made an unfair decision? Had I been totally selfish to marry Chen and come with him to Malaysia? My temples began to throb. I picked up my glass of water and plodded up the narrow stairs. I flopped on the bed. Memories of my family filled my head—memories of the worst day of our lives.

It was in the afternoon of March 14, just three months ago. My mother and I were having a cup of tea in the den when we heard the car door close and went to the window to see my dad trudging up the path. At the bottom of the stairs, he stopped as if he dreaded reaching the door. When he came in his face was ashen and his shoulders slumped. I knew something was very wrong.

"You look so tired, Nolton! I'm glad you've come home early."

He stared at her blankly. I felt motionless— frozen with fear. She grabbed his hand, saying impatiently, "What is it, Nolton?"

He, whose job as a medical doctor had often required him to deliver bad news, was speechless. Finally, looking forlorn, he whispered, "It's Richard."

"Richard? Richard is Heli-skiing with Charlie

*and Jim. Richard?" There was silence. Then Mom
took Dad's arms and shook them hard. "Tell me
what's going on!" she demanded.*

Then quietly, he said, "In an avalanche."

*"No!" my mother shrieked. "Not Richard! Not
in an avalanche!" She began to sway. Dad put his
arms around her and held her tightly. I went to
them. We clung to each other, holding each other
up. Together we sobbed and shook as we struggled to
believe something that seemed so inconceivable.*

That was only four months ago. It still felt like a fresh wound.
I couldn't think of Richard without thinking of Mom and Dad,
too. I decided to email my parents. I picked up my lap-top, and
with a heavy heart, walked down the staircase. Back at the kitchen
table, I moved some Chinese newspapers aside and began to
type.

> Hi Mom and Dad,
>
> Things are going alright here. I'm having a
> crash course in Chinese family life. Lots to learn
> & adjustments to make. Differences from home
> are bigger than expected, though I knew I'd
> have some big challenges. Chen is so sweet &
> making a big effort to help me. Today is the first
> day I've been alone. Everyone's at work. Chen
> started at the klinik (clinic) this morning. He's
> only been gone a couple of hours but I already
> miss him. I get overwhelmed when I try to
> figure out what I will do here. Chen urges me to
> be patient—not my strongest suit, I'm sure you
> will agree!
>
> Tan's a busy lady. She seems to like me,
> though sometimes I'm not so sure. It's so very
> important to me, because Chen is so firmly tied

to his family. It will be very difficult for both of
us if she doesn't like me.

I think of you both 24-7 and often find
myself trying to see things through your eyes—
to get inside your minds & commune with
you—the best parents in the world.

Lots of love and hugs,

Lauren.

As I clicked *send,* I marvelled that my little message might
be on my parents' computer in minutes. Realizing how easily we
will be able to keep in touch, I gave my computer a loving pat.
My spirit lifted. I would go out in spite of the heat and see the
sights.

Ambling down the street, I stopped to look at some shoes.
Malaysians seemed to be forever taking off and putting on their
shoes. I needed some sandals that would slip off easily. The shoes
were stacked everywhere—everything from pink plastic flip-
flops topped with a pile of fake bananas to beaded gold and fake
crocodile skin,

"Do you have any size nines?" I asked.

"Yes, I get some," the saleslady said as she shuffled off, making
a loud *thwack* with each step. Just as I was about to give up,
the woman returned with some red sandals, reeking of cheap
plastic.

"These the biggest ones," she announced proudly. "You try
it, lah."

I turned the sandals over and read—size six.

"My feet are very big," I said, feeling as if it were somehow my
fault. "Thanks for looking."

I left muttering to myself as I continued down the street,
"Maybe all colours and all styles, but *not* all sizes."

Malay women doing their shopping captivated me. They
looked much more likely to be going to a party than buying

food and clothing. Wearing the most beautiful long silk dresses in delicate colours and patterns, with their large head scarves in coordinating colours, the ladies looked like beautiful butterflies. I felt like a heffalump. No wonder they thought I was huge. No wonder they don't sell shoes larger than size six!

Further down the street, I saw the sign *Tan's Hair Saloon*. Saloon? How could such an error occur? It looked like a bad joke! I felt sorry for Ma. I wondered how she would feel if I turned up without notice. She hadn't told me anything about her shop. I decided to stick my head in.

"Come, Lauren. Nice to see you. Meet my helper. Lim."

Lim, wearing a short and very tight skirt, twitched her way toward me and shook my hand limply. "Hi," I said, as we stared at each other's hair. Both of us had a mop of red curls! But my hair was the colour of sweet potatoes and Lim's the colour of candied apples, with jet black showing ever so slightly at the roots.

"When I said to Lim that Lauren have curly red hair, she wants red, too. And curly, too. It take me six hours for colouring and perming!" A sly smile broke over Lim's face and soon the three of us were laughing.

"Want me wash your hair, Lauren?" asked Tan.

I felt quite self-conscious about the thickness of my hair and tightness of my curls and didn't like *anyone* washing it—especially my mother-in-law! But I felt a bit cornered, so I agreed, and started towards the sink.

"No," Tan said. "I wash it here in chair." She swathed me in a sheet of red plastic (looking suspiciously like the red plastic tablecloth on her kitchen table) and put a towel around my neck. Then she squirted some water on my hair from a large white plastic bottle and squeezed a small handful of shampoo on top of my head. She kneaded the water and shampoo into my hair until my eyes widened at the sheer volume. She continued—more water, more shampoo, more kneading with her short but strong and supple fingers. At first I thought it was a bit ridiculous, but it *did* feel good. The volume increased. I looked like Marie Antoinette!

I couldn't suppress a giggle. When Tan began massaging my neck, I murmured, "Ooh… this is bliss." I could feel the tightness in the cords of my neck releasing as Tan's fingers slipped and slid through the meringues of shampoo. Eventually, she lifted handfuls of foam off my head and shook it into a sink. The rest was rinsed off and towel dried.

"What now?" Tan asked.

"Oh, I'll just tousle it with my fingers and let it dry. "You'd never get a comb through it without a product called *Friz-ease*. Thanks, Ma. That was a treat!"

"Welcome, Lauren. Anytime."

Walking along on the sidewalk on my way home, suddenly I felt a drop or two of rain. *Oh damn! I bet I'll be soaked!* Two minutes later rain drove down in sheets, sheets that seemed to be walking sideways. I was quickly drenched. I could feel my curls screwing tighter. I started to laugh. *This is a hoot!* I felt like dancing. Water flowed along the sidewalks and roads, finding its way into the deep storm drains. People scurried along holding a newspaper, a briefcase or whatever they had, over their heads. Motorcyclists congregated under the bridge, waiting for the rain to subside. Leaning on a light standard, I lifted my face to the sky. Raindrops landed on my skin and popped off instantly. I giggled. I felt revitalized. I stood there for five or ten minutes feeling no wish to rush home, just wanting to savour my first tropical rainstorm.

When Chen came home from his first day at work, I jumped up to meet him. Before I reached him, he turned to his father who was washing the car in front of the house. Pa Wong, in a white undershirt and beige shorts with big front snapped pockets and his feet bare, greeted Chen with "How much is he going to pay you?"

"Four thousand a month to start," Chen responded.

An incessant stream of words spewed forth from Wong.

"Four thousand! Not enough! Why didn't you say not good enough? I worked all my life to get you to university and you're getting four thousand! The man is crazy! Too stupid! You tell him tomorrow."

I stood close to Chen, looking at him with wide eyes. Tan heard the commotion and flew out from the kitchen, with her apron bulging like a sail..

"How much you going to get? You said four thousand? How many hours?" she asked without taking a breath.

So Ho, standing on the sidelines holding a cigarette between his thumb and index finger, said sourly, "Probably all you're worth. You think you're a big guy but you're just a kid."

I could feel my eyes filling with tears. I had to get out of there. I flew up the stairs and flung myself on the bed for the second time that day. Through the window, I heard Lee Fang arrive on the scene.

"What's the trouble?" he asked.

They all talked at once but Fang wasn't long in understanding the problem.

"Four thousand a month. Sounds wonderful to me!" he said with his usual propensity for lifting the mood.

Before long I could hear Chen walking up the stairs. He found me lying on my stomach on the bed with a pillow over my head.

"What's the matter, mon bijou?" he asked gently.

"Everything's the matter!" I said in an angry whisper.

Chen wiped his brow and said, "Tell me about it."

"I've been waiting all afternoon for you to come home and to hear about your new job. When I saw you coming, I stood up and was on my way to meet you. Then, all of a sudden I froze as everyone attacked you and yelled at you. They're so critical! So loud! Is money the only thing they think of? Is it really any of their business? Isn't your salary between you and me? I'm your wife! Did it ever occur to them that we want some privacy? And *you* completely ignored me! I don't think you even noticed when

I left—or for that matter that I was even there! I am your wife! I expect to come first; not last!"

Chen heaved a sigh and said, "Do you ever think how *I* feel? *Everyone* seems to expect to come first. There sure isn't any time for *me* to come first. I'm too busy trying to please everyone else. Money is a big concern for my parents. They think they've set me up to be rich. They don't like to wait."

"I don't like to wait either! I don't like to wait for us to have our own place. It's so crowded here! This room is so small! If I want some clothes I have to lift the suitcase up on the bed, shuffle through everything, *then* put it all back. And my crate hasn't even come yet. Where in hell is *it* going to go? And where am I supposed to *paint*?"

"See what I mean? I don't know where in hell your crate is going to go, but I'm sure we'll find a place!" he shouted.

I was the screecher. Chen had never raised his voice to me before. I knew he must feel in the eye of the storm. The way his hair flipped up made him look so young and vulnerable.

"I'm sorry, Chen," I said, taking his hand.

"I know this place must seem small to you Lauren… but we'll sort it out. You know we're sort of broke. Someday we'll have our own place."

"It can't happen too soon for me," I said, silently chastising myself for my temper that always returns to haunt me, in spite of my best intentions. I could understand that Chen felt in the eye of the storm, yet I was fast to blow more wind on it.

Later that night when the Wongs, including me, had simmered down, I told Chen about my impromptu visit to Ma's salon.

"I wondered what to expect, but Ma welcomed me. She even washed my hair! She did it in a way unique to me, but it felt great. We had a jolly time. Lim is quite the comedian with her candy-apple red hair and curls. She wanted to look like me! I was shocked to see Ma's sign, *Tan's Hair Saloon*. Doesn't she know that a saloon is a bar? I felt embarrassed for her."

"No, I'm sure she doesn't know. We don't use the word *saloon*. Don't you think it comes out of the North American Wild West?"

"I suppose it does. Even so, the spelling is wrong."

"She doesn't know that and it probably wouldn't bother her anyway—nor her customers."

"Okay then. I suppose it shouldn't bother me... but it will always make me smile.

Chapter 7

A T SIX FORTY-FIVE IN the morning, Tan and I arrived at the Wet Market. The sun was just thinking of rising and the air was heavy and moist. I didn't choose the hour; it was written with indelible ink on Tan's agenda.

In stalls outside the market building, chickens were laid out on tables with their feet in the air. Their claws resembled miniature, well-manicured human fingernails and their eyelids hung at half mast. Other chickens were squawking, marking time while they were confined in their cages, waiting their turn for the big chop. At one end I could see small chickens with black skins.

"What's with the black ones, Tan?"

"Called Telur Ayam Kampung. In English, egg hen village." I guessed that we would call them free range chickens. "Good for health. Use to make soup." Then Tan turned to the woman vendor who was holding a cleaver, and after a few words in Chinese, we were walking away with a few pounds of chicken whacked into small pieces with no regard for the bones. The vendor wrapped the chicken in a plastic bag which was popped into a bigger plastic bag. I couldn't help chuckling when I thought how far removed it was from the Canadian Safeway equivalent—boned, skinned chicken breasts sitting on a styrofoam plate, wrapped in clear plastic with a snip of green plastic grass on the side. What I saw before me lacked slickness, but certainly not freshness.

Our next stop was at the fish section. Some of the fish were still swimming in very large plastic containers; again, proving their freshness.

"Are you going to take the head, Ma?"

"Must. They charge for head. Anyway, best part, lah. Chen like meat in cheeks best."

They may charge for the head, but not much. I had just seen a sign, *5 fish heads one ringget*, (approximately thirty-three cents Canadian).

In the fish department, I felt even closer to nature than I had in the chicken department. I imagined my Vancouver pal, Robin, screwing up her nose and saying, "Oh, Buschy! How can you stand it? Don't you just feel like puking?"

I didn't quite feel like puking, but I did feel very self conscious, very much a visitor. People interrupted their animated chatter to stare at me. I asked Tan how to say *good morning* in Malay. She replied, *selamat pagi*. I repeated it softly several times before I tried it out. I smiled bravely as I greeted a Muslim woman who was patting her hand on each of the five smallish fish she was buying. I asked her if she was checking to see if they were fresh. Her response was, "No, I am thanking them for giving up their life for our dinner."

Tan didn't introduce me to anyone. In fact, she didn't speak to anyone. I wondered if I embarrassed her, and if so, why she had asked me to come along. Surely she realized this was a very different way of shopping for me. Maybe she thought I had to get used to it and the sooner the better. Perhaps she just wanted to get the shopping done so she could get on with her day. Whatever the reason, she seemed totally focused on the business at hand. The fish vendor wore high rubber boots. He chopped the head off the fish, slit the belly and in one smooth motion, deposited the innards into a floor drain and washed them away with a hose. The fish, including the head, was wrapped in newspaper then put in the everlasting plastic bag. Tan seemed to be haggling about the price, but it was soon settled and we were off to get vegetables.

Some vendors displayed well-stocked tables of spinach-like greens and root vegetables as well as some familiar ones, such as tomatoes, carrots, beans, cucumbers and corn. Things were priced in Malaysian ringgits per kilo but that didn't preclude haggling. I didn't relish the idea of bargaining. Apparently, it was very common, but it made me squirm.

With less to offer, some vendors sat on tarps outside on the ground surrounded by their produce. Some had only a few types of vegetables and little piles of chillies, fresh ginger and garlic. The ginger was the best I had ever seen. In contrast with the brown and somewhat shrivelled skin of ginger shown in Canadian stores, this was pale yellow with bits of green stalk protruding. The vendors looked up with pleading faces as they pointed to their meagre offerings. There was little price squabbling here. A small bowl with coins sat beside the vendors. Seemingly they would be happy with whatever was offered.

"Here's pork room," Tan said, opening the door. It was a pork room all right! Great slabs of pork hung from the ceiling on hooks. Trays of bacon, sausages, pig's feet, pig's ears, and some part of pigs I could only guess at, were exposed to the heat and flies.

"Why does this pork rate a separate room, Ma?"

"Muslims cannot eat pork. They cannot touch pork. They don't want even to *see* pork. Mohammed said *cannot*!" Tan followed this announcement with, "Chinese eats lots of pork. Really likes it. We get some next time."

Next time would be fine with me.

Coconuts appeared to be big business. As we walked around, we passed about a dozen identical machines processing coconuts. The operator would lift a coconut from a pile on the floor, deal it a perfectly placed crack with a cleaver and empty the watery juice into the drain. Then he would press one half at a time against a propelled projection, somewhat like an electric fruit juicer which grated it finely. The final step was to put it in a plastic bag and take it home to be made into coconut milk for cooking.

Everything was buzzing. The community's women had gathered. The Muslim ladies were clad in long silk dresses and the ever-present head-scarves, *tudungs*, even this early in the day. A few of the Indian women wore saris. Tan said most Indian women send their maid to do the shopping. Many of the Chinese ladies wore shorts. They looked as if they, like Tan, had a lot to accomplish and were working like efficient machines.

"Chen likes watermelon. We buy one and be gone."

Near the exit, we passed a booth where an Indian woman was stringing jasmine flowers and winding about a meter of them into a ball. I stopped to watch. The market was full of surprises. This one smelled divine.

"That for praying, Lauren. Some Indian girls put in their hair, around their kondai bun. I get some for you. Smell so good in your room."

"Thank you, Ma." I was touched that such a practical woman would give me this little luxury item. We trudged home carrying our plastic bags. I lugged three bags including the watermelon and the big fish. My arms felt as if they might come out of their sockets. *How did Tan manage day after day?*

Chapter 8

"**M**E? FLIRTING WITH WIWA? Are you serious?"

"There's a rumour, Lauren, that you were seen laughing and chatting with Wiwa for fifteen minutes."

Chen sounded like a prosecutor, and I didn't like it at all.

"Who said that?" I snapped.

"Someone told So Ho that they'd seen you with Wiwa last Monday morning."

"So Ho! The old prune! What a victory for him to get me in trouble! I *am* in trouble, it would seem. Do you want to hear *my* side of the story—or is your family's word all that counts?"

"Of course I want to hear your side. But the fact is, Ma and Pa are disturbed."

"I'm damned disturbed myself!"

"Talk."

"Well, I was sitting outside the front door with my sketch book on my knee when I saw Wiwa at his stand. I walked over and ordered one piece of roti canai. While he was cooking it, I asked politely if I could sketch him while he worked. He couldn't understand, so I explained about his movements being unique and my challenge to capture the motion. He was amazed at how alive he looked and wondered how... Damn it, Chen! I'm angry! This is beyond my realm of understanding. I feel as if I'm at confession and you're the priest. Why should I have to justify buying a piece of roti and chatting for a few minutes with the cook?"

"You shouldn't Lauren. I wouldn't have brought it up except that my mother said if I didn't, my dad would... and I thought you would prefer hearing it from me."

"Well, I'd prefer hearing it from *neither* of you! Where are they coming from?"

"They don't want you to tarnish their reputation. I heard someone say that a woman's reputation is a delicate thing. It's like a mynah bird in your hands— slacken your grip and away it flies."

"Don't give me that crap about women's reputations and mynah birds!" I snarled. "I don't see how treating Wiwa like a human being instead of a lowbrow servant was wrong. I have values, too. And I don't intend to tarnish them, either."

"We definitely have a conflict of values here. This is what I was dreading. We've got to learn how to deal with the conflicts."

"Even before that, *I* have to learn what will cause a conflict. Obviously, I don't know. But really, Chen, we'll have to learn to respect each other's values and I *want* to learn to do that. But, I'm *not* going to toss out my own values! It's important for me to hang on to mine, too!"

"Of course, you're right. But it's not as easy as it sounds. You can be very judgemental. You can't expect to come into this country and criticize people's customs and beliefs. Both sides will have to work to understand each other. Let's consider it a warning of my parent's expectations."

"Yikes!" I said. "I guess I shouldn't be surprised. You tried to tell me."

I wanted to confront the Wongs and set them straight, but willed myself to let it ride. I would put it in the hamper—unless, of course, they brought it up.

Chapter 9

"COME IN, LAUREN. I'M Dr. Chong's wife, Shanthi Vendesh," she said as she met me at the door. Her dark eyes sparkled and she held my hand like my mother might have. I liked this charming middle-aged woman instantly. Her sea-green sari had a gold border and the part that draped over her shoulder had a design in royal blue. Her gold earrings pulled heavily on her ears, and a cluster of narrow gold bangles tinkled softly on her arm. She led me into what she referred to as the *hall.* The hall was about twelve by eighteen feet. In Canada we would call it the living room. On the floor lay a thick Indian rug with a floral pattern in soft yellows, pinks, and greens. The windows had small panes of glass bordered by heavy brocade drapes. Several Indian statues sat on side tables. Shanthi noticed me staring at them and said, "Those are Hindu deities. The large wooden one with the human body, the elephant head, and the four hands, is Lord Ganesh. He's sitting on a nag cobra. Ganesh is one of the most revered gods, a symbol of fortune. My mother brought it for me when she visited from New Delhi. The brass statue is Lord Murga."

"Why does Lord Ganesh have four hands?" I asked.

"It's so he can help us better," she said patiently.

We sat on two couches facing each other with a large, ornately carved, glass-topped table between us. Beneath the glass spread a battle scene carved in a grey metal, probably pewter.

"Your house reminds me of a storybook English home," I said.

"That's not too surprising because it was built for a British agent over fifty years ago. Later it belonged to my husband's father and mother. At that time the house was in the country, but now we're surrounded by the town. At least we've got a big property, so we still have some privacy."

"How long have you lived here?"

"When Dr. Chong's father died, we moved in to care for his mother. That would be in 1965. She passed away ten years later. At that time we renovated the bathrooms and kitchen. But that's enough about us! What about you? What are your first impressions of Malaysia?"

"It's a beautiful country. I've enjoyed mooching around with Chen, meeting his family and seeing where he grew up. I'm anxious to see a lot more. I've felt somewhat aimless since Chen started work—a bit overwhelmed."

"What did you do in Canada?"

"I'm an artist. I have a BFA with a major in painting from UBC. That's where Chen studied."

"Will you paint here?"

"Oh, yes! My equipment should be here in a few more weeks."

"What kind of painting do you do?"

"Flowers and portraiture are my favourites."

"Really? If you're interested in flowers, I must show you my garden. How did you meet Chen?"

"When I attended university, I had a part-time job in the medical library. After I graduated, I kept the job while I sorted out my plans. That's where I met Chen. He spent a lot of time at the library bent over his books."

"Yes, I'm sure. He was an excellent student and showed great promise even when he was a child. He'll be a fine doctor. My husband is so happy he's home and wants to work with him. It's very apt that you two met in a library."

"Yes. At first I was impressed with Chen's focus on his studies, but I soon recognized and respected his commitment. Thats probably because my dad's a doctor and my brother was, too."

"What does your brother do now?"

I gulped air before going on.

"He was killed in a skiing accident last year." Tears welled up in my eyes and my chin was quivering. I was surprised at my reaction considering I was with a stranger. Perhaps it was because I felt so far from home or that I instinctively felt that Mrs. Chong would understand.

"I'm so sorry, Lauren. It must be very difficult for your parents… and you. Do you have any other siblings?"

"No. There was only Richard and me. It was very hard for me to leave my mom and dad."

"That's understandable."

"I couldn't have left if my mother hadn't supported me."

I remember it so well…

> *I was hysterical. My father had asked Chen to be*
> *his partner. It was a great opportunity to stay in*
> *Canada and he had turned it down. My dream*
> *was shattered!*
>
> *I thought it was so stupid!*
>
> *"No, Lauren," Mom said, "it's not stupid. He*
> *feels his commitment to his family strongly. You have*
> *to accept that. He was born into the Chinese culture;*
> *he has just been visiting in ours. Don't try to pull*

him away. You can let him go or you can choose to go with him."

"Go with him? Are you serious? Leave you and Dad? My friends? My painting? What about my own culture?"

Mom leaned forward and put her arm around me. "Poor darling, you've got such a lot to think about. I wish I could help you."

I looked into my mother's concerned eyes. "You have helped me, Mom. You've shown me that I do have choices and best of all you've given me freedom to make them. I'm so lucky to have you and Dad for parents."

Mrs. Chong's voice brought me back to the moment. "I understand better than you might think. Dr. Chong and I have only one child. Her name is Nisha and she lives in England with her husband and three children. We really miss her."

"Freedom. It's the greatest gift a parent can give a child. It's right up there with love," I said. "Some parents seem to worry that giving their children freedom to follow their dreams will weaken family bonds. But from my experience, Mrs. Chong, I think it *strengthens* them."

Her head nodded in agreement. I sensed that she was impressed by my little spout of wisdom. "I think you're right," she said. "We certainly feel close to our daughter. The distance doesn't change that. Of course, we're very fortunate that we are able to travel back and forth from England as frequently as we do. Actually, *I'm* the lucky one. Often it hasn't been easy for Dr. Chong to get away. Would you like some tea, dear?"

"Yes, I would, Mrs. Chong. Thanks."

"Lauren, Chinese and Indian people don't take our husband's name when we marry."

"Oh! I'm sorry. I forgot that. In Canada, the practice of women keeping their name is getting more common. I'm certainly happy to be keeping mine! It's part of my identity."

"Lauren, I feel we're going to be good friends. Please call me Shanthi. Come, you must see my garden. It's my biggest joy. I'll ask Lavinya to bring tea out to us."

From the formal dining room we stepped into Eden. I tried to take it all in—the rattan lawn furniture, the pond with big orange and cream-coloured fish, the herbaceous borders of tropical flowers, the lushness of the shrubs and the backdrop of the dark green hedge interspersed with large-leafed lime bushes.

"It's magnificent!" I said.

With her hand on my elbow, Shanthi said, "Come, I'll show you around."

"What are those big, red flowers with the yellow edge and the thick petals? Over there against the hedge."

"They're Heliconias. They belong to the banana family. The leaves are similar to those of banana trees. Come and feel them; they're very woody. Some are upright and some varieties bend right over. The thick *petals*, as you called them, are called bracts. Local people call them lobster claws."

Over one corner of the garden reigned a canopy-shaped tree with clusters of pink flowers and shiny green leaves. Shanthi saw me looking at it and said, "It's a frangipani. You can smell the blossoms from here. They have one of the strongest scents of any flower. Almost as powerful as jasmine."

"Wonderful!" I mused. With my eyes shut, and inhaling deeply, I felt intoxicated by the beauty around me and the warm, perfumed air.

"The Buddhists call the frangipani the *Emblem of Immortality* because even after they are uprooted they show signs of growth and new blooms. Oh, here's Lavinya with our tea. She seems to have made iced tea. Is that alright?"

"Oh, sure. Even better. I'm struggling with the heat."

"Yes, I'm sure. Would you prefer to go in?"

"No, I want to stay right here. We'll get some shade from the umbrella."

"It's nice to read out here in the early morning, but by nine o'clock it's getting a bit too warm."

"Yes, I've discovered that. Do you have any help with this astonishing creation?"

"Oh, yes. Parveen comes two days a week all year—more if we're doing a project. I've taught him a lot over the years and he has built himself a business."

When it was time to go, I asked Shanthi if I could take some of the frangipani blossoms that had fallen on the ground.

Shanthi hesitated. "We tend to think of frangipani as a funeral flower. But of course you can. I'll get you a bag."

I picked about a dozen perfect blossoms off the ground and placed them carefully in the bag. When I left I told Shanthi I had really enjoyed meeting her and seeing her garden. I don't think she could imagine how true that was—certainly not that I had a dream her garden would become my studio.

Chapter 10

Aᴼꜰᴛᴇʀ ʙʀᴇᴀᴋꜰᴀꜱᴛ ᴛʜᴇ ɴᴇxᴛ morning I sat at the kitchen table enjoying the fragrance of Shanthi's frangipani blossoms floating in a shallow bowl of water. I admired the sheer beauty of their perfect design and colouring: five equally spaced, soft shell-pink petals radiating from a strong orange center. As I watched this bowl of wonder, I had a strong urge to explore. *Why not take a bus? Why not just go… see this tropical land?*

At eight-thirty I climbed on the bus. My ticket to freedom cost ninety sen—the equivalent of thirty-five cents Canadian. The bus was high, large, and rank with fumes. I felt heady with my quick decision. I didn't really care where I went; I was off to explore the countryside. Half the passengers were teen-aged Muslim school girls in turquoise uniforms and white blouses. Their round, happy faces were framed by no-nonsense white tudungs. They were pristine and jabbered and laughed in spite of the huge backpacks of homework they carried. I sat by the window. A girl with a sweet smile joined me.

"Where you from?" she said, shyly.

"Canada."

"Tourist?"

"No, I live here." A few of the other girls stopped chatting and strained to overhear our conversation.

"Where you going?"

"Umm, ah… I'm just riding on the bus… going to see the country. Where is your school?"

"In Temerluh."

"Is there a park there?"

"Big one in town and on opposite side, some nature… tracks."

"You mean trails to walk on?"

"Yes. Walks."

"Do they have guides?"

"Guides?"

"People to go with you."

"Don't know. Never went."

"Probably that's just what I want. Thanks."

The trails were near the Pahang River. A weathered sign said, *Keselamatan anda adalah tanggung jawab sendiri.* Thinking these might be useful words to know, I wrote them on my arm with a black ball-point pen. Feeling flutters of excitement and well equipped with my sturdy shoes, bottle of water and camera, I walked along an abandoned road flanked by scrubby fields. In the distance, I spied some banana trees in a clump. As I walked closer, I saw one with a huge cluster of small grass-green bananas clinging to a hefty stem. They were arranged in circles. I calculated that there were about ninety bananas in that one bunch. Their weight had pulled the whole branch over. Cascading from the end was an exotic, (some might say erotic), flower with a fuzzy lobe at least ten inches long with a single large crimson petal at the top and a small crimson tip at the end. Never had I seen a banana tree this close up. I photographed it from every angle, then continued along the path and headed up toward a hill. The sun was stinking hot, but in my excitement I was hardly conscious of my wet shirt and steaming feet. I saw a large opening in the hill and went over to investigate. A huge cave beckoned me. I calculated it must have been a hundred feet high. Entering, I saw the walls were covered with an eerie iridescent green moss. The only light was filtering through from an opening at the top. Looking up I could see what I instinctively knew were bats. They were not number one on my list of favourite critters, but they seemed content to stay high up above me. I climbed some narrow steps. The concave treads were slippery with a build-up of droppings from above. The whole place resembled a setting for a mystery book written for teen-aged boys. For that matter, I guess I was acting like a teen-aged boy. I went up about twelve steps and stood with my head tilted back, watching the bats swoop in the cave heavens above. The dank air smelt of mold, and predictably, like poop. Long shafts of light streamed through particles of dust. My mouth felt like it was stuffed with a wool sock. The fact that my water bottle was now empty made me crave a drink even more. Feeling slightly light-headed, I decided to get back out in the sunshine. As I turned around on the top step, I lost my balance and slipped on the guck. I fell to the bottom, sliding and bumping on each step and landing on a sharp spike at the bottom puncturing the right cheek of my bum. I was skewered like an olive on a pick. I couldn't move in any direction until I freed myself from the spike that held me captive. Pain hammered my butt and radiated out like rays from the sun.

Realizing action was required, I steeled myself and got my breathing under control. Then with my left hand firmly braced around my wound and my right hand grasping the spike, I tore the two apart with all the courage and strength I could command. I was as free as a newborn severed from his umbilical cord. Unfortunately, though I was severed from the weapon, the pain continued to mercilessly throb.

As if that wasn't enough, I realized my ankle felt twisted! I could feel the wetness from the muck mixed with blood, seeping through my cotton slacks. I couldn't contemplate moving. I just wanted to stay put and wait for an ambulance to drive up and whisk me away. But there would be no ambulance and I knew that sitting in the muck wasn't a luxury I could afford for long. Sooner or later I'd have to get out of there. Shifting around until I was in the prayer position, I grabbed the railing and pulled myself slowly up. Painfully I took a few steps toward the opening. My options were few. Walking would hurt my ankle, rolling would torture my bum, travelling on my knees would shake up both. I decided to do a mixture and really doddle. Along the path I found what looked like a broken and weathered broomstick. I used it as a walking stick. It didn't really help, but it comforted me. By the time I hobbled to the trail entrance, it was mid-afternoon. My posterior and my ankle were competing for first prize in throbbing. Aside from the physical pain, I felt exhausted and frustrated that what I had earnestly tried to do had turned out so badly. I propped myself against a grassy bank beside the road and prepared to wait for a bus. This wasn't exactly downtown Vancouver. I guessed that a car would be more helpful to me than a bus anyway. Cars sped by but none stopped. I needed something to draw attention to myself. I took off my cadmium yellow headscarf and tied it to the broom handle to make a flag. A breeze was shaking the dead leaves out of the trees and whirling them through the air. I thought of the Chinese superstition that if you hear a crow caw between seven and eleven you could expect rain and wind. I guess I had missed the warning. I could hear monkeys shrieking and knew that was a sign of a heavy rainstorm approaching. *God, help me!* Thunder rumbled in the distance. Rain fell gently for about a minute before the sky opened and unleashed its load. Rain fell in sheets, blown along by the wind. The thunder was no longer rumbling, it was c-c-cracking! Lightning split the sky. I had become used to these immediate violent rains, but this was the first time I'd been out in thunder and lightning. I waved my broomstick flag until my shoulders ached with the effort. At least the rain cooled me off and relieved my mind from my injured body and soul. After about fifteen minutes, the storm stopped and the sun burnt its way through the moisture. Steam rose from my wet clothes. No one had wanted to pick me up when I was dry, and now I was drenched, I certainly hadn't improved my prospects. Just when I was beginning to despair, a lorry came along, slowed, and yes, stopped.

By late afternoon I had shocked Padma and the patients, not to mention Chen, by hobbling into the office in my muddy, soggy clothes. Chen whisked me into a cubical and asked me what had happened. It wrenched me to have to tell him. The moment I mentioned *bats*, he looked at my open wound. He asked a nurse to clean me up and scurried off to talk to Dr. Chong, leaving me with a sense of foreboding.

On his return, Chen explained that bat saliva and guano could carry rabies. "Sounds like you were sliding around in it."

"But Chen, they were so high up!"

"Sure. But caves can harbour thousands of bats… and you got yourself an open wound. You were sitting in the saliva and guano. That's an invitation for infection."

"What's guano?"

"It's excrement of some seabirds, small furry animals, and bats."

"Rabies is dangerous, isn't it?"

Chen hesitated, before saying, "Yes. Extremely. Hopefully you are fine, but we can't take any chances."

"What's the treatment?"

"Post exposure prophylaxis (PEP). It just means preventive or protective treatment for disease. In this case it's a vaccine against rabies. Have a shower and I'll get you some scrubs to put on. Then you can have the injection. Ordinarily we would have had to order the serum from KL, but we needed some for a patient two days ago, and there is plenty left for you. You'll get the injection in your arm. Be prepared to feel significant discomfort from the shot. At least you don't need a tetanus shot, since it was part of your shot program before you came to Malaysia. I'll borrow Dr. Chong's car and take you home."

Arriving at 88 Jalan Kupas, I slowly mounted the spiral staircase. Awkwardly, I perched on the bed. Chen propped me up with pillows. He sounded like a broken record.

"What were you thinking of? What did you suppose the *muck* was? Did it occur to you that it was bat excrement, souped-up with rain? The place would be full of snakes. Snakes love to eat bats. What if you had broken your leg and couldn't have got out? Can't you hear me saying, *"Oh, Lauren's not home. Let's look for her in the bat cave outside of Temerluh!* Damn it, Lauren, you didn't even tell anyone where you were going! You really are a Dragon."

"I didn't *know* where I was going," I said defensively. "I just wanted to get out… see the country. This morning I realized there was beauty everywhere; I just had to open my eyes and look around. I felt uplifted and wanted to go out and explore the surrounding area. I have to do *something,* Chen."

"I know you do. I'm sorry if I sound critical, but I was really worried when you arrived at my office looking like you'd been swimming in a tank of molasses. I should be getting back to work. Don't worry about low grade fever or muscle aches. That's normal. The office was quite busy this afternoon. Is there anything more you need?"

"No, I'm fine. Thanks for the mangosteens and the bottle of *100 PLUS.* I'll read the *New Straits Times* and maybe have a nap."

"Okay. Careful of the mangosteens. They'll stain your clothes. I'll see you at seven." He gave me a quick hug and turned to go.

"By the way," I said extending my arm. "What's *"Keselamatan anda adalah tanggung jawab sendiri?"*

Chen laughed. "It means *your safety is your own responsibility.* Guess it's time for language lessons! Now, I really must go."

As I lay propped on the pillows, I opened a mangosteen the way I had been shown, by squeezing it gently between my two palms to release the white lobes from the thick pulpy shell. While I savoured the lemony, marshmallowy fruit, I thought how my escapade would seem to Chen—and worse, to his family.

Thankfully, they would be saved the embarrassment of hearing me admit to a student that I was on the bus but didn't know where I was going, or me sitting by the side of the road with disgustingly filthy, smelly, wet slacks with a rip in the back, pathetically waving a broom stick with a yellow bandana tied to the end while I waited for help. Then walking into Chen's clinic with everyone staring at *the doctor's wife* in her disheveled state. No doubt the Wongs would find out enough to damage my already questionable credibility. I felt weighted down from being constantly studied under the Wong's—and the whole town's microscope. Wherever I went, I stood out. It felt like being in the courtroom with every man and woman in the town on the jury. I sighed and picked up the newspaper.

After a restless night my aching muscles had not improved noticeably. I could feel the swelling on my bruised backside. Chen told me to stay home and rest. He brought me an ice pack to reduce the swelling. Soon after he had gone to work, Tan came into my bedroom and asked the predictable Malaysian greeting, *have you eaten?* I told her Chen had brought me some coffee before he went to work.

"You feel better?"

"Not much, Ma. I ache all over."

Then she announced, "You need a *hot ginger compress* for your ankle. I will make it. You will watch. You will know next time."

I felt caught in the middle, with Chen saying *ice* and Tan saying *hot*—both with considerable authority. I wasn't prepared to challenge Tan. Besides, I was curious about Traditional Chinese Medicine. I thumped down the stairs, grabbing the rail and holding my bandaged right foot in front of me. I sat at the table and Tan brought me a cup of green tea and congee topped with peanuts, spring onions and hard-boiled egg. While I ate it, she gathered up the ingredients for the hot compress: gingerroot, spoon, knife, waxed paper, elastic bandage, a gas burner, and to my chagrin, a cleaver! "This is how we treat a joint that has *wind,*

Ma said." I had to curb an irreverent laugh. My joint had *wind*? What next? Tan was going to treat it with *hot ginger*? Why the cleaver? I watched as she cut the gingerroot into one inch pieces and put them directly on the gas burner element until they sizzled. Then she put the ginger on a board and gave it a blow with the cleaver to release the juices. That went on the waxed paper that was in turn put on a tea towel. Finally, the whole thing was slapped on my ankle and held there with the elastic bandage. With the room temperature probably thirty-three degrees and the skin on my ankle cooking, I said with some distress, "It's very hot, Ma."

"If it's very too hot, we can off the bandage. Cool it a minute."

I wanted to be a stoic but was forced to ask her to take it off *quickly*. I wondered, briefly, if she were out to get me! The procedure was repeated several times before I could relax and admit that it felt soothing.

When Chen got home at seven, I told him about Tan's treatment.

"It's an ancient practice," Chen said.

"Does that mean it's good?"

"If it has been used for centuries, there's bound to be some justification for it."

"I was worried that you would be cross with me."

"No, I'm not cross, but the next time do me the honour of following my orders. I'm relieved that at least Ma put the compress on your ankle and not on your open wound."

I didn't like the tone of his voice, but I recognized by the furrows of his brow that he was worried about me.

Three days later I still felt battered. I was nurturing my wounds and trying to be up-beat, when Chen announced it was time to have my *second* shot! Again, I had major discomfort, more swelling and tenderness.

"You didn't tell me I'd have to have two shots, Chen! Is this the last?"

"Actually, not. It's a series of three."

"Three! Why didn't you tell me that in the first place?"

"Come on, Lauren, I know these shots are not fun. Just keep in mind that rabies is almost always fatal. No matter how unlikely it might be, I would never take the slightest chance of infection."

"Thanks, Chen. I promise I'll pack up my whining. You've been very tolerant."

Chapter 11

AFTER TWO WEEKS OF limping around and positioning myself carefully to protect my fanny, I sought some action. I phoned Auntie Lai.

"Is there *any* time that Zi Qing and I can get together?"

Apparently the dear little boy was still fully booked.

"When I promised him we would get together to make some pictures, he sounded so excited. I don't want him to think I've forgotten."

"I hope he *has* forgotten. He doesn't have time for anything more. He has Tae Kwon Do on Monday, Chinese lessons on Tuesday and Thursday, Math tutorial on Wednesday, and gymnastics on Friday. So that leaves the weekend."

"That's not good for me. I see so little of Chen that I really want to keep my weekends free."

"Okay, lah. I'll call you if Zi Qing gets a cancellation. Thanks, lah."

The following Friday we had our chance. The gymnasium was

needed for a meeting of all teachers in the district and gymnastics class was cancelled.

"Go over at three-thirty. The maid will let you in. Zi Qing will be there. Make him change his clothes," Auntie Lai said. "Tell the maid to make you tea and whatever else you feel like. "I'll be home at six. Zi Meng won't be there. She's at violin practice. Bye."

I couldn't believe this woman. By comparison, Tan was a tower of compassion. Again, I wondered how such polar opposites could be sisters. I should have figured Lai out on the first night when I saw her prancing around in her stiletto heels while everyone else was in bare feet, shoes neatly stacked on the rack outside the front door.

At four o'clock, I knocked on the door of Auntie Lai's row house. A small wisp of a woman with her black hair wound into a bun at the nape of her neck cautiously opened the door.

"Hello, I'm Lauren," I said to the maid. "What's your name?"

"My name Risa," she said quietly. "M'am said you come."

I took my shoes off and stepped inside to face an altar similar to Tan's. That's where the similarity stopped. Where Tan's floors were covered with linoleum, Auntie Lai's were ceramic tiles. Tan's house was full of clutter; Auntie Lai's was in blank order. The white walls showcased three pieces of black lacquered Chinoiserie furniture: a cabinet with scenes of landscapes and battles from ancient China painted in gold, and two side chairs with straight backs and horseshoe arms. Although the chairs looked grand, the seats looked like butt-busters. No pictures hung on the walls and no books, newspapers or plants cluttered the surfaces. The whole room suggested there might be more to come.

"Auntie Lauren!" Zi Qing screeched as he flew down the stairs pulling his T-shirt over his head. "Is your ankle better now? And your bum?"

"Yes, they're much better, but I still have to be careful how I move."

"Ma said you slipped in some poop in a bat cave. Is that true?"

"Yes, it's true. The real name for bat poop is *guano*. It might be hard to remember, but it sounds nicer."

"Oh. Wish I was there to take care of you," he said with his eyes full of concern. "I've waited to see you so long. Did you bring paints?"

"Actually, I brought some chalks. They're called pastels. The colours are lovely. Look," I said, opening the box.

"Aiyo!" he said, picking one up. "Can I try them?"

"Sure, they're for you. Here's some paper. See? You have a fat pad of it."

"These… what do you call them?"

"Pastels. They're called that because they are soft colours."

"They're even prettier on the paper. They look like candy colours."

"Then let's draw candies."

"Candies?"

"Yes. Why not? Think of your favourite candies and use your favourite colours."

"I like gummy bears and jelly worms and ginger jellies."

"I think those might be some of your Uncle Chen's favourites, too. I'm going to ask Risa for a glass of water. Would you like one?"

"Not now. I'm busy," he said, kneeling on the hard floor and picking up a green chalk.

I stayed in the kitchen chatting with Risa, wanting Zi Qing to have a chance to work without me hovering over him like a helicopter.

I asked her how long she had worked here.

"Ten month," she said, holding up her ten fingers.

"Where do you live?"

"Here. Sleep by kitchen."

"Are you Malaysian?

"Indonesia. I get money, bring husband and daughter."

"How long will that take?"

"Three year or five."

"Do you ever talk with your husband and daughter?"

"Ma'm is good. Let me phone one time month. Fifteen minute."

"Oh, Risa. You must miss them so much!"

"Yes, miss them."

Fifteen minutes a month! "M'am is good," Risa had said.

"What do you do with your time off?" I asked.

"No time off, M'am."

Thinking she had misunderstood, I said, "The days that you don't have to work, Risa. Where do you go? What do you do?"

"No days off, M'am. For one year. Contract."

"Are you sure?"

"Yes. Two year, two Sunday month."

Speechless and distressed, I thought I should get back to Zi Qing. *No time off for a year? Could I have misunderstood?* I'd made my decision. Auntie Lai was a *Dragon Lady!* Passing through the dining room, I stopped at the aquarium. I stood there watching at least six varieties of tropical fish swim over stones, fake rocks, and tunnels. The water looked sparkling clean and bubbles rose up to the surface. Several boxes of fish food sat on top the tank.

"How's it going?" I asked, looking over Zi Qing's shoulder.

"It's fun," he said. "See? Doesn't it look yummy?"

"Yes, yummy," I said, conscious of my ankle as I knelt down on the floor beside him. "It looks as if you emptied the candy bag right on your page. The heads of your gummy bears are facing in all directions. That's great. Do you want to know a secret?"

"Yes. First time I saw you, you said you would tell me some secrets. Are you going to whisper?"

"Yes, I am," I whispered. "See this jelly worm?"

"Can," he whispered back.

"Well it looks flat. But really it's round. So if we take a finger and rub it across the center and smudge it a bit, it makes the colour lighter, and now it looks…"

"Round," we said together.

"That's neat! I'm going to do it to the others."

"What do you think should be behind the candies?" I asked him. "A dish? A floor… or maybe more candies? I'm going to watch the fish," I said, "while you decide what to do."

In a few minutes, he said, "I'm finished. That's coloured sugar floating around the candies!"

"Great!" I said.

"I want to give it to Uncle Chen," he said writing his name on it.

I wanted his parents to see it, but something told me they wouldn't think drawing candies was an activity worthy of their only son's time.

"Uncle Chen will be happy if you give it to him," I said. "Come and tell me about your fish."

"Okay. There's nine… four orange, two black, two yellow and one black and white—it's the big one. The orange ones are small. Sometimes they get eaten by big black and white one. Least I think so but I've never seen it. Ma lets me, not Risa, throw the dead ones out. She won't touch them."

"Oh, you are a brave boy. You must have to put your arm in the tank till the water's right up to your shoulder. Would you like to draw a fish story?"

"Yes. Should I bring my paper pad up on the dining room table so I can see the fish?"

"That's a good idea."

"I don't know how to draw water."

"Maybe you should draw some fish. Then I'll whisper you a secret about the water. I'm going to read the newspaper while you make the fish."

Zi Qing worked intently drawing fish. I could see him looking up at the tank as he went.

Finally he said, "I'm finished the fish, so can you come and tell me how to make water? It looks white to me."

"Okay, let's hold a piece of your white paper up beside the water. Do you still think the water looks white?"

"No, but what colour *is* it?"

"It's secret time again. Let me whisper. It's a lot of colours because water is clear and it reflects the colours around it. It reflects the brown from the table, some orange from the fish, some green from the seaweed and even some blue from your shirt. Let's lay some bits of those colours through the water. Now... move your fingers through the colours like this... smudge it... and keep it going, back and forth, the way the water moves. We have to make it look like it's moving because the fish are swimming through the water. The bubbles will help to put some motion in the water, too—and they're easy to draw. That's good!"

"Won't Mummy be surprised to see the water moving?"

Again, I said I was sure she would. Again, I wouldn't have bet on it.

"I have to go now, Zi Qing. I had a good time watching you make pictures."

"Can you come again?" he said.

"I want to. You make pictures as often as you can and keep them to show me the next time I see you."

Zi Qing disappeared and I went into the kitchen to say goodbye to Risa.

"Bye, M'am," she said.

"Please call me Lauren," I said.

"Can not. M'am not like. Problem."

"Then call me Lauren when she is not here."

"Will try."

Zi Qing was quickly back saying, "Here, take this picture to Uncle Chen." He reached up and gave me a hug.

"Thanks for the fun—and the hug, Zi Qing. And thanks from Uncle Chen for the picture."

Chapter 12

In Shanthi's garden I sat on a teak chair with a yellow, canvas-covered cushion on the seat, making detailed sketches of clusters of frangipani blossoms. The branches, I noticed, were not tapered like other branches. They were straight as a half-inch pipe, all the way from where they left the trunk to their tips. Coarse, leathery leaves and waxy blossoms sprouted forth from the branches. The glow from my time spent with Zi Qing the day before had caused me to phone Shanthi and ask if she would mind if I spent the afternoon sketching in her garden. She sounded more than pleased; as if I would be doing *her* a favour.

Another plant I was attracted to was the red ginger growing in the shade at the back of the herbaceous border. The stems grew a couple of feet tall, and the leaves attached in a way that strengthened the stem to support the stunning large, red flowers. Shanthi saw me studying it and came to tell me that the red bracts were not the flower. Technically, the real flowers were white and quite insignificant. We certainly eyed the garden from different perspectives. I saw the flowers through artist's glasses, Shanthi through a textbook. For my purposes, the gorgeous red bracts standing straight and reaching for the sky were the flowers.

"They are very easy to propagate, which explains the huge clumps."

To the left of the red ginger, stood one lone yucca with sword-like leaves.

"The yucca adds a bit of contrast because of its sculptured form," she said, "but I only want a token one. They're not popular with serious gardeners, they're just for people who want low-maintenance gardens."

There was no doubt that she was a serious gardener. "You sound like a botanist, Shanthi."

"I *am* a botanist. I studied botany at the University of Edinburgh which is where I met Dr. Chong."

So that explains it. "Were you from Malaysia originally?"

"No, I was from New Delhi. Dr. Chong is the Malaysian."

Similar to Chen and me. No wonder we're bonding easily!

My pencil rolled off my lap and my sketch book slipped down to meet it.

"How was it for you, when you first came to Malaysia?" I asked eagerly.

"Not easy at all. My father-in-law was upset—to the point of not recognizing me as a part of the family. The only thing that made the situation tolerable was that my mother-in-law accepted me from the beginning. But she was forbidden to have me in their house. Dr. Chong and I lived over a shop house for the first year. People ostracized me. I'm talking about a generation ago, don't forget."

I felt shivers on the skin of my upper arms. "I understand how you must have felt." My heartbeat picked up speed. I needed to talk with Shanthi. "Let's sit down under the umbrella," I said.

"Imagine Dr. Chong trying to start a new practice while coping with his father's attitude and knowing that I was so alone and unhappy."

"Why didn't you just go somewhere else?"

"In those days, it was even harder to push aside the eldest son's role as caregiver for his parents. Dr. Chong kept hoping things would change, and they did—six months before his father died."

"That must have been a relief, but how sad that he alienated you for so long. How did you deal with it?"

"Dr. Chong's mother and I used to meet in the privacy of this very garden. This is where we got to know each other. She was a very dear lady."

"How long did you feel shunned by the community?"

"Always… still some. Culture shift doesn't happen in a day. Nor a year. Try a decade, or two."

"Oh! That's terrible." Not for a moment had I ever considered that I would *never* feel part of the Malaysian community. "How did you manage?"

"At first I threw all my energy into looking after Dr Chong, and later, nursing his mother and caring for Nisha. Gradually I became obsessed with this garden."

The phone rang, and Shanthi excused herself.

I tried to imagine her living in a fortress with her family and her garden, year after year. Did that mean she had no friends? Surely there were some Indian people who would befriend her. Had her father-in-law turned people against her? How did this bode for me? Would my future be one of loneliness and isolation? My head reeled at the new insight Shanthi had given me. I hardly knew her, yet she had shared so much.

I stared, without seeing, at Shanthi's duranta plumier—to me, the golden dewdrop. Slowly I reigned in my attention and looked at the trumpet-shaped periwinkle flowers with little yellow sacks in the center, growing about four meters high then draping over a piece of lattice. Add to that show, yellow grape-shaped berries hanging side by side with the flowers. I moved my stool over and sketched details of the trumpets, the fruit and the leaves. I would come back to this. It might be my first large painting since coming to this land of tropical beauty.

Just as I was about to leave, I heard a loud engine and what sounded like a muffler dragging behind a lorry, followed by the slamming of a door. A man jumped out. I figured it must be Parveen. He was slight with narrow shoulders and sun-damaged skin. The only thing round about him was his straw hat. His smile exposed perfectly aligned teeth white as alabaster. He hustled back and forth from the lorry to the pond with flats of something pink.

I left my sketching and went to see what he was carrying. He didn't shake my hand, but he did tell me his name.

"Do you like the garden?" he asked, beaming as if from ownership.

"It's a paradise!" I said. He looked puzzled so I said, "It couldn't be more beautiful, Parveen. It's an oasis."

"I don't know oasis but glad you like it."

"I mean it's a special place that gives joy and peace in the middle of the ordinary."

"Not peaceful for me," he chuckled. "But pretty. I put lotus plants in pond now."

That night I told Chen about the personal things Shanthi had shared with me.

"You will have a lot of challenges, but not nearly as severe as hers." he said. "I feel encouraged because I can see the progress made in one generation. It gives me hope that greater respect and acceptance of individual differences will continue to grow in the future. And you, my dear, will be in a position to be a catalyst for the process."

I was very moved by his vision and his expression of it. I hoped I could live up to the challenge. It would probably confound me at times, but I suppose that's part of the process.

In a lighter tone, I said, "What is Dr. Chong's name? Shanthi calls him 'Dr. Chong' all the time! She says it in a very respectful and endearing manner, but I find it quite strange."

"I'm not sure what his name is. I can't help you out because everyone at work calls him Dr. Chong, too. I'd say it's out of respect and also because of his age. As for Shanthi, I think she does it out of respect and no doubt a hint of pride."

"By the way, what do they call *you* at work?"

"Padma, and I guess most of the staff, call me Dr. Wong, but Dr Chong calls me Chen. He seems to feel rather fatherly toward me. I like it."

Chapter 13

ONE NIGHT, AFTER DINNER, Wong gave a big burp and rubbed his stomach. Then he said, "Lauren, do you feel ready to come to the plantation with us tomorrow? You will come when we go to work. Fang will drive you home when you're ready."

I liked that he had remembered my wanting to go and agreed quickly.

The next morning I woke to the tinny sound of the alarm clock. The darkness would last for another hour and a half. Faintly, I heard the Imam calling the Muslims to prayer. I imagined the faithful getting out of bed in their night clothes and kneeling on their prayer mat for the first of five times that day. Chen was sprawled over two thirds of the bed and didn't budge when I got up. I kissed him gently. Tan would wake him up in time to get to the clinic. I put on some old clothes as Wong had suggested, and went downstairs to have congee and coffee with Wong, Uncle So Ho and Fang.

I tried to sit with my weight on the left of my backside as we bumped and rattled along country roads in Wong's Proton Saga. The windows were open and the brothers were dragging smoke into their lungs. I sat beside Fang in the back seat, choking on country road dust and cigarette smoke. Calmly I told myself that they were just part of the adventure.

Finally, we came to an impressive sign—measuring about six feet by five, and emblazoned with WONGSHOPE RUBBER PLANTATION in large black capitals. Below that, in smaller letters: Wong So Kwok, Owner; Wong So Ho, General Foreman; Wong Lee Fang, Head Planter.

"That's quite a sign, Pa," I exclaimed.

"That's how it must look. The law. The numbers at the bottom are registration and license numbers."

We turned down a narrower road and drove along a nondescript variety of shrubs growing along a wooden fence. I could smell whiffs of latex before I got out of the car, but they were nothing compared to the stink that greeted me as I stood up. Before me stretched rows of rubber trees, (*Heveas*, Shanthi would call them), climbing up an incline for as far as I could see.

"Does any sun get in there, Pa?"

"Not much. Some days it's almost dark. The lorry paths are the brightest. Come inside, Lauren. It's cooler in there."

The office was in a run-down bungalow with peeling paint, dirty windows, and a tin roof. The largest room was Pa's office. So Ho's office was considerably smaller. The third room had a bed and chair used by the night watchman or in the case of an emergency. The kitchen space was used up by a sink with one tap, a table with four chairs and a small refrigerator. The bathroom had a corner shower. One grey towel hung limply from a hook. Offensive smells came from the straddle toilet. A bottle of Javex sat on the floor and a bar of soap on the window sill.

"These are pictures from the old days," Wong said, pointing to the framed sepia water-stained pictures on his office walls. This is a labourer cleaning a coagulating tank. This one shows dried sheets coming out of a smokehouse, and the third one shows tapping the trees. They used to let the latex drip into small china cups. Now, as you'll see, it drips out of carefully crafted slits in the bark into black cast iron pots."

"Do they make one cut at a time?"

"Yes. One cut at a time. When the cut heals, we make a new cut. Fang, take Lauren in the lorry. Show her what it looks like in there. Don't go in too far. Get her a pair of rubber boots. Get some repellent from the office. Drive carefully."

"Sure, Pa," Fang said with a saintly look.

"This is cool!" Fang said, revving the engine. "What do you think so far?"

"I am impressed by the density and the sheer size of the plantation. It goes on as far as I can see."

"Oh, it goes *farther* than you can see! I'll show you."

We rumbled along narrow, barely passable roads, climbing and turning in all directions on the grid.

"Everything looks the same, Fang! How do you know where we are?"

"It doesn't all look the same to me. I work here every day. Let's get out. I'll show you the latex, and what's under the trees."

"What exactly *is* under the trees?"

"There's mimosa planted between the trees. It doesn't get sun, just damp, so it rots and fertilizes the rubber tree. Also, lots of surprises crawl on the soil—like snakes, rats, worms, centipedes, scorpions and cicadas. Look, Sis—there's a spider. Must be four inches across."

"I don't want to get out, Fang. For one thing, I know scorpions are poisonous."

"Don't be afraid. That's what the boots and the Deet are for."

True enough. I got out. The air was laden with moisture. Cicadas sang seamlessly on one shrill note. My back and forehead were beaded with sweat.

"See how rich the earth is," Fang said, picking up a handful of dark, loamy soil. The trees grow fast. After six or seven years, the trees are ready to tap. Most of the trees grow fast. Like Dad says, you can almost see them grow. One big problem is that the native tropical trees get cleared to plant the rubber, but they are determined to grow back. We have to keep clearing them out. While we're here, look at the latex in the pail. It's liquid."

"Yes. It looks like the Bondfast glue we use in Canada. Does latex get sold just as it is?"

"No. It coagulates fast. Concentrated latex is used for making glue, gloves, condoms, catheters, balloons, carpet backing... all sorts of stuff."

I felt very damp and somewhat claustrophobic. Breathing was difficult. I had to drag the air into my lungs.

"I think we should go back, Fang."

"Really? It's fun for me to show you something you haven't seen before."

"It's interesting for me to see all this, but I really want to go back. Why haven't I seen any workers?"

"They are working in different parts of the plantation. Believe me. You only saw a small corner. They're tapping, collecting latex, killing pests and trying to clear out the native trees over and over—all sorts of stuff."

Back at the office, I heard about a variety of estate problems—pests, destruction during the Japanese occupation, competition from synthetic rubber, escalating costs, recessions, weak markets and tariffs.

Pa Wong looked very serious. "Actually," he said, "I want to give up the rubber plantation and go into the palm oil business. That would make us more money."

I knew his head was full of plans for the conversion. He had mentioned it before, leaving me wondering if he would ask us for financial aid. Obviously it was lack of money holding him up.

"Was rubber the first big industry in Malaysia?" I asked.

"No, tin. Tin was not just the first, it was the most successful.

You probably don't know, but oil palm was grown here before rubber. Way back in 1875 the first oil palm seeds arrived in South East Asia from West Africa. Four seeds! And from those four seeds a huge industry started. It became an Estate Crop that had ups and downs but became a huge financial boom for Malaysia. The trees grew well, but apparently it was a fussy crop—needed special soil, the fruit (which looked like grapes) was easily bruised and rats destroyed the trees even after they were mature. Workers would kill three-hundred rats a day at one and a half cents a rat. The trees had to be grown on a hill, and that brought on erosion problems. Worst of all, the oil was difficult to market."

"Pa, that seems like a lot of good reasons *not* to get into oil palm again."

"I suppose… but that was in 1845. That's 125 years ago. The market is *excellent* now. Markets call the shots."

"Yes, I suppose," I said lamely. My brain was saturated. It was time to split.

"Thanks, Pa. I've learned a lot. If Fang is free, I'll leave and let you go back to work."

"Sure, Lauren. I'm happy you are interested in knowing about our business. I'm glad for that."

Chapter 14

LATE THURSDAY AFTERNOON THE Mahjong tiles were clacking at 88 Jalan Kupas.

"Come, Lauren. Come see. Called 'twittering of birds' when we mix up tiles. My friends—Pong and Ping. They're twins! And that's Chow Kit," Tan said, hardly pausing for me to acknowledge them. "Now we build Great Wall of China." They arranged the 144 tiles face down in a square with eighteen tiles per side and two tiles deep. "I am East Wind. I start the game," she said picking up four tiles and putting them in her rack. She babbled fast—all the time preparing for a new game to start.

"It looks like fun!" *Really it scares me—winds, dragons, characters, circles, flowers, bamboos, pungs, kongs, chows—yikes!*

"I'm going to meet Chen now. Enjoy yourselves." No one looked up from the game. I just smiled and walked out. I wondered if Ma would want to teach me Mahjong. It looked intriguing, but their speed was off-putting and I didn't like the gambling aspect.

Meeting Chen at his office after work was the tip-top of my

day. We craved the privacy and peace of hanging out together and chatting, with the river flowing by and the moon shining coyly down. There wasn't much daylight left by the time he got off work around seven. In fact, it was almost dark. Still, the evenings were warm and pleasant. Never did we even consider taking a sweater. The light and dark pattern varied very little all year long because of Malaysia's proximity to the equator.

That night we strolled through the night market and picked up a snack of chicken satay with peanut sauce and two bags of guava juice. With our plastic bags swinging from their plastic strings we wended our way toward the river. We leaned against a large acacia tree, both sitting on padded straw mats—Chen to protect his good pants and me to protect my tender rear.

"How was your adventure to the plantation today?"

"Stellar. Fang drove me around seeming proud to show me as much as we could fit in. I was uncomfortable getting out of the lorry after he told me there were scorpions under the trees. In fact, near the end, between the endless trees and heavy air, I felt quite claustrophobic."

"Yeah. All of it was so new to you. It's sort of like taking a rubber tree planter and plunking him down in a UBC anatomy lecture."

The thought of that made me laugh until peanut sauce shot up my nose and sobered me.

"You know, Chen, the natural rubber industry is really environmentally sound."

"You're right. Replanting guarantees an endless renewable resource."

"Pa talked about oil palm—starting way back in 1875 when four seeds were sent to Malaysia from West Africa. That was the start of a booming industry. Then he talked about all the problems and trials involved with growing oil palm trees until I got the courage to ask why he would want to produce oil palm."

"Yes, quite brave. What did he say?"

"Something about 1875 was 125 years ago and there was a

good market then and a *great* market today. It would make him much more money. That's when I bowed out. I chose to escape before he repeated a subtle cry that he needed money. I'd like to know why he doesn't borrow from the bank."

"He already owes the bank a lot of money, and he doesn't want to pay interest."

"So what? The rest of the world does."

"Chinese people like to borrow from other family members."

"Then why doesn't he borrow from your rich uncle in Singapore?"

"It's because my uncle says if he's going to lend a big amount, he wants to own half the company. Of course my father will never consent to giving half the profits to his brother. Even within families, a deal is wangled shrewdly. They say that ten percent of the Chinese are very wealthy, and the other ninety percent are working like hell to become so."

"That's not hard to believe. Do you think he will stop hinting, and actually ask us for funds?"

"You have a lot of questions tonight. I doubt if he will ask us because he knows we are paying him back for my education in amounts that leave us with only a pittance."

"I just hope he won't want us to live with them until our debts are paid." I shivered in spite of the warm evening.

"Come on. Don't borrow trouble. I'll do my best not to let that happen."

"I know you will, babe. Give me a hug and let me see your everything-will-be-alright face."

He gave a rascally look. It did the trick. We picked up our cushions and the plastic bags from our snacks and headed home to have dinner with the family.

Chapter 15

Two nights later we returned to our favourite spot on the bank of the river. As we listened to the familiar sound of the water flowing by, I put my arm around Chen and said, "How was work today?"

"Okay. So far I've mainly been looking at medical records and meeting patients. Dr. Chong introduces me to everyone who comes in. Some of them seem to be coming in just to check out the Wong boy. The interesting thing is to see how the patients want to mix the old cures with the new: TCM and western medicine."

"What's TCM?"

"Traditional Chinese Medicine. It goes back for many centuries. Chinese people have grown up with those treatments, and want to use them first. Only if they haven't been cured will they think of trying western remedies."

"Did you study TCM at UBC?"

"Actually, yes—sort of. I took one elective called DPAS: Doctor, Patient, and Society."

"Was it interesting?"

"Sure, everything was interesting. It's probably not the type of course I could have had in Malaysia."

"What do the Malaysians really think of the western countries?"

"Do you mean western medicine, or just generally?"

"Both."

"Okay. Medicine first. The way I see it, there are three things. Asians think people in the western countries don't pay enough attention to preventative medicine; they take too many pills, and they want fast cures. An herbal treatment requires patience. It may help, but not instantly."

"Those things don't surprise me, but don't you think the tables are turning? Westerners *are* more interested in preventative medicine now. And they *are* looking to alternatives—like acupuncture, various massage techniques and herbal medicines."

"You're right. The ultimate would be people using the best of both systems. I expect to see big progress in that during my lifetime. As for what Asians think of westerners in general, I think they secretly admire them—or at least what they *have* and can *do*. But they're also critical. Malaysia has put up with centuries of domination—by Portuguese, the Dutch, and then the British."

"Didn't those countries help Malaysia?"

"Yeah. They did. But Malaysians rightly believe that the Europeans *took* far more than they *gave*. It's not surprising that the resentment, even bitterness, carries on."

"Sometimes Malaysians seem to idolize westerners. Like in their movies, and music, and clothes."

"Right again—and sometimes they actually seem to hate them. They think westerners are arrogant, crass and rude. They feel that westerners don't understand Asian culture—they don't respect it or, even worse, they don't even recognize its existence."

"I've sensed that, already."

"Sure, Lauren, you would. What first attracted you to me was that you really wanted to know about my family, my country and culture. No one else had shown more than a superficial interest. I think the other students thought of me as one of those damned Asian students who took all the prizes and wore out the facilities.

"Do you remember how rude Richard was when you came to meet my family?"

"Sort of. I remember that he fired comments about my brain, the fact that I didn't drink beer, but worst of all I felt out of place with your family. I liked your dad, but I couldn't imagine ever feeling like one of you."

"At the time I remember being outraged with Richard's rude and totally inappropriate and unrelenting remarks to you. But it's interesting, since my brother's fatal accident those feelings have faded. Now, I tend to remember the good times I shared with Richard. It's like I still carry a heavy burden of loss. There's no room for anger."

"I guess I can understand that. I suppose we should head home. I sure hate to leave our little oasis," Chen said.

"Me, too. But dinner will be ready. We must go."

When we walked in the door, Tan said, "Glad you're home, I have something to say."

We all sat down and were slurping up the noodles in our Won Ton soup when Tan said, "Pa and me think we should have wedding."

Chen and I lifted our heads, our chopsticks poised in mid-air, and listened.

"Tea ceremony will be here. Then wedding dinner at *restauran*. Everyone would come. Yes?"

"Aiyo!" Fang hooted.

"Sure," said Chen. "If that's what you would like, it's okay with us. Right, Lauren?"

I couldn't believe what was happening. There had been no mention of a Chinese wedding. What motivated them? To show off Chen? To show off me? To have a party? Or maybe the celebration was to pull in the little red envelopes. Probably some of all of that, I mused.

"Yes, of course," I said.

We continued our dinner. So Ho was looking especially blanched.

"Can I be Master of Ceremonies?" asked Fang. Then we all took a cue from him and joined in the spirit.

"Do I have to wear a suit?" asked Pa Wong.

"Can I do your hair, Lauren?" asked Tan.

"Can I stay home?" asked So Ho, almost smiling.

"We can't have the wedding until my crate comes because my shoes are in it," I said. "And I'm not prepared to fold my feet into a pair of Malaysian size sixes."

"Can we have a Lion Dance?" asked Fang. "Or at least a drum band?" We laughed, but even I knew he was not joking.

It seemed everyone wanted to be involved. That was fine with me. I'd done my thing in Vancouver...

The day of the wedding was bright and warm. Chen arrived in a sand-coloured summer-weight suit, a cream shirt and a sand tie with narrow dark brown and peach stripes. His roommate, Jason, had driven him and was staying close by his side. From my bedroom window I watched them as they walked into the garden. Chen seemed to pause to take in the beauty of the spring garden. The dogwood tree was in full bloom and the flowerbeds were massed with irises, tulips and Canterbury bells. When Dad and I came into the garden I was wearing the white cotton voile dress embroidered with flowers that had been my mother's wedding dress, daisies in my red hair and the gold chain with the Chinese symbol of love around my neck. I held a bouquet of Bonnie Marie peach camellias and lily of the valley. Even Chen's conservative nature couldn't conceal his happiness.

We were both filled with joy as I walked toward him. We stood in front of the ivy-covered arbour with Robin and Jason beside us and our guests around us. After we had said our vows and slipped a gold band on each other's finger, we embraced. Everyone clapped. Chen's Uncle Tan Soon Fatt and Auntie Chu Pei Kee who lived in Vancouver and had included us in their Chinese New Year celebrations, were beaming.

Caterers scurried about filling the punch bowl and putting food on the trestle tables they had assembled a few hours earlier. Everyone mingled easily and happily. In the beauty of the wedding and the uniqueness of our situation, the big change in our lifestyle that lay ahead could only be seen in a positive way.

Before we left on our honeymoon, I hugged my mother and dad and said, "Thank you for being champions of our marriage."

Dad replied, "In this marriage there are only champions."

Our Chinese wedding would be Tan's party. I would do my best to play it her way.

Chapter 16

O N TUESDAY MORNING THE phone rang. It was Wong.

"Lauren? Your shipment is in Port Klang."

"Oh, that's great, Pa."

"I arranged it be taken through customs. Agent's name is Abdullah. I will send Fang in my lorry. He will get it for you."

"That would be perfect. Thanks so much."

"It's okay. You stay home to wait for it."

"Actually, I should go. There'll be papers to sign."

"You're right. Take your passport. Fang will come soon."

"Thanks for the reminder about the passport. Thanks for everything, Pa."

"Welcome. Bye"

"Hey, I like this," Fang said as we rumbled along in Wong's lorry. "I get to spend some time with my new sister-in-law and I get the day off work!"

"And I'm excited because I get to spend time with my new brother-in-law and at last, I will have my things! I thought this lorry stayed on the plantation."

"It's really for work, but it's a good lorry. How big's the container?"

"Four by six by eight feet, I think. I'm wondering if I should leave my stuff in the container or take out the individual boxes and pile them in the lorry."

"Why do you want to keep the container?"

"I thought I might use it for storage. Just take out what I need."

"It should fit in the lorry, but not much more room."

"Do you think your parents would mind me leaving it outside by the front door?"

"No, they don't mind. They know there's not much of space."

"I feel guilty about the space we're using."

"It's okay with us. Chinese people are used to living in small places. The only one who might mind is Uncle So Ho. Before he used to sleep in your room and now he shares my room."

I had labelled him a recalcitrant old codger and hadn't given any thought to the inconvenience we were piling on him.

"How long has So Ho lived with your family?"

"About six years, I guess. He moved in after his wife died."

"*Wife*? I didn't know he was even married! How did she die?"

"That's a very sad story. Uncle So Ho and my Auntie Ooi were driving on the highway. Uncle So Ho was passing a long lorry. His judgment was bad. They collided with an on-coming van and my Auntie was hurt bad—cut very bad on her neck, lost a lot of blood. There was nobody to help them. She died before they could go to a hospital."

"Oh. That's terrible! I had no idea."

"Yes, it was terrible, already. My Uncle had only a broken knee. That's why he limps. In case you wonder about his two missing teeth, now you know. He won't get them fixed. Maybe he's afraid or maybe he wants a constant reminder of his guilt. His nerves were bad and he was often drunk. Ma said to come live with us. It was hard for So Ho because he's the eldest son, but it's my father that takes charge for him."

I felt as if an explosion had gone off in my head. How could I have been so unfair? Why hadn't Chen told me? Even though I had only been part of the household a few weeks, I could see how generous Wong and Tan were in their support of So Ho—employing him, feeding him and literally taking care of him, year after year. Then I thought of what they had done for us, taking us into their already crowded home, with no concern for themselves, and the extra work and inconvenience we caused them—so that we could have some time to organize our lives and finances. Again, I recognized those generosities as graphic examples of the strength and commitment of the Chinese family.

"You're very quiet, Lauren. Are you okay?"

"Yes. I was thinking of your family and how little I actually know of them. Thank you for telling me about your Uncle, Fang. I was thinking of your father, too. He knew I was anxious to get my things. And here we are, an hour later, on our way to collect them."

"My dad is a strong man. He takes care of us all."

"Where do your Dad and So Ho go after dinner?"

"They like to gamble and drink some beer. So Ho wouldn't go out by himself, but he likes to go with Dad. Dad keeps an eye on him. So Ho still has depression. Sometimes quite bad. But my dad likes to gamble. Don't get me wrong, it's not just for Uncle So Ho. All Chinese men like to gamble."

"Your mother likes it, too. I've watched her play mahjong with her friends. They play lightning-fast and take it very seriously."

"It's her entertainment."

"Yes. She really enjoys it. I'm sort of glad she hasn't asked me to play. I know it would slow down the game and frankly, I have no interest in the gambling aspect."

Fang's eyes opened and chin dropped as if he were a marionette that had just had his strings jerked.

At least I hadn't admitted I don't even like to buy raffle tickets.

Wanting to change the subject, I told him I really enjoyed my ride into the depth of the rubber plantation last week. I asked him to tell me more about his responsibilities on the job.

"The main thing I do is be planter. Sometimes I help with the tapping. I suppose it's something like tapping maple trees in Canada. Surely the maple sap smells nicer than latex. I'm used to it, but you must think the latex stinks."

"Let's just say it's not a perfume created by Dior. Odour aside, do you like the job?"

"Not really. It's boring and tiring. My father wants me to be a sort of cop. Some of the workers are lazy and sleep under the trees. They know I'm the son of the boss so they work hard to keep out of trouble when I'm around. It makes me work hard, too. What did you think of the plantation?"

"I thought it was neat. I was surprised to hear about the many problems. Most of them seemed to be out of your Father's control. Do you think of getting a different job some day?"

"Maybe someday but this one is good now. The best part is that my dad, he lets me have time off when I have work with the troupe doing Lion Dance, Dragon Dance or drums. That's what makes me most happy. But at times of the year there isn't much work for the troupe so I need the plantation job to earn money—and to help my dad, lah."

"I know what a good feeling comes from feeling passionate about your work," I said.

"You're passionate about painting, aren't you Lauren?"

"Yes. Just before I met your brother, my parents helped me create a studio above our garage. It took my mother and me two weeks just to empty the loft.

"After we cleaned it, we put two coats of paint on the walls and ceiling. I insisted that the walls be white."

"Why?"

"I wanted the walls to be like big blank canvases, waiting to be filled with vibrant paintings. It makes me feel excited just to talk about it."

"You've got good parents."

"Yes I do… and so do you, bro."

At three-thirty Fang backed the lorry through the gate at 88 Jalan Kupas. "I guess we have to pry the top off the container and unload the boxes so you can see where things are," he suggested.

"Should you go back to work, Fang?"

"Heck no. I want to see what's in the boxes."

"I'll bet you do! Let's get on with this, partner."

"Right away, Ma'm. I'll get a crowbar," Fang said, with a mock bow.

"I'd like to empty the container, then put it beside the front door and fill it up again—except for the things I need now. Is that a problem?"

"No, Ma'm. Anything you say, Ma'm. Let's keep moving." He climbed into the back of the lorry and started the process in good spirit. "You'll be glad to see this," he said, tugging on something.

"Oh. My easel," I screeched.

I took it from him and swung it around like a dancing partner. Then I propped it up beside the container. An hour later, boxes of books and wedding presents were back in the crate with my paints and rolled canvas on top. Fang and I had taken cartons of clothes and gifts to my bedroom where we stacked them in a corner.

"Well done, Fang. I can't thank you enough."

"It was no problem for me. It was fun to be with you. Let's get a drink of water. Then I should probably get the lorry back to the plantation."

The remainder of the afternoon was spent unpacking. I opened a box labelled IMPORTANT. On top, bound in bubble wrap, were pictures of my family: my mom and dad, brother Richard, and one of my dear grandmama. She had been so excited about my wearing Mom's wedding dress. I pulled out the dress. It was quite wrinkled. I decided to iron it in case Tan might want to see it. Then I searched for our gift for Wong and Tan, a framed eight by ten graduation photo of Chen. I had wrapped it, but the wrappings were looking a bit tattered. Suddenly I had a great yearning to see the photo again. I tore off the wrapping and there he was, smiling back at me. He looked so bright, so wise, so very dear. I brought the photo to my lips and gave it quick peck. I was so proud of him that day. Mom had invited him for a special luncheon…

It was the first week in May. The wedding plans were cast aside while Chen graduated with High Honours from the Faculty of Medicine at UBC. We invited Chen's Vancouver relatives, his Uncle Tan Soon Fatt, Auntie Chu Pei Kee and their son, Tan Lee Guan, for lunch.

"Should I attempt to make some traditional Chinese food?" Mom asked.

"Forget that!" I said. "That's Auntie's territory. Don't try to compete with it."

"Well, okay, but I can't help thinking it would be a nice gesture."

"I suppose it would be. What about starting the meal with Shark's Fin Soup? We could buy it. There are lots of good Chinese restaurants on Broadway. It's a very auspicious food; healthy, too. They'd love it! Then we could have cold salmon, salad, rolls and some kind of dessert. How does that sound?"

In honour of the special occasion our dining room table was set with the best china, sparkling crystal and silver. Chen's relatives seemed quiet as they sat around the table. But in spite of that, they looked fairly comfortable and smiled warmly. I sensed they liked me. They no doubt remembered how happily and enthusiastically I had accepted their home and food last Chinese New Year. I noticed Auntie Chu

Pei Kee admiring the bouquet of cherry blossoms on the buffet. As Dad served the Shark's Fin Soup from the tureen, Uncle Tan's eyes widened.

"This soup very auspicious, too," he said. "Brings good luck to Chen, good health, too.

"Speaking of luck, I propose we make a toast to Chen," Dad said. "Hearty congratulations, Chen. May you have a long life of happiness and prosperity!"

"To Chen!" we said as we raised our glasses and the others followed suit.

I marvelled that Dad always says the right thing. How did he know that prosperity and long life are the best wishes one could give Chinese people? The soup was highly rated by Chen and his family. Mom commented on its crunchy, gelatinous texture with her eyebrows furrowed. When the soup tureen was completely empty Dad carried it to the kitchen. He returned with a platter of deep coloured, cold, sockeye salmon, garnished with watercress and lemon. My mother followed with potato salad and a basket of whole-wheat bread and some white rolls. Salmon was a favourite of Chen's.

"Remember how you used to say salmon with the "l" pronounced?" I teased.

Chen chuckled. "Yes. I had trouble with silent letters. Most Malaysians do—the Malay language doesn't have any silent letters."

"You shouldn't be criticizing Chen's English, Lauren. He does so well!"

"Sure he does. That's why I can rib him a bit."

Uncle Tan smiled widely and said, "We very, very proud, Chen."

"I'm sure you are. We all feel the same way. He's a truly remarkable young man," Dad said,

as he spooned whipping cream on our strawberry shortcake.

After Chen had thanked Mom and Dad for inviting him and his family for lunch, I drove him to UBC where he would meet up with his class. "Dad will bring us all over about one forty-five. I've got the passes. We'll be cheering for you, sweetie! Look for us on the west side, near the front. I've got my camera loaded. I want to get good pics to take to your mother and father. I wish so much that they could be here today."

"I'm glad you're going to get photos."

Chen got out of the car and stretched. You can't imagine how relieved I am to be finished!" he said. "I actually feel kinda giddy."

I was still holding the picture of Chen on my lap. I almost wished I hadn't been so reckless in tearing off the wrappings, but I had enjoyed my little reverie.

By the time Chen got home from work, I had found all the gifts and, miraculously, some gift bags and *red* tissue. I lined the parcels up on our bed—grad picture and smoked salmon in a Vac-Pac for Wong and Tan, a can of maple syrup and a book called *Festivals Around the World* for Fang, and a picture book of British Columbia for Uncle So Ho.

As soon as dinner was finished, Chen brought the bags down to the table.

"Gifts from Canada," he said, as he passed them around.

Tan held Chen's portrait and Wong looked over her shoulder. They gave a guarded smile. "It's nice," Tan said, in a voice that could easily go unheard. The salmon pack lay on the table. So Ho said nothing. They were as enthusiastic as tepid tea. Were they disappointed? What had they expected? Something bigger or more expensive?

Once more, Fang turned the tide. "Hey! Maple syrup. Lauren was just telling me about it this afternoon on the way home from Port Klang. They make it from sap from the maple tree... and Dad, they tap the maple trees just the same as we tap the rubber trees."

"What does it taste like?" Wong asked me.

"It's very sweet. We put it on pancakes. My dad pours it on vanilla ice cream. But the real treat is having it boiling hot and poured on snow. When it congeals, just as latex does, we pick it off the snow with a fork and eat it like candy. There is a big maple syrup industry in Quebec where my grandmama lives. We used to plan our visits during the spring when the sap was running. The whole family would go into the sugar bush for big parties and eat maple candy. It was like eating toffee. It could pull the fillings right out of your teeth. Another treat was making maple butter by patiently pushing the new maple syrup back and forth on a wooden paddle until it was creamy. When we couldn't eat another mouthful, we'd have a pickle, and go back for more syrup."

"Maybe Lauren would make us some pancakes on the weekend," Chen said.

"Sure I would," I said, sounding more confident than I felt.

Later that night when we were in bed, I whispered to Chen, "Why didn't you tell me about So Ho?"

"What about him?"

"Why he's so moody, grumpy and edgy. Why he lives here. Why your dad takes him out every night and watches out for him. About his *wife!* About the accident."

"Sounds like Fang beat me to it."

"Beat you to it! You've had plenty of time. I thought of him as a miserable old curmudgeon. Now that I've unravelled the skein of his family story, I feel so guilty."

"Don't feel guilty. He had serious depression and he was a big strain on the household. I was concerned about how you would like my family and country. I thought the last thing you needed was to hear about my spaced-out uncle. He seems much better now than before I went away, but perhaps he'll never be the same as before."

"I needed to know, sweetie. I've been so unfair to him. I realized, again, how little I know about your family. By the way, do you think they liked the things we gave them?"

"Probably. Chinese people don't show appreciation. They think it would seem as if they *needed* the gift and that hurts their ego."

"Do you think we should have bought more expensive stuff?"

"Maybe. They think expensive gifts are a sign of wealth and that's important to them. They also think everyone in North America is rich."

"Yes, there are many things I don't know about your country, but I've learnt the importance of wealth. My feeling about gifts is just the opposite. For me, gifts are never measured by their cost."

"I know that... but only because I learned from you. You're doing great, *mon bijou*—and you did so well to sort out your things and get the gifts organized. Were you nervous riding in the old lorry with Fang?"

"No. Fang was a hero. We had fun together. He's a cutie."

"A *cutie*? Do I have to be jealous of my brother?"

"Nope! He is cute, but not as cute as you," I said, planting a kiss on the end of his nose.

Chapter 17

I WAS WASHING SALAD greens in the outer kitchen sink when Tan came in from work, waving a wedding invitation.

"Come see," she said. "For me, this is nicest."

After drying my hands, I picked up the sample invitation: a large red card with a double fold toward the center, held together with a gold Chinese character (representing double happiness, Ma said). Inside, on a pink liner the invitation would be written vertically in Chinese on the left and horizontally in English on the right.

"You like it, Lauren?"

"Yes, the card is very pretty. But I'm wondering... does the envelope have to be pink?"

"Almost always is, already," Tan said.

"There's no glue on these envelopes," I said in surprise.

"Never any glue on Malaysian envelopes. Because of weather. The air so damp that glue stick together before it is time. You can use glue at the *Pos* Office. Now I know you like it I will order. One hundred fifty."

"That's a good job done, Ma. If you like, I'll help you address them when they come."

"Okay, lah."

The pink and red combination had startled me, but never mind. They certainly were interesting.

My mind traveled back to three months ago when I was shopping for invitations in Vancouver. The invitations all looked so formal, so common. I decided to make my own. At a specialty store on Hastings Street, Mom and I found some crisp, kiwi-green parchment for the folder and some rice paper for the message. I adorned the front with sketches of bamboo. They were quite stunning. Dad was pleased about the Chinese touches. I remembered the satisfaction I felt making those invitations so personal. The difference between the ones I made and the ones Tan chose, was amusing.

Chapter 18

"LAUREN, WE NEED TO talk about wedding," Tan said. "Let's talk tonight if Wong at home. Should be the four, anyway for some things. You and me can talk about your dress. What you like to wear?"

"I thought I would wear the dress I was married in last month in Canada. Actually, it was the dress my mother had been married in thirty-three years ago," I said.

Tan's almond-shaped eyes became rounder and her head gave an involuntary shake. "Your *mother's* dress? Why wear your *mother's* dress? To save money, already? Don't want your *own* dress?"

I willed myself to be patient. "No, it wasn't to save money. I *wanted* to wear my mother's dress. To me it was very sweet. It had a lot of sentimental importance." I knew if I talked until midnight, Tan would not understand.

"What do *you* think I should wear, Ma?" I asked, jerking my own preference aside.

"Chinese brides wear a white wedding dress for the tea ceremony at home and a red wedding dress for the dinner at restauran. You can wear your mother's white dress to restauran and then change to red one during the dinner."

Now it was my turn to be flabbergasted. "Do you mean I would leave in the middle of the meal and change from my white dress to my red dress?"

"Yes. That way the people see you have two dresses. They think you are more rich, lah. There's two shops in town—Zaboon Bride Fashions. They rent. D & R Wedding Gowns and Dress Maker, they rent, too. Both on Jalan Imbi."

The custom of wearing two dresses to demonstrate wealth knocked me back, but I was determined to avoid conflict whenever possible. Tan must lead, I kept repeating to myself.

I simply said, "I'll check out both stores tomorrow."

That evening Wong, Tan, Chen and I sat around the table to discuss the wedding.

"We should wait until August. The eighth month is auspicious," Wong said. "Is the eighth day of the eighth month on a weekend?"

"No, it's Tuesday… no good, but maybe eighth month is enough good," Tan said. "Where we have it?"

Wong said. "The Jade Garden or Eng Fok Restoran. Jade Garden is best. Will cost six hundred ringgit a table of ten. How many people?"

"Near 150," Tan said.

"That's nine thousand ringgit! A lot of money already. Lauren can we ask your father to give forty-five hundred ringgit? That's half."

While I was trying to digest what I thought I'd heard, Chen said, "No, Pa. That is totally inappropriate!"

"Sorry, lah. I thought he is so rich maybe he would help us."

"Dr. Busch paid for our Canadian wedding and our honeymoon trip to the Banff Springs Hotel in the Rocky Mountains. As well, he gave us a substantial wedding gift. There is no way we would even consider asking him for more."

"Sorry, already. We'll work it out. Tan, I'll choose the menu later."

And with that, the meeting was adjourned.

"Let's get some air," I mumbled to Chen.

"Your father! The audacity of him!" I said, working to restrain from raising my voice as we walked along Jalan Kupas.

"I don't know the word *audacity*."

"Okay, the nerve of him. Honestly, sweetie, I'm really trying to think of this wedding as their party and to let it be just that. After all, I had things exactly as I wanted at our Canadian wedding—my father didn't even choose the menu!"

"I know you are trying to give them the opportunity to have the Chinese wedding they want for us."

"You were very sweet to come to my defense so quickly."

"It was automatic, *mon bijou*," he said taking my hand in his.

"And that's not all of it. This afternoon your mother asked me what I was going to wear to the wedding. I shook the status quo by saying that I thought I'd wear the dress I wore to our Vancouver wedding. When I mentioned it had been my mother's dress she asked me if it was to save money, and I told her it was because it was what I *wanted* to wear. We were the distance between Canada and Malaysia apart. I just let it drop."

"Perhaps you should look in town. It wouldn't do any harm."

"Oh, I've already planned to do that. Ma gave the names of two places. They're close to each other, on Jalan Imbi. I'm going in the morning."

"Don't worry about it too much."

I wasn't worrying about it excessively, but cringed at the underlying idea of either displaying wealth—or faking it.

"Is it true that Chinese brides have two dresses and change in the middle of the dinner?"

"Yes, it's true. Some have three or more dresses for the wedding."

"No kidding! Sounds like a bloody fashion show. I can't handle more than two, especially since one needs to be red. I've spent my life avoiding red! You know, I feel like having a glass of beer."

"Then let's do that. Let's go to Choy's Bar and Kafe."

I finished with Zaboom Bride Fashions at 11:05. One walk around the ballerina-like dresses, with a small, determined Chinese saleslady following close behind me, was all that was necessary.

Putting my faith in D & R Wedding Gowns and Dress Maker, I made my next stop. Again, the dresses didn't interest me. In fact, I was losing interest in the whole exercise and had just decided to leave when I was attracted to a rack with bolts of fabric at one end of the store. My eye quickly caught a deep emerald green Thai silk. That would be my first choice. *But Chinese brides wear red*, Tan had declared. I could believe it. Three quarters of the fabrics were reds. They were brilliant, but really fought with my red hair and over-powered my blue-white skin. I would look my best in the emerald green. The sales-lady had been hovering over me as I was agonizing about colours.

"You want I call seamstress?" she asked.

"Not yet. I'm just thinking."

"You want see Fashion magazines?"

"Sure, thanks. I'd like that."

I sat on a white rattan chair with a lacy pink cushion and perused the well-thumbed fashion magazines. The sales lady brought a cup of Oolong tea and put it down beside me.

"It's Mimi that sews," she said. "You see something you like?"

"Not yet."

"You don't need picture. Just tell her and she make what you want."

"Can't she use a pattern?" I asked.

"Can not. Does not want pattern. She measure you, she does just what you want."

I felt very confused. I looked at the fabrics again, one at a time.

Hey! I muttered to myself. This claret silk might be just right. It's a beautiful tone. It would look good—maybe even stunning on me. And maybe Tan would think it was close enough to red. Feeling encouraged, I jumped up and turning to the saleslady, I asked if I could borrow the magazines for a day.

"Can. Leave phone number," she said.

I spent the afternoon outside, the shade of the breezeway taming the heat. Beside my chair were the borrowed magazines and on my lap, my sketch pad. Sketches lay beside my bare feet on the concrete floor. My concentration was broken by the sound of a bicycle bell. *Jiling! Jiling! Jiling!* I jumped up instantly, recognizing it as the watermelon vendor. For twenty ringgit, I chose a triangle of cold, red watermelon and a slice of yellow. The yellow didn't taste much different from the red, but was pretty. I said *terima kasih (thank you)*—the only pair of words I now used habitually, and not without a touch of pride. Unlike Canadians, who say *thank you* routinely for everything—from the offer of a cookie, to having a tooth pulled, Malaysians use the phrase only for exceptional service or kindness and never for something considered to be the person's job.

Feeling refreshed, I continued to plan my wedding dress. I envisioned a simple, sleeveless dress with a low neckline to accommodate my gold chain from Chen. A simple train could flow out from the waistband at the back, and slightly beyond the rest of the hem. The Thai silk was a good weight for the design and the claret would be more than okay. I would remember to call it "dark red" when talking to Tan. Chinese brides may wear Chinese red; but then, I'm not a Chinese bride. I wondered if dark red would at least be more lucky than green.

I was basking in my success. Choosing a wedding dress is never a snap. My mind traveled back to shopping for a gown in Vancouver, just a few months ago. They were all so pouffy, puffy and excessive! Mom got a little fed up as I kept rejecting her suggestions and asked me just what it was that I *did* want. I responded that I wanted something simple, sweet, and summery. It didn't take long before I realized I wanted one like my mother's. Mom phoned my grandmama who was delighted to look for it. Three days later it arrived in the mail. It was going to work. I was ecstatic.

That night on the way up to bed, I stopped in my parents' room to look at the picture of their wedding. I thought how young they looked and how happy. The dress gave Mom a look of innocence and sweetness. Her hair was black and curly. Richard's hair was just like it. Tears filled my eyes. "Dear God," I murmured, "Why? Why did it happen? Comfort us—especially Mom and Dad."

Chapter 19

I WAS TREATING MYSELF to a day with my new sister, Yee Lee. When the bus pulled up to the stop in Buar, I could see her waiting for me. She looked perky in a crisp white top just barely meeting the waistband of her short, red skirt. After a warm greeting, we went off in her royal blue Wira.

"Nice, car. Is it *yours?*" I asked her.

"Yes. Actually, it's Ma's, but she seldom drives it. I guess ownership is a control thing; it leaves her free to call the shots."

When we turned on to Jalan Bintulu, her mother-in-law saw us coming and walked toward the driveway.

Lee Yee jumped out of the car and announced, "This is my new sister. Lauren, this is my mother-in-law, Chua."

"How do you do, Chua," I said. She was plump, with doughy features, but neither forbade her an air of primness. Her dress, with its pleated skirt and white collar made her look more like the matron of a girl's school than a Chinese housewife. We shook hands and she said, "So this is Wong Lee Chen's wife," and went into the house. Seemingly I hadn't scored very high and there didn't seem to be any room for recovery, at least for the present.

The house was large. Lee Yee and Mok had a suite near the back, with a living area, bedroom and bathroom. That there was no kitchen would certainly tie Lee Yee to her mother-in-law. I thought about when we were in Vancouver and Chen had heard from his mother about Yee Lee's marriage.

Oct.19,1999

Dear first son,

  Your sister Lee Yee will be marry to Mok Ping Kwai in two month. We think that would be best time for you so you have the Christmas holiday. He is good man his parents live in Buar. His family will take good care for her. We glad you work hard an do good. Good we see you soon. Your father send money for ticket. I think of you. I wait for you come home.

Your Mother

"First son" had phoned me. I knew he was very upset about something and asked him to meet me in my studio. Without even greeting me, he threw back his head and squeezed his eyes tightly. As if attempting to make it real, he repeated over and over, "Lee Yee is getting married. Lee Yee is getting married. Why didn't she tell me? She was going to go to university! I was going to help her. How can this be happening? What can I do?" He pounded his fists on his thighs. He took the letter out of his shirt pocket and read it to me."I can change nothing," he said.

  "You sound as if her life were over," I said.

  "Well, her life isn't over, but her plans to go to university sure are."

  "Oh, Chen, I am so sorry. Are you sure she

couldn't continue her education…maybe wait awhile to get married?"

"Yes, I'm sure!" Chen snapped in frustration. "My parents will expect her to marry Mok Ping Kwai and his parents will expect her to live with them. This is Chinese tradition! It's what my parents want for her. She will no longer be their responsibility. Try to understand that!

"I can't. It's barbaric! I can't even talk about it. I'm sorry Chen, but I just can't understand it! How could a daughter's life be so controlled by her parents? How could Lee Yee be expected to leave her own family and be handed over to her husband's family like a possession? How? Why? I will never be able to understand it. Part of me doesn't even want to try!"

My outburst was the last thing Chen needed. I put my arms around him and said,

"I'm sorry I was so abrupt with you. I know you're upset and instead of comforting you, I made judgements.

Now I was seeing the situation in action. My reaction was the same, but I was determined it wouldn't dampen our time together. "This is nice, Lee Yee. A private home within a house. You must like it."

"Yes. We're too close to Mok's parents, but at least we can have some space and privacy. How's living with my Ma and Pa?"

"They're very good to us, but honestly, I'm so anxious for us to have our own place. I don't care where it is, but Chen says a flat over a shop is not appropriate."

"That's no surprise. How are the wedding plans?"

I told her about Tan ordering the invitations and the search for a dress.

"I'm glad you are getting the dress you want, and that Ma let it go."

Lee Yee showed me her wedding photographs. The pictures of the tea ceremony especially interested me. Mok's mom and dad were sitting in chairs and Lee Yee and Mok were serving them tea in small cups.

"The idea is that if the parents accept the tea, they are accepting the daughter-in-law. Then the rest of the family is served tea starting with the eldest. Don't worry about it. It's really simple."

"Did you know that Fang is providing a Lion Dance?"

"No, I didn't hear that."

"I think it will be great fun. His excitement is contagious."

"I know. He has a way of lifting up everyone around him. Every family would be lucky to have someone like him. Who's doing the formal photographs?"

"I've no idea. I thought guests would just take candid shots."

"You can be sure Ma will want you to have a formal one. At least you won't have to get your face whitened," she chuckled. "You'll get the photos done at least a week before the wedding."

I knew Lee Yee's formal picture was on the wall at home. Now Chen's grad picture hung beside it.

"'That reminds me, I have something for you." I reached in my bag and handed her the wrapped gift. She took it from me and laid it on the table. Chen had told me that Chinese people do not open gifts until they're in private, and I was well aware they do not thank you for them.

I boldly told her I would like her to open it.

"Alright," she said unwrapping it carefully. "Oh, Chen's grad picture. Doesn't he look handsome?" She laid it on the shelf beside some books. That was that. I debated whether she was giving me the Chinese reaction to a gift, or if she was maybe a bit jealous of Chen's education.

"Let's go out for lunch. Is that okay? If we stay here we should eat with Mok's mother."

"Sure, let's go."

"Just a minute. I'll check out with Ma."

We had a lovely chat over clay pot chicken and rice in the dining room at the local hotel. Lee Yee ordered in Chinese. The Wong family's English was so good that I was still slightly surprised when they broke into a gush of Chinese.

"You make Cantonese sound so easy," I said.

"No. It's not easy. People find it hard to learn. What does Chen call you—sounds something like *mou bigou*, seems like a code."

"Oh," I laughed. "He's saying *mon bijou*. That's French for *my jewel*. My mother is French. She was born in Quebec. Her English is perfect, but she still sprinkles in the odd French word. Chen heard her calling me *mon bijou*, and he continued the tradition. He seemed a bit shy about using endearments and I think he found a French one easier—more private."

"So that's it. Sounds very romantic... and cosmopolitan. I had no idea your mother is French. Is she from Quebec?"

"Yes. She met Dad when he was going to McGill. They moved to Vancouver and have been there ever since."

"Do you still have family in Quebec?"

"Yes. My grandmama, whom I adore, and all my mother's family is there. We used to love to visit them but it was a five hour flight."

"We have so much to learn about each other," Lee Yee said.

"Yes, when Fang took me to Port Klang last week, he told me about your Uncle So Ho. I had no idea what he is dealing with. I realized, as you say, that we have so much to learn about each other's family."

"Uncle So Ho has had a hard time. I haven't had much patience with him, probably because he's been such a drag on my parents. He's a cranky old guy, and it seems like it's not going to get better. By the way, have your paints come yet?"

"Yes they were in the crate that Fang and I brought home.

Now I need to search out Mr. Yap Chug Chin and get him to stretch some canvases for me."

"I know him. I took black ink drawing lessons from him. I loved it."

"Did you study art at school?"

"Definitely not. No such luck."

"I'll be happy to help you," I said, feeling like a big sister."

"That will make two of us happy."

I told Yee Lee that Shanthi had offered to let me use her marvelous garden as an outdoor studio.

"That's so kind of her. I've heard she is very nice. Does Chen like working with Dr. Chong?"

"I think so. He's getting good experience and seems to feel confident and useful. The hours are long: seven in the morning till seven at night. I find the days never-ending."

"Have you any plans?"

"I have a few ideas. I'd like to have a studio and sell my paintings. I need to go to Kuala Lumpur and get to know some galleries. I sometimes think of having an art school for children, with a bit of drama and music around the edges. I just don't know how it would take. Chen begs me to be patient. He's so conservative… probably just what I need to keep me in check."

"We all seem to need being held in check," Lee Yee said, with a hint of bitterness.

"What would *you* like to do?"

"I don't know. But sometimes I feel really trapped here. Like I'm the maid. I sense pressure on me to produce a son. I'm *twenty*, Lauren."

"I know. Don't rush. Have courage to crack the mold," I said, wondering if I had sounded hurtfully western.

"It's not easy. I appreciate your support."

We drank endless cups of Jasmine tea and had quality conversation. At three o'clock, I suggested she might drop me at the bus terminal.

"Oh, no!" she said. "I'll drive you home. I had forgotten about your ankle, or I'd have come to get you this morning."

"Actually it's almost as good as new now, but if you have time, I'll grab a ride."

As we took off in her Wira, I couldn't help feeling a bit envious. After all, I hadn't even been able to negotiate a bicycle!

"This was fun, Lauren. We should get together again soon. I'll be glad to help with the wedding decorations, or anything else. Just ring me."

"Thanks. Your mother and I are going to make a tapioca cake for the wedding. Probably tomorrow."

We chatted about wedding plans all the way home. When we got there I asked her if she could come in.

"No, I need to get back to help with dinner," she said wistfully. We had a hug and off she went.

Tan was not home. I sat in one of the only two truly comfortable chairs in the house, Wong's chair. My time with Lee Yee revealed some of our differences. She had a car of her own. She and Mok had private rooms. She was very pretty. She seemed very clever. But she was trapped—bound in tradition. Her heritage was determined to trounce her modern womanhood. Her dreams and aspirations would be given over to serving Mok's family. They would expect her to bear children: hopefully male, and hopefully soon.

On the other hand, I had no car (or bicycle!). Chen and I had one private room, our bedroom. I was not pretty in the Chinese way and if you judge my cleverness by the marks I got in algebra, I wouldn't fare well. But I would *not* be trapped! While in that frame of mind, I felt like a raging lion, when really I was a gentle lamb wanting desperately to please Chen's family. I couldn't afford to rage. I believed a solid relationship with the Wongs was essential in the turning of the wheel of the Chinese family.

Half an hour later, I was changing into shorts, when I heard a loud, persistent knocking on the door. I flew down the stairs, buttoning my blouse as I went. The knock continued with the desperation of a child needing to pee. *I coming, you egg head,* I muttered. I opened the door. A delivery boy handed me a box and left. I sat at the kitchen table with the fan whirring. I felt sure the box contained the wedding invitations. Briefly, I considered waiting for Tan, but decided to undo the paper, and slide one out. It read—

Mr. & Mrs. Wong So Kwok
Together with
Dr. and Mrs. Nolton Busch
Request the pleasure of your company
To attend a wedding dinner at
Jade Garden Restoran
24 Bukit Bendera 26
Taman Damai, Pahang D.M.
Saturday, August 19th 2000
At 6:30 p.m.
On the occasion of the marriage of
Mr. Wong Lee Chen
(Eldest son)
and
Miss. Lauren Marie Busch

RVSP— 019-9609237

Why on earth were my mother and dad's names on it? As I thought about it, an ugly possibility came to mind. I grabbed the phone and dialled my dad's office. There was no answer. I quickly realized I had forgotten the time difference and that it was eleven o'clock at night in Vancouver. I dialled home and Dad answered.

"Hi Dad. Sorry to call so late."

"That's okay, Snooks. Is everything alright?"

"I'm not sure. How are you and Mom?"

"We're fine. It's lovely to hear from you. Mom is getting on the other phone."

"Hi, Mom. I hope I didn't startle you by calling so late. Were you in bed?"

"Yes, but not asleep. How are the wedding plans?"

"Stressful. I just wondered... has Pa Wong been in touch with you?"

"Yes," Dad said, "he sent me an email last week. He asked me if I would contribute to the cost of the Chinese wedding dinner. I sent him a cheque right away."

"That's what I was afraid of. He asked us if he could approach you to pay half the cost of the dinner. Chen quickly said, definitely not; it would be very inappropriate. I assumed that would be the end of it. I feel terrible."

"Well, don't. It's okay. I realize that it is a cultural thing. Hopefully it will be a very happy event for you and Chen."

"You're so generous, as usual... to pay the money and not be bitter about it."

"Anything for you, sweetie."

"Are you wearing my wedding dress again?" Mom asked.

"Yes, and a red one as well! Actually, it's claret and I think it will look pretty sharp. I'll email you about it. I should get off the phone. I don't imagine international calls are very popular in this household."

"Well, feel free to reverse the charges anytime," Mom said.

"Thanks. You're both the greatest."

I hung up and sat in silence. I felt violated. Chen explicitly told Pa not to ask Dad for half the money for the wedding dinner. Wong had apologized, then went right ahead and did it. What a two-face!

"Damn him!" I muttered. "Money reigns. Again!"

I met Chen after work, anxious to tell him privately what had happened.

"I'm disappointed." Chen said. "More disappointed than surprised."

"Why aren't you surprised? He *said* he wouldn't do it!"

"I'm not proud of it… but the fact is, Lauren, Chinese people tend to be deceitful. Sun Tzu said, *All life is based on deception.* "

"Who's Sun Tzu? I've never heard of him."

"He wrote a famous book in the fifth century BC called, *The Art of War.* The essence of it is to use espionage and mystification in every enterprise. All life is based on deception."

I felt the back of my neck tingle and my face was sweating harder than the heat of the evening warranted. "That makes me sick, Chen!" Trying to be rational, I said, "But that was fifteen *centuries* ago!"

"Yes, but *The Art of War* is still studied by some Asian investors and businessmen today. Even overseas Chinese people give credit to Sun Tzu's philosophy for their success."

"I feel I won't ever be able to trust him again," I said. "In fact, I don't know who I *can* trust."

"It isn't that bad. Just be aware. What was your dad's reaction to being asked for money?"

"Oh, he was fine with it. He said he understood it was a cultural thing and seemed glad to participate in the occasion. He hoped it would be very special for us."

"That's really decent of him. You know, it'll really help us, because otherwise the money for the wedding dinner would have come out of our wedding gifts, the money in the ang pows."

"Really? At this point that would seem like robbing Peter to pay Paul. And Chen, I don't like that the invitations refer to me as *Miss*. I'm not *Miss*; I'm married and proud of it. And to top it all off, it says RVSP instead of RSVP," I said with my voice rising.

"Don't worry about that because I don't even know the difference. I know it means *reply,* but have no idea what the words are, and neither will the others."

"Okay, babe. Just for your information, it's a French acronym for *Répondez, s'il vous plait.*"

"Okay. It's no big deal. How was your day with Yee Lee?"

"It was great. I *think* she was pleased to have your grad picture."

"Good. Did you notice that my mother hung her picture of my grad beside Lee Yee's wedding picture?"

"Yes, and apparently we will be expected to have a formal portrait of our wedding, too. Probably as soon as my dress is ready."

"Another photograph for the gallery. I just wish it would someday include a portrait marking Lee Yee's graduation."

Chapter 20

"THESE TAPIOCA ROOTS LOOK as if they were whacked off a tree with an axe," I said. Tan was back from the wet market and I was at the sink scrubbing the three roots we would need to make tapioca cake for the wedding. I asked Tan if tapioca cake was a traditional wedding cake.

"No," she said, "but Chen like it. We buy more little cakes from bake shop at the market. Hard part for tapioca cake is peel and grate the root."

I was anxious to help, and figured I couldn't go wrong with jobs like peeling and grating. "I can do that for you, Ma," I said.

"Okay. Here's grater."

The hand-held grater, was made of tin and about the size of a small pocket book. I started to peel the woody skin which was like smooth bark and definitely a chipping job. When that was finally finished, I undertook the grating. It was astonishingly difficult and I had two-and-a-half kilos of root staring up at me from the sink. The hardest thing I had ever grated was cheddar cheese—well, maybe it was a whole nutmeg, but that was only the size of a thimble. I worked at it with determination. After all, I was a strong lass compared to Tan—or so I thought. Several times I stopped to uncramp my nicked hands. By the time I'd finished I was limp and wet, but my pride was intact. I presented Tan with two-and-a-half kilos of grated tapioca root in a big metal bowl. She set it down and dumped in a bag of brown sugar. Then she dumped in about a cup of white sugar and stirred it briskly. Sticking her finger in the mixture, she tasted it. Then she added more sugar, stirred and tasted again... and again. Finally, she added two cups of coconut milk and poured in some vanilla and pandan leaf essence.

"Should make pandan flavour myself, not from bottle," she said.

"You don't need to apologize to me, Ma. The aroma is heavenly."

She beat the whole mixture with great fervour, then opened a bottle of red food colouring, poured in a bit, and stirred again. She divided the mixture into two square cake pans and put them in the oven.

"It cooks for how long it takes," she said.

"Chen may like tapioca cake," I said, "but it's a lot of work."

"It's for my boy, my eldest son," his ma said reverently.

Just a few months ago my own mother made my wedding cake; a fruitcake, soaked in brandy overnight, and left it to ripen for six weeks. Just thinking about it made me salivate. When the cake was ready, Mom took it to a professional, along with a picture from a cookbook showing an elaborate three tiered cake. I was touched that she remembered how as a child I had often turned to that page in complete awe.

I thought of the two mothers making cakes for their children's weddings. Both were major jobs, although I guess Tan's cake took the prize for more physical labour.

"Let's have tea while the cake bakes. Want? Want not."

"Thanks, I'd like it. Tan, I keep thinking I smell moth balls."

"Yes. Under the sink."

"Oh! Why?"

"Keeps away cockroaches. Chen said you don't like cockroaches. We don't like, too. Very dirty. Very hard to catch. Even geckoes cannot catch. You like geckoes?"

"I don't mind them. I know they eat a lot of bugs, but sometimes they startle me; like when I open the blinds and one drops down and takes off as if it were running the Boston Marathon."

Tan brought two cups of tea to the table—hers with condensed milk, mine with powdered skim.

"I made appointment for you and Chen for pictures. Saturday afternoon," Tan announced. "I can do your hair in morning. It's good time to see how it looks, so I can change it if you don't like. Then I take a week off the *saloon* to get ready for the wedding."

"You'll have to tell me how I can help you, Ma."

"Can. Lee Yee's wedding this year. Easy now."

"I'm looking forward to meeting all the relatives."

"Hard to remember them. So many."

When the cake came out of the oven, it was surprisingly flat. It looked more like a square than a cake. Tan pronounced it perfect. The heavenly smell of pandan essence, vanilla and coconut milk filled the room, over-riding the pungent odour of mothballs.

With all the fussing over wedding dresses, I realized I hadn't given an iota of thought to my husband's outfit. Assuming he would wear his beige suit, I folded and bagged it, and started out to find a cleaner. Tan had told me that the Chinese word for cleaner is dobi and I should go to the one on Jalan Sri Layang. I spotted it quickly, and went inside. The short Chinese owner, wearing a blue-white shirt, was being attacked by a threatening customer yelling, *"You have my laundry done by five o'clock, or I'll knock your head to smithereens, you old opium chest!"* He spun around and walked out.

Feeling sorry for the dobi man, I smiled especially sweetly, and asked him to please dry-clean the suit. He said, "Yes, lah. Come tomorrow at three."

The next day, I was at the Kedai Dobi at three. The little man produced the suit and hung it on a hook while he made out the bill. My heart sank. The suit jacket looked as if it had gone through the washing machine. I was *sure* it had. The fabric seemed matted and the seams shriveled. I changed my allegiance back to that of the customer who had shouted at him so rudely the previous day.

"Did you put this in the washing machine?" I asked.

"Yes, did already," he said.

"I asked you to dry-clean it. It looks very bad. I will ask my husband to come and see it. I don't think it will even fit him now."

I wasn't looking forward to telling Chen that his only suit was ruined, but I needn't have worried. His response was, "I haven't got time to go there. If it's as bad as you say, let's just leave it. I'll rent something. Don't think about it."

Chapter 21

Hi Mom and Dad!

The wedding was *fantastique!* I felt demure in your sweet wedding dress, with my hair (arranged by Tan) piled up on the crown of my head and anchored by a hoop, with jasmine flowers and green leaves tucked into the bed of curls. The groom is supposed to go to the bride's house to worship ancestors, serve tea and get an ang pow from the parents. Then they go to the groom's house to do the same, but of course we're both here. Tan and Wong accepted the tea I offered which means that they accept me as their daughter-in-law. Whew! Hee, hee! Then we passed tea to aunties and uncles working through from eldest to youngest, bowing slightly before each. That was strictly a family gathering—sixty-three of us with joss sticks smouldering in the entrance and red banners over the doors. A lot of the family came from out of town. The rich uncle and his

Irish wife, Morraine, came from Singapore. They invited Chen and me to visit them anytime. Hope we can do that soon—it's only six hours drive from here, though nobody mentions making the trip.

Some people stood outside in the breezeway. They were served curry puffs, little cookies, tapioca cake, which Tan and I made, (I'd give you the recipe but you'd never get the main ingredient, tapioca root) and fruit punch with watermelon juice, pink guava, black currant and lime. It was a marvellous light raspberry colour and tasted fresh. We drank gallons of it. Most of the young men drank beer and the older men drank cognac. Chen and I did a lot of mingling and the guests were friendly on the whole, though the odd one seemed unsure just what to think about me.

Two little fertility rites: the bed had been sprinkled with lotus seeds to hasten conception, and at one point all the children gathered on our bed and jumped full steam—rather hard on our bedsprings, but considered necessary to plant the idea of the bed moving up and down!

Then the wedding dinner. I wore the claret silk dress I'd had made locally. Chen loved it. I must say I felt almost regal. I wore some of the gold jewellery I had been given in the afternoon. Get this—a gold bracelet with jade insets from Wong and Tan (the jade is to protect me from danger), three narrow gold bangles from Auntie Lai, a gold ring with three emeralds from the Singapore Wongs. They also gave us a cheque for RM1,000—actually it was for RM999 (for good luck!) The other gifts were ang pows. People seemed to be giving the red envelopes to Wong!

After his last antics, I wondered if we'd ever see those little red envelopes again. However, he passed over (at least some of them), amounting to RM2500. Nice, eh? But I'm getting side-tracked. When we arrived at the restaurant there seemed to be a sea of people and red tablecloths. The meal was ten courses—the minimum for a wedding dinner. I'll attach a menu. We ate for two and a half hours! During the meal we were constantly interrupted for toasts. They all lifted up their glasses and yelled *Yam Sengggggggggggg* until they ran out of breath, then swilled their drinks. It was wild. Then the highlight! We heard the drum and gong band—loud and metallic—pounding out a repetitive rhythm which got louder and louder until they got inside the door. Two lions, with two men in each wearing costumes ablaze with bright satin, feathers, sequins gold cords—huge heads with much exaggerated eyes, long eyelashes and huge mouth, pranced in playfully right up to our table. I knew Fang was in the head of the first lion. When he got in front of Chen and me, he waved his head back and forth and put his paws on our shoulders. Then the two lions did a dance. Someone threw mandarin oranges up in the air. Fang's end rose up and caught one mid-air, right into its mouth. Everyone cheered. The lions chased the oranges and danced around patting the heads of the people at our table, then moving in and around tables as much as room permitted. The whole body moved in fluid, undulating motions and the heads rose and fell, acknowledging as many people as they could. They even went in the kitchen (the owner asked for that when he heard there would be a Lion Dance), to bring good luck to his business. Some of the children were a bit overwhelmed and a couple of young ones were really howling. The drum band kept up the beat until the lions left the room. Fang was back in half an hour to join us at the head table. Chen and I praised and thanked him for giving us this special entertainment for our wedding gift. He is so full of life—loves everyone and everything. You'd love *him*! One of Fangs friends made a video. I'll send you a copy of it soon, with some photos and other mementos.

Oh, yes! Dr. Chong gave us three days of holidays and a voucher for accommodation at the Awana Kijal Resort on the east coast. It's on the South China Sea. Doesn't that sound romantic? And his wife, Shanthi, made me a bouquet of *The Love of White Moth* Orchids. She's my friend, the botanist. She knows *everything* about plants. These have been genetically improved to be larger and longer lasting. She said they should last at least a month or two. Amazing or what!

We're off to the resort in two days—very excited! We're going by bus—we'll see new territory and be very carefree.

Will be in touch as soon as we get back.

Thanks again for your major contribution to the Chinese wedding. Wish you had been with us!

Bushels of love,

Lauren

P.S. We signed the register after the Tea Ceremony— we've tied the knot in two countries. That's final!

Chapter 22

W<small>E WERE LYING IN</small> the buff with warm breezes from the South China Sea blowing over our happy bodies. Chen had bowed to my wish to leave the windows open for the night. Never mind the bugs and the geckos and whatever else that might want to come in. I felt so free. So relaxed. So in love.

"Let's go jump in the sea, Chen."

"Lauren it's eleven o'clock!" Then, not wanting to thwart my excitement, he quickly said, "Why not?"

We wiggled into our wet bathing suits, wrapped up in the resort's thick, white robes and headed for the elevator. Avoiding the lobby, we went directly to the lower-ground floor. People were having late-night snacks at the outside café and we could hear music and laughter coming from the lounge. The beach and water were brightly lit with spotlights and dozens of garden lights. We sauntered toward it and sat on the sand watching the waves rush in and roll out... rush in and roll out. We sat, lost in our own thoughts. The sight was mesmerizing. Such power and volume! I visualized the South China Sea fading into the Pacific

Ocean. I thought of Mom and Dad at the opposite end of this unimaginably vast body of water. They might be strolling along a beach themselves, or sitting on the beach watching wind surfers with colourful sails rising up on huge waves and down the other side, or maybe a Holland America cruise boat heading up to Alaska.

"You're looking far too serious, my dear. Time to lighten up."

"You're right, Chen. Come on, let's play in those babies."

We shed our robes and walked toward the water, our feet delving into the shifting sand. The water was like a warm milk bath.

"Canadian water never felt like this."

"That's right. No market for wet-suits here!"

"As well as feeling warm, the water feels so soft."

We jumped in the waves getting tossed and pitched and laughing gleefully as we played. I had an urge to take off my bathing suit and feel the undulating water stroke my skin. On impulse I tugged at my suit until it was freed then slipped it around my neck. I just wanted to let the motion of the water carry me along, its grey-green saltiness keeping me buoyant.

"You look like a tropical fish with that blue ruffle around your neck," Chen said.

"Come on! Here comes a big one!"

We both jumped high up toward the crest of the wave, tossing and turning, tense with excitement. We reached the finish line just in time to see my blue bathing suit being pulled away by the undertow.

"Get it, babe," I called.

"Not a chance. It's gone, mon bijou. Never mind, you look like a beautiful mermaid swimming around me, he said, as he slid his hands under my newly-freed breasts. "Tonight the South China Sea belongs to us."

Though my bathing suit might be difficult to replace, my spirits could not be dampened.

Back in our room we jumped into the shower together, rinsing the sand and salt off each other. To speed up the drying of my thick hair, I took my hair blower over to a seat in front of the window to reinforce the breeze blowing through my curls. Chen sat on the corner of the bed and massaged my feet with lemon grass oil. I felt so pampered that I didn't care if my hair ever got dry. Finally, we were back in bed where we had been an hour before, with the sea breeze blowing gently over our damp bodies. Even with a five-hour bus trip, it had been a wonderful day—and we still had two full days left.

"That was some breakfast," I said. Buffets are hard on people like me who like everything from waffles and syrup to nasi lemak, and one of our favourites, roti canai (which I'll probably never be able to say without remembering the flirting accusation)."

Going through the lobby on the way back to our room, we passed a gift shop with bathing suits in the window. I told Chen I wanted to have a look. There wasn't much selection but I found three in my size and tried them on. The best bet was a floral bikini. It would be great for the resort.

"If you couldn't look after one piece, how are you going to look after *two*," Chen teased.

"Surely it can't happen twice."

"Not if you leave it on, ma chérie."

We were ensconced under an umbrella fashioned from palm fronds, lying on long beach chairs with royal blue mattresses topped with blue and white striped beach towels. I wore my grey-blue straw hat with the accordion top and wide brim: an umbrella in its own right. Chen had slathered me with sunscreen, all the while warning me of the consequences of too much sun. We people who have paper white skin and freckles know the rules and get tired of well-meaning people trying to warn us about sun—even if our cheeks *do* look as if they'd been rubbed with raspberry coulis.

My book was about a family saga with a grand matriarch ruler written by a Malaysian Indian. It covered three generations. At that moment, they were coping with the Japanese Occupation. Malaysia was being ripped apart by Japanese soldiers, pillaging and raping as they went. Chen had a couple of magazines and the *New Straits Times*. During the morning, several times we would find that we both had our books in our laps and were gazing out at the sea. The beach stretched for several miles and was virtually empty. I watched layers of action. Boats on the horizon… where were they going? Australia? Japan? China? What were they carrying… mobile phones? Tiger Balm? Mandarin oranges? Knock-off Taylor-Made golf clubs? Closer in, young people roared around on sea-doos, water-skied and manoeuvred colourful fibreglass kayaks. Closer in again, on the beach children built castles in the sand, flooded them and built them again. Vendors crept onto the property to sell colourful sarongs, kites, windmills and flip-flops.

"Let's buy one of these fruit drinks and skip lunch," Chen suggested.

"Good idea. Penance for eating the equivalent of two or three meals at breakfast."

Chen beckoned to the waiter and we chose, a glass of watermelon juice for me and mango for Chen. We felt sleepy in spite of having had such a relaxing morning.

"I suggest we get out of the mid-day sun for a couple of hours. Maybe have a nap, and come back later, when the sun isn't as strong," Chen said.

Mid-afternoon, we left our air-conditioned room and sauntered back to the beach. Chairs were a bit scarcer. It seemed that people were leaving a towel on their chair to reserve it while they went off to do something else. We wandered around and found some chairs farther back from the water. Happily for me, we also found a reflexologist and I made an appointment for a treatment. He couldn't speak English, but had a paper with times and names. Two others had signed before me. I didn't mind— it just gave me time to enjoy the anticipation.

Forty-five minutes later, the man wearing shorts, white shirt, and a sun hat, kneaded and lubricated my feet and calves. The scent of lavender, sage and sandalwood wafted through the air. He sat on a stool at the end of my beach chair, massaging my feet. I closed my eyes and enjoyed the treatment he gave me with his strong, skilled hands. The cost was only forty ringgit. I charged it to our room. Just as I was signing, Chen came along with two coconuts with the outer shell hacked off and a long straw jutting out. He looked so cute, so happy to be bringing me this treat, and so anxious for me to like it.

"It's coconut milk," he said. "Very refreshing."

"Wow. That's neat!" The taste was hard to describe. Watery and clean tasting… maybe slightly sour, certainly not sweet—as totally au natural as drinking milk from the cow's teat.

"Let's have a toast to Dr. Chong, babe."

We lifted our coconut containers, "To Dr. Chong!"

It was eight-thirty p.m., and we watched the sun go down on the beach for the last time. We had considered taking a tour, thinking we might go north to see Kuala Terengganu and the oil refineries, but decided against it. We were too happy just lazing on the beach, swimming in the pools and walking on the sand. I had sketched the sea, the trees, rocks, children flying kites and a teenager playing chess with his grandfather on a giant chess board painted on a concrete slab and two feet tall chessmen. My favourite was a sketch of a frail, elderly woman wearing a two-piece bathing suit. She was slight and withered but seemed so comfortable in her body.

That evening we checked out the *Windows* restaurant. Tomorrow we would spend a large part of the day on the bus, inching back to the realities of life. Time to think of that tomorrow.

We tucked into our meals. I ordered lobster bisque and the first steak I'd had since leaving Canada. Chen chose Chicken Kong Pao—stir-fried chicken and vegetables with spicy oyster sauce and steamed fragrant rice. For dessert I splurged on Crepes Suzette and Chen had Lin Chee Kang—chilled sweet syrup served with white fungus, dry longan, red beans and corn. How nice for each of us to have so many choices.

After dinner we sat in the lobby with Bailey's Irish Cream and coffee. The wood ceiling was seven floors above and a soft sea breeze floated over us. A female singer belted out songs to a small crowd, subdued by the day's sun and a good meal. I couldn't remember ever being happier.

Chapter 23

I LANDED AT THE Wong home with a thud. Everyone was at work. I sat on a red plastic chair in the breezeway, a bottle of water on the floor beside me. I felt nearly as lost as I had on the first day Chen went to the office. Surely I'd made progress in the nearly two months I'd been here. Lazily I turned to the back page of my sketchbook and began to note my progress:

- Better understanding of the strength of the Chinese family
- Sweet new *sister*
- Really like Fang a lot
- Understand Uncle So Ho better
- Shared a few bonding times with Tan
- Wong - arrogant and bossy but seems to feel protective of me
- Shanthi—a delightful friend and soul-mate
- My stuff arrived safely
- Adventure at the cave—complete with bats, snakes, slimy stairs and two injuries

- Our finances are taking shape—sort of
- We've had an unexpected and excruciatingly delightful holiday

Not so bad. In fact, darned good! Now, what next? I had to get some canvases stretched before I could paint. I knew how to do it but didn't have the equipment. With my spirit renewed, I decided to visit Mr. Yap at Art Supply and Lesson. I sketched a plan and went happily down Jalan Kupas to the center of town with my roll of canvas slung over my shoulder. The shop hadn't opened. When would I remember? I decided to have a cup of coffee next door

"A cup of *kopi* with fresh milk, *sila*," I said.

I thought the waitress was trying to suppress a chuckle. "Anything else?" she said.

"No, *terima kasih.*"

"Sit. I'll bring it."

She was still smiling when she delivered my coffee. "Here," she said. "Nice to hear you try speak Malay. What's your name?"

"Lauren. And yours?"

"Siew Kee."

"Do you work here every day?"

"Do not. I go to college. My father owns the *kafe*. I'm helping him out while I'm on break for semester."

"What college do you go to?"

"I go to Malaysian Art Institute in Kuala Lumpur. MAI is what we call it."

"You *do*?" I couldn't have been more surprised if she'd said she went to MIT in Massachusetts.

"I have a Fine Arts degree from UBC. That's the University of British Columbia in Canada."

Our surprise seemed mutual. She sat down on a chair beside me.

"Taman Damai is a small town, but isn't it a surprise that we find each other, already?"

"Yes, it sure is! Tell me what courses you're taking."

"The first year, some of everything. Then I choose sculpture. I like it best."

"Do you work with clay, Siew Kee?"

"Mostly. Sometimes with wood or stone or mix all kinds. What do you do?"

"Like you, when I started I did a bit of everything. But I chose painting as my major."

"Oh, I'd like to see it."

"My supplies just came recently, so I haven't done anything yet—except sketching which I do every day. Actually I came here to have some canvas stretched next door. As usual, I forgot how late the shops open, so I came in here for some *kopi*."

"That's Yap. He's my uncle. He'll do that. He teaches and sells supplies."

"Yes, I know. My sister-in-law took some lessons from him when she was in high school. Guess I'm supposed to say Form 4 or 5."

"What's her name… and why are you here?"

"Her name is Wong Lee Yee. I'm married to her brother, Wong Lee Chen."

"Really? The doctor? Studied in Canada, already?"

"Yes, to all of that. I should let you get back to work, but I'm so excited to have met you. We'll keep in touch. When do you go back to school, Siew Kee?"

"In two weeks. Hope you will come here soon."

"You can be sure I will."

I hopped into Mr Yap's shop, Art Supply and Lesson, with my rolled canvas under my arm. He was a slight man with elongated, Buddha-type ears and two gold teeth shining from the front of his mouth. I explained what I wanted, and we discussed dimensions and widths of the stripping for the frames. He didn't have the right size of stripping but he would order it, and I could pick the canvases up on Friday.

That night I asked Chen if anything unusual had happened at work.

"Actually, yes. Very unusual."

"Can you tell me?"

"Yes. In trust. Agreed?"

"Of course."

"An unconscious man was brought into the hospital from his workplace by ambulance. They called Dr. Chong because he had seen the man twice before. His records showed the same scenario each time—arriving from work by ambulance, unconscious. Each time he had tests and all tests showed negative. The next day he would be discharged. The doctors were perplexed. Dr. Chong suggested that the psychologist and a Human Resources rep from his workplace be included in a meeting after lunch."

"Isn't it a psychiatrist they needed?" I asked.

"Maybe, but there isn't one in the area, so they asked the psychologist."

"Did he gain consciousness fairly quickly?"

"No. He was out for half an hour. So at the meeting, the rep from his work said that the patient had been under a lot of stress. He had married a second wife—Muslims can marry up to five wives, you know."

"They *can*? You're joking!"

"No, I'm not. But they have to be able to support their wives and treat them equally.

"Ha. That's a tall order."

"Yes, but let me get back to my story. So when he was discharged the first time, his new wife looked after him. She was a widow with three children and he already had two from his first wife... so, five children. His first wife was mad at him, *her* parents were mad at him, and *his* parents were mad at him... he's twenty-nine years old!"

When I found my voice, I said, "Yes, I think it's safe to say he's under stress. What a mess! Then what?"

"The psychologist says we should consider that the man is

dealing with his stress by making himself go unconscious—sort of like getting drunk, but he gets more pity and attention this way."

"It sounds like an adult version of a child who gets attention by holding his breath until he turns blue. Does he really make himself unconscious, or does he fake it?"

"That's a good question, but yes, he is really unconscious. Dr. Chong said that while the patient was unconscious, he pinched his arm hard and the man's arm jumped. To me that suggests his unconsciousness was not very deep."

"Doesn't it break your heart?"

"No. I feel sorry for him, but I have to stay detached to do my job well. You must know that from your dad."

"Yeah, but when people have such overwhelming problems—physical or mental, it must be depressing for you."

"Could be, but being depressed takes energy and it's better to just feel good that you are probably in a position to help the situation in one way or another. Anyway, let's not get too heavy. What did *you* do today?"

"I had a great day! I decided that number one on my want list was to get some canvases stretched *so* I headed out to see Mr. Yap. After a lot of discussion, he said I could pick them up on Friday."

"Don't be surprised if he doesn't have them ready. Malaysians want to be positive, always—to the point of saying something that isn't true just to tell the person what he wants to hear. It can cause confusion."

"Hey, Chen! I've got things in the wrong order of importance. I met a wonderful girl at the kafe while I was waiting for Yap to open! Her name is Siew Kee and she's studying art at the Malaysian Institute of Art! Can you imagine that? She'll be a good contact for me at MIA. We are both excited that we happened to meet each other."

"I'm so happy for you, Lauren. Sounds like you two will have a lot in common."

"You're right. The things that happened today made me realize that I should learn to speak Bahasa Malaysia. Siew Kee was so pleased when I asked for a cup of *kopi* and said *terima kasih*. The only other word I know is *selamat pagi*. People are visibly warmed when I smile and say good morning in their language. It makes me feel good, too. I've thought I should learn the national language since the day I couldn't read the sign at the caves warning me to pass at my own risk. If I didn't get along so well speaking just English, my motivation would have urged me on sooner. Anyway, now I'm ready. How should I go about it?"

"I think learning Bahasa Malaysia is a great idea. It will open opportunities for you. I'm sure you won't regret it. You should have a private tutor. We'll probably find a listing in the newspaper. I'm really pleased that you want to do that."

"Thanks, Chen. I'm starting to feel that my life is on track."

"Well, let's celebrate!" Chen said, putting his arms tightly around me with a grin.

The next morning, I was sitting outside with my tea beside me and my sketch pad on my lap. I felt elevated by my plan to learn the Malay language. I thought of how many words were just naturally understandable—like having *kopi* at a *kafe*. I decided to make a list. At the top of the list were the first words I had discovered: *bas sekolah*, school bus. The list grew with *klinik, foto, teksi, bas mini, telefon, restoran, poskod, projek,* and my favourite, *fisio terapi*.

Chapter 24

ON SEPTEMBER 26 SHANTHI, as a Hindu, celebrated Deepavali, a festival which signifies victory of light over dark and good over evil. She and Dr. Chong invited Chen and me to their Open House. The house and garden were ablaze with lights. I pondered how often lights play a significant role in religious festivals around the world as symbols of celebration and hope. On a flat area beside the front door, Shanthi had made a clever design with coloured rice. It was perfect, but would only take a cat or civit walking through it to muck it up.

The guests were doctors and their wives, most from out of town. The Indian ladies wore brilliantly coloured silk saris embellished by gold jewellery hanging from their earlobes and on their wrists. Several had decorated their hands with intricate patterns drawn with henna dye. I was no match in my two-piece cotton outfit and sandals.

Chen knew that Deepavali was a gift-giving time and that sweets were appropriate. Our gift was a carved wooden bowl full of sweets wrapped in cellophane and brought together with a bow. Shanthi took it from us and put it in another room. Not a word was spoken. I shouldn't have been surprised, but I'd expected more from my dear friend.

Shanthi introduced me to her friends. I chatted with a woman I'd just met about the wonderful aromas of the curries. "The food looks incredible," I said.

"In some areas Deepavali is marketed as a food festival, rather than a time of religious rituals," she said. "Let me tell you about the food." Pointing with her fist enclosing her thumb, she said, "that's a chicken curry, a goat curry and a lamb curry". We walked around the table. She lifted the top of a large urn and said, "This is *dhal* soup. Over there, in bowls are vegetable *raita* and beside it, yellow dhal—that's lentils, and in the yellow bowl, saagwala murgh—that's chicken and spinach. The salad is watercress and mustard leaves, and the breads are naan and poris—that's the puffy one. Laddu is a lacy pancake. The dough is put through a piping tube."

"I see *roti canai*," I interrupted. "I love that. I buy it at a hawker stall, from a man named Wiwa. The first time was the day after I arrived."

"When was that?"

"At the end of June."

"Are you American?"

"No, I'm Canadian."

"Is there much difference? Aren't the countries joined together?"

"Yes, they're joined together and yes, we think there's quite a difference," I laughed. "I met Chen in Canada when he was a student."

"Oh," she said, "a big venture for him... and an even bigger one for you to come to live in Malaysia." I resisted saying, "You're not kiddin'!"

Walking home later, I said, "Shanthi couldn't have made all that food herself, surely."

"Probably not. Lavinya would help a lot and probably she bought some items."

"I thought Shanthi didn't have any friends."

"She said she didn't have any friends in Taman Damai. It's all about the Indian caste system. The Indian people at the party are professionals. That means they are Brahmins: social equals. In Taman Damai, I suppose most of the Indians were born into lower castes—scribes, traders, labourers or untouchables. It's complex, but the basis is that people socialize with others in the caste they were born into."

"It sounds archaic and unfair."

"It is what it is. That's not for us to judge, Lauren. I was just trying to give you a bit of background so you would understand Shanthi's predicament."

"You're good at accepting 'what it is' aren't you Chen?"

"I guess so. I think it's admirable in any situation, but it's especially important when you live in a small country with three quite distinct cultures."

Again, Chen had chastised me for being judgemental and insensitive. Again, I felt that I was travelling in a new carriage on a narrow street. Would I ever *get it*?

Chapter 25

"**C**OME IN. I'M HALIMAH," she said softly. This young
Malay woman swathed in a peach silk *kabaya* and
a white beaded headscarf was my Bahasa Malay
language teacher. She had a very sweet round face and eyes that
were a blend of bright and soft.

"I'm Lauren Busch," I said, extending my hand.

"Can I show the Malay greeting?" she asked. Without waiting
for an answer, she put her fingers of both hands quickly to her
heart before bringing her hands together with a light touch of
palm to palm. "We do it quite quickly. You try."

My attempts were embarrassingly awkward and slow. She
showed me again and soon I had mastered it. "It's nice. I like
it. It gives a message… of warmth," I said. "Mind you, the firm
hand clasp used in the western world gives a message, too—of
trust and goodwill."

"That's interesting," Halimah said. "I think we can learn
much together."

She led me into a room with mauve walls. The only ornament
was a large, green velvet picture with a message written in eight-

inch, graceful, fluid Arabic script in lustrous gold thread. A Turkish rug, woven with intricate red, blue, and green patterns, covered part of the floor. Florescent light shone starkly from the ceiling. We sat at a small wooden table with two metal chairs with blue, crimson, and gold patterned cotton pads. A plastic box of toys was in one corner.

"Before we start, I want ask questions," Halimah said. "How long are you in Malaysia?"

"Three months."

That was followed by: Where did you come from? Why did you come? How long will you stay? Why you want to learn *Bahasa Malay*? No doubt she wondered what kind of student I would be—how great was my commitment.

I told her that as well as wanting to learn the language, I saw this as an opportunity to learn about the Malay culture.

"Good. The two can work together. I want to know about your culture, too. I know only little. All I heard is westerners are rich and bossy and loud."

I swallowed that direct assessment without choking. I had heard the same from Chen. "We probably deserve some of that, but surely there's more to us than that."

"Yes. People in West probably say us lazy, poor, and a crazy religion. Unfortunate that different is bad. We will talk more. We start *Bahasa*. Today I teach you about the sounds vowels and consonants."

After many repetitions, Halimah gave me a reference chart to take home. Next she taught me some greetings. She started with *selamat pagi*—good morning. I didn't tell her that I knew that because I thought it would be to my advantage if she thought of me as a blank page, which was close enough to the truth.

"*Selamat petang* is good afternoon; *selamat malam*, good night. In Bahasa Malay, we say every letter. I was drilled until the words were slipping off my tongue almost easily. Now I wouldn't have to use "good morning" around the clock!

When Halimah announced she was going to teach me how

to make nouns plural, I groaned, thinking how complex English plurals can be. I was relieved when she said, "All you do is repeat the noun two times. *Buku*—one book; *buku buku*—two or more books."

That was an encouraging way to end the lesson. I left feeling up-beat and anxious to tell Chen what I had learned.

That night, I was sitting up in bed, re-reading my Malay notes when my guy came in.

"*Selamat malam*, Chen."

"*Sama, sama*, Lauren."

"What's *sama sama*?"

"It means *same for you*."

"That's a good one to know. I like the sound of it. Listen to me count: *satu, dua, tiga, empat, lima, enam, tujuh, delapan, sembilan, sepuluh*. Isn't that *good*?" I asked proudly.

"It's a good start, chérie."

Chapter 26

FOR RENT
Upstairs flat.
Ask for Mr. Fong.

WELL WHY NOT? WHAT'S there to lose? I stepped inside
the office of the Fly Away Travel Agency. On the wall
hung some faded posters of the Great Wall of China,
the Tan Si Chong Su Temple in Singapore, and the statue of
the Goddess of Mercy towering above the Kek Lok Si Temple
in Penang. A wire rack held half a dozen brochures. Two agents
engaged in talking on the phone didn't even glance up. I picked
up a brochure for Bangkok and Pattai Beach. Maybe if they
thought I was a customer they would acknowledge me sooner.
They kept talking. I looked at my watch as if time were a concern.
They kept talking. I wrote a note—Can I please talk to Mr. Fong?
She returned with—He's not here. I wrote—When is he coming
back? She returned with—2:00. I wrote—I'll come back. She
nodded. They kept talking.

I was back at two. Not so, Mr. Fong. To kill time, I wandered into a bookstore next door. I gravitated to the Malaysian culture and religion sections. There wasn't a huge selection and many of the books were wrapped in cellophane and taped. I'd been thinking I would like to have a better understanding of the Wong's religion which Chen told me was a mixture of Taoism, Confucianism and Buddhism. I saw a book about Taoism and love. I bought it and went back to Fly Away Travel Agency. Mr. Fong had arrived and was expecting me.

"Could you show me the flat that's for rent?" I asked.

"Can. It's upstairs. The people just move out."

Following the odour of urine and cigarette butts, I followed Mr. Fong up a long, narrow set of stairs with one light bulb hanging from the ceiling by a cord. There was a dead bolt on the door. Inside, the white walls were various shades of grime. The past tenants had left a lot of stray junk, including the coke cans and McDonald's take-out containers from their last meal. The small kitchen was at one end of a large open space. Even the appliances were small. The stove had two burners and the fridge sat on a counter. The front door opened into a ten by ten-foot room. The rest of the space was divided among two small bedrooms and a tiny bathroom with a toilet that apparently didn't flush. I erased all the negatives from my mind and replaced them with a scrubbed version, freshly painted with good light. It could be such a nice nest for Chen and me…

"How much is the rent?" I asked.

"It's RM325 a month. You pay the power."

"Okay, but I need two things—I want the toilet to be fixed and I want to be able to paint the walls."

"Okay, but you buy the paint."

"I will do that. I'll talk to my husband tonight. Do you have a card?"

"Yes. You have to be fast. This will be gone."

"But I *want* it Chen! I'll scrub it up. I'll paint it. It's not very expensive. He said it would go fast."

"It won't go fast. He was just putting pressure on you. Did you bargain?"

"No. It seemed like a fair price, so why would I bargain?"

"If it was his first price, it was too high. It's as simple as that. The game is they offer too high—you counter too low—they come down a bit—you go up a bit and you meet somewhere in between. Always! You want them to think you're nice, but they'll think you're just dumb!"

"I didn't want to risk losing it. I thought I was pushing my luck to insist they let me paint."

"Are they buying the paint?"

"No," I said wearily. "But I *want* to buy the paint! I don't want take some left over paint pot from heaven-knows-where! The main room is a good size… and I insisted he fix the toilet."

"Yeah… and they'll have to come back half a dozen times before it's right. It's not exactly a prestigious address."

"Okay! Now the truth surfaces. I see. Well, Chen, *you* find us a place. Tomorrow is Saturday. You can start then," I snapped.

"Do you want to come with me on this mission?" Chen asked.

"Of course! I need to learn how to bargain."

The previous night I had apologized for my rude remarks, but I could feel my crankiness returning. At least I got him moving. I resolved to be flexible and patient. We looked in the newspaper to see what was available and wrote down a few addresses.

The first place, like the one I'd seen yesterday, was over a shop: a sheet metal shop manufacturing woks. Chen said it would be noisy and he wanted to scrap it without looking.

"We should look at it Chen. We need a reference point."

"Okay. There seems to be some action up there. Let's see if we can get in."

Shades of yesterday's experience, we walked up a narrow staircase. One man was painting, one was changing a light fixture and a third was fixing the toilet.

"It's similar to the one I looked at yesterday, Chen. Except that they're fixing this one up. Ask them if they know how much the rent is."

Chen argued that they were just workmen and wouldn't know. I gave him a look of helplessness; he responded in Chinese, asking if they knew what the rent would be.

One of them said that he thought it was going to be RM500. Chen thanked him and we traipsed back down the stairs.

"Too expensive." Chen said.

"But you could bargain. The game is…" I chided.

"Hey! Don't pick on me. Remember I'm here, doing just what you told me to do. Anyway, getting back to this particular place, it would be too noisy with the welding and hammering below. Let's look at the new development near the river."

"But they're row houses aren't they?"

"Yes. I'd just like to see them."

We drove to the outskirts of town and there they were— large-scale row houses, still under construction. I could see that Chen liked them. We walked around, dodging boxes, tiles, bricks, shingles, bathtubs and bags of cement. Everything smelled of newness and wet plaster. Dust from the cement bags went up our nostrils and dried our throats. Light poured through the glassless window frames into the large rooms.

"You like them, don't you Chen?"

"Yes, I do. But they are too expensive for us now. It's too soon for us to buy. Our plans aren't firm enough. I'm sorry."

"Don't feel sorry for me. I find them much too *rowish*."

"Too *rowish*, eh?" he said. Even after all this time, we heckled each other over the Chinese use of "lah" and the Canadian equivalent, "eh."

We seemed to be getting nowhere. Chen said, "Let's go to the kampung (Malay village) area and see if we can buy a fish." We drove along the river. Buying a river fish was not exactly what I had hoped for. I felt defeated. The house hunt was finished. At least we had a start, albeit a shaky one.

"Chen, look over there! There's a dear little house on the

riverbank with trees all around it and a 'For Sale' sign in front. Let's stop, babe. *Pleeease…*"

"Okay. We'll have a look, but I see lots of problems."

"I'm sure you do," I snarked.

No one seemed to be living in it. There was a number to call on the front door.

"It's darling, Chen. I'd be so happy here, surrounded by beauty and watching the river go by."

"Darling, is it? It would need lots of work, my dear," Chen said, trying to peer through the filthy windows.

"I'll do it! Really, I will!"

We continued to circle the house, peeking in windows. There seemed to be two small bedrooms, a kitchen, bathroom and a living area. Just right for us.

"Can I help you?" someone said. We turned around as a man in his fifties got out of his car. "I'm Goon. I own the house."

"I'm Wong Lee Chen and this is my wife, Lauren Busch. We're wondering if you would rent this place."

"I really want to *sell* it. But it's been on the market quite a long time. It would need lot repairs."

"Maybe we could work on it together," I said. "Can we see inside?"

"Can." He unlocked the door and we followed him in. The air was stale—more than stale, definitely dead. There were cushions of dust on everything. The windows were full of cobwebs and I hoped Chen wasn't noticing the floor was deep in mouse droppings. Even I would have to admit the bathroom was bad and the kitchen not much better. The wind was knocked out of my sails… but I still wanted this house and was ready to tackle it.

"This is not what we want," Chen whispered to me.

My heart sank. Then I squared my shoulders and asked, "How much would the rent be?"

"If you want to fix it up, I could rent it for two hundred ringgit a month. You'd be better to buy it. I'd sell it to you for twenty thousand ringgit. The land is worth more than that."

"I'll have to think about it," Chen said.

"Here's my card. Call anytime." We shook hands and off he went.

"I *want* it!" I said.

"That's the second time in two days I've heard that, Lauren. You're sounding like a spoiled Canadian doctor's daughter. *Slow down!*"

"Be fair, Chen. I think we *should* buy it. It's a lovely property and it will only increase in value. Look at the Chongs—their property used to be outside of town, now it's surrounded by houses and is probably worth fifty times as much as Dr Chong's father paid. We have to think of the *future*."

"I say we have to think of the *present*. We'd have to get a loan for the place. Then we'd have to put in a new kitchen and bathroom and what have you got? A little old house on the bank of a river."

"Sounds wonderful to me."

"We'd have to get a car if we lived here."

"We need to get one anyway," I said flatly.

"I'll have to ask my father."

"Ask your *father*? Ask him *what*?"

"Ask him if we should buy it. He'll expect me to. He knows a lot more about what to look for than I do. That's if we're thinking of buying it. If we're just going to rent, it might be okay.

"We could rent, but it bugs me that I'll spend months of time and money fixing it up and when I'm finished Goon could kick us out, and he'd have a much more attractive place to sell—thanks to our toil."

The next day Chen had heard from his pa. "Dad says we have to have the water supply and plumbing checked. He says the price is good but make them come down. He says he and I should do it together. I've told him that you really want it, and that I want you to have it if he thinks it's a good deal."

"Fine, go for it."

Chapter 27

Hi Mom and Dad,

WE'VE BOUGHT A LITTLE HOUSE! It happened quite quickly and I'm so excited. It's a little cottage built on a bank of the Pahang River, just outside of town. It's on about an acre—quite flat, and has some well developed trees. The house is in poor condition but Chen and his Dad managed to get it for RM18,000 because it had been on the market for quite a long time and was in bad shape—make that *disastrous* shape! Probably most people would tear it down and build a new one. I really wanted it and promised I would do the work. I'm glad to. You know I've never been short on ideas—nor energy.

Chen says there shouldn't be any problem getting a mortgage and we'll add a few thousand so we can have some money for a new bathroom and some improvements to the little kitchen. My eyes were open all night. Just couldn't believe it. It's so peaceful out there. I always thought it would be the ultimate to live beside water. It's going to make us a darling little home.

I took some canvases to be stretched last week and I go (for the second time) to pick them up tomorrow. I think they'll have to wait for a bit while I shovel and scrape at the house. I won't know what to do first.

Fang says he's going to organize a *Gotong Royong*—that's what Malaysians call a work party.

I was glad to hear that you are going to Quebec to visit Grandmama next month. The autumn leaves should be lovely then. Give her a big hug for me.

Love to you both,

Lauren

P.S. I'll send pictures.

Chapter 28

I WAS A WOMAN with a one-track mind. Chen promised to look at cars the first chance he got, which was the following weekend. I decided in the meantime I would buy a bike. Chen might not like it, but I really needed it—besides, I could always dip into the money my dad had given me for contingencies. That would leave Chen only my safety to worry about. At ten o'clock I was on the main street looking randomly at kitchen appliances, bathroom fixtures, paint and tools, when I came across a bicycle shop. Thinking of all the things we had to buy, I looked at some filthy, used, bummed-up bikes. Then I noticed I could rent one for RM10 a day. I considered that only briefly. I wanted to *own* one. If we were going to live eight kilometers out of town, a bike would be good back-up transportation. I walked confidently to the new bikes and chose a royal blue beauty with three gears. I bought it. It was my first real purchase, since coming to Malaysia, and I hadn't asked Chen. I felt in control. Energized.

By eleven o'clock I was pedaling out of town to our cottage with a red plastic pail over the handlebar. The pail contained a package of sponges, soap, a bottle of water and a lunch of

Nasi Lemak plus some chocolate cookies. A note book, pencil, tape measure, and the key bulged my pocket. On the highway, I promised myself to focus on staying on the left side of the road and keeping very alert.

I arrived at the house with shaky legs and sweat running down my back. Wong had said the house was about eight kilometers from town. He certainly hadn't exaggerated. I pulled off my shirt and put it on a branch to dry. Then I took off the head scarf that had battened down my curls and fashioned a halter of sorts. At first I thought I must have the wrong key, but I persisted and eventually it turned. I gave the door a good whack with my glutes and it crunched open. I did the same with the back door. That would get the air circulating a bit. The kitchen window opened but the others were glued closed with paint. I wondered what the Feng Shui buffs would think about that!

I had to admit I was a bit daunted. Where should I start? A well-worn, hand-made broom propped up outside the back door was an antique lover's delight, but very stiff and coarse. I gave a cursory sweep to the whole house and used the great outdoors for a dustpan. Then I filled the pail with water to wash the counters. The water was the same colour as the river—brown. It was difficult to imagine improving anything with that, so I dumped it out. After letting the water run for a few minutes I tried again. This time it was a bit better—good enough for the top layer of debris. Gecko droppings lay on every surface. Chen had assured me they weren't from mice. There would be no need for the Pied Piper. I put my notebook down on the clean shelf and listed the equipment I would need to continue this cleaning project. I made sketches of the kitchen and bathroom as they were and how I visualized the end result. Then I noticed the container of nasi lemak and cookies I had brought for my lunch. I took it outside and was immediately drawn to a stump in the shade of a large acacia tree. It was relatively smooth and the side facing the river was slanted. Perfect. I claimed it as mine. I had a feeling of well-being as I ate my lunch and watched the river flow by. A soft breeze comforted me. Fishing nets were spread over bushes on the opposite side of the river. Then I noticed large charcoal-grey heads with horns sticking out of the water. I would ask Chen about them. I felt warmed by the sun and fully alive with the joy of ownership. I walked around our little cottage with its flaking brown paint and in a flash I could imagine bright yellow sides with white trim. Like sunshine! How happy it would look, and how happy its occupants.

That evening, I met Chen after work. While we were sauntering down Jalan Kupas, Chen listened to me burble and babble enthusiastically about my day.

"You did a lot today, mon bijou."

"Yes. It's a start. At least I have a plan. By the way, when I was eating my lunch, I could see big-horned grey heads floating in the river. What *are* they?"

"They're water buffalos. They get very hot while they work and their skin doesn't allow them to sweat, so they wallow in the river to cool off. They would die if they didn't. Sometimes all you can see is their noses sticking up!"

"*Water buffalos*! That makes me realize how far from home I really am. I never thought I'd be living on the banks of the muddy Pahang River watching water buffalos while eating nasi lemak with my chopsticks! What kind of work do the water buffalos do?"

"Lots of things. They pull farm machines and they can pull logs or containers of fish. They're very strong. In the old days, people in the villages used to race them for a bit of recreation."

"Today, they seem like a combination of tractor and race horse."

"Not a race horse," Chen said. "They're quite slow… but they are strong as a tractor."

I had stalled as long as I could. "I bought a bicycle this morning. It's blue. It's new. I love it." Before I could go farther, Chen interrupted. "You *did*? I asked you not to. I told you it was very dangerous. Did you ride it to the house?"

"Of course I did. And back. How else did you think I got there?"

"That really upsets me, Lauren."

"Well. Get over it. Give me some credit."

"I do. It's just that it's wild and crazy out there. I hope you didn't ride in rush hour."

"I didn't."

"I hope you kept well over on the edge and not too close to the water gutters."

"I did. Don't worry. I grew up riding bikes. It felt great." I didn't mention my wobbly legs and shirt so wet I had to take it off and hang it on a tree.

As promised, Fang and his friends turned up on Saturday morning for a *Gotong Royong*. Chen had planned to shop for a car, but I persuaded him it would look bad if he didn't show up at the work party.

The helpers checked the place out without comment. What did I want them to say? Surely they could at least say that it had potential. On the other hand, perhaps they couldn't *see* any potential. Maybe Malaysians just don't comment—good or bad. To give them credit, they had come equipped to work and went right at it. I had posted a list of suggested tasks and soon everyone was working away at something. What they lacked in speed, they made up for in enthusiasm. Fang's friend, Ling, brought a rake and was piling leaves and wayward branches. Auntie Lai was predictably absent, but her husband, Khoo, was washing windows with soap and water and wiping them dry with newspapers. Kim and Abdul had stiff brushes and were loosening debris from the roof and sweeping it off. Ling hollered up, "Hey, lah. How can I clean the yard if you keep sweeping stuff down from the roof?" Sam and Choo were washing the walls. Chen helped Fang and Lim pull up some unsightly floor covering in the kitchen. What we saw underneath was a shock. The floor boards were rotten! Bugs, like butterflies set free from a bottle, skittered over and around the boards. The stench of decay rose up. I felt sick—physically and emotionally. Chen was looking at me with a what-other- surprises-are-we-going-to-have look. As if that wasn't enough, Papa Wong would be coming in an hour with the lorry. He would not be impressed.

"We must check the bathroom floor as well," Chen announced.

I cringed. However, I knew it had to be done, since it had the same cracking linoleum and the same exposure to water. When they pulled out some nails and tore up some linoleum, sure enough, there were more rotting floor boards underneath.

"That gives us a new item on the high priority list," Chen said, wearily. "The floor will have to be renewed before anything else can be done in the kitchen and bathroom." He got together a little team to take away the floor covering and throw it on the refuse pile. I picked up some of the rotted floor and as I started toward the door Chen barked at me, "Lauren, this is men's work. Find something else to do."

"Not women's work, eh? Work has no gender. It's just plain work. Don't insult me. Move over," I said, giving him a push. I was the one who most wanted the house. I was determined to prove that I was more than just the director of clean-up.

Around two-thirty, Wong and Tan arrived with the lorry. Tan had brought lunch. She hadn't seen the house before. I fought tears in my eyes as she walked into the kitchen and watched the bugs perform. "Are they termites, Ma?"

"Wood worms. Aiyo! So dirty. So much work."

Wong strutted in, looked at the floor and said, "I know a man who will make a new floor. Cheap, too. He owes me. Let's eat. These people have worked hard."

Will I ever be able to read Wong? Now and then, compassion seemed to ooze through the veneer of this domineering man.

Tan put a plastic table cloth down on the ground by the river and spread out bowls of rice, curried mee noodles, sweet and sour pork, and a big jug of lime juice. Everyone smiled at the thought of a break. We washed our hands with a bit of Axion and brownish water. Chen and I were discouraged, but we put our problems aside and focussed on the big group of friends who had come to help us. Wong distributed a case of Tiger Beer. Good cheer reigned through lunch. It reminded me of stories of barn-raisings in North American pioneer days when the camaraderie and the meal were the reward for labour. In fact, in the early days, pioneers in Quebec formed a social group called *The Order of Good Cheer*. Seeing parallels in our different cultures was always fascinating.

When we had finished, Wong said, "Fill the lorry up. I'll take a load to the dump."

We bagged the yard refuse, cleaning rags and newspaper and pitched them into the back of the lorry. The offensive floor coverings were tied up and loaded. Two of the boys grabbed a badly rusted metal barrel and threw it on top. We had cracked the surface of the coconut.

Chapter 29

REVIVING THE HOUSE CONTINUED to drain our money, not to mention my energy. As is often the case, the process involved a series of highs and lows. The lights I needed in my studio, along with the extra power needed for our new appliances, caused the power breaker to trip regularly. The concrete foundation needed leveling before we could lay the new flooring. The thirsty walls slurped up paint by the gallon. Stains kept bleeding through until I was forced to splurge on a primer coat.

On the up-side, the kitchen and bathroom were finally functional and looking fresh with new floors, and fixtures. Our new car, a Chinese red Proton Vega, was a pleasure. Now I was able to drop Chen at work and carry on to the house with whatever I needed for the day.

Fang and I were watching an Indian drama on TV at Wong's one evening, when he said, "Let's go out to your house and finish painting the studio."

"Oh, no, Fang," I replied, yawning. "You've helped us far too much already. We don't need a night shift."

He knew I was anxious to have that room finished and get my easel up, so he said, "Come on Lauren, it will only take us a couple of hours. Let's go."

The thought of having the painting finished, over-rode the effort of the drive and the temptation to stay home and laze.

Fang wanted to drive our new car. I imagined how excited he would be to drive his elder brother's gleaming new red Vega. I was a little reticent, but remembered how carefully he had driven us to Port Klang to retrieve my belongings from customs.

"Sure you can," I said.

"Aiyo! This is great! How fast can it go?"

"Not very fast tonight, please!"

"Okay, lah. I'll be good."

When we got to the house we turned on some music, rolled up our sleeves, and started to paint. I appreciated having such a willing helper. Of course I understood Chen was busy at work and this was *my* project, but at times I felt overwhelmed, and wished he had been more willing, or able, to help me. Fang clowned around with his usual *joie-de-vivre*. We sang while we painted. Half an hour later, we had nearly reached our goal. "It's a shame to have to open a new can of paint with such a little bit left to do, but I guess we'll have to. Use my palette knife to pry it off, okay?"

"Sure, but only if you'll let me kiss you."

"Oh, you silly goose! Open the paint," I said.

He did open it, but then he came toward me and put his arms around me. He held me gently and looking at me with soulful eyes he said, "Lauren, I love you *so* much."

The look on his face made it clear it was not brotherly love he was feeling. "Sorry, sir," I said, "I'm in love with your elder brother."

"My elder brother doesn't deserve you, Lauren. All he loves is work."

"We're going home, Fang. Now! Put the top back on the paint can. I'll finish it when I come back in the morning." My friendship with Fang had been zapped and my pulse responded.

"Okay, if that's what you want," Fang said woefully.

We closed up shop and walked out to the car. Fang jumped in the driver's seat and we were off. I didn't need to worry that he would speed. He was not in a hurry. After we'd driven a few minutes, he put his hand on my knee. I ignored it briefly, but then he put his arm around my shoulders. My mouth felt like it had been sucked dry and my body tensed. "Stop it!" I said sharply, trying to push his arm away. Suddenly the car jolted with a loud, grating sound and a smashing of glass. Both front wheels were draped over the side of a five foot deep drainage ditch.

"Now see what you've done!" I shouted, like an exasperated mother of a young child.

We got out and anxiously looked the car over. The left headlight was broken. There was a dent in the left bumper and some deep scratches in the paint. So much for the good luck of having a Chinese red car. I felt confused and upset about the damaged car—and the whole evening. I cringed at the prospect of explaining the story to Chen, and having it inevitably filter down to Pa and Ma Wong. *Why were Lauren and Fang out together? Why were they painting at night? Why was Fang driving? Why did he go in the drain?* Fang, of course, was dealing with his own misery. I felt little mercy. "Here's my handphone, Fang. *You* call Chen. It's ten o'clock. He'll probably be home."

"Dad? Chen home? Not yet? I'm on Jalan Baru. I had a… a… little accident with Chen's car. It's not much. She's here. We went out to the house to paint. I need to be pulled out—only a *little* pull. Just took my eyes off the road… for just a little minute. I feel so sorry, lah. Yeah. I *said* I feel sorry! Yeah. Okay, lah." Fang closed the phone and handed it to me. "My dad, he knows a man… is sending him… says wait here. Pa's coming too. He'll ring Chen."

This was the hardest situation I'd dealt with since coming to

Malaysia. What was I going to tell Chen? I was afraid if I told him what Fang had done, the family dynamics would explode, leaving the status quo in shards. On the other hand, I liked Fang, and I felt sure it had been a "once only" exhibition. My goal was to be part of this tightly knit family. I decided to go for damage control.

It turned out I didn't have that option. Wong arrived to see Fang with tears on his cheeks, holding a blood-soaked, paint-splattered rag to his forehead, me with a swelling the size of a rambutan on my forehead, and the new car with its nose pushed into the side of the concrete ditch. He shook his head and shouted, "*Sow sang*! What the hell did you do Fang?"

"It wasn't my fault."

"Why wasn't it your fault?"

"Lauren poked me."

"Why did she poke you?

"I don't know."

"I'm not stupid, Fang. Why did she poke you?"

"We were disagreeing."

Wong scratched his head and said roughly, "Get in the car!"

Chen was in the driveway when we got home. He had seen his car. He was silent. Just when I was crediting his control, he swung his arm and gave Fang a punch in the nose. It was obviously broken. Then Chen grabbed Fang's nose and gave it a strong twist to reset the damage.

Tan came out and went directly to Chen. "Poor Chen. Your new car! Was Lauren driving? What happened Fang?"

"I was driving. Lauren poked me, Ma. Next thing I knew the car was in the ditch. Sorry, lah. It's not my fault. Not my fault at all."

"Shut up Fang!" Wong said.

Tan scowled at Wong and said, "Who are you going to believe, your son, or Chen's *kwai loh* wife? This would never happen if

Chen married a Chinese wife. We should know she would be trouble."

Chen was silent. I had to get out of there. My pumping adrenalin took me up the stairs in about four leaps. I was shaking, but tearless. I tried to sort out my feelings. I had thought Tan and I were building a good relationship, though I must admit sometimes I wasn't so sure. Now I knew what she *really* thought of me. Why had she welcomed me and tried to teach me the Chinese way of life? Of course, she had accepted me because of Chen. Actually, she had tried hard. But tonight her efforts had detonated. And Fang, the weasel! Imagine him saying the situation was not his fault! And Pa Wong—he had clearly defended and protected me, even to the point of going against his wife! And Chen—whacking his brother in the face and breaking his nose! What about myself? I certainly did not want to stay in this house. Yet what were my choices? Chen was climbing the stairs, and not by leaps. His expression mirrored distortion and sadness. I stood up to greet him. He threw his arms around me and held me tightly. We stood that way, wordless, wondering how this would shake down. Finally Chen said, "This is the toughest position I have ever been in." Silence again. "From my upbringing I know my duty to my mother, but in my heart, I want to be on your side and fight on your behalf."

Hey! You don't even know what went on! You don't know that he told me he loved me and tried to kiss me. He even said you didn't deserve me, and that you loved only your work. I insisted we go home. While Fang drove, he was trying to fondle me. That's when I yelled at him and gave him a poke with my elbow, and that's when he drove into the storm ditch. Then he says it's all my fault!"

"You and Fang have been such good buddies from the start. It's hard to believe what happened tonight."

"Yes, I know! I'm wondering if I confused him. In Canada women and men can be good friends and spend time together without being in love. Maybe he interpreted my friendship as love.

Anyway, whatever he thought, he sure messed things up for me! I don't want to stay in this house, Chen."

"I'm not surprised. I don't blame you."

"I can only see two options: *I* could go back to Canada, or *we* could move into our home."

"Please don't talk about going back to Canada! I can't stand it! I'm sure we can work this out. As for going to our cottage, there isn't even a bed there."

"We'll get a bed. Let's not let furniture get in the way of a solution."

We talked well into the night, sometimes with bitterness, but most often with sadness.

Chapter 30

TAN WAS OUT WHEN I woke up. Part of me wished Ma Tan would throw her arms around me and show her sorrow and another part of me wished she would magically drop out of my life. Chen phoned to say that Wong was lending us his car. He would use the lorry from the plantation to go back and forth to work. On top of that, he and his dad would be here at nine o'clock to take me and our things to the cottage. Dear Pa Wong—his support from last night had spilt over to this day of continued confusion and stress. I dressed, then stuffed the suitcases until they groaned and carried the unpacked wedding gifts to the driveway. I was still spinning around in circles stuffing our possessions into plastic bags, when Pa and Chen arrived. For them, time was of the essence. The three of us scurried back and forth, electing to dump everything in the living room. An hour later, I sat on the floor surrounded by all our worldly goods. My early morning energy seemed to have evaporated. My Chinese family was at odds. I thought of Tan. I wondered what she was doing, what she was thinking? I supposed she was carrying on as usual, but what was she *feeling*? I decided to go outside and sit on my stump. I wondered if the rest of the clan felt as disjointed as I did. I felt a bit shivery in spite of the heat from the tropical sun. Tan, Tan, Tan. I couldn't stop thinking about her, and the way I had tried to please her. Attempting to look on the bright side, I thought perhaps Tan and I just needed a break from each other. Surely this rift would heal. In the meantime, I must carry on, just as I assumed Tan was. I would feather the nest for my husband and me.

In the kitchen I unwrapped wedding presents that had dipsy-doodled across the Pacific Ocean. My heart leapt as I opened our dinner set of Italian dishes from Mom and Dad. Mom and I were so excited the day we found these! I'll think of her every time we use them. I washed each piece and stacked them on freshly lined shelves. And the humungous Tuscan yellow bowl from Robin—I had no table to put it on, but would leave it on the shelf where I could feel its warmth every time I looked at it. My spirits lifted. I really did love this place! Suddenly I had an irresistible urge to paint. As if I had known this urge could appear any moment, the easel had been assembled and a large canvas was blankly waiting. I wanted to paint outside, so I whipped the canvas off, folded the easel and dragged it through the door. Standing with the sun behind me, I painted my happiness: our little yellow house with the white trim and the crooked path leading up to the aquamarine door, the cocoa-coloured Pahang River flowing by and the strong sun filtering through the acacia trees while their hefty leaves occasionally floated down. The fact that the house had not yet been painted did not deter me. I knew exactly how it would look. I felt as if I had stored up my energy for painting too long. I worked frantically. Three hours later, I stood back to look at it. My loose, broad brush strokes had captured our home and its setting. I felt the tenseness of my neck and shoulder muscles and realized the intensity and concentration I had expended in a relatively short time. I stood farther back to admire it and declared it a winner. "It's damned good! Chen will love it."

Just as I was tidying my paints, a lorry pulled up delivering a bed, a small table, and two chairs!

"Did the bed and stuff come?" Chen asked, as he carried food from the hawker stalls into the house.

"Yes. You were good to think of a bed. I hadn't given it a thought," I admitted.

"I smell paint. Have you been painting? Really Lauren, how could you paint with all of this mess around?"

I hadn't considered that Chen would find my priorities skewed. I attempted to turn the tide by showing him the dishes all clean and neatly stacked in the cupboard.

"Don't the dishes look nice?"

"Yes. I hope the shelf is strong enough; they're very heavy."

"Relax, babe. They aren't *that* heavy."

"Lauren, I really hate it when you call me *babe*. I'm not a *babe*, and I will never be one. It sounds so silly to me." *Boy, Chen is touchy tonight.*

"That's a matter of opinion, but okay. Can I call you sweetie?"

"I don't mind that as much."

"Okay, sweetie, let's assemble the table."

It was just a matter of attaching the legs, but we didn't have the right tool. I suggested we eat outside on the river bank. Chen was reluctant but didn't have a better plan. After we ate our nasi lemang, chicken satay and watermelon, he wanted to deal with the bed.

"Sure Chen, but please—won't you take a minute to look at my painting?"

He said it was "very nice" then asked me to help him drag the bed into the bedroom. His reaction made me freeze.

"Chen try to understand. I was alone. I was upset. I had split your family up and was riddled with guilt and confusion. I tried to pull myself out of it. Painting takes me to another space. I painted my happiness with our home. I painted it exactly how it will be when we paint it yellow with white trim. I fed my creative urge."

"That's all good, Lauren. I'm proud that you could find happiness—a light in the dark." Fortunately, the bed frame was a snap. We lifted the mattress on top. Chen bounced on the bed like a child and pulled me toward him.

"I think we need to try this out."

"But what about the devil looking in the window?" I asked. "Your mother has been urging me to hang curtains, so the devil can't see in."

"To hell with the devil! Let's give him an eyeful."

Chapter 31

A WEEK LATER, OUR red Vega was back on the road and ready to simplify our life. Wong and Fang were sharing the cost of the repairs. The bed sported crisp periwinkle blue sheets and pillow cases with a green and blue striped cotton spread. Shiny pots and pans and new linens were stowed away. The refrigerator was full and the living room was empty—except for two giant yellow pillows and my large painting, full of sunshine and happiness.

The sad part was that I had had no contact with Ma Tan. Nor had Chen. Still, in my thoughts and movements Tan followed me, tormented me. Could I live in this birdcage?

Chen came home from work with a big smile. "This place looks good, ma chérie. I love being here with you. Just the two of us."

"*Sama, sama,*" I replied.

"Way to go! You have to use the words you're learning."

I agreed, and promised to call Halimah and reinstate my lessons.

"Everything is good, Chen. But everything will never be *great* until there is peace between your mother and me. What should I do? When? How? Please help me!"

"Sure I'll help you," he said. "Let's consider our options. First tell me what you think should happen."

"I think you should approach your mother and tell her what went on that night."

"Why me?"

"Beause you're at the top of the ladder and I'm at the bottom— always have been and probably always will be. I just want to get back *on* the ladder!"

"I don't want to do that. We should continue to wait for Ma to come to us. She *will* come, because she'll want to have a rein on me."

"Yes, but when? I'm tired of being tense and preoccupied. Really, all I want is for Ma to think I'm worthy of being your wife."

"I know that. I also know that Ma will believe me before anyone else. But I can't arrive at her door and tell her what to do. We need to be patient."

"How long do you think Ma will wait?"

"Damn it, Lauren. You North Americans are all the same when it comes to rushing. It doesn't happen like that here. It happens when it happens, and not necessarily at your convenience. You'll be happier when you learn that."

"Okay, okay! I'll try. But if you won't approach your Ma, will you at least talk to Fang?"

"What's your message?"

"Tell him you know everything that happened that night. Tell him I have suffered a lot of grief. Tell him, that in spite of everything, I want to be his friend."

"Okay. I'll do that. It's about time I talked to him with a few words of my own."

Chapter 32

I FOLDED A WHITE card and sketched our little house on the front; then picked up a pen and wrote:

Sept. 20, 2000

Dear Grandmama,

The pine armoire arrived yesterday! You'll be relieved to know that it was in good condition, especially considering it was over two months in transit. I can't thank you enough for giving us this piece of my heritage. For as long as I can remember it was in your kitchen, filled with food—fruit preserved in Mason jars, jams, pickles, cookies and all kinds of treats. There is still a faint smell of cinnamon, raspberries and dill—smells of summers past. You couldn't have given me anything that would have meant as much to me. It will be put to practical use, but beyond that, it will be a cord that binds together happy times I spent with you.

Chen and I are happily settled in our little house. His sister and brother-in-law came last weekend to help us paint the exterior. We worked hard but we had a lot of laughs, too. They worry about their skin getting dark, so they wear long sleeves, long pants, hats and probably sunscreen, too. Even then, they wanted to work on the shady side of the house. I was hot, so wore as little as was decent. Their skin is so lovely and the tone is so even, whereas my skin has three colours: white, red when I'm hot and blue when I'm cold—just like the water faucets!

Take good care of yourself, dear Grandmama.

Special love and great thanks!

Lauren

P.S. Must mention the horrendous freight charge you paid—a gift in itself!

Chen came in just as I was finishing up my note to Grandmama. He glanced down at it and said, "Can your grandmother read that?"

"Of course she can read it! What made you wonder if she could read it?"

"She's French, isn't she? You've always told me your mother's family is French."

"It is, but my grandmama grew up in Drummondville. Her mother was an English speaking Irish Catholic. The children in their family all spoke English and some French."

"How did your grandparents get together?"

"My grandmother was in Trois Rivières, attending a youth conference sponsored by the parish. The story goes that my grandfather fell in love with her rosy cheeks and they were married as soon as Grandmama finished high school. She tried to teach all *her* children to speak English, but there isn't much English spoken in Trois Rivières, so it must have been hard sledding—even downhill. My grandparent's family would definitely classify as French Canadian."

"Do the English and French in Quebec get along well together?"

"Some do and some don't. During some times in history the relationship was better than others. At one time the War Measures Act was used, due to a murder and riots in Montreal. They could use a lesson from Malaysians, where the Malays, Chinese and Indians co-exist happily."

"That's true, but I sometimes think it just seems that way on the surface. There will always be some jealousies, narrowness and competitiveness."

"The same could happen with you and me, if we let it."

"We'll have to knock it on the head if we see it happen."

"Let's eat. We're having curried rice and chocolate cake. Hey! How's that for bi-cultural cuisine?"

Chapter 33

W E DID OUR FIRST entertaining at mid-autumn Moon
Festival. The exact date is the fifteenth day of the
nineth month of the lunar calendar which usually
translates into late September on our calendar. That's when the
moon is considered to be at its very brightest—a *harvest moon*
we would call it at home. Traditionally, the family gathers at the
parent's house, but this year everyone (except probably Tan) was
anxious to come to our new home. Lee Yee and Auntie Lai offered
to bring food. I would cook the rice and make the soup. We would
all contribute Moon Cakes and other sweets.

For a month Chen had been bringing home moon cakes given
to him by his patients and co-workers. These little cakes, round as
the full moon, represent the family circle and the reunion families
would celebrate. Elaborately packaged, the pastry-type cakes with
Chinese writing pressed into the top, were dense and heavy. There
seemed to be dozens of varieties. Fillings might contain red bean
or lotus seed paste, fruit, walnuts, sesame seeds and sometimes
ham. Most were very sweet. In the center of some of the cakes
lurked a whole preserved ochre egg yolk, representing the moon.

I decided they were an acquired taste—like Roquefort cheese for some Canadians. I hoped next year I might like them better.

What I did find fun were the paper lanterns. They hung everywhere, but I found a shop-house with an irresistible selection. There were classic Chinese lantern shapes in red with yellow trim, fish, birds, flowers, moons. All were colourful and fitted with a candle holder inside. To my chagrin, even Disney cartoons had infiltrated this Chinese tradition. I bought a few more lanterns every time I passed a shop. They were feather light and swayed in the currents of the air-con. I was taping the lanterns to the ceiling in small groups when Lee Yee and Mok arrived with nine more lanterns for us.

"Hey! This is the first time we've been here that we haven't been handed a broom or a paintbrush! Looks nice, Lauren," said Mok.

"You'd better watch out, Mok, I could still find a job for you!"

He pretended to run away.

"Come back here, Mok. How would you like to hang these lanterns in the tree by the front door? Here are some candles for them."

"Where's Chen?" Lee Yee asked.

"He's working till seven. Dr. Chong has been home with bronchitis since Tuesday."

"He seems to be sick a lot."

"I think maybe he was just worn out by the time we got here. He has a big practice. His wife, Shanthi, sent her gardener over last week with the big blue ceramic pot full of chrysanthemums at our front door."

"That's so nice. The blue pot matches the door."

"Yes. She has an artist's eye for colour, shape and form; you can see it in her garden, her clothes and everything around her. She's got a big heart, too."

"I can understand what drew you together."

"Thanks. I don't see her a lot but we like being together. She's been over to talk about our garden. I want to keep it simple, but I don't think she knows about simple."

"What's this?" Lee Yee asked, pointing to my prized possession.

"It's an armoire. That's French for cupboard. It's a wedding present from my grandmama. I love it! Look inside."

"Aiyo! Holds a lot. Did those scratches happen in travel?"

"No, they came over many years of use. Pine is a very soft wood—used by the early French settlers. The armoire is part of my half-French heritage and has many memories for me.

I doubted she was impressed with my armoire. She might even think it was junk. My grandmother Busch would agree. Her house in Montreal had Chippendale tables and finely spindled chairs for little girls with smocked dresses—all in my memory bank, but not on the prime shelf with the farmhouse. Whatever Lee Yee thought about the armoire, it was balanced by her excitement over my paintings.

"They're incredible," she said. "It's like a gallery in here."

"I did the one of our house the day we moved in. My itch to paint had been bottled up after painting all those white walls in our house! I did it in one crack. The other painting I gave to Chen last Christmas. It was my first gift to him. The one I'm working on now is on the easel in the guest room. In fact, it's the *only* thing in the guest room. Want to see it?"

"Sure do."

"This is like a warm up. It's all about experimenting with darks and lights, to show both the strength and the grace of bamboo. I'm working on it out at the back by the river."

"Lauren, I really want to watch you paint. Can I?"

"Sure. Let's get together next week?"

Her face lit up. "That's perfect. I can't wait."

Pa and Ma Wong, Uncle So Ho, and Fang arrived with two folding Mah-jong tables. All of a sudden our kitchen was looking very small.

"I'm going to go outside where there's room to move," Wong huffed.

Tan stayed in the kitchen but didn't say anything to me. Nor had she brought food as she normally would. Fang was quieter than usual. In fact, he was understandingly forlorn. This was the first time he had been here since the night of his debauchery last month. I instinctively wanted to comfort him, but thought better of it.

In the middle of the hubbub, Auntie Lai, Khoo, Zi Meng, Zi Qing and the maid, Risa, arrived with more food and lanterns. The children gave me a hug and Risa produced a guarded smile.

"I'm so glad you came, Risa."

"Welcome everyone," Chen said, as he came into the kitchen, finally home from work and freshly showered.

We served the punch Lee Yee and I concocted- in my big Tuscan yellow bowl.

"This is a beautiful bowl, Lauren," Fang said.

"It was in my crate of things you brought home for me from Port Klang in your dad's lorry, a wedding present from my best friend, Robin."

"We had a good time that day, didn't we?" Fang said, looking wistful—as well he might.

"Yes, we did."

By eight o'clock we had finished our feast. The Moon Cakes, cut in quarters, were passed around and around.

"Do the dishes," Aunty Lai commanded Risa.

I was outraged with the Dragon Lady. "No! I didn't invite her here to do the dishes!"

"Well, that's why I allowed her to come."

"Then she and I'll do them together. The rest of you can go outside. We'll come out when we're finished." Auntie Lai flounced out as if she were wondering if all westerners were as ignorant as me. Risa washed and I dried and put the dishes away. I thanked her for helping me. She said "No, thanks. My job." I pulled her along when I went outside. The air was warm. The moon ruled the sky and reflected in the motion of the river. Despite its beauty, nobody pointed at the moon—*if you point at the moon, your ears might get chopped off.* Everyone sat on blankets or benches provided by Wong and Mok. So Ho sat on the riverbank by himself, smoking a cigarette. I felt sympathy for him now that I understood his suffering. No doubt he found festival times the most difficult. The lanterns shone from the trees and a light breeze blew. Zi Qing and Zi Ming paraded around with their favourite lanterns. Lee Yee called them to come and sit beside her to hear a story about the Moon Fairy.

When she finished, Zi Qing said, "That's a good story Auntie Lee Yee. But what about the one about the secret messages?"

"Oh. I can tell you that!" Chen said, and he told a story he had been told many times, about secret messages that were hidden inside moon cakes during an uprising that deposed the Mongol Dynasty.

"They were smart. That was a good hiding place," Zi Qing said seriously.

"We have to go home right now!" Auntie Lai announced. "Enough stories. Tomorrow is a school day. Risa! Get my bowls and get the kids in the car."

I winced. Such a control cop! In defiance, I asked Zi Ming and Zi Qing which lanterns they'd like to take home. We walked around the yard cutting down their favourites and blowing out the candles.

"There's no time for all this!" Lai sputtered. I gave Zi Ming and Zi Qing big hugs as they got in the car.

With the engine revving, I called out, "Thanks for helping with the dishes, Risa!" I could see Auntie Lai grimacing.

"Time for us to go, too. Call So Ho," Wong said."

"I'll get him," I said. I walked over to the spot where he had spent the whole evening. Cigarette stubs and several empty beer bottles lay on the ground beside him. I squatted down and put my arm around his shoulders. Simultaneously, his body began to quiver. It would have been easier to walk away, but I couldn't do it. "You are very sad, aren't you?" I said. He nodded. We sat, wordless, for several minutes before Wong bellowed loudly that they were leaving. I would never have suspected I could feel such a strong current running between Uncle So Ho and me. We stood up when we saw Wong coming toward us. We met him, hand in hand. Wong looked as if he'd seen a ghost. He, Ma, Fang and So Ho got on board. As they drove off So Ho waved briefly to me.

"*What* did you *say* to Uncle So Ho, Lauren?" Lee Yee asked.

"Not much. I just recognized his sadness and put my arm around him. We sat motionless until Pa called. We stood up and he put his hand around mine."

"You are a miracle-maker, Lauren."

"No, of course not. I just recognized his misery in a quiet, gentle way and he felt my caring and understanding. The thing that amazes me is that he had never even spoken to me in the four months we lived under the same roof."

"This is a big lesson for me," my *sister* said, throwing her arms around me. If Ma and Pa clued into what was happening, and I expect they did, they will be so grateful."

Ma? Grateful to me? Maybe…

It was Mok's turn to say, "Time to go." He climbed into the car. Yee Lee gave me another hug and whispered, *You are so strong!* As they pulled out she yelled, "I'll see you next week."

I had appreciated Tan's presence at our family party, but the battle was not over. Since Chen insisted we play the waiting game, I was determined to focus on my own life.

Chapter 34

ON MY BIRTHDAY MY heaviness was lifted when my sweetheart made one of my wishes come true. I was lying on the grass looking straight up at the Twin Towers in Kuala Lumpur—eighty-eight telescopic layers of glass and steel, stacked to the sky.

"I've never seen anything like it, Chen. Give-over the camera."

"Sure. You'd better hurry. Everyone's looking up. You'll get stepped on."

"Never mind. This is what I've longed to do. What a twenty-fourth birthday! I feel absolutely *pavlovian*.

"What's that?

"Pavlova is a wonderfully light meringue-like dessert. Can we go to the top, by any chance?"

"No. It's all office buildings. But we can get a ticket and go to the forty-second floor. Should be able to get a good look at the city."

We found the tickets (free, even) and were shepherded like school children up to the bridge that joined the two towers.

As we looked out at the city, we could hear the guide in the background… cost1.8 billion ringgit… based on an eight-pointed star seen often in Islamic architecture… signifies unity, harmony, stability… monuments to power and prosperity…

"See the humongous flag over there? That's Merdeka Square. Independence from Britain was declared there in 1957. Lots of parades and ceremonies happen in that square. The cream building with the turrets and towers is the old railway station— built by the British in 1913. I've read that its roof was built to withstand thirteen feet of *snow*! Isn't that a… hoot, as you would say? Guess the Brits had one set of specs for the whole empire. See the little building—the one with the large hexagonal window in the pitched copper roof. I think it's the Hong Leong Building. It's a huge international company. They would have chosen to construct that building small. Chinese people think if you can afford to put a small building on an expensive property, you are *really* wealthy. Let's get on with phase two now, okay?"

Chen hadn't told me much about his plan for my birthday treat. I only knew we were going to Kuala Lumpur for the whole weekend. We drove along wide tree-lined streets, with me ogling at the unique architecture of the National Mosque, museum, library, and a theatre, with its turquoise roof jutting out in angles reminiscent of the Sydney Opera House. When we got to the National Art Gallery, Chen stopped the car. He seemed unusually pleased with himself. As we moved around I suddenly saw it! An exhibit of Sam Carter's work—from Vancouver! I couldn't believe it. To be on the other side of the world and see work by an artist I knew of, from my hometown, seemed unbelievable. "Did you *know*, sweetie?"

"Yes. Actually, I read about it in a magazine."

The entire exhibit was of dragons—some were paintings, dozens were sculptures. Many would fit in the palm of your hand, some were breathing fire, all were to honour the year 2000—the year of the Golden Dragon. There would not be another for sixty years.

"You were born in 1976. That was the Year of the Dragon—just not the *Golden* dragon." I wondered if Mom and Dad knew I had been born in such an auspicious year. Not likely.

We strolled around the Lake Gardens and looked at the Orchid Orchard. The varieties amazed me. The blossoms were similar to my mother's irises. I saw a few Moth Orchids, the kind Shanthi had put in my wedding bouquet. I felt dizzy from the heat. My skin thermometer was red hot, and I knew I needed to get inside. Chen agreed when I suggested a break. We went back to the stately Mandarin Oriental Hotel to refresh and recoup.

The best was yet to come. My sweetie was feeding me treats one by one. The Twin Towers were next door to our hotel. As we stepped outside from the artificial chill of the hotel to the dark warmth of the night, the towers stood before us. What had been sensational by day became glorious by night. Lights glittered all the way to the top where they met a big orb of lights skewered to the building by a steel rod.

"It's my birthday cake, Chen."

"Anything for you, *chérie,* to quote your father. Here's another little surprise," he said, handing me an envelope.

Inside my birthday card were two tickets to the Malaysian Philharmonic Orchestra with Sarah Chang, an internationally known violinist, as special guest. The Dewan Filharmonik Petronas was the venue.

"Woo-hoo! Are we going *tonight*?" I asked.

"Yes. In about an hour to be exact. I thought we'd eat after, if that's okay. Let's look around a bit."

We went in through the Suria Shopping Complex at the base of the towers. "Look at this, Chen! Chanel... Cartier... Mont Blanc... Salvadore Ferragamo... Wow! Who buys this stuff?"

"The biggest customers are probably tourists, especially from the Middle East. I'm sure some local people buy, too, but from the look of things I'd say there's a lot of... what's the expression? Shopping windows?"

"Close. Try *window shopping,*" I laughed.

We walked to the center of the mall and looked up to five floors of stores with an enormous dome above. Decorations for the up-coming Muslim holiday, Hari Raya, hung from the ceiling and light fixtures.

"Let's walk through to the Concert Hall," Chen said.

"Is it in *here?*"

"Yeah. We go up those winding staircases," he said, pointing with his fist.

The high ceilings gave such a feeling of space. The walls were of a highly polished reddish-brown wood, a warm contrast to the stainless steel pillars and crystal chandeliers. The same materials had been used in the Concert Hall. The air was saturated with anticipation and excitement. The music was excellent and words couldn't explain Sarah Chang. I had never heard of her, but I would never forget her. This beautiful Chinese woman in her sensuous red gown played the violin with her hands, her head, and her heart. Her whole body lifted and bowed to the music. At times her hair flew as if she were in a windstorm. During one of the more boisterous parts, a string from her bow came loose and was whipping around over her head. One of her encores was Mendelssohn's "On Wings of Song." For the second time that day, I had tears of joy in my eyes. I held Chen's hand tightly and for once he didn't seem to mind.

Later, we had seafood pasta and red wine at Santini's at the ground level of the towers over-looking a kaleidoscope of water fountains and a park that stretched as far as night vision could see. Families, lovers and tourists strolled along paths, enjoying the beauty and freedom from the relentless sun of the daylight hours.

"What's left for tomorrow?" I asked.

"I thought we might enjoy a sleep-in, then breakfast at the Shangri-la. Later in the morning we could head down to Chinatown."

A sleep-in? Actually, I'd prefer an early walk in the park. In fact, I'd overheard someone talking about a rubber jogging track. I knew Chen would come with me, but I also knew it would be a big treat for him to sleep. I turned off the alarm clock.

"I want you to remember your first birthday in Malaysia."

"I'll certainly do that, sweetie! It's wonderful being with you in this beautiful city. You've planned it all so carefully, so lovingly."

That night I was too excited to sleep. Chen lay beside me, breathing softly. I gazed at his clear skin and the fullness of his lips. I thought of the wonderful day we had spent. This had been a *Lauren day.* My mind wandered back in time to the romance I had had with a guy named Clarence. He, too, was a med student, but arrogant and wholly in love with himself. He would have been challenged to organize a picnic, let alone a weekend in the city focusing on things he knew would delight me. I gave a sigh of relief and wiggled closer to Chen to feel his warmth as cold air pushed down from the air-con.

Chapter 35

I HAD PROMISED MYSELF I would focus more on my own life. Today was Day One. Chen came home to daisies on the front door and a sign saying Wet paint. He opened the door and called out, "What's with the daisies on the door?" I threw my arms around him and said, "Read this!"

DAISY DOOR CREATIVE ARTS PROGRAM

Help your child to develop his or her creativity
with this program using a variety of Visual Arts
PAINTING
SCULPTURE
MUSIC and DANCE
WHO? Children aged 4 – 7
WHEN? Wednesday 3:00 – 5:00
COST? RM30 per session, payable monthly
WHERE? Painting studio, 454 Jalan Kota Belud
To register or for further information please call 2164-7874
Lauren Busch, BFA, University of British Columbia, Canada

"Wow. You move fast! One minute you have an idea and the next minute there are daisies on the door. I'm sure there's more. Tell me."

"You *know* I have been thinking about creativity classes for children. Ideas have been brewing in the right side of my brain for some time now. I phoned Lee Yee to ask her if she'd like to help me and she was delighted. I plan to talk to Siew Kee about teaching sculpture whenever she can fit it in, and I'm hoping Fang will be able to find some time to help with rhythm and motion... and, I'd love to have him demonstrate the costumes for the Lion Dance. That could open up a lot of things—*papier mache,* head masks, drumming, dancing... I'm sure your dad will know a man who could knock together some little fold-up easels. I've started a collection of music and materials for costumes and props, not to mention painting supplies."

"Whoa! I can't keep up. How many children do you expect to have?"

"I could handle a dozen at a time and I could easily have the program on several days, with other age groups. I'm just going to do some advertising and take it from there."

"How are you planning to advertise?"

"I'm going to put the notices around—the one I gave you to read when you came in. I expect that you, Dr. Wong, will put a notice on the bulletin board in your office. There are places for public notices at *The Store* and at the *Pejabat Pos.* Do you think the school would promote it? Probably Auntie Lai will spread the word... tell her friends about it. Won't Zi Qing be excited?"

"Who knows what Auntie Lai will do? She might tell her friends, but... that may not work to your advantage. As for Zi Qing, yes he would love it, but you know how hard it was to get a date with him. And no, I don't think the school would promote it. They wouldn't be likely to support something that they saw as a distraction from the school program and homework."

"You're not exactly encouraging, sweetie, but don't worry. I'm sure this is going to take off like gangbusters. I just hope I can accommodate them all."

"I don't want you to be disappointed," Chen said lamely.

The next day I phoned Siew Kee. She was keen to be involved whenever she was in town or not working for her dad. She offered to take a stack of notices to her Uncle Yap to give out at Art Supply and Lesson. Wong did indeed know a man who would make some easels, but he thought I should hold off till I knew how many I'd need. *What is the matter with these Wongs—they're such a bunch of cynical nay-sayers. I'll show them what I can do! Fang is the only one I can count on to be excited. Oh, and of course, Yee Lee.*

I sat down at the kitchen table with my new binder and reflected. The Wongs were not the first ones to be negative. My own father, who loved me dearly, had been disappointed with my choice of art as a career...

"Mom, why do you think Dad wanted me to be a doctor so badly?"

My mother scrunched her eyebrows and said, "I think that the question is really why you wanted to be a doctor. You talked about it from the days when you put Band Aids on your dolls. Dad tried to encourage you because he thought you were interested."

"I guess I was interested, but eventually I realized that it was just a dream from my childhood. When Richard was in med school I was aware of the tensions—Richard trying to cope with the demands of school, you worrying about him not getting enough sleep, and Dad worrying about heaven-knows-what..."

"Reste tranquille, Lauren! Calm down! Your father only wanted what's best for you."

"I'm sure he did. I'm just trying to figure out

what's eating him! Why he's so focused on looking at life through a stethoscope."

"It's probably that focus that makes him such a respected doctor. Your dad has always been a champion of women choosing professions that were largely male-oriented, and besides, I think the idea of both his children following in his footsteps would have made him doubly proud."

"Proud? Why can't he be proud of me as an artist? He acts as if artists are not to be taken seriously... as if art is just self-amusement! A hobby! A bohemian way of life. Proud! I've always been proud of him! I admired him because he helped people. Well, I think I can help people with art, too! For that matter, I read just the other day that hospital rooms and corridors where families wait for loved ones undergoing surgery often have no windows and no colour. There is no respite from the harsh reality of crisis. It's completely soulless and devoid of creative expression. I'd love to get in there and remedy the situation. It's that feeling of starting with a blank surface and going where your spirit takes you. Just thinking about it makes me feel so alive! So inspired! Like I want to share my love of beautiful things with the world," I said, as I widened my arms and hugged my mother.

"Ma chérie, I feel good vibes for your career," Mom said.

Always, my mother has cheered loudly for me. The confidence I felt about my Daisy Door Creative Arts program came directly from years of her genuine interest and encouragement of my endeavours.

Carrying a glass of guava juice, I picked my way over tree roots to the elevated bank of the river behind our house and sat on my stump. Sun filtered through the leaves above, making dappled patterns on my white legs. I stared at the brown water flowing by, and listened to the cacophony of the birds. I felt a mixture of calm and excitement. Opening my binder, I started to develop a work purpose statement. *ARTS* was circled in the center with painting, sculpture, music and dance radiating out like spokes. Ideas, clustered at the sides and end of each spoke, came quickly. Each one got written down—the possible and the outrageous, the safe and the courageous. I began to see possibilities for weaving the four categories together. The framework would be in month long modules with one major goal—to provide children opportunities to develop their creativity in a stimulating environment. In the process we would consider the moods and light of colour, harmony, texture, space, movement, setting...

All of a sudden I had a change of mood. I needed to get going. I dropped my binder on the kitchen table, put some money in my pocket, and set off to town on my bike. I wanted to check out materials. I felt obsessed with texture. There was no shortage of fabric stores. I wandered into one and went straight to a large remnant box at the back. Pawing through the treasure chest, I found pieces of bright silks, smooth satins, some glittery stuff, and a piece of what my grandmama called *oil cloth*. In a dark, narrow craft store down the street I found beads, sequins, pipe cleaners and spools of ribbon and even feathers.

I might as well have been rotating on a spit, the heat was so intense. As I walked past a dried food shop, I stopped to admire containers piled high with beautiful curries—Buddhist-yellow, saffron, paprika, brick-red, terracotta, and masala. They shouted *autumn leaves in Quebec* at me. As I stared at them I had an urge to use them to paint a picture. That quickly developed into a vision of a room full of youngsters smearing curry powders onto long-toothed paper. Minutes later I was on my way home with small plastic bags of multi-coloured curries and a big bag of fabric remnants and bric-a-brac.

Back in my kitchen, I tried to paint the powdered curry on

construction paper with a brush. It didn't grab, so I added a bit of oil to bind it. That was better but of course the oil bled into the paper. A wee bit of water was the answer. The curries produced a grainy effect that made it all the more interesting. To me this was like baking powder to a cake. I was working away when I heard someone banging at my door. Lee Yee bounced in smiling.

"Hi", she said. "I came to Taman Damai for a dentist appointment and thought I'd come in for a visit."

"I'm glad you did," I said giving her a hug.

When we walked into the kitchen she said, "*What* are you *doing?*"

I told her. By this time, I not only had six saucers of "curry paint", but a jar of mustard and containers of black and brown shoe polish. Yee Lee still looked as if she were trying to decide whether to phone the doctor or the psychiatrist. "I don't understand," she admitted.

"Do you like the picture?" I asked.

"Yes... I think I do. It looks very woodsy."

"That's good. That's just what I was trying to say."

"To say? Are you trying to say something when you paint?"

"Always. Art is communication, an expression of thought and feeling. That's what I want for the children. I want them to explore new mediums, try new ideas, and not be stifled by conventions. Children aren't born with conventions—just watch toddlers draw with their strained spinach, or even their feces, if the opportunity arises. Their natural creativity can be nourished or wiped out. Well-meaning parents and teachers can destroy it easily. All they have to do is to be critical or judgemental or put too many limitations on their kids. Even not wanting the children to get dirty can be stifling. There's a poem that floats around teachers' college about a little boy who loved to paint and sculpt. Obviously, he was one of the lucky ones whose mother let him create things without interference. When he got to school, he wasn't that fortunate. His teacher wanted to "teach" the children how to draw. She drew; the class copied. He learned to make things just like the teacher's. Eventually, he didn't make things of his own anymore."

Lee Yee looked reflective. "Yes," she said, "I know. I understand that. I think I'm going to learn as much as the kids."

I looked at her affectionately and said, "You're going to be a big help to me."

Chapter 36

THREE WEEKS LATER, I sat on my stump. But that day the river did not soothe me. My shoulders felt heavy and my eyes were stinging. Only four children had applied for the Daisy Door Arts Program. Each day I thought surely the next day there would be lots of applicants. I slouched in humiliation. What hurt most was that Zi Qing wouldn't be able to come because he had no time. Furthermore, the *Dragon Lady* said she was sure none of the other kids would have time, either. The inference was that they were too busy with things that were more important.

I imagined the Wongs taking at least some small pleasure in the fact that I had gone out on a limb, fallen off the branch, and had mud on my face. Tan would be asking how I could possibly know what Malaysian children need. Were Malaysian children different from any other children? Of course not! I still felt confident in my plan, even though public opinion would have it that I had failed.

By the time Chen got home from work, I was a steaming stew of righteous indignation and self-pity.

"Four kids, Chen! FOUR KIDS! What am I supposed to do with *four kids*?

What's the matter with everybody? Do they think I've landed from outer space and plan to turn their kids into robots? Robots are what they are now! I want to free them up, not shackle them! Damn it! No wonder these kids have trouble thinking outside of the box. They might not even recognize it until they get to university and have to come up with original thoughts and ideas."

"Come on, Lauren. Calm down. I know you're disappointed, but let's analyze what's going on."

"It's plain to see what's going on. It doesn't need much analyzing. Nobody wants their children to take part in my program!"

"Look at it this way, Lauren. Four is a start."

"I thought four is an unlucky number. Is it, or isn't it?"

"Not always. Do you remember what Dad told you when you went to his rubber plantation?"

"No. What?"

"He told you that in 1875, four rubber tree seeds were mailed to Malaysia from West Africa, and from those four seeds a huge industry began. Maybe the four children will be prophetic."

"Prophetic. That's quite a word, Dr. Wong! Are you saying that from these four children a huge school may develop?"

"Can. Maybe can. Maybe it will grow by people who send their children telling others how good it is."

"Are you saying I shouldn't give up? Work with the four and see what develops?"

"I'm saying it's an option. One of two options—and I don't think you would consider the second. You are not a quitter."

"I guess you're right." I looked at him sheepishly. "What would I do without you to defuse me?"

"You're too hard on yourself, mon bijou. Seems like this is a good night to go out for some grub."

"Hell, yeah!"

"Do you want to go to Khoo's KFC?"

"No, I'd rather go to Fook Kee's and have butter prawns and pigeon."

"Ooo… I wouldn't have predicted that choice. Sounds great! Let's go dig into some pigeon!"

Chapter 37

Hi Mom and Dad,

The kids just left. I'm so excited! Had to tell someone and you two got the lucky draw. Session 3 just finished a fascinating mural! We call it, "What's to See in the Sea?" Started last week by painting the sea with thick paint, then made waves by dragging a coarse comb through it. Kids thought they'd been very clever. We talked about what was on the bottom of the sea & how we could make sand and stones. Had tons of things for them to choose from and watched as they decided to make the stones with dried beans and lentils. Chee Meng and Farhana argued about what to use for the sand. Farhana said that her sand would have gold glitter, "because the sun is shining through the water." Zheng You added some small shells I'd brought back from the east coast. This week they made fish from coloured papers—all sizes and shapes.

Some had pleated tissue paper fins. Others had feather fins. Tze Chin was adamant that feathers were for   birds, not fish. Chee Meng was equally convinced that the feathers looked really good for fins. The bubbles were the coup-de-grace. Some used buttons, others sequins, and Zheng You made tiny tin foil balls. He wasn't sure how to put them on, but decided to put a pin through each one and hold it with tape on back side. Wish you could see it. More than you wanted to know?? You won't be surprised by my enthusiasm. After all, I am a *Dragon* and they're noted for having vitality and enthusiasm. Tee-hee. Next week they'll sign up for November. These 4 will renew. Hopefully others will join.

I'll keep you posted.

Love and hugs,

L. xx

I thought about emailing Robin but decided to wait until next week after the registrations for November. She wouldn't be impressed that I was working with four children. I took an Oreo bikkie out of a package and poured some lime juice to go with it. Then I picked up the package again and had another bikkie. I was reaching for a *fifth* when I realized what I was doing. I twisted the top of the bag, put it at the back of the top shelf and slammed the cupboard door. What I needed was exercise, not a bag of Oreos. I stomped outside and sat on the step to put on my Nikes. After tying up one shoe, I put my foot into the second one. Something was in the toe. I had a habit of rolling my two socks together and stuffing them into my shoe. I reached in to retrieve the socks, but couldn't seem to get hold of them. The same thing happened on my second attempt, so I peered inside. There, pushed into the toe tightly, was a *frog!* I gave a startled screech as I flung my shoe across the path. They were my only running shoes; I needed to wear them. I banged on the heel of the upturned shoe. Still no frog. Then I got serious and whacked the shoe, heel down, against a big rock. Out it jumped and away it limped. In spite of my disgust at my cookie binge, I laughed. It would be a funny story to tell Chen that night.

A breeze was blowing—the kind of breeze that precedes the late afternoon tropical rain. With a token warm-up, I took off down the road. Running felt good. I could feel my tension release. Predictably, it started to rain, cleansing my sweat and cooling my skin. Huge puddles formed quickly in my path. I plodded on with squishy shoes and my T-shirt glued to my skin. My curls were tight and heavy. There wasn't much daylight left, so I turned around and headed for home. Cars passing by washed me with sheets of muddy water. It made me think of the day I had fallen in the cave and waited in the rain for a ride. At least this time I didn't have a sprained ankle or damaged bum.. Nor would the Wongs be flapping around.

When Chen got home, I was fresh as the daisies on the door and wrapped in a batik sarong. As he stood behind me with his arms around my waist, kissing my neck, he mumbled how glad he was to be home with me.

"I've brought you a dragon fruit," he said handing me an egg-shaped fruit that filled the palm of my hand.

"No *hot pink* could be hotter pink than this. It's beautiful. I'm curious to see the inside."

Chen sliced through its middle. The pulp was white and filled with small black seeds. He urged me to have a taste. It was almost like a kiwi fruit—cool, juicy, but sweeter and wrapped like a gift in pink paper. I thanked him for the treat, and sliced it on a plate.

"Seeing all those seeds makes me think… how were your *seeds* today?"

"Just great! Come and see the mural," I said, pulling him along.

"I agree. It *is* great! I don't know where to look first. These fish are amazing."

"I told Farhana that her fish looked like a blue-ringed angelfish and quick as a flash she pointed to another one and said, "That one looks like a green-*face* angelfish!" Then they all started naming them. I told them that the fish in Malaysia were much more colourful than fish in Canada."

"That's good they know their country is beautiful. We all take our own country for granted, especially when we're children. It took me four years away to realize the beauty of Malaysia. What are you going to do with this mural? I suppose you could cut it and give each of the children a piece."

"Oh no! It has to stay in one piece. I'm thinking maybe we could give it to the hospital for the children's ward. I'll ask the kids about it next week. After all, it belongs to them."

"What's Yee Lee think of all this?"

"I think she likes it. She seems to have the concept of being a facilitator. Hey! Get a load of this—Mok's mother, Chua, doesn't like Lee Yee spending time with me (that kwai loh)! She thinks her daughter-in-law is getting a lot of *ideas* about art and schools—even *university*!"

"What is Lee Yee's response to that?"

"She's going to clam-up about me and my interests, and where she's going. We're both going to try to drum up more business. We decided to invite any parent who wants to see what we're doing, to come for the last half hour next week."

"That's a good strategy, Lauren. Good luck, mon bijou."

Chapter 38

THE WEEK PASSED QUICKLY. I put a notice in the newspaper, explaining the program and its potential to develop the right side of the brain and inviting anyone who was interested to drop in at four thirty on Wednesday. Lee Yee, living in Buar, had others to contact. Her enthusiasm was bound to be infectious. My head was full of it. I kept a long narrow notebook in the pocket of my jeans shorts and jotted down everything that filtered through my grey cells.

When my four *seeds* met on Wednesday, I asked them what they wanted to do with their mural. Chee Meng said she wanted to take it home. The other three quickly said, "Can not, lah."

Tze Chin said, "We have to cut it in four and everyone takes a piece."

Farhana said "I want it to stay big."

I planted a 'seed' that they should think about someone we could give it to—someone who would be very happy to have it. Maybe someone who is sad and needs something pretty to cheer them."

"You mean like someone who is sick?"

"Maybe. It's a big picture so it needs to be somewhere with a big wall."

"Maybe it should go to the hospital. They must have big walls."

"Yes. Then a lot of kids can see it."

"Does anyone have a better idea?" I asked.

"No, we got the best idea. But what if the doctors don't want it?"

"Of course they'll want it!" Farhana said. "They want the kids to be happy."

Then Zheng You said, "If we have to give it away, why don't we each make a little one that we can keep for ourselves?"

"Fine," I said, "We've got lots of materials to do that. Let's start."

The kids went at it like old hands—which they were. They were not just repeating what they had already done on the mural. I was proud of their confidence and the fact that they took the project to another level.

At four-thirty two new mothers arrived, each with a shy child clinging to her. The mothers whose kids had been coming for a month, drifted in close to finishing time. They were whispering to each other and shaking their heads. The children of the new mothers broke loose from their mother's skirts and got down on their knees. One took a handful of sequins and looked at them lovingly. Another asked for a paper and some paint which I quickly provided.

I sensed tension amongst the mothers. They looked at the mural hanging on a wall by itself with the names of the children in the lower right hand corner.

Chee Meng's mother said, as if she was thinking out loud, "I don't get it, lah. It's just a lot of stuff! What do they learn by pasting stuff on a big paper? It's just a waste of time, already. There is nothing here for my child." She wound up and threw the ball.

"Chee Meng will not be coming back. Get your shoes on, Chee Meng!"

Chee Meng was not quite finished her sea picture and continued to work. Her mother grabbed her by the arm and said sharply, "I said put your shoes on. Leave the picture alone."

I reeled. I wondered what I could say. I willed myself to be calm. Words came. "I'm sorry you don't understand the value of the program, Mrs. Ng. Thank you for giving the program a try. I've enjoyed working with your daughter, and I think she has enjoyed being here."

"Enjoying isn't what it's about."

"What's it about, Mrs. Ng?

"About learning, achieving."

"And you don't think your daughter can do that here?"

"Can not," she said as she pushed Chee Meng out the door.

After they left, two other mothers admitted that they, too, had decided that their children would not benefit from my classes. That left Farhana. It crossed my mind that her mother might assume that the classes would die a certain death, so she would save face and say nothing. The two mothers who came to watch were not in a hurry to make a commitment, but the cheapskates were determined to take full advantage of the free half hour. They watched their children intently. Maybe they were confused. I tried to explain the project they were viewing and gave them some idea of my future plans. When five o'clock came, I thanked them for coming and offered to talk to them if they wanted more information. They left. Their car doors slammed shut.

I was flattened. Flattened and folded, just like a roti canai. I gave a primeval scream—so loud it made my throat sore. I flew into my studio and grabbed a brush and some blue paint. I flung the door open and smeared blue paint over the daisies. My program stayed alive for one month. It was finished! I was scuppered! One seed. Maybe four could have survived, but not just one. My throat felt raw and my head ached.

Tan phoned. Even though I felt as if I'd been thrown into drain ditch with alligators, I rejoiced in her long awaited call.

"So Ho smiles more now. Started at Moon Festival. Nice to have him around. How are you?"

To resist talking to her about the art program, I told her about my sore throat.

"Do you want to learn something today?" she asked, in a tone that indicated she thought I had to start somewhere. "I'm coming now."

Tan was coming. Well. She hadn't exactly apologized, but I guessed she was giving me some credit for So Ho's escape from dark clouds. Saving face, especially important to the Chinese, was what Tan had done. It was good enough for me!

Tan marched into our home with a plastic bag full of oranges and some pieces of crystallized sugar. Each piece of sugar was the size of a mini marshmallow and looked like a lump of white granite. She punctured holes in the top of the orange with a knife, and pushed a lump of sugar into each hole. "Now you have to steam the orange for one or five hours. I'll come back."

"Thanks, Ma."

Tan came back in three hours. Seemingly, the time the orange simmered was dependant on your schedule. "Now you squeeze the juice and drink. Hot. I'll do it. You sit down and put a blanket on. I'll squeeze."

She wasn't going to take her eyes off me until I finished. The brew was too sweet and too hot. I remembered the hot ginger compresses and wondered why everything needed to be so hot—especially in a country where the daily temperature was thirty-two degrees all year around. It's not as if you had frost bite on your cheeks.

When I had sipped the last drop of my cure, Tan said, "You make it three times every day till your throat are better. I'll leave oranges and crystal sugar lump here for you."

"Thanks, Ma. I'll do just what you said."

I did do just what she had said. It was messy and time consuming. The next day my throat felt somewhat better; certainly enough better to give myself a break from impregnating oranges with lumps of sugar. I put the plastic bag with the remaining crystallized sugar in the very back of my highest cupboard. The old Ma was back. Chen was right when he insisted we should wait for Tan to come to us. I had learnt more than how to make a remedy for my sore throat.

Chapter 39

M Y SORE THROAT WAS long gone, but I still felt limp. The closure of my Arts Program had crushed my spirit. Chen had tried to console me, but I couldn't seem to rekindle my fire. He explained that Chinese children have to get high marks. High marks are the ultimate. They open doors for the student's own betterment and protection for the parents who brought them up. In Malaysia there are limited places for Chinese students at university, making the competition harsh. This all made sense intellectually, but didn't comfort me. The program I had planned was sacred to me. It enveloped my love of art, and my belief in its ability to add to mental and spiritual growth for people of all ages. It had been thrown back in my face. It had no value. Consequently, nor did I. Nothing soothed me. Instead of moving on, I brought other aches to the surface. I had hoped to be pregnant by now. Why wasn't I? Was I going to be a failure in that department as well? And always there to haunt me was the memory of Richard and the loneliness of my uncomplaining and adoring parents.

Even the weather conspired to hold me down. What had been

late afternoon downpours, now seemed to start in the morning and last most of the day. The vegetation was greener than ever, but the sun had been replaced by heavy, grey clouds.

The street drains were working overtime to redirect the water. With the flash floods gnawing away at the edges of the road, I didn't have any desire to run. I watched with considerable interest as the Pahang River rose. I noticed that when Chen drove into the yard, he walked to the riverbank before he came in the house.

"It's higher tonight, isn't it Chen?" I said, sensing his concern.

"Yes, it seems to be. Nothing to worry about though. It's common for the water level to fluctuate. I don't think the rain is quite as intense at the moment. It will probably let up in the night. How are you, my dear bijou?"

"I'm okay. This rain is giving me something more urgent to think about. I'm glad you're home. We're having Szechuan pork and broccoli stir-fried with garlic and prawns."

"And rice?"

"But, of course. Surely you don't have to ask *that*."

"You're right. I love the way you cook Chinese food."

All night the water pounded on the roof and on the window panes. I was starting to feel more uneasy than I wanted to admit. In the morning, the first thing Chen did was check the river. He went into the bathroom and I went into the kitchen to put on some coffee. We both shrieked in alarm, "It's *wet* in here!" We looked up and sure enough, water was dripping from the ceiling. The roof must be leaking. Chen took the mop and I took a couple of big sponges. We used the two plastic pails we owned, and a few kitchen pots. Before long things were under control—at least temporarily.

When Chen came in, with a jacket over his pyjamas and untied running shoes, he announced that the river level was up.

"Well, that's not exactly a surprise," I said. "Is it dangerous?"

"Not really. Surely the rain will stop soon. I'm going to phone my dad and see if he knows someone who would patch the roof, for now."

Of course Papa Wong knew a man who would patch the roof. He wasn't sure when Chu would come because he would be busy. He also said I should stay home. I didn't like being told where I should stay, but under the circumstances I let it go. The last thing I wanted to do was go out, anyway. I wanted to guard our home.

"Dad says that there is a lot of flooding down by Kampong Warip. Fortunately, most of the homes were built on stilts. I'm expecting to be very busy today, too." Setting his coffee mug on the shelf and pulling on his boots, he said, "Guess I'd better scram."

Before sending him on his way, I hugged Chen and promised to phone him if I needed anything. With my second cup of coffee, I had brown toast with butter and a thick layer of marmalade. I lamented that it was so sweet. I certainly preferred the Seville marmalade my mother bought.

A leak above the fridge had dripped on the list of Malay words I'd taped to the fridge. The ink had run. I took it down and tried to decipher: who—siapa; where—kemana; what—berapa; when—bila; why—kenapa, and how—berapa. Below the list were some useful words: Saya tidak faham—I don't understand.

The rain seemed to be letting up. Instead of running off the window panes in sheets it was dripping like cleansing tears.

At ten o'clock the phone rang. Tan was calling to check on me.

"You okay, Lauren?" she asked.

"Sure, Ma, I'm fine. I've never seen so much rain, though. Vancouver is probably the rainiest city in Canada, but I've seen nothing like this."

"Wong said to me you got holes in the roof. You and Chen want to come for dinner tonight?"

"Thanks, Ma, but I think we should stay right here till the rain stops."

"Okay. I call again this afternoon. Phone me if you want something, lah."

"Sure, Ma. Thanks. Are you going to stay in, too?"

"Yes. It's Thursday. Girls come for Mahjong at one. They walk."

"That's nice, Ma. Have fun."

An hour later the phone rang again. This time it was Shanthi wanting to know if I was alright.

"Yes, Shanthi, I'm just fine. Everyone is being so thoughtful. How are *you*?"

"I'm fine, too, but Dr. Chong is ill. He has pains in his chest again. That happens every time he gets too tired. He's planning to stay home and get a lot of rest for a few days. Is there anything you need?"

"No thanks. We have a couple of leaks in the roof but Pa Wong is sending someone over to fix them today. Tell Dr. Chong I hope he feels better soon."

"Thanks, Lauren. Keep cheerful. This rain won't last forever. Bye, dear."

I was concerned about Dr. Chong, but I was also concerned about Chen. Half the town was in a knot and Chen would be in charge of the practice. "Keep cheerful," Shanthi had admonished. I wondered if she thought the rain would make me depressed. Perhaps she had heard of my recent discouragements. I thought of Tan, playing Mahjong with her friends… building the Great Wall of China, twittering like the birds and laughing with her friends. How simple her life seemed. But what did I know about her life? Not a lot, but I *had* lived with her for a few months… long enough to see how she shopped at the wet market when it was barely light, kept fit with Tai Chi, ran the Hair *Saloon,* cooked multi course meals every evening, tended the altar and the spiritual requirements for the family, prayed for the ancestors … heck, just living with Wong and So Ho for all these years couldn't have been easy. And *me*! I'm sure I stretched her coping skills and threatened her authority with her dear eldest son. Thinking of her almost always led to renewed admiration and respect. She does what she has to do. I vowed to try to do the same.

"What I have to do now," I said in an audible voice and with a smirk, "is empty the pails!" I was not a minute too soon. They were too heavy to lift, so I got down on my knees and yanked one pail at a time toward the door. With every tug there was a slosh until I was finally able to tip the pail and let the water cascade to the ground. I mopped up the water I had spilt on the floor, placed the pails strategically and set the oven timer for thirty minutes. I had to do something between emptying pails. I decided to make cookies, ginger cookies. Chen liked them and I would take some to Dr. Chong tomorrow.

Chapter 40

AT FOUR O'CLOCK, I was emptying the pails every fifteen minutes. There had been no contact with Chu, so I decided to phone Chen. I was told by Padma that Chen was at the hospital and had been there since two o'clock. She asked if it was urgent.

"I think it might be soon… but don't alarm him. Thanks."

"Okay, Lauren. I'll see what I can do."

An hour later Chen had not called. Nor had Chu come. I decided to phone Wong myself.

"Hi Pa. It's Lauren."

"Hi Lauren. Everything is okay?"

"I guess so, but the roof is leaking in three places now, and I'm working hard to keep ahead of it. I haven't heard from Chu, and I called Chen but he's not available."

"Not available?"

"No. There have been some road accidents. He's at the hospital. Could you give me Chu's number?"

"No. I'll call him myself. Expect him soon."

"Okay. Thanks."

I hung up the phone, wondering what Chu owed Wong.

Half an hour later Chu drove up. Flushed and haggard, he took a ladder from the back of his lorry. I grabbed the jacket Chen had worn early this morning and put it over my shoulders. It was still wet. How cold and miserable it would have felt in Vancouver! Not so here, where the air always holds such a high intensity of tropical heat and humidity.

"Show me leaks," he said, walking into the house with his work boots on. I recognized that as very unusual Malaysian behaviour, but it certainly didn't matter today.

After a brief look at the leaks, he said, "Needs new roof. Can't fix today, lah."

"Can't fix today?" I parroted.

"I put some covers on roof. Big ones. Bricks hold them. Will be some better, lah."

"Can I help you?" I asked.

Chu looked at me with disbelieving ears. He checked me out from top to bottom, then said, "Yeah... can. Need shoes with rubber. It goin be slips."

"Have a cookie," I said, putting on some rubber-soled shoes.

He took four. *Had he eaten?* "Would you like something to drink?" I asked.

"Had water. Fix first."

That suited me fine. He took some huge tarps from his lorry, and I helped him drag them to the bottom of the ladder. He climbed with a piece of the tarp, while I stood at the bottom and fed more up to him. While he placed it, I carried bricks up the ladder to hold the thing in place. We worked together and soon it was done.

"You good help," Chu admitted.

"When did you last eat?" I asked.

"Six," he said. "Had good cookies."

"You haven't eaten since six? What would you like?"

"Anything. But I go now."

I went into the kitchen and quickly found some cold chicken and a tetra-pak of soy milk. I handed it to him and he refused it.

The water continued to drip from above but more and more slowly for about fifteen minutes when it virtually stopped. Wet clothes were draped around the house. They wouldn't dry anytime soon. I had a shower and made a cup of tea. I felt fairly relaxed. I felt something else that I couldn't identify. A few seconds later, I realized I felt strong, and *useful*. A team member. I thought of Chen, so absorbed that he hadn't taken time to phone me. How lucky doctors were to have so many opportunities to help people. To treat their illnesses, but also to comfort and encourage them.

It was nine o'clock when Chen got home. He apologized that he hadn't phoned. He'd intended to, but had simply forgotten. In addition to traffic accidents and an influx of minor injuries, one man, a father of six, had drowned trying to rescue his boat. Then on the way home he had stopped to see Dr. Chong.

"Oh, Shanthi phoned this morning. She told me Dr. Chong was taking a few days of bed rest. She said he had chest pains. That sounds serious to me. Is he okay?"

"Probably. I suggested that he get a complete assessment at the Cardiac Diagnostic Center in KL. He seemed to think it would be a good idea. Tell me about your day, Lauren. Did Chu come this morning?"

"No. Not till four-thirty. I had to phone your dad again. He phoned Chu and I don't know what Pa said to him, but Chu was here half an hour later. He said we need a new roof ! In the meantime he covered half the roof with tarps. It stopped the leaks quite quickly. I was able to fire the bucket brigade—just have a couple of small towels down now."

"Sounds as if you've done a great job here. I knew I could count on that," he said, giving me a hug. "Do I smell ginger cookies?"

"Yes. I was feeling restless this morning and needed something to do between dumping pails," I said, getting up to fix us a snack.

"I'm sorry you had to deal with that. I think the worst is over now. It's still raining but very lightly. I think we'll sleep well tonight!"

We did indeed sleep well. Physical and emotional stresses had kept us wired for several days now and the easing of the rain gave us a sense of relief.

Just before dawn I dreamt that the rain had started again and was beating against the windows with violence. But wait—I was awake! This was not a dream. In fact, it had the possibility of being a *nightmare*. I woke Chen abruptly. We both got out of bed at once. We were standing in water above our ankles! We waded to the kitchen. The first thing I saw was my beloved armoire standing solemnly in five inches of water.

"What are we going to do about *this*?" I demanded.

Chen ignored me and opened the door to investigate. The Pahang River had threatened to overflow its banks and tonight, and while we were innocently sleeping, it had fulfilled its intention. The yard was like a lake with a few higher areas sticking up like islands in the water.

"This is worse than I ever imagined," Chen said. "I feel stunned. I'm not even sure where to start. I guess I'll do what I always do—call my Pa."

He turned and went into the house. I followed. At this point all I could think of was the armoire.

"Chen, what can we do with the armoire?"

"If it's so damned important, Lauren, *empty it*!"

"But there's nowhere to put the stuff. It's so *full*!"

"*Sow sang*!" he said angrily. "You figure it out. I'm calling Pa."

Never had my sweet, gentle husband spoken to me so roughly. I burst into tears. Besides my armoire which my grandmama had waxed so faithfully for sixty years, our new floors were deep in

221

muddy water. The worst part was that we didn't know what was still to come. I prayed that the rain would stop and that no more damage would be done. As I prayed, I wondered why God should help someone who prays only when her feet are under water. As if to make amends, I prayed for others in distress and especially the family whose father had drowned.

Fifteen minutes later, Wong's lorry stopped on the street outside. Tan had come in their car. The whole family—Wong, Tan, Fang and So Ho climbed out of the vehicle and traipsed through the water into the house.

"*Tiu!*" Wong cursed in disgust. "This is bad! I *told* you not to buy this house! You bought it anyway. You bought it because your little woman *wanted* it. It didn't matter that I said it could flood! Maybe you will listen to me next time."

"Come on, Pa, we may have made a mistake, but don't treat us like children."

"And I resent being called *the little woman*," I said, feeling cheeky.

"Okay. Sorry, lah. You tell me what you want me to do."

Then without waiting for us to speak, he was giving orders again.

"The first thing we have to do is turn the power off. Got candles, Lauren?"

I did have candles, though I had envisioned them being used at a romantic dinner, rather than a disaster. I produced them and matches as well. I was furious with Wong. Both of us had been attacked. Nevertheless, once again, we needed him. On the other hand, we didn't need him being so cruel in the middle of the disaster around us. The rain was still pounding down.

"Since we don't know when the rain will stop, you have to come home with us," Wong said. "Bring what's important."

"What's important to me is the French Canadian armoire," I said stubbornly. "Can we get it out of here?"

"No, Lauren. It's heavy and I don't want to bring the lorry into the yard in case I can't get it out. It won't hurt your cupboard to stand in the water for a day and we hope the rain will be stopped by then," Wong said.

"What happens when it stops raining? Does the water just drain out like a bath tub when the stopper's pulled?" I asked.

"Can, lah. Water can go down quite fast," said Wong.

Tan and So Ho were agreeing whole-heartedly with Wong. Fang, the little Romeo, was the one who understood how I felt.

"Let's take the stuff out and stack it up on the shelves, Fang said. I think then we can lift the armoire up and put some blocks under it."

"That's a great idea. I'll empty as much as I have room for, and someone can look for some blocks to hold it up"

Tan looked as if the armoire could sit in the water for a week for all she cared. However, she had come to help, and help she would. We stacked dishes on our limited shelf space and dry foods on top of them. The remainder we put on chairs. As we worked, a little miracle occurred. So Ho had found four tires in the trees and brought them proudly into the kitchen.

"They're just what we needed, Uncle So Ho. Thank you, so much."

So Ho smiled. I thought I saw a full set of teeth. I looked again. I *did* see a full set of teeth! I wanted to hug him and tell him he looked great. Fortunately I realized that might embarrass him. When the right moment came, I quietly said, "Uncle So Ho, you have a lovely smile now."

"I used to never smile. Now I sometimes do... special for you."

He was probably still being chased by devils, but it would seem that he had slain some of them.

Lifting the *cupboard*, as they liked to call it, was a family affair. Rescuing the armoire seemed to have a calming effect on us all. There was not much else we could do. The sky was starting to lighten.

At 88 Jalan Kupas, I felt the Wong's house enfold me. Summing up the previous night, I realized again how the whole family stuck together. They had all come—and today that seemed more important than the finger-pointing and confusion they had brought with them. I fell asleep on the couch and when I awoke, I could smell the coffee and knew Tan would have made congee for breakfast. Everyone else had left for work. We ate together, this little, time-worn lady and me.

"When you going to have baby?" she asked.

"I don't know, Tan. Soon, I hope."

"I hope, too. Give you something to do. Make me happy, too. Nice boy baby."

I shouldn't have been surprised, but I was. I knew Chinese parents want male children but was somehow surprised to be personally involved with this, what seemed to me, unremitting nonsense.

"I would be delighted to have either a girl or a boy, Ma." I felt tears close to the surface.

"Need a boy. Gives you good start. I go to market now, Lauren."

"I'll drive you. I need a few things, too."

"Why need food? You stay here with us."

"I guess you're right. Well, we'll get the groceries, and then I'm going to drive out and see what's up."

"Then come back. Stay here."

I wondered if she were being helpful, possessive, or possessively helpful.

"We'll see, Tan. I have a feeling the sun may shine today."

Chapter 41

OUR LITTLE HOUSE LOOKED as if it were floating in chocolate milk from the river. The Malaysians would say it looked like *teh tarik,* pulled tea— which has a slightly redder tone, and did describe the river water even more accurately. Bright blue tarps covered much of the roof. As I stopped the car by the curb, I recalled a story from my childhood called *Kingcup Cottage*—about a frog who invited her friends to a party, but nobody came because her house was too wet. I took off my shoes and rolled up my pants. Lifting my feet high, I made my way slowly to the front door. With difficulty I opened the door. It looked about the same as when we left it last night. With the power off, the kitchen looked dreary. Ghostly, almost. I lit the candle stubs we used at the height of the crisis. They had missed their chance to add sparkle to a celebration or create a mood. It occurred to me that they *were* creating a mood now, too—one of bleakness and sadness. I watched as my movements made the water ripple and gleam as the candle light reflected off it. I looked at the armoire standing crooked and humbled as it perched on top of the rubber tires. In spite of our combined efforts to raise it, part of it was still standing in water and was sure to have a permanent black ring. Whereas yesterday that thought would have upset me, today I saw it as simply another scar, marking another experience in its history. My Chinese family had seen it as old and damaged, but I saw it as a part of my family's history. *Who had made those marks? Had my mother run into it with her doll carriage? Had her older sister, Denise, accidentally swung around and hit the door with her skates? Did her youngest brother, Pierre, hammer three nails into its right side? Might my grandmama have covered the holes with a calendar to prevent my grandfather from spanking Pierre? Was the black watermark on top from Grandmama's bouquet of pale pink peonies placed in her pickling pot to support them? Now it would have a black watermark on its lower edge, much worse than the one on top—because it had been in a flood in Malaysia in the year 2000. Life goes on, like the Pahang River, sometimes high and sometimes low.*

When I came out of my reverie, the kitchen was bright. The sun was shining!

Halleluiah! Thanks be to God! I opened the window and could feel the heat beating down. The phone rang. It was Chen.

"Good morning, *mon bijou*. Has the bathtub stopper been pulled?"

"Well… yes. But the tub is far from empty!"

"Never mind, the worst is over. How's the armoire today?"

"It's fine, sweetie! Just fine! It will always improve as it ages. And hopefully, so will we."

"Aren't you philosophical on this sunny day? Maybe you should go to town and give the yard and house a chance to drain."

"No. I'm going to paint."

"Standing in the water?"

"Sure… why not? My pants are already rolled up."

"Okay. What can I say?" he said, laughing. I don't pretend to understand you sometimes. When you sought refuge from my family and were sitting in our cottage with everything we own dumped into one room, you paint. When you're home has two inches of water on the floors, you paint. Have fun!"

My painting was inspired by relief and thanksgiving. Our little house stood in muddy water with its windows fairly grinning through the brown residue left by the storm. Birds were singing in the trees, and the yellow chrysanthemums in the blue pot were looking tired but relieved. The general issue of royal blue tarps on the roof, which Chu and I had put in place less than twenty-four hours previously, matched the large blue plant pot. Light flooded the entire painting.

My light-hearted rejoicing became a bit heavier as the water level receded. Outside the yard was muddy and mooshy. Inside the floors were the same—muddy and mooshy. Forget brooms and mops. I needed a trowel. I found a piece of masonite and on my hands and knees, I started near the doors and pulled the sloppy mud along until I could deposit it outside. The residue was wet and heavy, almost like sloppy cement. I could only do a bit at a time. I needed a shovel—a snow shovel would be great. I chuckled to myself. Who would have a snow shovel? No one. But Shanthi would have a *garden* shovel.

"You're going to get the mud out of your house with a shovel? Oh! You poor dear! Come on in," Shanthi said, giving me a hug. "Come and see Dr. Chong. I think he's getting tired of sitting around with just me to look at. Lavinya will make some tea."

"I really do need a shovel for the mud on our floors, Shanthi. I shouldn't stop, but I will! I've brought you some ginger cookies."

"Thanks, Lauren," she said, "Dr. Chong will enjoy one with his tea. I'm so sorry you've had such a hard time. Was there really enough water to leave all that mud?"

"Believe me. It's like thick soup in every room in the house!"

The patient sauntered into the room saying, "You can't do that yourself. You should call the town office and see who they suggest."

"I *can* do it, Dr. Chong. I helped Chu put the tarps on the roof," I said with child-like pride. "What about *you*? Are you feeling better?"

"Yes. Just tired. All I've done is sleep, read and eat."

"Sounds like good medicine to me." Actually, he looked decidedly thinner and what my mom would call *pasty*.

"Have you seen these pictures of Nisha and her children?" Dr. Chong asked, as he stood up stiffly and motioned me to come to the piano. I *had* seen them, but enjoyed looking at them with him. "They're a wonderful family. We're so proud of them… wish they weren't so far away…" he said with his voice fading away and his chin giving a slight quiver.

Lavinya brought the tea tray in and put it on the table. We had scones and strawberry jam and my ginger cookies.

"Having tea at ten-thirty in the morning with two lovely ladies, is quite a departure from my usual schedule," Dr. Chong laughed. "I like it!"

"Canadians have the same feeling when there is a bad snowstorm. For those who have the luxury of staying inside, it can be relaxing and cozy.

When I got ready to go, Shanthi said, "You know, Lauren, Parveen is working in the garden, cleaning up after the storm. I'm going to tell him to go home with you and give you a hand. That will put a smile on his face. He has liked you since he first saw how you enjoyed our garden."

"That's a great idea," Dr. Chong interjected.

"Really? That would be great! He'll probably have some better ideas than I do. Thanks so much. I hope you'll feel better soon, Dr. Chong."

"Thanks for coming," he said.

"Don't thank me," I said. "I came with some cookies and am leaving with some tools and a helper.

"Can I follow you?" Parveen asked.

"Sure," I said, surprised that he didn't know the way, since he had delivered the planted pot from Shanthi previously.

With that settled, he proceeded to put various tools in the boot of my car. He took off his cover-all and straw hat and put them in the boot as well. Then he jumped in the front seat beside me. I couldn't imagine why he had asked if he could *follow* me, if he intended to come with me. I guess it's just a localism. I'd remember next time.

With garden tools over his shoulder, Parveen and I made our way to the house, every step creating a suction with the mud.

"Aiyo! This is bad," he said.

"This isn't bad. It was bad yesterday and the day before. This is *good*. When Parveen opened the door he said again, "This is ba-a-ad!"

"Well, what's the best way to deal with it?"

"With shovels, like you said."

We each took one and slowly pulled the wet muck to the door. I pulled toward the front door, and Parveen to the back. It was slow but ever so much better to be able to work standing up. What seemed like hours later, I was exhausted and I suspected Parveen was tired, too. Bit by bit, we'd removed the mud and hosed the floors. They still needed more cleaning, but we'd made a lot of progress.

"This is enough for today," I said. "Thanks so much for your help! You've given me a real boost. I'll drive you back now."

After nearly a week of living with Chen's parents, we were back in our house. We felt discouraged. The walls were still damp and the new flooring no longer shone. I had kept the windows and doors open while I worked, but in spite of my efforts we were plagued by the musty smell of mildew. Chen thought the flooring would have to be replaced before the smell would dissipate. A new roof was going to be expensive. Worst of all, was the realization that powerful brute, the Pahang River, could punch us again.

We had eaten our dinner and were having a cup of tea in the living room. I was haunted by Pa Wong's remark on the night of the flood. Until today his remarks had lain quietly in my subconscious. I took a deep breath and dove in. "Did your father say, "I told you not to buy this house! You did it anyway!"

"Yes. That's what he said."

"Then why did you buy it?"

"Why *did* I? Why *did* I? I knew you wanted it! It was *just darling*, if you'll recall. You pleaded. You wanted to get out of my parent's house. This little cottage would be *a wonderful little nest* for us. Do you remember that? Besides, you always said that I did everything my father told me to. I decided I was going to fight for this house because *you* wanted it! I argued with my dad till he backed off. That was a big step for me. I did it for *you*."

"I don't know what to say, Chen. I had no idea things happened that way. No wonder you didn't admit to your dad how threatened we were by the water level of the river—at least not until we were desperate. You knew he would say *I told you so!* And he did. He acted like the domineering father he is. I'm very proud you told him you were doing it for me, even if it was a bad decision."

"I'm not sure it was a bad decision, Lauren. You had a lot of enjoyment fixing it up. And you did a good job—most of it single-handed."

"Thanks, sweetie. We do have to think seriously whether to fix it up or sell it, though. What do you think it needs?"

"It needs a new roof—no doubt about that. And the floor coverings probably have to be replaced. I'm not sure what all needs to be done."

"And it needs to be protected somehow from further floods. Maybe some kind of retaining wall," I said.

"Sounds right to me. The trouble is, with Dr. Chong still away, I have no time to make inquiries."

"I'll give it a go."

"You'll never get a good price. You'll get expat rates."

"I'm not an expat. I live here! I'll flash my green eyes at them and they'll know I mean business."

"Maybe you're right. You could always ask Pa," Chen winked. We both knew I wouldn't be asking Pa.

"I can deal with it. I'll get three quotes, then we—you and I—will make a decision."

"Yes, Ma'm. I think we should start with the roof."

"I don't. I think we should live with the tarps until we sort out the stinking floors… before they rot any further. We have to get something water-proof under the linoleum."

"Okay, okay! You're probably right. Go, girl! Go!"

After the flood, flooring dealers were enjoying brisk business. Not one of the stores was interested in investigating our problem. I was thinking I would have to stoop to asking Pa Wong, when Lee Yee phoned.

"Hi Lauren. Guess what? I'm pregnant!" she blurted.

I felt like a pouting child being told by a friend that she was going to Disneyland and I couldn't go.

I forced myself to say, "That's… great!"

"I wanted to tell you so badly, but I couldn't do it while your house was flooded. How is it now?"

"Well, we're living in it, but we still have some problems to resolve. I've been trying to find someone who can tell us what to do with the sub-floors before we put down the new linoleum. No one seems to know or care. The smell is driving us whacko."

"I know a guy who would help you. He's from Temerluh, and he knows everything about floors."

I let out a guffaw and said, "You sound just like your dad!"

Lee Yee laughed, too. "Just a minute. I'll give you his number."

A minute is just about all it took, but it was long enough for me to get the conversation back to the new mother-to-be.

"Mok's mother must be pleased… and yours, too."

"Yes, they are. Both have put in an order for a boy. I hope it's a boy, too. It would be so much easier if they got their way."

"I suppose it would," I said, trying to imagine the potential problems if the stork brought a girl. "How are you feeling?"

"Perfect. Mok's mother is fussing about what I should and shouldn't do."

"Oh, no! How do you *stand* it?"

"It's okay. It's what Chinese mother-in-laws do," she said with a laugh.

Frankly, I didn't think it was very funny. *We'll see.*

"Thanks for calling with the good news… oh, and thanks for giving me Mr En's number."

"Okay. I hope he does good work for you. Bye."

It was often seven-thirty before Chen got home for dinner at night. Tonight it was eight. Days were long for both of us, with the result that our time together was very precious.

"Guess what the news of the day is?" I asked.

"You found a floor doctor."

"Yes, actually I did, but that's not the right answer."

"Lauren, I'm too tired for guessing games. Just tell me."

"Okay. How about this? Lee Yee is pregnant!"

"Hey, that *is* big news. Did she phone?"

"Yup! Said she didn't tell us sooner because of our flood problems. Actually, I was very surprised because the last time we talked about babies, she was feeling pressure from Mok's mother and simply didn't feel ready. I was even more surprised at my own reaction. I'm afraid it boiled down to bald jealousy. She's twenty-one and I'm twenty-four—seemed as if I should have been dealt the bairn first."

"What's a bairn?" Chen asked because he didn't know and possibly to defuse the tension he could sense in me.

"It's a Scottish word for *child*. Chen, do you hear what I'm saying?"

"I do. And I can tell you, you *will* have bairns. Obsessing about it is not what the doctor prescribes. Let's be happy for Lee Yee."

"You're right! I'm going to be an Auntie! All the children I know here call me Auntie Lauren… but now I'll be a real one."

"Very real and very wonderful. Ummm," Chen said, nuzzling into my neck.

Chapter 42

SIX WEEKS LATER, THE house was healthier than we had
known it. New sub-floors had solved the moldy odour.
We felt relieved to have a new roof and felt more secure
with a three foot brick retaining wall bordering the back of
our property. Everything had fallen into place. The down side
of this accomplishment was that I began to feel restless again.
Fortunately, it wasn't long before my doldrums were punctured
by an unexpected turn of events. Dr. Chong had been to the
Heart Center in Kuala Lumpur for tests. He had been given
medications and was told to take some time off work. He and
Shanthi had decided to go to England for six weeks to visit their
daughter, Nisha, and her family. They asked if we would consider
house-sitting for them. Would we! Living in Chong's big house,
with maid and gardener in place, would be a delightful change.
Chen would get valuable experience from being in charge of the
practice. He'd certainly had a taste of being in charge, but always
with Dr. Chong nearby. The decision was easy. We'd *do* it.

The Chongs were planning to leave on December fifteenth,

and return at the end of January. The same night we told them we would stay in their house, I was sound asleep when I felt Chen shaking me.

"I've got a great idea," he said.

"Oh Chen, I was asleep!"

"Never mind. This idea can't wait. Why don't we invite your parents to come for Christmas?"

Instantly I was awake. "Oh, yes, sweetie!" I said brightly. "What time is it?"

"It's two-thirty."

"Okay, that's late morning in Vancouver. I'll call my mother."

"Now?"

"Yes. Now!

"Mon Dieu, ma petite, quelle bonne chance!" was my mother's response. That told me two things— her mind was boggled and she was very excited. The problem, she was quick to point out, was Dad's practice. He couldn't just close the door and walk away from it. She'd talk to him and they'd phone later. Was I sure a month wasn't too long? She'd have to get out her summer clothes. She'd have to send Christmas gifts to her family in Quebec right away. Had we asked the Chongs if they'd mind? How was our own house? Had everything been fixed? Would she and Dad be in the way? Would they need to get shots? Would they need to buy ringgits before they came?

I reminded Mom that it was two-thirty in the morning and though we were wide awake, we should try to get back to sleep. We signed off reluctantly. Chen was in the kitchen having a slice of watermelon.

"The next time I get a great idea, I'm definitely not going to tell you until morning," he said, throwing the watermelon rind in the dust bin. "I gather your mother is quite happy about it."

"Quite isn't the word of choice," I said, laughing. "You're brilliant, sweetie." I threw my arms around him and said,

"Nothing could be more perfect—for so many reasons. Let's go back to bed now. Your brain has produced enough for one night. Give it the rest it deserves."

Chen did drift off easily, but adrenalin was coursing through my body. As I rolled around in bed, realizing that the *condition*, and it was a big one, was that Dad had to find someone to do a locum. For Mom to come without him was unthinkable. Both of them needed a break. Dad had waited anxiously for Richard to finish his residency and become his partner. Finally, the time came. Once more, I recalled in detail, the skiing experience that had left my parents and me utterly shocked and devastated. Dad had gone on with life stoically, though he must have endured incredible torment. A month with us in Malaysia would inject excitement and joy into both of their lives. Chen was the first to realize how workable the plan would be now that we were going to be in Chong's house.

As I tried to drift off, I remembered another wonderful idea that had been formed in the early morning hours. Back then, Chen would soon graduate from medical school and go home to Malaysia. I was pretty messed up about it, until all of a sudden I saw a solution...

> *The next morning at nine, I bounced into the clinic. "Hi, Sylvia!" I said cheerfully. "I need to talk to Dad. Is he busy?"*
>
> *"He's on the phone, but his first appointment isn't for fifteen minutes. Why don't you just slip in?"*
>
> *A few minutes later, he hung up the phone and said, "This is a pleasant surprise! What's up?"*
>
> *"Dad, I need to talk to you."*
>
> *"Of course, Snooks, what's on your mind?"*
>
> *"I'm sure you realize I've been pretty unhinged about Chen leaving in two months. Last night, as I was hashing it over for the hundredth time, I had a flash of brilliance. To be very direct, I'm*

wondering if you would consider taking Chen into your practice."

"Actually, I've thought about it, Lauren, thought about it quite a bit, as a matter of fact. Chen's a fine person with a brilliant mind. He'd be a definite asset to my practice."

I was dumbfounded. "Why haven't you said anything?"

"Probably because making the offer had such potential to change the course of your lives. First, I had to have input from you and Chen."

"That's just what I want! To change the course of our lives! I love him, Dad. I don't want him to go."

Dad stood up and put his arm around me. "We understand that, Lauren. If that's what you want, I'll give him a call. I'll do it this morning."

"Thanks, Dad," I said. "You have given me a solution when I didn't think there was one. I couldn't be happier!" I bounded out of the office. The doctor had given good medicine.

Back in my studio, I pictured Chen at Dad's office. He would probably miss his eleven o'clock class. I'm sure he was curious—maybe even a bit worried. I suspected he was as loath to leave me as I was to have him leave. Now, he could stay in Canada and be Dad's partner! I felt flushed as I looked at my watch. Where was he?

He looked excited as he reached the top of the stairs. He told me about Dad's offer, how honoured he was, and how he had never dreamed he would be so lucky.

"I know!" I said, throwing my arms around him. "You deserve it! Dad will be lucky to have you. We'll both have a wonderful life here."

The blood left Chen's face giving him a sickly pallor. "Oh, Lauren... I couldn't accept the offer."

"You couldn't accept? Are you telling me you didn't accept?"

"Listen, Lauren. My parents have fulfilled their responsibilities to me. Now I have to fulfill my responsibilities to them!

"You listen, Chen. I'm fed up with your damned responsibilities. March out, you nerd!"

I barged ahead of him and went into the den to talk to my mother. Through tears of anger, my voice fluctuated from whispers to shrieks as I poured out my story. I was dripping with frustration and self-pity. It was then my mother pointed out that Chen had to do what he had to do, and that it was me who had to make a decision. I could wave goodbye as he returned to his family in Malaysia, or go with him.

I was overwhelmed by my mother's suggestion. How could she lose her son in the most unexpected and immediate way, and three months later stand there telling me the choice was mine—stay home, or go with Chen to Malaysia? Actually, I knew at least in part, where her strength came from. I had gathered the insight when I overheard my mother talking to Richard in the kitchen late one afternoon in the early spring. I had been on the path to the back door when I heard voices steeped with emotion...

"Is Chen coming again tonight?" Richard asked as he watched our mother putting a pie into the oven. "If you ask me, he's around here far too much. I told Lauren the other day that she's crazy to be involved with him. She was really cheesed-off and told me to mind my own business. I don't like it. She's getting much too struck on him. I'll be glad when May *rolls around and he goes back to* Malaysia *where he belongs."*

"Richard! For goodness sake! Don't talk like that!" our mother snapped.

"Mom, I can't understand you! You don't seem to mind that they're together every possible minute— usually holed up in the privacy of Lauren's studio! Well, you'll mind when they tell you that they want to get married! That will be a mess that won't be easy to clean."

"Calm down, Richard. You're right. You don't understand me. Our feelings and values are shaped by our experience." Mom stood at the sink staring pensively with a potato in one hand and a peeler in the other.

"What experience could you possibly have had that could let you tolerate that foreigner hanging around Lauren and wheedling his way into our family?"

Mom dropped her potato peeler and stared out the window. "Richard, the experience I am referring to happened before you were even born. Your father and I fell in love in Montreal while he was studying medicine at McGill. When we wanted to get married, his parents were devastated." Although Richard could not see his mother's face, he was aware that what she was sharing with him was coming from her inner core.

"I am French and as if that wasn't bad enough, I am Catholic. Your grandparents knew the Catholic Church would require any children we might have to be brought up in the Catholic faith. They didn't even want to meet me! Three months later, when Nolton told them we were going to get married in Montreal, *they said they wouldn't come to the*

wedding. Everyone was hurt, angry and stubborn. It was only after you were born, Richard, that they asked us if they could come to visit." Tears ran down her cheeks. "So much hurt, Richard. I could never do that to Lauren or you." Richard stood up, put his arms around our mother's sagging shoulders, and whispered, "Thanks for telling me that Mom. We think we know each other so well, but we can only know what has been shared."

As I said to Shanthi several months ago, freedom is the best gift a parent can give a child—second only to love. Feeling secure and thankful, I rolled over and drifted off to sleep.

Chapter 43

DECEMBER EIGHTEENTH CREPT UP slowly. Chen arranged a private taxi that specialized in longer trips and I was on the way to the airport to meet Mom and Dad. In spite of the fact that we'd had some anxious moments, everything had worked out. The Chongs were delighted that Chen and I would stay in their house, and happy for my parents to stay with us while they were in Malaysia. Their clothes were taken out and our clothes were put in. It was almost that simple. Dad's replacement had not been that easy, but after several failed attempts, he contacted Dr. Wells, a colleague whose Christmas plans had been canned at the last minute. With that settled, I let my excitement flow. We were all overjoyed, with the possible exception of Ma, who had been non-committal. Pa and Fang were enthusiastic—maybe just more curious. Chen was happy in his own quiet way but fully occupied with work. He had asked the taxi driver, Rosali, to make a stop in Kuala Lumpur on the way home. I needed to go to the grocery store, but more importantly, I wanted Mom and Dad to have a preview of the city that had captured my heart. I remembered my own flight just six months ago, how endless the trip seemed and how disappointed I'd been to be by-passing Kuala Lumpur. I hoped my parents wouldn't be too tired to enjoy my plan.

When I saw them coming into the Arrivals Hall— Mom with her red sweater and stuffed shoulder bag, looking like a young Mrs. Santa and Dad pushing the trolley and looking a bit stooped and tired, but very dear; tears of joy dripped down my cheeks. As I hugged them, I said, "I seem to remember we were weeping the last time we saw each other, too… but this is much happier!"

"Yes, much happier. I'm *so* delighted to be here, Lauren."

"Me, too," Dad said, "In more ways than one. That's by far the longest flight I've ever taken."

"Did you sleep?" I asked, as we ambled along.

"Dad sure did, but I was too excited. I could hardly believe what was happening and wanted to stay awake to be sure I wasn't dreaming."

I took Mom's bag, put my arm around her, and we walked along together. I relived my own experience, walking out of the air-conditioned airport into the stifling heat, packing the luggage creatively to accommodate it and trying to take in everything, including that I had just flown half way around the world. Dad stretched out his long legs in front with the taxi driver, Rosali, and Mom and I squirreled-up in the back seat.

"We're going to do a little detour to Kuala Lumpur to give you a quick peek and go to Hock Choon's to pick up a frozen turkey and some orchids—if you're not too tired."

"Sounds good to me. How about you, Marie-Claire?"

"I feel fine. Riding around in a taxi doesn't sound too strenuous."

Mom and Dad commented on the Malay signs, the roadside decorations and flowers, the palm trees and housing developments. Long before we got to the city, we could see the skyline with the Petronas Twin Towers dominating and construction cranes stretching their necks as new skyscrapers rose in the downtown core. We circled the Twin Towers and their surrounding park, then drove past some of the historical buildings from the British era and Merdeka Square where independence from Britain was declared.

"You seem like quite a tour guide. You've only been to KL once, haven't you?" Dad asked.

"Yes. On my birthday. We spent the weekend here. It was really fascinating and I hope we can come back while you're here. We'll go to the grocery store now please, Rosali. "

"Yes, M'am. Hock Choons."

While we drove along Jalan Ampang, Dad commented on the embassies.

"I'll drive on Jalan U Thant? Many more there, and on Jalan Golf is Canadian High Commission," Rosali said.

"Okay, thanks."

"How do they come up with a name like Jalan Golf?" Dad asked.

"Well, Jalan means *street* and it backs onto the Royal Selangor Golf and Country Club," I said in my best guide voice.

When we got to Hock Choon's, Mom looked quite surprised that it was so small. She probably thought it looked dingy, too.

"Never mind, Mom, they have everything… and all we really need is a turkey and some cranberries. With that accomplished, Dad headed to the imported wines, and Mom and I went to a shed behind the store to buy flowers. Mom tip-toed over puddles on the wet floors and bent over to examine the pails full of flowers. I tried to build a Christmassy bouquet with three large red ginger flowers, a mass of white orchids and a smattering of yellow and purple ones. Then I added some green ferns and young stalks of bamboo. When Rosali saw us coming towards the taxi, he threw back his head as if he wondered where we intended to put our purchases. Although his taxi was considered deluxe, it was small. Dad tucked his four bottles of wine into tight crannies in the trunk and put the frozen turkey on the floor between his feet. Mom and I had the bouquet in the back with us. It was wrapped in no-nonsense newspaper, but neither of us had difficulty appreciating the beauty of the flowers.

We chatted like the early morning birds, about Malaysia, Vancouver, Grandmama, the flood, and the miracle of having Chong's house at Christmas time.

My mother's eyes closed periodically and eventually she drifted off.

We arrived in Taman Damai in the late afternoon. Mom was charmed by the garden and the relaxed comfort of the Chong's house. Dad found a soft chair with a footstool and picked up the local newspaper. Lavinya brought us Earl Grey tea and curry puffs.

"When are we going to meet the Wongs?" Dad asked.

"Ma wanted us to come for dinner tonight, but I told her you would be too tired. I said we would like to come tomorrow night. She seemed a trifle disappointed— you know she can't imagine the length of the trip."

"It sounds funny to hear you calling her 'Ma'."

"Believe me, it seemed strange to me, too. When I first came, we were actually walking toward Wong at the airport, when I realized I didn't know how to address him. When I asked Chen, he quickly responded, "Call him Pa". It sounded very hillbilly to me, but I hardly think of it now."

A few hours later, Chen came home and the four of us sat at Chong's dining room table. We considered sitting in a row so we would all have a prime view of the garden, but we decided that for tonight a view of each other was even better, so we sat two on each side. Lavinya cooked her last meal for us. I preferred she not be around while Mom and Dad were visiting, and she was happy to spend two weeks with her cousin in Maran. Tonight she had steamed prawns with butter sauce and fried rice full of bits of mushroom and finely chopped vegetables. Dad opened a bottle of wine so we could toast the occasion. We had a hard time finding wine glasses. The closest we came were small glasses that looked more ornamental than functional.

"This is very pleasant. Here's to a wonderful time together," Dad said, raising his glass.

"Here's to the travellers," Chen said, proposing another toast. "Thank you for coming."

"And while we're at it, here's to the Chongs!" I said.

"And to Dr. Wells," Dad laughed.

We had a relaxed evening chatting together. It made me happy to see Dad and Chen conversing so comfortably.

"What activities have you planned to do with your parents?" Chen asked.

"Any suggestions?"

"I think a lot of tourists go to Taman Negara, our national park. You go up the Tembeling River by boat for about three hours. I think there's a resort up there and lots of camping."

"I'd like to take them to the east coast to see the amazing beaches on the South China Sea, and to spend some time in Kuala Lumpur."

"Those are the only places you've been, Lauren. Go somewhere you haven't seen either."

"That all sounds lovely", Mom said, "but let's start with tomorrow."

"Yes. The first thing I want is to show you our little cottage. Then we can look around town and we'll go to Wong's for dinner at night."

"That sounds good. I'm really looking forward to seeing your home," Mom said.

Before long, Dad said, "If you'll excuse us, I think Mom and I should go to bed."

"Good idea. I'll show you how to operate the instant hot water for the shower and the air conditioner, too."

I saw them tucked into bed and said, "I feel like jumping in there with you."

I smiled as I thought how surprised Chen would be to see the three of us in bed.

Chapter 44

AFTER A LAZY BREAKFAST, we drove to our cottage. The sun beat down on our yellow abode with the blue door. The gentlest hint of breeze was stirring the leaves of our acacia trees.

"Ooh, Lauren. *Que c'est jolie!* No wonder you wanted this place. Look at the river, Nolton. It's like a riverbed flowing with chocolate milk."

Pointing to my stump, I said, "That's where I meditate and contemplate. It knows my joys and sorrows, that stump."

"Doesn't look all that comfortable," Dad said.

"Well it's magic, for me. Come and see inside."

The armoire was the first thing Mom's eyes went to.

"Doesn't it look great?"

"Yes, it sure does. It's quite a conversation piece. Not everyone sees it as we do, but that's okay now. When it first arrived, I used to get cranked up when people seemed totally unimpressed with it."

Dad was engrossed in the structure. He pronounced it *light weight*.

"Sure it is," I said. "Don't forget it doesn't have to withstand winters."

"Just floods," Dad chuckled.

"Come on, Dad. Don't laugh at our house."

"I'm not laughing at your house, but I think you've made a smart move, having that wall built at the edge of the bank."

"I think it's charming," Mom said.

"Oh Mom, that's so generous. I call it EELD—early essential living decor.

"There's nothing EELD about a house with your beautiful paintings on the walls."

"Thanks, Mom. Look, these are some 'before' photos we took."

"Gosh! Look at these, Nolton. It looks like a tear-down. I wouldn't have known where to start."

"You're not the first person to think that. I'm the one with the dubious distinction of having saved its life. Dubious, because we've had to put a lot of money into it. At times it seemed like pouring tea through a strainer, but for now I think things are under control. This picture was taken at the Gotong Royong, the work party organized by Chen's brother Fang. That's the clean-up crew on the roof, in the yard, in the kitchen and bathroom pulling up the linoleum and finding it alive with termites—Ma called them wood worms. There's lots more that could be done, but we're happy here."

"I suppose this is the water line from the flood," Dad said, pointing to the damaged lowest three inches of the wall."

"Yes, and there's a matching stain line at the bottom of the armoire. That's what upset me most... until I had a few philosophical moments."

"You poor children! What a nasty experience for you."

"It was. The worst part was wondering how bad it would get. We felt so out of control; just had to wait it out. Wong said it might not happen again for years. Anyway, as you said, we'll feel a lot better with our new retaining wall in place. Would you like some tea? I'm sure I could find some bikkies. I usually have them hidden all over the place."

We felt a bit as if we were on our way to a tribunal as we drove to Wong's for dinner that evening. For once, I joined Chen as the middleperson.

When we reached the door, I whispered, "Take your shoes off. Put them on the shelves over here."

"I can't think in my bare feet," Dad muttered.

Standing between the front door and the altar, I said, "Pa, this is my father, Nolton, and my mother, Marie-Claire." Wong shook Dad's hand with surprising gusto and my mother's more dutifully. *I introduced the men first without even thinking. Good for me!* Then I turned to Tan and said, "Ma, this is my father, Nolton, and my mother, Marie-Claire."

Tan said meekly, "Glad to meet you at last." *Did she think we should have come sooner? Was I putting my family first? Damned right!*

We shuffled into the main living area and the introductions continued with So Ho, Mok, Lee Yee and Fang. It wasn't long before everyone was chatting. Wong, with So Ho standing quietly by his side, was monopolizing Dad. Fang and Lee Yee were exuding charm and keeping Mom entertained. Tan went back to the kitchen and I followed to see if I could help her.

"Your mother very pretty, skin very fair," Tan said quietly. "Looks rich."

"She's very kind and very loving and happy, Ma. I hope you will like her. I have told her lots of nice things about you."

"Nice things?"

"Yes, Ma." I put my arm around her narrow shoulders. "You are both very good mothers. Try to remember that. Can I help you?"

"All done. We will eat now?"

"Sure, Ma. We'll eat whenever you want."

As we sat at the round kitchen table, one dish of food after another kept appearing. Steamed patin garnished with Chinese parsley and thinly shredded green onions, was the star of the show, with its head pointed at Dad, as honoured guest. The fish was followed by crispy chicken, sweet and sour pork, butter prawns and fried rice. Lee Yee popped up every four or five minutes to pour Chinese tea into our small cups.

"The only way to avoid a top-up is to leave your cup full, or empty it and turn it upside down," I said for the benefit of my parents.

"I've eaten in a lot of Chinese restaurants in a lot of places, but I've never had Chinese food as good as this, Tan," Dad said.

"Yes," Chen said, "Chinese restaurants are everywhere, but the food is sometimes not so good."

"It must have been so much work," Mom said. "How do you get it ready all at the same time?"

Tan looked a bit confused so I explained that in tropical countries, food is eaten at room temperature and keeping food hot is not an issue—whereas in cold climates we try to keep everything hot, so the timing is more crucial. Actually, I made that up. I'm not sure *why* we are so fussed about having everything hot.

"I work in two kitchens. Same time. Boil inside. Fry outside. Same time," Tan said, proudly.

"Chen told us about the two kitchens the first time we met him," Mom recalled. "I remember I had made a garlic and chilli sauce for the steak and Chen was so surprised and pleased."

Tan looked as if she were trying to imagine Chen having dinner with the Busch family so far away in a land so foreign to her. She stood up, and I was quick to follow, taking dishes to the kitchen and bringing back a big bowl of lychee nuts with wide strips of shaved coconut in syrup.

Mom and Dad enjoyed the meal and were lavish with their praise. Everyone else seemed to take it for granted. I sensed that the praise suggested to Tan that what they had eaten was more or better than usual, whereas she would have preferred them to think they had eaten normal fare.

"We would like you all to have Christmas dinner with us next Monday," I said while we were still all together at the table.

There seemed to be a bit of apprehension. No one was jumping with joy except Fang who said, "That's great! Can you get one of those big turkeys?"

"We've already got it, Fang. We picked it up in KL on the way home from the airport."

"Can I help?" Tan asked.

I knew she really wanted to, so I asked her if she would look after the vegetables.

"Can," Tan said, with a trace of a smile.

Chapter 45

CHRISTMAS EVE ARRIVED. WE had taken the liberty of bringing one of Shanthi's large potted plants into the house. We didn't know its biological name, but it was green and looked charming with the gold-edged red bows Mom and I had concocted the previous day. As well, each of us had made an angel with supplies from the Daisy Door disaster. Mom made one with curly red hair and mine had black curls.

"No angels have black hair!" Mom said, looking at my creation.

"I know one who does," I said, patting her head.

We put both angels together at the top of the plant, and stood back to admire our *tree*. Then Mom went bustling off saying she'd just remembered something.

She handed me a mailing envelope with my name and Malaysian address on the front. When I opened it, I shrieked, "It's the snowflakes Grandmama crocheted! You were going to mail them to me, weren't you? That's so thoughtful." I put them lovingly on the plant. The bouquet we bought on the way home from the airport was still fresh and looked tropically splendid. Dad's CD of the Vienna Boys Choir played in the background.

"How is Santa Claus supposed to find our stockings if there's no fireplace to hang them on?" Dad said, with an appropriately worried look on his face.

Chen suggested that Santa would probably take a few roof tiles off and come down through the attic opening into the bathroom.

"I refuse to hang my Christmas stocking in the bathroom!" I said.

"Then let's hang them on the dining room chairs and just hope Santa figures it out," Chen said.

Mom said she didn't know how Santa was going to find us anyway. She never did understand how he got all around the world in one night.

"Anyway, how would *you* like to bustle through Malaysian houses dressed for the North Pole?"

"One thing we should do for sure is put out a few lychee nuts for Santa and some bok choy for the reindeer. We'll show him some Malaysian hospitality," Chen said.

He had spent last Christmas with us, so knew our traditions—decorating the tree, hanging our stockings on the fireplace, walking to mass and wishing for snow, indulging in tortière, eggnog spiked with rum, fruitcake and shortbread.

Here we were a year later, trying to implement our Christmas Eve traditions in the tropics. With the problem of not having a fireplace solved, the four of us drove to the Catholic Church in BUAR where Lee Yee lived. The Catholic school and the church shared one building. As we drove into a field-cum-parking lot at the side of the school, we could hear the church choir singing outside. We rolled down the window. Their pretty voices were singing... "I'm dreaming of a white Christmas!" In spite of the hour, the temperature must have been at least thirty degrees.

"Dream on," Dad said. We all laughed, Chen included.

The church smelled of wax and incense. Everything seemed to

sparkle. Coloured lights flickered on a Christmas tree and, to my dismay, even the Virgin Mary was bound up with red lights! The church was packed with over a hundred people sitting on chairs and benches and some standing at the back. The congregation seemed to be about two thirds Indian and one third Chinese, and the three of us. We each held a candle. The brilliant colours of the silk saris, the gleam of the gold borders and pounds of gold jewellery were stunning. The black-haired heads were shining, too. Dad and I were the only people with red hair. Adoring parents held adorable wiggling children.

The priest spoke in Tamil, Chinese, and English. He based his Christmas message on the song, "Let Every Day Be Christmas Day," and ended by playing a recording of it. The carols were accompanied by three guitars and the voices were straining. There was a definite air of joy and celebration.

When we got home, we opened the doors to the garden where Dad had put white lights on some of the shrubs. Chen made us teh tarik which was very good— though Dad probably missed the rum. We had some shortbread cookies and some gingerbread men.

"It's a good thing you thought to pack the cookie cutter, Mom. Making those gingerbread men with you was fun."

"I really enjoyed going to that church service, Lauren. Everyone was so friendly—wishing us Merry Christmas. The Father at home would envy the fact that there were so many young people there."

"Yes. And so many *men*," Dad said.

Christmas morning we slept in until nine. Santa *had* managed to find our stockings. I had put them together quickly, decorating them with painted snowy trees, and some silver glitter. Their bulgy shapes were hanging from the dining room chairs by large loops.

The Wong clan arrived about four. Tan and Mok were carrying covered bowls of vegetables. So Ho was standing tall and flashing his new teeth. I saw a small gift wrapped in red tissue paper which almost fit in his pocket. I took gifts from Wong and Yee Lee and put them under our tropical tree. "Joy to The World" played in the background.

"That turkey smells good!" Fang said. "Can I see it?"

"Sure, come and have a look," I said, walking into the kitchen.

The bird, looking massive in the small oven, had already started to brown.

"Looks great, Lauren. It's fun to be here, all together."

"Yes, it sure is." *Amazing even, when you think back to the rifts of a couple of months ago.* The Wong family thinks we're all together, but we're *not* all here. This was the first Christmas without my brother Richard. Memories of him hovered. What good fortune that Mom and Dad were here with us. I put on my organizational hat, went into the living room, and suggested we open our gifts. Dad handed Pa and So Ho bottles of cognac and Pa gave Dad three bottles of wine. I was thinking all this booze was looking anything but wholesome, when Ma hopped up and distributed well-received *lottery* tickets to everyone present—well received, by everyone but prudish me, that is.

The gift opening continued. Mom gave Tan two silver serving ladles with Canadian Native Indian designs and Tan reciprocated with a Chinese tea pot with five small bowl-shaped teacups for Mom. There was a book of Impressionist paintings for Lee Yee, and for Mom, a straw beach bag filled with sunscreen, sun hat, flip-flops and a journal constructed with handmade paper with a cover designed using coconut husk fibres and dried anise pods. Chen couldn't contain his pleasure with the Palm Pilot from Dad and Mom. Then Dad announced that he had wrapped nothing up, but his gift to Mom and me was a trip to Taman Negara, *and* a holiday at a beach resort on the east coast.

"Aren't we the lucky ones!" I said, giving him a big hug.

"Let's pick up the wrapping paper," Chen said, to no one in particular.

"Oh, Chen," I said, "Please don't. It looks so festive."

"I'm going to the kitchen now, Pa. Keep an eye on Chen. Don't let him pick up the paper yet."

"I'll help him with it," Wong said with a wink.

So Ho followed me into the kitchen. Almost whispering, he said, "This is for you, Lauren. A long time ago I give it to my wife, Ooi.

I unwrapped the little box. So Ho was very quiet. A gold bracelet with a flock of sparkling diamond chips winked at me. I gave him a hug, and told him it was very beautiful and I would treasure it. I let him know I was honoured he wanted me to have it. He said, "I want to give it to only you." What a sweet man! I felt aglow, thinking that my words to him seemed to have been the catalyst that sparked his new confidence.

The dinner turned out really well, thanks to Mom. No one but she and I knew that the oven rack had caved in with the weight of the turkey spilling considerable fat on the oven floor.

Dad said grace: "Thank you God for bringing our families together at this meal. Bless us and help us to remember the needs of those less fortunate than ourselves. In Jesus' name, Amen." Lee Yee broke the silence by saying, "That sounds nice."

Turkey, mashed potatoes and gravy, bread stuffing with sausage, sage and thyme, cranberries and plum pudding with lemon sauce were all new tastes for the Wongs. But… there were some new tastes for the Busch family as well. Tan had brought black mushrooms with dried oysters and black moss, and taro in red and green beans. Mok and Lee Yee joined us in drinking Sauvignon Blanc and the others had Tiger beer or Chinese tea. However you looked at it, it was a feast and everyone felt part of it.

Chapter 46

W E WERE SITTING LOW in a flat-bottomed boat with our knees pointed up to the tin roof above us. Mom, Dad and I were on the Tembeling River on our way to Taman Negara, the world's oldest tropical forest, which means it's been around for at least 130,000,000 years. A small motor, not much larger than an egg beater, propelled us through the quiet, murky water.

"Doesn't it look like we're on a river of steaming hot cocoa?" Mom asked.

"Yes, and look down there where the rapids are. That looks like a cup of foaming cappuccino," I quipped.

And from Dad, "You two rascals are making me wish for a mug of good, strong coffee."

"Here, have some bottled water," I teased. "This is a serious adventure we're on. Actually, it's making me feel quite poetic."

I fished around in my bag until I found a pencil and sketchbook then started to make notes. On the shore a show unfolds... trees tall as masts and just as straight... topped with branches spreading out like veins... vines mounting trunks... camouflaging their host... red fruit the size of crab apples clinging to trunks in clumps... flowers in tangerine blots... thick greens... collared kingfishers in brilliant turquoise swoop with bursts of energy... water buffalo congregate and fishermen shake out nets.

The hum of the motor and the increasing heat made me feel very relaxed. I slipped into the empty seat behind Mom and Dad and started to sketch them as they sat contentedly watching ahead, totally unaware of me. With my ever-present pad and a few soft lead pencils, I captured Dad's Tilley hat with his curly red hair showing slightly below, his strong shoulders stretching his navy and white striped shirt, and Mom's smartly shaped black hair topped with a jaunty red visor, her crisp white shirt with a Chinese collar, and the edge of her round silver earrings. I framed it all by the low roof of the boat and the back of the seat cushioned by orange life jackets. I tore the page out of my book and passed it to them.

Mom said, "We can't take our eyes off you for a moment."

"You know, Lauren, this is very good." Dad said.

"You know, Dad," I said mimicking him, "This is one of the few times you've ever said that." It was just a quick sketch, but the sun seemed to shine even brighter with his comment. I kissed the back of his neck.

After our two and a half hour boat ride we unfolded ourselves and struggled, with our back packs, up a long flight of stairs to the top of the bank. Our accommodation was a one room chalet made of wood with a thatched roof lined with rattan woven in clever patterns, in tune with the woven floor mats. At the back, a porch looked as if it wasn't sure whether it was part of the chalet or part of the jungle. Whichever it was, it would be perfect for reading and communing with nature. The screens (here called *netting)* were blocked by flowering vines. The windows were a bit cobwebby but we could forgive that when we thought of the tourists in the dorms and the campsites down the way.

There was only one restaurant at the resort and every meal

was a buffet with an incredible array of food. We were astonished. How did all that food get here? We were expecting to be roughing it with bacon and beans and here we were, eating as if we were in downtown Kuala Lumpur.

The first night, we went on a Night Jungle Walk with our guide, Amri. Thinking of the jungle in the dark gave me the whim-whams, but when we met with our walking shoes and flashlights, I felt calmer and full of anticipation. The cicadas were singing one note with high, shrill determination. They must sing in shifts because they produced a seamless screech. Against this background noise, Amri pointed out a Huntsman spider (just a *little bit* poisonous) whose wife eats him! Another female badge was the six inch stick insect, twice as big as her husband. Other sightings were a stark-white spider, glow worms, florescent fungi, and ropes of rattan swinging from branches, covered with harsh thorns (which disappear at maturity), and all manner of parasites and elements of wonder. The biggest wonder of all was that we felt so safe on our first walk in the jungle... and at night!

When we got back to our chalet, there was a cicada in our room. We decided to ignore it. Ha! As soon as we turned out the light, its one note concerto began. Mom and I were happy to let Dad deal with it. With model patience, he coaxed it into his hat and took it gently outside where it jumped to freedom; no doubt at least as relieved as we were.

In the morning, Amri took us along the Canopy Walk. The rope bridge dimensions were four hundred meters long and twenty-five to forty meters above the ground, putting us right up there in the tree tops. Looking *down* on a tropical jungle gave an interesting dimension. Coupled with the unusual vantage point was the sway and bounce of the walkway with each step I took. I forged along with a white fine mesh cap covering my head and neck, and sweat running down my back and even beading on the backs of my hands. Fantasy grabbed me. I imagined falling off the bridge and landing in a nice bowl-like tuft of large leaves. That was fine, until I felt snakes writhing underneath me. I held tighter to the rope rails and kept my eyes focussed straight ahead. How far could four hundred meters be?

In the afternoon, we were taken by riverboat to Lata Berkoh Cascades to swim. Mom and I, assuming we were being taken to a beachy swimming spot, wore sandals. After a twenty minute boat ride, came the unexpected half hour walk over rough terrain. By the time we got to the swimming hole, we felt blistered, pooped and drooped. Dad peered at us from under his Tilley hat, with a *see me—fresh-as-when-I-left* look. We shed our clothes and walked toward the water in our bathing suits. To get to the swimming area we had to slide over humungous, smooth and incredibly slippery rocks. I, by far the youngest of our trio, thought I was going to break my neck. We had fun swirling around in the pool, but we all knew that if getting *in* the pool was a challenge, getting *out* of there was going to be worse. Mom and I fumbled around and lost our balance, but after several aborted attempts, we reached the top of the rocks. It was Dad's turn to be humbled. He couldn't seem to get a grip on anything even remotely able to support his weight. Amri and other men tried to make encouraging suggestions, but to no avail. Finally, Dad flopped back into the pool and relaxed for a bit. Amri got a *skookum* (a British Columbian localism) rope from the boat which Dad tied around his waist for some support. He tried a different angle and with great effort, and to everyone's relief, he inched his way up. On the way back, Dad grumbled that the excursion had not been properly represented and that it hadn't shown good sense from a safety point of view. When we got back we relaxed with cold glasses of beer and some Asian pizza with chicken, chillies, squid and prawns.

"Too bad Chen isn't here with us, but I suppose he's been here often."

"No. Actually, he's never been here. The Wongs didn't venture far off their vision, Chen's education. Their life was quite narrow, bordered by the rubber plantation and their home and village. The trip that Dr Chong gave us to the Awana Resort was Chen's only break ever that we would call a holiday. Except, of course our honeymoon trip in the Canadian Rockies, thanks to you, Dad."

"You and Chen will have some nice trips, I'm sure. Obviously, this is not the time, when he's been entrusted with Dr. Chong's practice," Dad said.

"You've both been real troopers on this jungle tour. I hope you think it has been worthwhile," I said.

"Oh, yes!" Mom said. "I never thought I would be walking above the trees in a Malaysian jungle."

"Me, neither," Dad said. "I feel far from my usual responsibilities at home. But I was hoping to see more animals. I suppose with all the tourists, the wild-life has escaped to privacy deeper in the jungle. The only sign of animals has been the monkeys constantly being shooed out of the open dining room."

In spite of that, we agreed that we'd had a great experience— even if it did almost take mountain-climbing equipment to get Dad up the rocks.

Chapter 47

WE HAD BEEN ADMIRING orchids at the night market, when we suddenly found ourselves staring at bras—rows and rows of them. They were folded with padded cups pointed up, giving the impression of goose eggs in a huge sectioned crate.

"What are these?" Dad asked, bending over to have a better look. Mom and I, only seconds ahead of him, laughed heartily. Dad regained his composure at the next stall featuring watches and Gucci purses. We shuffled down the closed-off street, past vegetable stands, racks of dresses, safety pins, elastic bands, medicines, work pants, plastic toys and pirated videos.

"This is what you could safely call one-stop shopping," Dad said. "*Walmart* has nothing on this."

"It's more than one-stop shopping; it's a social event," Mom said. The air was soft and warm. Swallows sat wing to wing on the telephone lines. There were teens in jeans and grandmothers in silks. Bahasa Malaysia, Mandarin, Cantonese, Tamil and English floated through the warm evening. Handphones connected the shoppers to the community beyond.

"Let's get something to eat," Mom said.

"Sure, we'll walk up the other side."

"I'd like some of that satay," Dad said. "Let's take some home for Chen. Look at those Peking ducks with the glaze. They look as if they'd been coated with walnut varnish."

"Hey, that's what we should be taking home. Chen loves duck, especially the crackle. He should be home by nine. Let's get some other stuff, too."

An hour later, the four of us were sitting at a glass-topped table in Chong's garden eating outside—*en plein air* as Mom would say. Spotlights twinkled beside the walks and the perfume of frangipani lingered in the moist air. Chen was indeed delighted with the glazed duck and the *lemang panas* to go with it.

"You should have seen it, Chen. The rice was cooked in bamboo about a foot long. They split open the bamboo and there it was—rice, all wrapped in banana leaves. They sliced it for us and popped it in a pink plastic bag."

Chen smiled. "I've seen it many times, Dr. Busch. It's very popular all over the country. On the highways there are often a string of stalls selling only *lemang panas*. It's sticky rice and doesn't crumble, so I guess it's a good snack for the car."

After he removed the crackle in strips, Chen cut the duck into pieces. "This will bring us good luck."

"Oh, sweetie. Don't be so silly," I chided.

"You'll see!" he said defensively.

"Actually, I can't imagine feeling any luckier than I do tonight—sitting in this beautiful garden with my three favourite people, sipping Sauvignon Blanc and nibbling duck and *lemang panas*," I said. "I wish you were going to meet the Chongs. They have been unbelievably good to us. With their interracial marriage, study abroad and similar interests, we're almost soul mates."

"Yes, I can see that," Dad said. "I'm sure they really appreciate you, Chen… and you, too, Lauren."

After dinner Dad picked up a pile of brochures.

"Where are you going next?" Chen asked.

"I want to take my parents to a resort on the east coast," I said. "We had *such* a good time there. Yeah, I know, it was our honeymoon," I said, releasing my legs from the lotus position and getting off the chair to give him a hug.

Dad had done a good job of picking up brochures and Shanthi had left a pile, as well. We lined them up and were overwhelmed at the choices. It seemed as if we could pick one blindfolded and do fine.

"Why don't you go to Pulau Redang," Chen said. "I've heard it's the greatest. You might as well go for the best. It's an island up north—a bit hard to get to. You should take the car. I'll stay with Pa and Ma so I'll be closer to work."

"Dear Chen, wanting us to have the best—even giving us the car, while he stays home to work. Isn't he the sweetest?" I asked.

"He's the sweetest!" Dad said.

"Yes! He *is* the *sweetest*," Mom said.

Chapter 48

PULAU REDANG WON THE draw. We were happily ensconced in our red Vega, driving east to Kuantan and north along the coast. We had holiday weather—not surprising since almost every day of the year is holiday weather. Dad was singing "It's a jolly 'oliday with Lauren…" and we all joined in substituting each other's names. We saw the occasional cow on the side of the road… or chicken, or goat and lots of stalls selling local food.

"Hey. There's that sticky rice like what we got at the Night Market… *lemang panas*, the glutinous rice cooked in a bamboo tube," Dad said.

A lot of the stalls had traditional Malay clothing in batik, straw hats, hand-made brooms… *and much more,* as they say in Canadian garage sale ads.

Awana Kijal Resort was a must. We stopped for lunch so I could show my folks the amazing architecture and miles of beach. I guided them through the lobby. They were as agog as Chen and I had been. Especially they admired the openness—with sea breezes wafting through.

We walked to the beach and sat under a blue umbrella watching the South China Sea.

Mom was murmuring, *heavenly... just heavenly.*

"Let's order a sandwich and a drink and eat right here," Dad said.

"Great idea—but we shouldn't spend more than an hour because we have to catch the four o'clock ferry from Kuala Terengganu and we need to allow for time to find the jetty."

An hour later, when we got back into the hot car, I think we were all privately wondering why we weren't just staying where we were. We drove north past the oil fields. Dad was impressed. "The oil industry must be *huge*," he said.

"Yes, Petronas is nationalized. It financed the Twin Towers, and also sponsors a race car in the International Formula One races."

"That's astonishing. How did it all happen?" Dad asked.

"The Prime Minister, Dr. Mahathir, seems to get the credit. He's been in power for years, He's a man with huge vision— dedicated to bringing Malaysia out of its third world status by the year 2020."

"I have a hard time thinking of Malaysia as a third world country," said Dad.

"So do I. You should see Putra Jaya! Dr. Mahathir wanted to get the government out of KL so he literally built a city to house the Government. The Prime Minister's home sits on a hill and might rival Buckingham Palace in size and presence. The streets are wide and the part leading up to the Prime Minister's residence resembles the *Champs Élysées*. No kidding! The whole city was built and landscaped in *five* years."

"I haven't heard of it," Dad said. "Have you been there?"

"No, not yet, but I've seen it on TV. Oh, and there's a huge and absolutely exquisite mosque. The public can go in at certain times, but if they are wearing shorts, they must cover up in long pink robes. Pa Wong thinks it was all a waste of money, but Chen argues that it's all a "See us! See what we can do!" tactic and that it will reap rewards in economic development."

"Amazing. Didn't Malaysia hold the Commonwealth Games in 1998?" Dad asked.

"Yes, and apparently they did a spectacular job. Again, it focussed on showing the world what Malaysia could do. There were over sixty thousand people from around the world. Kuala Lumpur was left with a legacy of amazing venues and sport facilities. The people who said they'd have a flop were left eating humble pie. Dr. M, as he's called, sees what has to be done and makes it happen. He lectures the people in the newspaper, almost daily. He even tells them they must clean up their toilets."

"He's a practical man," Dad laughed.

We followed signs to the Marang jetty and parked the car in a large lot. After lugging our gear to the office, we bought tickets to the island of Pulau Redang. The usual late afternoon breeze was coming up, and we could see the waves starting to chop farther out. Because of the low tide, we needed to go into a small boat to get to the catamaran. The narrow ramp swayed as we moved awkwardly along with our backpacks. The first boat probably had about a dozen people over the safety limit. You have to wonder what good rules are if they are not enforced. We sat on benches around the outside edge and propped our feet on all the luggage, golf clubs, and diving equipment dropped in the center.

Three small boat loads later, we were ready to depart for Pulau Redang. We tossed and heaved for forty-five minutes before we reached the island. I figured we had used up all the good luck Chen promised when we were eating the duck crackle a few nights ago. Mom and even Dad took it all in stride, much to their credit. We got off at a charming fishing village with brightly painted houses up on stilts, embellished with lines of clothes from the daily wash. Boats painted in primary colours, often with stripes, were tied to the stilts and fish nets were strung up for the night.

Children played everywhere we looked. We were seeing a fishing community, one more slice of Malaysian life.

For the last lap in getting to the resort, we were trundled into a vehicle that looked like an extended golf cart. Dad said our adventure made him think of the old comedy, *"Planes, Trains and Automobiles."* Mom and I agreed.

At the registration desk, we felt weary and somewhat doubtful. But as we went into our "sea-view deluxe" room and walked out on the balcony, our chins dropped. Before us lay a full view of a long, wide beach with the finest, whitest sand we had ever seen. The South China Sea was fading from turquoise to ink blue and a row of tall coconut palms swayed gracefully in the breeze. Dad broke our stunned silence with, "Well, this ought to do us. Let's slather on some sunscreen and get down there."

Truly, this was paradise. Hour after hour we sat on beach chairs, staring at the sand and sea. The sand was coral, which meant it never got hot on the feet. It resembled Roger's white flour. An image flittered though my mind, of a giant mother with a giant sifter, standing on a cloud, dispensing refined sand along the edge of the sea.

A matter of footsteps into the water, Dad discovered that the water was clear enough to see picture-book tropical fish. In fact, he discovered the bottom could be seen, probably for a depth of fifteen feet. Everything seemed so pristine. Our bubble broke when I was telling a staff member about our amazement at the depth we could see in the water. He wistfully replied that whatever depth we saw today would have been twice that when he was a boy. The resort had taken a toll. The problem is universal. As Mom said, "It's sobering."

After our buffet breakfast the next morning, Mom said she just wanted to play in the coral sand.

"Do you mean you want to make a sand castle?" I asked in mock seriousness.

"No," she said, "but I'd like to relax with my feet in it... maybe go for a walk in my bare feet."

Dad announced he was fascinated with the fish and wanted to rent a snorkel and fins.

Half an hour later, the three of us were fulfilling our desires. Dad was about fifty meters out, his snorkel barely visible. Mom was sitting on the beach wearing a large sunhat. I had completely buried her feet and legs. She said she felt as if she were at a spa.

I decided to do the same for myself. It was a bit more challenging, but I managed it. We sat there like chattering mermaids when we heard someone call, "Help!" There weren't many people around, so it didn't take us long to deduce that it was Dad. Sand blew in all directions as Mom and I squirmed out of our sand packs. Someone had left a plastic row boat on the edge of the water. I jumped in and rowed as fast as I could. Dad had been bitten by something and said it was very painful. With only one hand to work with, he struggled to get into the boat. He had no idea what he had touched. His fin strap had come unfastened and the fin had fallen to the bottom. He was trying to retrieve it when his hand and wrist were suddenly blazing with pain. When we reached the beach, Mom came toward us with Nizan, the man who rented the water toys. Her eyes were full of concern. Nizan took one look at Dad's hand and said, "Sea urchin! They sting bad."

"How's the best way to handle this?" Dad asked, humbly.

"Depends who you ask. Most people, they say work fast. Pull out spines you can get hold of. I'll do it for you. Will hurt."

Dad told him to go ahead. With care and concentration, Nizan captured some of the spines. Judging by the contortions of Dad's face, it was an ordeal. Finally Nizan said the rest would have to come out when they were ready. He poured vinegar over the affected area and went off to get some hot water. It was hot alright. Hot, just like Tan would use.

Poor Dad! Nizan finished by saying, "Before bed, wrap area

with towel soak in vinegar. Wrap everything in plastic bag and tape."

"I'm curious," Dad said, "what other remedies do people use?"

"Some get lime juice. Get at the bar. Some guys say use razor blade, careful cut, pull out spine. Some people say *pee on it*."

"Hey! That's a bit over the top. My dad is a doctor. You'd have a hard time convincing him to pee on his wound!

Dad chuckled. "Only as a last resort. Thank you for helping me, Nizan." Dad handed him fifty ringgit and Nizan walked off with a smile.

The next morning Dad was tired. He hadn't slept well and his wrist felt almost as bad as it had the day before. He seemed bent on getting some antiseptic cream, so I offered to see what I could find. I thought I was on Mission Impossible, but someone suggested I look in the gift shop. Sure enough, there it was—good old *Polysporin*.

Dad was relieved. Grinning, he said he was beginning to think he might have to resort to peeing on it.

We had only that day left. Dad's golf game had been scuppered. It seemed unfair that he had had a problem on both of our trips, but Dad being Dad, made the best of his bad luck.

"Let's order some Tiger beer and hang-loose on this beautiful beach." Dad had made the suggestion, but Mom and I were glad to join him on both accounts.

Chapter 49

M Y PARENTS WERE LEAVING the next day and I hadn't slept well. I woke up feeling as if my heart had slipped almost to my waist. We had spent such a happy time hanging out together and the thought of my parents flying to the other side of the world made me feel physically ill. And then, to top it off, Ma wanted us all to come for dinner. We hadn't spent much time with the Wongs. There was no way I could refuse their invitation.

After the somewhat harsh start to my day, I found Dad reading in the garden. Mom had set the breakfast table beside him.

"I just love eating out here amidst the flowers, birds, and the fish in the pond. It seems so far from the cold rain and dismal January days at home," Mom said.

"It *is* so far!" I snapped. Tears unleashed, landing on my lap. I was as surprised as my parents were.

Mom put her arms around me. We didn't need words to know what the other was thinking. My fix-everything-dad didn't look all that in charge of things either.

"I cooked bacon and eggs for our breakfast, Lauren," Mom said.

"Yes, I could smell the bacon," I said, trying to get a grip. Bacon and eggs. Yuck. But I would eat them. I would stop acting like a child. My resolve to be up-beat was short-lived as I told my parents about our dinner invitation from Wongs.

"Of course. That's fine," Dad said.

"Thanks, Dad. You're a good poppa. Now, what would *you* like to do today?"

"We've done so much. What's left?" Mom asked. Then she added, "I know. I'd like to go to the Tea House to buy one of those china tea sets for Grandmama—the kind they use for the Tea Ceremony—like the one Tan gave me for Christmas. Maybe I'd better get two. What about you, Nolton?"

"I'd like to take something home for Dr. Wells. The other day I saw a Mahjong set in a nice leather case."

"That's a fine idea, Dad. There's a home for blind people, not too far from here. They're taught to weave and there's a shop selling their products. I found it fascinating."

"Sure. That sounds like a good outing."

Two hours later we had finished the shopping and were driving up a steep driveway to check out the school. The sun was set on high. There were several buildings. Everyone was inside. No one seemed to notice us. We could hear singing in the background, competing with percussion instruments. I went into the main structure to announce our presence.

Adult men and women were sitting on the floor, concentrating on their projects. Their white eyes stared straight ahead, blankly. Obviously, they were operating only by touch. One man was weaving a seat for a square stool. The detailed pattern used four colours of plastic cord. Dad was watching fishing baskets being woven. The shape was unique. The bases were square and flat but the sides became a circle by the time it neared the neck. Mom found some twenty-four inch square woven boxes with lids.

"I like these, Lauren. I'd like a few. You should get some, too. They'd be clever little end tables for your living room."

"Just how do you think you could carry those on the plane?" I asked.

"I'll mail them. This afternoon. If Grandmama could ship an armoire, I certainly can send some wicker boxes!"

"That's right, Marie-Claire. And I can put some of those fishing baskets inside your boxes. What are these cones?"

"I think they're covers to put over food to keep the insects away. You don't need those, Dad. There aren't many bugs in Vancouver."

Mom was looking at some crab traps. "Wouldn't these make good lamp shades?"

"Gosh you guys, I think we'd better get out of here. Let's pay up."

The whole hay stack came to two hundred and fifty-five ringgit—roughly eighty-five dollars Canadian. Dad picked up a folder advertising the weaving and singing program and also a course for blind computer students in KL. He paid the bill and left a donation for the school.

Chapter 50

A FEW DAYS AFTER my parents left, Chen and I cuddled up on the Chong's sofa. I felt as if I'd been up in the clouds and landed splat in a rain gutter. I persuaded myself to crawl out of the ditch and focus on Chen.

"You did well to cope with the commotion here after long days manning the practice alone. I always feel that you can handle anything. I never think of you being stressed or suffering from over-load. I only think about how much I miss you—twelve or more hours each day. How *do* you feel about being at the helm?"

"Basically, it's good. Certainly there's no shortage of patients. I miss having Dr. Chong to discuss things with, but there's always someone more experienced than me at the hospital. Your dad and I had some good discussions, too."

"Yes, I could tell you two were often having serious dialogue. One of my happy memories of their visit was watching the two of you—Dad sitting in the big armchair and you on the ottoman, almost knee to knee, far away in the land of wisdom and respect."

"The Chongs should be coming home soon. It's strange that I haven't heard from them. Maybe they're waiting until Chinese New Year is over. It's been nice for us living in their house, hasn't it?"

"Yes. It was the only way we could have invited my parents here for Christmas. But you know, I'm going to be happy to go back to our own little home with our own things."

"That's good. You really meant it when you said you wanted that funny little place, didn't you?"

"Yeah. I really like it. I fantasize turning the second bedroom into a nursery with yellow walls and ruffled white cotton curtains on the window. No pinks or blues. Girl or boy welcome! In the meantime, I'll use it for a studio. I've missed painting. Since we've been here I've had all the space I'd yearned for, but I've been joyfully wrapped up with Christmas and my parent's visit. I want to do a painting for the Chongs. I should do it before we leave here because I want it to be of their garden."

"That's good, *mon bijou*. We couldn't thank them in a better way."

Chapter 51

Jan. 23/01

Hi Mom and Dad,

Dizzying preps for the Chinese New Year are underway. The Pa has to conclude all business deals, pay his debts and apologize for any wrongs. But it's the Ma who gets the lion's share. She has to clean the house (and hide the broom so the family's luck won't be swept away), buy new clothes and presents for all the family, and cook mountains of delicacies and must-have foods. Ang pows have to be organized—large amounts for their children and small amounts, in even numbered denominations, for guests and others. Greeting cards must be sent, and the house has to be decorated with artificial cherry blossoms, pussy willows, red bows, and red banners inscribed with poems written in Chinese and put on the side panels of the door. Oh… and she has to buy oranges—*bowls* of mandarins, *boxes* of mandarins, *crates* of mandarins to exchange with family and friends to wish them good luck. Right now Ma is cleaning the altar. It's the same hustle-bustle you have before Christmas, but CNY goes on for fifteen days!

I've really missed you since you left, but will be cheered by the celebration to come.

Lauren xx

Jan. 24/01
Dear Mom and Dad,

GONG XI FA CAI! Happy New Year! Welcome to the Year Of The Snake!

Last night, the eve of the new lunar year, we all gathered for an elaborate meal. The special feature was the Yee Sang Prosperity Salad. Each person puts one ingredient into a big bowl. Then, with chop sticks, they all toss the ingredients as high in the air as possible. shouting LOH HEI (life, prosperity, and longevity). The higher they toss, the better their luck will be in the new year. The recipe is below.

Even the ancestors are considered present! The living honour the departed with thanksgiving & great respect. A week ago I would have thought it was just another weird custom. But now I'm seeing some merit in it. They are recognizing the contribution of their ancestors who have laid down the foundation for the fortune and glory of the present day descendents. I think that's something for us westerners to think about, don't you?

Today, they continue to worship their
ancestors & welcome the gods of heaven &
earth. Immediate family members visit each
other. Tomorrow, the sons-in-law will pay
respect to *their* in-laws. Mok and Lee Yee will
spend the afternoon with us at Ma and Pa's.
Can you imagine *me* having to wait 3 days to
see you at Christmas because I had to be with
my in-laws? Not a chance!

Next year you should consider coming for
this celebration.

Take good care of each other.

Lauren xx

Yee Sang Prosperity Salad
Raw salmon or abalone, finely sliced
Carrots, shredded
White radish, shredded
Preserved winter melon, shredded
Pomelo (like a giant grapefruit)
Gingerroot, sliced thinly
Ginger pickle
Sweet-sour plum sauce
Drizzle veg oil, lime juice
White pepper, crispy crackers, and sesame seeds

Jan.29/01
Dear Mom and Dad,
Today we're staying home to welcome the
God of Wealth.

The next ten days will be dinner parties
and Open House parties. It's all about food,

food, food. How are these for dishes… double-
boiled bird's nest with red dates and black moss
seaweed for exceeding in wealth, dried bean
curd for fulfillment of wealth and happiness,
longevity noodles, and especially for me—lots
and lots of lotus seeds to insure I have many
male offspring!

On the 13th day they eat only rice congee
and mustard greens to give their bodies a break.

Love, L.

Feb.7

Mom and Dad—I'm sure I've told you more
about C.N.Y. than you wanted to hear but take
an Aspirin, because I haven't told you about
Fang and his Lion Dance.

We haven't seen much of him around here.
Their small troupe has danced and drummed
and gonged in the stores, restaurants, businesses
& private homes. Anyone who can afford it
invites the Lions to dance into their home to
bring good luck for the coming year. Pa asked
Fang's troop to visit the rubber plantation and
the house as well. I've watched it every chance
I get. The Lion Dance with its vibrant colours
& Tong! Tong! Chang! Chang! really gets your
blood pumping, and your nerves tingling—like
the emotion evoked by the Scots playing the
bagpipes, but with a lot more noise and racket.
Fire crackers (they're illegal) can be heard all
night, every night. Between the smoke from the
joss sticks and the smoke from the firecrackers,
it was like each house having a campfire.

Thanks for the nice email.

Bushels of love,

Lauren

I sat gazing at the paper pineapples and paper lanterns hanging from the ceiling, the red fabric draped around the doors, and ang pows pinned onto a fake cherry tree—all so important to this family I had joined. Although I thought everything was fascinating, I had to admit that I felt quite detached from it. As I finished the email, I was reminded of its speed and that, posted, it might not even have moved out of the mailbox for days. Everything comes to a halt, or seriously slows down, during the Chinese New Year, while people put their labour aside, and tighten their family unity by celebrating their ancient customs.

Chapter 52

THE LAST WEEK IN January, Dr Chong's daughter, Nisha, phoned to say her father had bronchitis and was quite weak. She thought her parents should extend their visit until the end of February. They hoped Chen would continue to look after the practice and the house in the meantime.

Of course, Chen would carry on. And so would I. We were as dependable as the late afternoon showers. Nevertheless, I was disappointed not to be heading back to our wee abode. Humble as it was, it was special to us. Chen had settled into a routine of twelve-hour days, leaving no time or energy for much else. Now that pace would be extended for another month. I yearned to visit his family in Singapore, to go to the "hill resorts" (Frazer's Hill or the Cameron Highlands), or spend some time in KL. All those places were quite near, certainly by Canadian standards, but required more time than was available. I'd even be happy if Chen would at least get some exercise. Our time together was spent sitting in the garden after a late dinner. Enjoyable as that was, it could hardly count as aerobic exercise.

The alarm clock sounded loud and persistently as Chen fumbled to turn it off. It was five forty-five. I sprang to my feet. Chen rolled over.

"Come on, sweetie. You promised," I said.

"I know. I'll get up and run with you. But come back to bed. Just for a minute. Just for a cuddle."

"You drive a hard bargain," I said.

The neighbourhood was still asleep. Only the birds were alert and planning their day. The running shoes Chen bought in Canada eight months ago looked as if they had just been taken out of the box. His freshly pressed shorts and his slicked with gel hair completed the image of a novice jogger. When I brought this to his attention, he said, "Okay, don't be too hard on me. I'm not used to this."

"We'll only do a fast walk for twenty minutes this morning, and work up from there."

"Oh, no! Not twenty minutes. I'll be late for work."

We walked along the empty road carrying our water bottles. Darkness would last for another hour. The warm air was heavy with moisture and the scent of bougainvillea. Every few minutes, both of us wiped sweat from our brows and necks. In Canada I had cringed at the sound of the word *sweat,* but in Malaysia, it was the best word to describe the wetness that issued from our pores and clung to our skin. Yes, in spite of the *sweat,* this was the best time of the day to exercise. I felt good when we got home, physically jump-started and pleased that Chen had agreed to come with me.

After we showered and downed our congee, Chen left for work. Without missing a beat, I started to paint. Realizing that the Chongs would be home in a couple of weeks and wanting to make the most of their garden, a painting frenzy overtook me.

I stood gazing critically at the painting of the Golden Dewdrop—Duranta Plumieri, I think Shanthi had called it. I would be proud to give it to the Chongs when they returned. I must say that I captured well the exquisite beauty of the periwinkle blue trumpet-shaped blossoms with the little yellow centers and yellow berries growing from the same vine. I adjusted some shadows and highlights. The whole composition was well-balanced with some lattice in the background. I felt confident that Shanthi would be delighted with it. Thinking how glad I would be to see her, gave me a little shiver.

With a fresh canvas on the easel, I smiled as I remembered how in the beginning Mr.Yap had struggled to make the canvasses the way I wanted. That made me recall meeting Siew Kee at the café beside Mr. Yap's shop. I hadn't seen her for quite awhile. Having amassed six or more paintings, I was on my way to getting serious about selling my work. My problem was that I painted sporadically… always waiting for a flash of inspiration. Also, the better the painting, the more I wanted to keep it for myself.

Chapter 53

THE LAST PART OF February, I packed up some of our personal things at Chongs and cleaned our own little house for our imminent return. I had stopped for a break and was sitting in the garden under the umbrella, when I heard someone in the driveway. It was Chen—home a shocking three hours early. Being home early was so out of character for him that I felt myself shiver with foreboding. I heard him call to me and went in. He looked a bit stunned—even his hair seemed to stand up straighter on the top of his head. He stood in front of me holding a paper. His lips were moving, but he wasn't saying anything. Then he thrust the paper at me and said, "It's from Dr. Chong's daughter, Nisha."

"Oh. When are they coming home?"

"Read it!"

Nisha explained that her father had had a moderately severe heart attack the previous week. They had decided it was time for her parents to live with them in Britain. The practice would have to be sold, as would the house. She herself would come to settle things at the appropriate time. Chen would have first bid on both the practice and the house. She appreciated any help he could give her and would like a reply when he had had time to consider the offer. The paper slipped from my hand and flew gracefully to the floor. Less gracefully, I slumped into a chair.

"It's overwhelming, isn't it, Lauren? When I read it I wished I could go into the waiting room and shoo out the patients. I wanted to have peace to think. I felt I'd been handed an enormous, shining gift—one so heavy I couldn't lift it. What do you think?"

"I feel as if I'm opening a gift—one that I don't think I want and am trying to decide if I can return it. What do *you* think?"

"I think it would give us real stability. We would probably stay here in Taman Damai forever," Chen said.

Unbidden tears came like tropical rain. They rolled down my cheeks and dampened my white denim shorts. "That's the trouble!" I sobbed. "Where's the adventure in that? It's like being dead-ended before you get started."

As if he hadn't heard me, Chen said, "We'd have a better salary, and I'd be able to give my dad the money he wants to turn the rubber plantation into oil palm!"

The tears came faster. Clearly Pa Wong came first; and furthermore, he always had, and it seemed likely he always would!

Reading my mind, Chen said, "I need to help him, Lauren. I thought you would really like living in this house."

My thoughts were bouncing around like nuts in a food processor. Shanthi was my best friend in Taman Damai. Nobody else in this country understood me like she did. No one could replace her. And she wasn't coming back! Chen's idea of adventure was watching National Geographic programs from his armchair. As if that wasn't enough, his father ranked higher than his wife. I felt defeated. Defeated by Chen and defeated by his culture. I thought of the other people involved. "I wonder what Nisha thinks about having her parents live with her?" I asked.

"It doesn't really matter what she thinks. She is the only child and it is her responsibility to look after her parents' needs."

"That doesn't mean they have to live with her, does it?"

Chen lifted his chin and said curtly, "I'm going out. I think we need some time by ourselves. I'll see you later."

He hadn't shown one sign of affection. Nor had he understood or even recognized my tumult. I wondered where he was going to do his thinking. I hoped he would be sitting on a magic mushroom. Certainly we were wrestling with a thorny burr.

I had some thinking to do myself. My thoughts were as tangled as my red hair. I tried to think of this big house, the garden I loved, Tan and even Wong, the smallness of the community and the difficulty in feeling part of it—all interspersed with the things I'd like to do and the places I'd like to go. Even alone in this big house, I did not have room to think. My stump by the river at our little house beckoned to me. I would go there! Chen had taken the car somewhere. I would use my bike.

Twenty minutes later, I arrived at our house. Our car was there. I looked to see if Chen was in it. All I could see was a pile of medical journals. He couldn't be in the house because his key was in my bag. I walked around the house and there he was—sitting on my stump! In spite of our troubles, we smiled at each other. He moved over to make a place for me. There we sat like two toads on a stool.

Chen broke the silence. "I'm sorry I upset you. I'm confused and I feel pressure to decide and let the Chongs know our decision."

"That's ridiculous, Chen. It's a *huge* decision. They can't possibly expect to you to decide quickly."

"They will. They probably expect an answer tomorrow… and that the answer will be *yes*—on both accounts. Let's go back and make a list."

"No, Chen. We don't need a list. We need to base these decisions on our gut feelings. Let's go home and sleep on it."

We both suffered. We spoke only when necessary. Answers did not present themselves.

Chapter 54

TWO DAYS LATER, IT was my turn to have a startling message. My dad phoned as soon as he thought I'd be awake, to say that my grandmama had died suddenly. I was speechless.

Waves of disbelief dizzied me. My grandmama, who had rocked me many times in her Canadiana chair with the down-filled cushions, was not there. Right now, I longed to be rocked again. Another part of my soul had been ripped from me. I felt helpless and so far away. I thought of my mother. I knew she would need *me* to rock *her*. I told Dad I'd come as soon as I could get there, and I would let him know what flight I'd be on.

I flew out of Kuala Lumpur that evening. In the last few days Chen had closed the office early twice—once to deliver Nisha's letter, and today to drive me to the airport. He did not want me to go. When I told him he was being selfish and thoughtless, he got tears in his eyes and said in a soft voice, "I'm worried that you won't come back."

"I expect to come back, Chen. We'll have some chats on the

phone. Right now, with all my heart, I want to be with my mother."
I wanted to further reassure him but, in truth, I was not completely
sure what I would do. *Fish gotta swim, birds gotta fly*. I had not
bought a return ticket.

Chapter 55

I ARRIVED IN VANCOUVER after a seventeen-hour flight and a one-hour stop-over in Taiwan, with tight muscles, swollen feet, and dry, burning eyes. I had left my husband with our relationship on sandy footings and I was going to my Canadian home at a time of sadness and sorrow at the sudden loss of my grandmama. Throughout the hours, my mind flipped from my past to my future. The one thing saving me from desperation was that I would soon be with my mother and father.

At noon, I walked by the familiar sign *Welcome To Canada / Bienvenue Au Canada*. Mom and Dad seemed to stand taller when they saw me coming. Looking into my mother's face, I thought the fine lines around her eyes seemed deeper. She clutched me and mumbled "… so glad you're here" into my neck. Dad enfolded me in a hug, then included Mom in the huddle. As he stood there with an arm around each of us I sensed him thinking, *here are the two people I love most in this world*. We headed to the luggage carousel to collect my big case. I had packed far more than I needed, but I just felt so unsettled.

Riding home from the airport, I was shocked to see how bleak my country looked. March winds blew. The trees were bare, the sky grey. I shivered. Although I was on a *home mission*, a vision of Malaysia's bright sun and palm trees settled in my head. Never before had I thought about how lame Vancouver looks just before the burst of spring.

An hour later we were sitting at the kitchen table eating lasagne sent over by one of the neighbours.

"I haven't had lasagne since I left Canada. It's real comfort food, isn't it?"

"Yes, and I've taken an apple pie out of the freezer."

Dad made a fire in the fireplace and we ate our pie and drank Earl Grey tea cuddled together on the sofa—me wrapped in a mohair throw. The fire looked so cheerful. For several reasons I felt weepy; I had left Chen on the other side of the world and in turmoil, my dear grandmama had died... and just because it seemed so magical to be here with my parents.

The next day, we were on our way to Montreal via Air Canada. From there we would transfer to a smaller plane for the trip to Trois Rivières, and finally to my mother's family homestead. Since my grand-père died, the farm had shrunk from two hundred acres to twenty. Oncle Étienne came in the spring to tap the maple trees that covered most of the property. It provided enough syrup for everyone in the family and Oncle Étienne easily sold what was left. Mom, Dad and I would stay in Grandmama's house with Aunt Veronique who had lived with my grandmama all her life.

"Aunt Veronique will be the most directly affected by Grandmama's death. I wonder what she'll do?"

"I hope she will sell the old house and move to an apartment in town," Mom said.

"She has always been my favourite—probably because I knew her best. She was always so glad to see us and didn't they have an endless supply of maple syrup? They put it on everything, even fried eggs. It's a wonder that they didn't all have diabetes."

"Three out of eight of us did—Étienne, Louise, and Suzette, who died in childbirth at the age of twenty-nine having her seventh child. And there was little Fernande, who died when he was two."

"Oh, I'd forgotten. What happened?"

"There was an epidemic of scarlet fever." My mother's eyes misted and mine followed. I tried to imagine the many disappointments and tragedies that Grandmama must have suffered through bringing up eight children plus losing two others, not to mention Grand-père.

"How did she *do* it, Mom?"

"I think her strong belief in God helped her cope."

"Did you break her heart by leaving the North Shore and going to Montreal? And then, as if that wasn't enough, to British Columbia?"

"I'm not sure what she thought in her heart, but she encouraged me to go. She was amazing—for her generation. She was tuned in to the revolution caused by the birth control pill. Those little pills had a lot of power—the power to change women's lives; to give them a chance to do more than churn out babies."

Eureka! I felt a wave of enlightenment. Of course my mother had freed me, her only surviving child, to go to Malaysia—just the way her mother had freed *her* to go to Montreal a generation before.

The night we arrived I felt I was in another world. Many of the family gathered in the old family homestead. The house was alive with greetings, hugging and tears. Sorrowing aside, they were obviously happy to be together. Even though they lived in Trois Rivières and towns surrounding, it was probably rare that they came together in such force. My immediate family, especially my mother, got a lot of attention—by means of our travelling the farthest, Mom being the youngest of her siblings and me being the youngest of the second string. Added to that, I had married a Chinese doctor and moved to Asia. If they thought Vancouver was a great distance, imagine what they thought of Malaysia. The small photo album I had brought was being passed around. How was Chen? When would they ever see him? What did we eat over there? Is that where they grow rice? Were there any churches there? Were there any cars? Does it cost a lot of money to go there? Did I like living there? Would I ever come back to Vancouver to live? (*Now there's a question!*) Only a few showed no interest at all— probably because my situation was just too far out of their comfort zone.

Aunt Veronique wended her way through the crowd putting more and more food on the table. The noise level was high. Uncle Jacques, a priest, put up his hand. He welcomed everybody in French. After saying some things about Grandmama, he said grace. He spoke very fast, but I understood some of it. He followed with more or less the same thing in broken English. There was no doubt that this was a French Canadian family. All the *rellies* filled their plates with an array of food, including tortière (pork pies), saumon poche, des oeufs en gelée, and paté. Dad and Bastien had brought wine and beer and were dispensing it from the open porch. It was a party! I beamed at Dad who appeared so comfortable in this crowd of men, many leaning against the railing with a cigarette and a can of beer. Even though it was March, the temperature was mild—ten degrees centigrade. The snow had melted considerably. I saw my Uncle Étienne, the one who looks after the sugar bush.

"Ah, Uncle Étienne!" I said, "It's good to see you. The warmth of the evening made me wonder if the sap has started to run yet."

"Lauren, good see you. The sap she start when the air she's warm. Maybe now. Be checking in the morning. You want to come?"

"Okay. I'll have to borrow some boots."

"Got many bots. We go at nine-thirty."

I awoke in my narrower-than-twin sized bed in the small room under the eaves: mine because it was the same one I'd slept in whenever I'd been at the farm since childhood. The mattress seemed to be a bit lumpier but the same braided rug, made by braiding long strips cut from worn out clothes, and sewing them together in an oval, lay on the hardwood floor. Even more amazing, the same Log Cabin quilt covered me. Grandmama had made quilts for all the beds—quite a feat as each one took her most of a winter. She lived in an era when everything was used and reused, an era of waste-not, want-not. But Grandmama was not here. She was not here to tell me stories. She was not here to call me her *petite chou,* little cabbage, or to tie an apron on me and let me play in the flour while she was making bread or to put her hand on my red curls and say, "They're your blazing glory." I lay on my tummy and wept into my pillow. Then I realized that rain was pounding on the metal roof. No, it was louder than rain. It must be frozen rain, sleet. That would make driving very difficult. I didn't worry about it for long. I still felt sleepy and so comfy...

When I went down to the kitchen for breakfast, Dad was reading the local newspaper—*Le Trifluvien.* There was a small picture of Grandmama—an announcement of her death, as well as a brief account of her long life in this area, her large family, and the contribution she made to the parish and to Trois Rivières.

Oncle Étienne came as he had promised. His twelve-year-old granddaughter, Eloise was with him. He found some rubber boots for me to wear and Tante Veronique gave me a duffle coat and a red cable-striped hand-knit scarf from the rack. We started off across the field walking to the sugar bush. I wished Chen was with us. I'd told him about spring in the sugar bush, but it was something that needed to experienced first-hand. Each step we took required some force to break the icy layer that had formed during the night. The weather was wild, but I loved the sound of our feet punching holes in the snow and the frozen rain picking at my face.

Eloise was a chatterbox. She asked me more questions about Malaysia than a lot of adults had the night before. She said she was going to learn a lot of English so she could come to visit me when she got enough money.

"You going to have some babies?" Eloise asked.

"I sure hope so!" I said, wistfully.

"Babies be white or Chinese?

"I don't really know. I guess they'll be a mixture."

Then Uncle Étienne told her not to talk so much.

"Don't tell her that," I said. "I think it's wonderful that she's so interested."

"Too bad your husband can't come. See your family."

"He's very busy. The doctor he works for is in England, so he has to look after the whole thing."

"Oh. You never have froze rain?'

I stifled a laugh and said, "No never. I live near the equator. The days are hot every day of the year —thirty to thirty-four degrees Celsius every day.

"How you work in that?"

"We have air-con."

"Air-con?"

"Yes, air-conditioning. It's in a lot of the houses and almost all of the restaurants and offices… and cars."

"Too old for me to go see. Hope you can go, Eloise, someday."

"Yes, I hope you can come too," I said holding her hand. "It would be big-time fun to show you around our beautiful country." I was startled that those words had come out of my mouth.

Three days later we were on the first leg of our trip back to Vancouver.

"Look down," Mom said, from her seat on Flight 506. "That's the mouth of the St. Maurice River. It looks as if there are three different rivers pouring into the St. Laurence. That's why they called this town Three Rivers—but really it's just one."

No one commented. We had been saturated with chatter since we arrived in Trois Rivières and now sat in silence, each with his own thoughts.

Grandmama's funeral had been held in the Cathedral—a huge cavern of organ pipes, chandeliers, candles, statues and gargoyles. Through the intricate stained glass windows, light shone down on a spray of yellow roses covering the top of her coffin. Even our family, plus cousins, neighbours, friends and parish members, were dwarfed by the vastness of the cathedral. Safe to say, some people were kept at home by the icy roads and sidewalks. The service followed the doctrine of all Catholic funerals, but it was personalized by virtue of Uncle Jacques celebrating the mass and Uncle Pierre's grandson lighting the candles. Grandmama's death had brought the whole family together. Each one of us must have remembered different parts of our life: times when we had been closest to our mother, or grandmother. Without doubt, we had loved and appreciated her. At least some of us must have been left wondering if we had expressed those feeling sufficiently while she was alive.

This was the second funeral I had attended this year. In fact, I realized, it was a year ago to the week that Richard had been the victim of his favourite sport, heli-skiing. Grandmama's long life of highs and lows showed visible accomplishments; whereas all that was visible of Richard's short life were possibilities and probabilities. I pondered how I could miss him so much when he felt so close. How could so much have happened in just one year? My mind was whirling. I thought about the differences in the culture and customs between English Canada and French Canada. Great as they may seem at times, they were nothing compared to those of Canada and Malaysia. I missed my homeland. Would I ever feel the same about Malaysia? Did I love Chen enough to be so far from my family? According to my remarks to Eloise, I loved my beautiful country, Malaysia.

Patiently, I had waited for the appropriate moment to tell my parents about Chen's offer to buy Dr.Chong's practice and house, but as we sat on the plane, three in a row, for six hours, it just slipped out. Surprise registered on their faces, but they didn't rush to comment. Finally, Dad said, "What does Chen think of that?"

"He seems to think he should grab it," I said.

"I imagine it's a good opportunity for him. What about you? You're not showing a lot of enthusiasm."

"You're right. His reasons for celebrating the offer were two. The first was because it would give us *stability*—and to quote him *we would probably stay in Taman Damai forever!*

The second reason was that he would earn more money and be able to help Pa Wong change the rubber plantation into an oil palm plantation. Frankly, I think both reasons *stink*!"

"Don't you like living in Taman Damai?" Mom asked. "The house is so nice, Lauren. We had so much fun there!"

"We had a fabulous time," I agreed. Then sounding harsher than I had intended, I added, "But the house is not the issue, Mom. The issue is that Chen figures we will live in Taman Damai forever. I can't even *think* of it!"

"Where do you *want* to live, Lauren?"

"Kuala Lumpur... Singapore... even Penang!"

"Lauren, try to think how Chen feels. He wants to be near his family, and he wants to help them financially," Dad said. "That is where he's coming from. I don't think it should surprise you."

"Come on, Dad! What future is there for him in Taman Damai? Why is he so damned narrow-minded?"

"My feeling is that you shouldn't expect so much so fast. Go with it, but share your vision with him—and don't expect big changes overnight."

The sense of what Dad said slowly crept through my stubborn membrane. I do have more vision than Chen. I am impatient, always have been. Maybe I needed to change... and maybe Chen would change some, too. I was not ready to leave this discussion with my folks. "What do you think of Chen wanting to help finance his Dad's financial projects?" I asked.

"I don't know much about that. It may be a very good investment for Wong and Tan. Maybe ultimately, for you and Chen. Don't be afraid to at least get some information and ask some questions."

I felt as if a heavy cloud had lifted and been replaced by a short ray of sunshine. Who did I think I was? A woman who saw only impossibilities? A woman who was ready to give up before even trying? Where was my courage? Had I not, just this week, been face to face with the courage of my grandmama? And my mother? Too tired to say another word, I put the small pillow behind my neck and holding the right hand of my father and the left hand of my mother, I fell asleep.

Chapter 56

A T EIGHT P.M. WE were back in our Dunbar home. I decided
to phone Chen.

"Thank you for phoning me. I've been sleepless,
worrying about the decisions we have to make. I'm worried about
you too," he said.

"Fill me in, Chen."

"I've thought of the offer all day and night. I talked to Dr.
Chong and the money angle sounds good. Even Pa thinks so. I've
also talked to the banker about financing. I'd really like to say yes
to the Chongs."

"Then I think you should do it."

"Really? I know it's not what you want. You want to be in a
city and away from my family."

"That's putting a bad spin on it, Chen. I just found it
overwhelming to hear you talk about staying in Taman Damai
forever. It sounded like the map of our life summed up in one
page. I promise I'll try to live more in the present and be more
flexible."

"I understand that you need more stimulation than you've

found in Taman Damai. I'll really try to encourage you in that department."

"That's so sweet, Chen."

"You sound as if you're coming home!"

"You can count on that. I'll probably come in a week or two—I'll let you know."

"I really miss you, Lauren. The house is too big for one. I've spent quite a bit of time with Pa and Ma."

"I'll bet they are excited about the offer."

"Definitely. If it's okay with you, I'd like to tell the Chongs that I'll buy the practice. I'll say we haven't decided about the house."

"Okay. I'm off to bed. I've been especially tired lately."

"You've spent a lot of time on planes and had a lot on your mind. Sleep as much as you can. Good-night, mon bijou."

He was certainly troubled, and to give him credit, he had made a decision and waited for my approval. But why hadn't he asked me anything about my sorrowing family.

The next day when Dad came home for lunch, I was just getting up. I came downstairs with my hair awry and my slippers flopping.

Dad said he was concerned about how tired I'd been and suggested I should stop in at Dr. Ray's for a check-up.

"Hey man! I've traveled half way around the world, then to Quebec and back! I think some jet-lag should not alarm you."

"True enough, but I still think you should follow my suggestion."

Dr. Ray had been my doctor since I was a kid. Actually, I'd like to see him again. I agreed to go. Maybe I'd get together with my friend, Robin, later in the afternoon.

Dr. Ray was surprised to see me and keen to hear about my life in Malaysia. After some comfy chat, he asked what had brought me in to see him. I told him I'd been very tired and Dad had expressed concern, and left it at that. He took my temperature, blood pressure and all that stuff, then asked, "When did you have your last period?"

I struggled to remember. Finally I said, "I think it was about six weeks ago!" I stood up. "Do you think I'm *pregnant?*" I shrieked.

"I think you might be. Is that good?"

"It's fantastic!"

One further test confirmed that Chen and I were going to be parents. "Looks like you should make a Christmas stocking for your December baby!" I gave Dr. Ray a hug, picked up my purse and said, "I've got to go! The next time I see you I will have a little... boy, if my Chinese mother-in-law gets her way."

I felt wired. Where would I go first? I wanted most to tell my mother, but Dad's office was on a different floor in this same medical building, so he drew the lucky number. Dad had come to the front desk for some information. I tweaked his arm and said I needed to see him in private. As soon as he had shut the door behind us, he asked me if I was all right.

"Yes, I'm very all right. I'm pregnant!"

"I'm not too surprised. That's great news," he said throwing his arms around me. "That explains why you were so tired. The first trimester is when you'll probably be the most tired. As far as your body is concerned, you might as well be running a marathon every day."

"That's interesting. I suppose a lot of energy is used in building the biological nest."

"That's exactly right. Now scurry home and tell your mother. I'll see you two tonight."

My mother was in the kitchen making my favourite meal, *Boeuf Bourguignon*: the king of beef stews. I knew it took a lot of preparation. Already I could smell the rich, fruity flavour of beef with tomatoes, garlic, thyme, bay leaves and onions simmering in a whole bottle of Burgundy wine.

"The *boeuf* smells fabulous! Good choice for a celebration. Guess what!"

"What?" my mother said, as she looked at me adoringly.

"I'm pregnant!"

Sparks of exuberance shone in Mom's face. "Oh, *ma petite chou. Que c'est bon*! Oh, won't we have fun!" For just a moment it seemed she had forgotten that her grandchild would be growing up on the other side of the globe. Her expression changed and she gulped air. Just as quickly, my mother's excitement returned. I knew she would make the best of things. She would enjoy the moment and she would cherish her time with me. Marie-Claire would be the best grandmother she could be. I had learned to expect that of her. I held her close and sensed her resolve.

I phoned Chen knowing he would be asleep, but I couldn't wait. His happiness equalled mine. He wished he were with me. I suggested he tell Tan, but he said it was much too early to do that.

"I thought she'd be happy, Chen."

"Sure, she'll be delighted!"

"Then why not tell her?"

He hesitated, then said, "I think she's going to drive you nuts, Lauren, telling you what to do—as though there was only one recipe for a perfect pregnancy."

"I'm not too surprised to hear that because Yee Lee told me about her mother-in-law calling the shots."

"When are you coming home?"

"I'll think about it tonight and let you know tomorrow. Go back to bed. I know you'll be asleep in two minutes."

"Tonight I think I'll need quite a bit longer—maybe *ten* minutes. I'm sure I'll have happy dreams and hope you do, too."

"It's only mid-afternoon, but yes, I'm sure my dreams will be happy, too."

The next call I made was to Robin. Tensed with excitement to spill my news, I said, "Guess what? Sophie is going to have a special friend!"

"No! You're not serious! That's great. When can we get together?"

I really wanted time with Robin, but every minute with my mother was precious. I didn't have to explain that to her. Robin would know. We agreed to meet with Mom at the golf course the next day.

I slept in late again. I stretched my arms over my head then lazily caressed my belly. It didn't feel a bit different. I tried to imagine that a new life was tucked inside me. Even though I was feeling dopey, I looked forward to the day.

After breakfast with Mom, we drove to UBC and walked on trails in the endowment lands. Layers of last year's soggy leaves were squashed on the paths and the birds chirped about spring.

At noon, we had just sat down, when Robin arrived with her sweet little six month old Sophie in tow. She was aglow. We hugged each other joyfully, and I bent over to admire Sophie. She smiled broadly. I touched her cheek. I wanted to pick her up, but couldn't chance it. What if I dropped her? I realized how little I knew about babies. All I knew was how much I wanted one like her.

"You're looking wonderfully happy, and so trim," I said.

"I signed up for an exercise program for expectant mothers and didn't miss a day. Would you be able to do that in Malaysia?"

"I strongly doubt it. But, I must say, Chinese mothers take good care of themselves and snap back quickly after the birth—helped on by their mothers-in-law. The post-natal period is a month long, full-time project. No one is even supposed to visit."

"Do you have to do what your mother-in-law says?"

"I have to try, at least. If the baby is deformed or has an imperfection, it will be my fault."

"Oh, Buschy. How do you do it?"

"I'm learning. Sometimes I think I'm making progress."

Mom and Robin ordered spinach salads and tea. I ordered a hamburger and a milk shake. I felt a tinge of guilt, but couldn't resist. I hadn't tasted a juicy, salty, fatty burger, with onions, catsup, relish, mustard, tomato and cheese, for nearly a year, and I started salivating before it arrived.

While chatting with Robin, I noticed my mother holding Sophie. They both looked so comfortable. Would I look that relaxed with my baby? Sophie had dropped a sock. I picked it up and wiggled it back on her foot.

The food arrived. Mom held Sophie and picked daintily at her salad, and I dove into my fat man's burger, savouring every bite.

Robin commented on her baby's contentment with Mom; then, with a flash of brilliance, suggested that Mom might like to look after Sophie once in awhile. It was an emotional moment. I imagined Mom enjoying Robin's baby while her own grandchild was on the other side of the world. Feelings of sadness and guilt mixed with a twinge of jealousy. I left the last third of my Mama Burger on my plate.

Chapter 57

I HAD BEEN BACK in Malaysia for a week. The sun blazed down, warming and relaxing me. I lay stretched out on a reclining chair in Shanthi's garden, actually *our* garden. In the light of our child-to-be, we had decided to buy Chong's house. We would have room to grow and room for our families and friends when they visit. Yes, it was our garden, but in my heart I would always share it with Shanthi. Parveen would continue to help for a while, but I hoped to learn from him and eventually do most of it myself.

A sensational reunion had greeted me on my return from Canada. Expecting to get an airport taxi, I looked twice at the tall, slim, well-groomed young man with the wide grin. I ran toward him. He looked first into my eyes, then below my waist; as if, in spite of his profession, he expected to see a bulge. Then he gave me a hug in public; something he would never have contemplated a few months ago. I got into the car, expecting to drive directly home, as we had when Pa Wong had picked us up on our arrival in Malaysia last June. But, no. Chen was not by-passing Kuala Lumpur.

"I thought we'd have lunch at the Shangri-la," he said. "Then we might walk in the park at KLCC."

"That sounds idyllic, Chen. Who's holding the fort?"

"It's Sunday. I thought you must have planned your flight to arrive on Sunday morning."

"I have to admit it was purely accidental, but what a great accident!"

The Malaysian-sized brunch buffet was in a room with a grand piano and a heavenly-high ceiling. As usual, there was a mixture of people, including many Muslim families with mothers swathed in black. Some even had black cloth from one ear to the other—like a trap door across their faces. This was a first for me. I hadn't seen any Muslims in black or with their faces covered. I asked Chen if they were Malaysians.

"Probably not. Most likely they are from the Middle East. They like to come to Malaysia to shop and holiday. Many of them are very wealthy."

I wanted to know more, but this was not the time to ask. I told Chen about my time in Canada: the visits with my mother and father, the Vancouver Art Gallery downtown, my lunch with Mom and Robin, and the afternoon with Robin—getting to hold her baby without fear, and even to change her diaper.

"I'm glad you had a good time. How are your folks?"

"They're fine. It's only been three months since they were here at Christmas. I thought they were a bit droopier, but it was probably due to the stress of Grandmama's death and the travel. They're both very excited at the thought of being grandparents, of course."

"Yes. No surprise there. Would you like to go to the park—or are you too tired?"

"I'll have lots of time to sleep when I get home. Let's go." We changed our shoes and sauntered off. "Have you been walking before work since I left?"

"You ask hard questions. Do I have to answer?"

I gathered he hadn't been walking but forgave him when he said he'd spent all the time when he wasn't working pondering life-changing decisions.

"I think you've made good decisions, Chen. Anyway, they aren't irreversible."

"I didn't think they were. You're the one who helped me see that."

Hoards of people were meandering on the walking track, giving the illusion that Chen and I were gazelles.

"Oh Chen… I saw the funniest thing in the hotel dining room this morning. One of the Muslim ladies who you said were from the Middle East, was eating with her black face cover still on. Only her glasses were sort of visible. She had a pile of four or five pancakes on her plate and I saw her put syrup on them. I tried not to gawk, but I had to keep glimpsing. I couldn't imagine how she was going to eat. The fork, with a piece of pancake, travelled under the long black cape and presumably from there into her mouth. She repeated the process until her plate was empty. The poor woman probably had her chin sticking to the mask. She's a prisoner in that garb."

Chen didn't find it as funny as I did. His mouth drooped and his eyes were beady.

"Of course that looked very strange to you, but it's the culture thing again. Some Muslims are more orthodox than others. Middle Eastern wives are clothed in volumes of black so other men won't covet them. She belongs to her husband. I think they dress however they want at home but are wrapped up when they are in public. To be a good Malaysian, you have to respect everyone. That's essential when you live in a multicultural society."

"That's quite a lecture," I said quietly.

"Sorry, lah. I didn't mean to be critical. That's just the way it is."

Once again, I felt chastised, humbled and hurt, but I also knew Chen was right. Even at that, I couldn't resist just one more comment. "How come her husband wears shorts? I could walk over to him and say, "You have adorable knee caps. Can I join your harem?" Chen smiled ever so slightly, and took my hand as we walked along. The sun's heat blasted down. I wiped my wet face with a strong Canadian kleenex from my pocket. Three quarters of the way around the track, I told Chen I felt a bit woozy.

"I'm so sorry, Lauren. I wasn't thinking. You've had a seventeen-hour trip and a major temperature change. I've been very thoughtless. Why don't you sit on the bench and I'll get us some drinks?"

As I waited, I watched Chen's long legs striding across the lawn toward the restaurant and realized how much I loved him. I realized, too, that I was glad to be back in Malaysia. I enjoyed watching the children. Slight, adorable and always looking so clean and well-dressed, they never failed to catch my attention. I fantasized about bringing our own child here a year from now. Despite the heat, a little shiver of anticipation whipped up my arms. Lots of people were sitting on the grass, drinking juice from plastic bags and eating snacks with trans-fats that would no doubt rival western nibbles... with maybe a shot of MSG thrown in. Teens were in groups, laughing exuberantly. Probably their homework had been completed and was piled, ready to be packed up in the morning. Occasionally, Muslim teens were holding hands, risking punishment for showing affection in public. Elaborate fountains spraying water high up gave a fleeting illusion of coolness. I kicked off my shoes. When Chen got back he was carrying two coconut milks, each in its own shell with its own thick husk insulating the refreshing juice.

"The last time we had this drink was on our honeymoon at Awana Kijal seven months ago." We sat quietly, sipping our drinks. I felt comfortable and happy.

Chapter 58

NISHA FLEW IN AND efficiently sorted out her parents'
possessions. She seemed relieved that Chen was buying
the practice and the house, relieved that things had fallen
into place, and ready to cope with the new curves life had dealt
her. Fortunately for us, the financial arrangements had reflected
her relief.

Severing the contract of maids was not my forte. We needed
to dismiss Lavinya, but I worried about any inconvenience and
hardship it might cause her. When I expressed my concern to
Nisha, she said she'd look after it. When did I *want* her to go?

I asked her to find out when she would *like* to go.

"That's not the way it's done," she said, with a twisted smile.
"What about the end of April?"

"That's okay… if it's okay with her."

"It will be."

A large crate at one end of the dining room waited for Dr.
Chong and Shanthi's personal belongings to be selected. Nisha
chose the things her parents would most like— a few books, some
heirlooms from Shanthi's family, antique urns and bowls from

China, and of course photographs. I wondered about the painting, lovingly done to thank Shanthi and Dr Chong for letting us live in their house for the one month that became so much longer. *Would it make the cut?* I felt uneasy. After all, the painting was large, and furthermore, it would be displayed in Nisha's house. My doubts were unfounded. When Nisha saw it, she said, "Oh yes! My mother will be delighted with a painting of her garden. I'm sure it will bring her a lot of happiness. We'll all enjoy it. My happiest memories of life in Malaysia were in that garden."

Though Nisha was a woman in command, I didn't miss the emotional undertones. The home and garden were alive with memories for her.

"My mother read to me there, by the hour. She was so gentle and looked so beautiful to me in her silk saris. She used to wear a cotton sari in the morning, but always a silk one in the afternoon. At a young age, I knew the names of the flowers, birds, bugs and butterflies. My mother is very fond of you, Lauren."

"We are kindred spirits. We shared a lot and I will miss her big time." I confided that when I first heard her mother wasn't coming back, I'd thought that, without her, I couldn't stay in Taman Damai. But in spite of my loss and the enormous change for her parents, there was no doubt that Dr. Chong and Shanthi would be content and happy to be in England with their daughter and grandchildren.

Nisha tied things up unbelievably quickly. I assured her that she could stay with us if she wanted to visit some friends while she was here. She answered that she had no friends here. She had gone to school in England and later to her mother's alma mater in Edinburgh. Like her, she is a biologist. I pondered how hard it must have been for Shanthi to let her only child go so far away. Certainly it underlined the importance Asians place on education. My thoughts turned to the new life within me. Could I send my child to school in North America. At this point, I could not even consider a separation.

Chapter 59

WE WERE HANGING OUT, lying on the Indian rug in our living room, looking up to the elaborately plastered ceiling. From the center of a huge medallion, edged with leaves, sprouted a brass light fixture and fan. The fan seldom rested, day or night. As it churned, so did our thoughts. We were silent. We had bought a house filled with someone else's things. Eight miles away our little house by the river sat empty. Chen had a practice to foster and changes to consider. We owed a lot of money. We were expecting a baby. I had just come back from Canada, where I had travelled from west to east and back and had spent an emotional time with the French Canadian arm of my family. I hadn't yet seen Ma and Pa Wong…

Chen broke the silence. "What should we do first, Lauren?"

"I think we need to refurbish your office first."

"Why would we do *that*?"

I sat up on the floor and said, "Because it looks like a dump. It's dirty. It's drab. It's depressing."

"You may think it's a dump, but it works. I think we should

sell our first house. We need the money. It can't just sit there empty."

I put a thumb on each cheek and massaged my forehead. The thought of selling our little house literally gave me a headache.

"I can see that you're not happy about that! There's no choice," he said firmly. "I think we should clean it up, get our things out, and list it at the end of the week."

"Listen, Chen. We should leave our things in. The whole place will look much more appealing and sell faster."

"You seem determined to keep us in a muddle. Let's forget it all for now. I think we should go to see Ma and Pa."

I knew we should do that. They would be waiting to see us and it would postpone dealing with *the muddle.*

"Did you bring presents from Canada for my parents?"

"No! I didn't even think of it. Should I have?"

"They'll expect it. Travellers always bring gifts."

"I didn't even bring something for you... or me, for that matter. Other than a few maternity clothes, all I brought back was some music and a Baby Einstein tape for our child."

I sensed that Chen didn't think I had had my priorities in the right slots. I didn't want to disappoint Ma and Pa when I'd just climbed back on the ship. There'd no doubt be plenty of time for that. Then I remembered the two pound box of Purdy's chocolates. "How about if I give them the chocolates?"

"Better than nothing, I suppose."

Obviously, he didn't have any idea how much it choked me to give up my Purdy's chocolates.

We arrived at 88 Jalan Kupas to find Tan alone. She was in the kitchen and hoped we would stay for supper. She wiped her hands and took the chocolates. She put them on a shelf without saying a word. I knew that she would have done the same thing if it had been a gift from Tiffany's. I wasn't hurt—hopefully a sign that I was learning to make some allowances and be more accepting.

"I'll make tea," Ma said. "We'll talk."

"Your trip to Canada was good?"

"I was extremely happy to see my mother and father… and all my French Canadian relatives. But, of course, my grandmama's death was a very sad occasion.

"Why sad? Chinese, we think if death is an old person it's a happy funeral. Only death for young is sad. For your grandmother it should be happy funeral. Family will wear some red. We have happy music and sometimes vendors for ice cream. Did she have a very nice coffin?"

"Yes. I suppose it was. A nice wooden coffin."

"Shows lots of money. Did she have a nice plot?"

"What makes a nice plot?" I was not enjoying this inquisition.

"Nice plot is high on the hill—so then the deceased can see the living family. Watch them. Give them good luck and protect them. Best plot cost one million ringgit. Friends give money, too. Someone we trust take it and make record so we can pay back same amount one day to them. Even poor friends give. They give two sweets—tie together. You put offerings for your grandmother?"

"We offer prayers and remember the life of the person who died. We had Grandmama's funeral in a big church called a *cathedral*. We said prayers. It's called a *mass*. My Uncle Jacques is a priest and he said the mass."

"Chinese, we put real offerings of chicken, rice, oranges, cakes with pretty, bright pink icing. We give money made from paper— all night we make it. Also we buy big paper TV, big paper car, big paper boat for trip, give paper tickets and money to spend, too… even passport we make, so deceased can go on trip— never travelled far before—never had big car, big TV."

"Okay, Ma let's have tea," Chen said.

A long evening loomed ahead.

I told Chen on the way home that I had not enjoyed what felt like a collision with Ma.

"She is *so* blunt. So insensitive."

"Yes, sometimes she is… but she's my mother. The problem with the death issues is that the whole matter has such opposite fundamentals. Let me tell you. Christians believe that the body dies but the soul lives on. Right? But, the Chinese believe that the *body* goes on. So… it will need treats, comforts and attention. Right?"

"I guess so. But have you ever seen the body of your ancestor riding down the street in a paper car?"

"Let's not get technical," Chen smiled.

"No danger of that!" I quipped. "It all seems such a fantasy. Another thing I continue to have trouble with, is the commercial attitude painted over everything. In death as in life, *money speaks!* I hate it!"

"Let it be, Lauren."

Chapter 60

THE NEXT MORNING, I was still sleeping when Chen went to work. In fact, it was mid-morning before I rallied. The rice congee was thick in the pot. After scraping it out for disposal (something I did gleefully), I sat under the umbrella in the garden munching on a piece of watermelon. I could smell the Madagascar jasmine. The beauty of the clear sky and the flowers, dappled by the sun shining through the trees, made me a feel both peaceful and thankful. Several empty boxes were left from Nisha's packing. I put them in the car along with a stack of newspapers and drove to the little house. Like a magnet, the stump drew me. I sat down and watched the muddy river flow by. A breeze was moving through the leaves of the Acacia tree and the birds were talking. How lucky I was to have lived in this little paradise. I knew I would miss it. A narrow shaft of self-pity flickered on me. Then, I thought of Shanthi's garden and saw the parallel—it too, was a paradise. My move would be from one paradise to another. I couldn't afford any self-pity. I hopped up and went into the house. I packed the contents of our cupboards and drawers but left everything else—even my paintings. Tomorrow, Sunday, Chen could do some yard work and I would bring flowering plants to freshen up the large blue pot by the front door. We'd take the boxes to Shanthi's, and list our little house. Voila!

When I submitted my progress report to Chen that night, he was impressed.

"Today I was thinking about what you said about my office. I faced it straight on, and I had to agree with you. It *is* bleak. I appreciated the fact that you gave it such high priority. Why don't you draw up a plan. Just two restrictions—be kind to the budget and minimize the time we'd have to close the office."

"Wow! That will be fun. Give me an hour."

Two weeks later, Chen's office sported pale azure blue walls (oiled based paint). The worn out red vinyl benches in the waiting room had been re-covered in heavy cotton with multi-coloured stripes. Two small tables held chubby lamps and magazines. There were no ashtrays in sight. Beside the bouquet of white and purple orchids on the desk, was a sign saying NO SMOKING. The flooring would have to wait as neither Chen nor the budget could handle any more mayhem. In the meantime, it looked both fresh and calming. Chen was impressed with the result and declared it worth the inconvenience. My biggest frustration had been that he forbade me to do the painting myself on the grounds that the fumes might be harmful to our child. When I told him I wished I could have contributed more, he sweetly said, "Never mind. It was your idea, your plan and you made it happen."

Chapter 61

M OK SENG HAI was born to Mok Ping Kuai and Wong Yee Lee on August 8th, 2001. Everyone was delighted. Yee Lee had done everything right. She had delivered a son who would ensure the continuance of the family name and ancestor worship. Added to that, her baby boy arrived two weeks early, on an auspicious date—August eighth, the eighth day of the eighth month. Chen was suspicious that his sister had engineered the date of birth.

"How could she do *that*?" I asked.

"Think, Lauren!"

"I can't guess. Doesn't a baby come when it chooses?"

"Not if there's a chance of arriving on an auspicious date. I would bet Lee Yee had her labour induced on August eighth. Most doctors would be alright with that."

"Isn't there a downside?"

"Hopefully not. Canadian doctors would frown on it because it's playing with nature."

I was anxious to see the baby and wanted to go immediately.

Chen told me it was too soon. Even Tan would not have seen the new-born yet.

"Mok Seng Hai is a Mok baby, not a Wong baby. Yee Lee is their property. Now you see what I tried to tell you when we were in Vancouver and she was about to be married."

"It's still weird for me. But yes, I see what you mean."

"Our baby will be much more important to Ma than Yee Lee's baby is."

"Okay, but my parents are going to have equal status with yours. That is the way it will be. And Ma and Pa will be just that: Ma and Pa. But I will never, never, be their property." There was no response.

Two weeks later, I gained entry to Lee Yee's quarters. She was halfway through her *confinement* month. Mok's mother told me not to stay too long. She acted as if her grandson might sprout feathers if I lingered.

In truth, Lee Yee was thrilled to see me. After all, we had declared ourselves *sisters*—not to mention that in a couple of months I would be giving birth to her niece or nephew. I threw my arms around her, saying, "Congratulations! How's it going, Sis?"

"It's going better every day," Yee Lee said. "Sometimes Hai sleeps four hours in the night. That's good. Then I can get more sleep. Mok doesn't even hear him in the night. Even in the daytime he doesn't seem overly interested in him, but I know he's proud to have a son. I hope you have a son, Lauren."

I felt impatience mounting. How many times did I have to tell her that I would welcome a girl just as much as a boy? Then it hit me; I was being as stubborn as she was. Of course she was pleased to have a son. She had lucked out! Everyone was delighted.

"What would they think if you'd had a girl?"

"They would think that it was too bad, but the next time I would have better luck."

"Mok Seng Hai is a bonny wee babe," I said. He was swaddled in a light-weight wrap and sleeping blissfully.

"Is bonnie good?"

"Yes, bonnie is good. It's a Scottish word—meaning he looks strong and handsome." At that, Hai crunched up his face as if to recognize the compliment.

"Oh, he's so sweet, Lee Yee. Can I hold him?"

"Sure," she said.

Thankful that I'd recently had a dry run with Robin's Sophie, I awkwardly lifted Hai from his cot. I could feel the weight of his head, and supported it carefully on my arm. He slept on. I felt elated that he felt such trust in me, in spite of the fact that I wasn't his mother. My rapture was interrupted by the entrance of Lee Yee's mother-in-law who walked up to Lee Yee, handed her a cup, then turned to me and said, "I will take the baby now. He needs to be changed." I vindictively hoped the diaper was poopy.

"What's in the cup?"

"It's an elixir to lighten and soften the skin and keep a youthful appearance. It comes in a box of thirty vials of liquid bird nests, with wild ginseng and rock sugar. The bird's nests are spun from the saliva of a certain kind of swallow."

"Yes," I said. "I saw it in the drugstore in KL. It cost two thousand ringgit for a box. I couldn't believe it! Chen says it sells in the USA for about $34,000. Apparently, western medicine would think of it as a potent tonic. But I still don't understand what makes it so expensive!"

"Mainly it's because it takes one hundred of those special nests to make one kilogram of essence."

"Do you think Tan will make me take that?" I asked.

"No, you won't be as lucky as me. She won't give it to you because she won't be able to afford it. Instead, she will probably buy you vials of chicken essence and a root called cordyceps. It will be the best she can do."

"I wish she wouldn't even do that. It means nothing to me."

Mok's mother came with the baby and put him back in his cot. She said I should go soon. I took the cue. I kissed Hai on the forehead and with a hug to Lee Yee, I was gone.

Chapter 62

"HE DIDN'T *BUY* IT? Why not? I suppose the Feng Shui wasn't right, or some dumb thing!"

"Lauren, you don't know much about Feng Shui. It's very important to many Chinese people. Yes, you're right. The couple who looked at it had a problem with the river."

"The *river?* I thought the river was *good* Feng Shui! I guess you're right. I don't know much about it. I just know that I had an affair with our cottage."

"Calm down, Lauren. It's not the river that's the problem; it's the fact that neither door directly faces the river. The chi comes down the river but doesn't have a direct entry into the house."

"Well, why don't they put up a mirror or a crystal to reflect it? Isn't that supposed to fix all problems?"

Chen whisked himself out of the living room like a brisk breeze. I heard him getting a glass of water and I knew I had done it again. I had over reacted, and he was frustrated. He thought I should accept everything as it was, but that was more than I could do. Faking was not high on my list of attributes. I went to the window and looked out on the garden. Without making a conscious decision, I did the first Tai Chi exercise I had learnt. I bent over slowly, putting my hands together, palms up. Then with controlled evenness, I spread my arms while straightening up until my hands, palms touching, came together above my head as I looked upward toward the ceiling. In that position I imagined that I was drinking in the sun; drinking in all of its warmth and comfort. Feeling calmed and renewed, I went into the kitchen and apologized in a soft voice. "Does your mother practice Feng Shui?"

"Sure she does. You know the ivy wound around the handrail of our spiral staircase?" I nodded and he said, "Energy, or chi, shoots down the staircase, taking energy and fortunes with it. The energy from the ivy slows and counteracts the negative effect of the stairs."

"Really? I thought the ivy was just your mother's idea of a decoration. Actually, to me, it renders the handrail almost useless."

"It may do that, but it's overlooked because of the benefits of feeling your life is being uplifted."

"That's fine until someone falls down and breaks his neck!" I said, seemingly determined to bash Feng Shui. "Are there any other reasons that the family didn't want to buy?"

"They didn't like the slanted ceilings."

"Isn't there an antidote?"

"Yeah. I think they could hang a wind chime from the lowest parts of the ceiling, or place flutes hung vertically under the slant."

"You know, I'm beginning to think they were looking for excuses because they couldn't afford it.

"Maybe you're right—but don't worry your head. It *will* sell."

Chapter 63

A S WE PREDICTED, TAN was over the moon to hear she was going to be a grandmother. Among her first comments were—"At last! First child is very special. It should be a boy. That is what we need for ancestor worship and name carries on. I am sure it will be a boy. You must get very healthy. You will need good foods. You will need cooling foods. Lots of chicken broth. I will take it to your house. I will show you how to make it in case I am too busy. I can show how to make it right now if I had the potion and chicken." The rules went on—hammering nails will cause the baby to be deformed; bad language will cause curse on baby; if a rat is struck the baby will look (and act) like a rat...

Ma was getting me fixed up for the chicken broth lesson. We met at the shop of a Chinese apothecary. Everything looked old and mysterious, including the apothecary himself. Near the entrance there was a counter with some rusty weights for measuring the product and a cash register, both of the same vintage—as well as a lizard in a cage. There were herbs, roots, and other unknowns in every jar on every shelf on every wall. Some of the jars appeared as if they hadn't been opened for years. Ma chatted-up the apothecary in Chinese. They both talked constantly while he pulled a root from a jar and using a small cleaver, sliced it thinly. The result resembled sliced almonds with the texture of wood shavings. Then, from another jar, he produced what could have been from a different part of a tree and using a fork-like tool he shredded it into pieces that could have made a fine bird's nest. He wrapped the two ingredients separately in brown paper, tied them with string and wrote in Chinese on the paper. Ma gave him twenty-seven ringgit and we left. I was having a struggle to be excited about this potion for my health which I would probably be expected to take on a regular basis.

Back in her kitchen, Tan produced a black chicken. By this time I'd had some practice chopping up a chicken, but the fact that its skin was black did nothing for my queasy stomach I should have known; I'd been told on my first trip to the market that the black skinned chickens were the healthiest.

"Now," Ma said, wielding a double-boiler, "water boils in bottom pan. In top pan we put the potion and chicken. Now we put it on stove for one hour and one half."

I must say that there was not much odour while it was steaming. I offered to prepare vegetables for dinner and Tan took me up on it. She did some ironing while I chopped.

When the time was up, Ma threw the potion, and the chicken, black skin, bones and all, into the garbage. The broth from the lower pot was poured into a jug. "Let it cool, Lauren. Then you can drink glassful," Ma said.

Ten minutes later, the moment arrived. How bad could it be? I would down it fast. I gulped about a quarter of a cup. A moment later, most of that quarter of a cup was on the floor and I was spluttering. It was horrendous—as bitter as bile, to quote my grandmama. I rinsed my mouth with water, but the taste would not leave my tongue. Tan cleaned up the floor. Poor Ma had put so much time and energy into making the soup for me.

"I'm so sorry, Ma. I had no idea how bitter it would be."

"That's okay, lah. Take it home and try some again tomorrow. You get use to it. Think how strong it makes you."

That night when Chen got home from work I poured out my story. "It was awful, Chen. Bad from the start. I felt like an alien at the shop. Your mother acted as if I weren't there. Everything was so foreign to me. I put my faith in the two of them and tried to remember that the Chinese had benefitted from these mixtures for thousands of years, and I would, too. *You* taste it."

I poured a glass of the broth for him and he drank just enough to test. "Yes, it's pretty bad," he said. "It tastes like really strong green tea with a hint of ginseng... and a bit of lye," he chuckled.

"Well, I'm going to throw it down the sink!"

"That should be good for cleansing the pipes," Chen said.

I appreciated his sense of humour and his support, and didn't miss the fact that he had put effort into walking the line between the Chinese culture and my own.

Chapter 64

M Y HOUSE WAS NOT mine. Of course it *was* mine; but my soul-mate, Shanthi, followed me every step I took. Often it was comforting to feel her near me. Other times I needed privacy. I wanted to put my mark on my new home. Chen could not understand my plight at all. He insisted with a firm jaw that we had no money for anything we could do without. I hoped he would loosen up his pockets somewhat when we sold our little house by the river.

Nisha had taken so little. Perhaps her house was over-flowing with her own things. I didn't feel I could throw anything out. What if Shanthi wanted something she treasured and I had pitched it out? I grabbed a large plastic bag and went from cupboard to cupboard, filling it with things most of us would agree were garbage—old slippers, postcards, ash trays, note pads, partly used candles, recipe cards, magazines, empty boxes and jars. After that, I felt ready for a bolder move. I chose one bedroom and consolidated the furniture in one corner. Then, with great resolve, I removed seven of Shanthi's pictures from the living room walls and stacked them in the newly appointed storage room. Aha!

This felt good! One by one I carried in my own paintings and found homes for four of the largest ones. The statues were not that easy. I knew Shanthi had revered them. Staunchly, I demoted them to the store room and laid them on the bed. There was one exception—the statue of Ganesh, the elephant head god. After all, he was the god who destroyed obstacles. We needed him around. He would sit on a rubber wood table and bring us good luck. I'd give Ganesh the benefit of the doubt. Now I would plug in the kettle and pick some flowers while the tea brewed. I was stoked.

A few minutes later, I sat under the living room fan sipping Jasmine green tea; basking in a mixture of pride, delight and comfort. This house had possibilities and I had ideas. All that was lacking was money.

Tan had laid-off with the chicken soup. I assured her I was making it and eating well. Today she phoned to say that for the first three months you could change the sex of your child. "This is what you do," she advised. "If you think you are going to have a girl, you can get it changed to a boy. Go to the temple and buy a white chrysanthemum if you want a boy. If someone happen to want a girl, they buy pink," she said, as if that were extremely unlikely. Then you have to pray, often. Maybe you want to do that. Just to be sure."

I struggled not to laugh. "No, Ma. I'm not looking for any changes. Either a boy or a girl will be perfect."

Chapter 65

A T SEVEN MONTHS OF pregnancy, I was fed up. Thirty pounds had found their way to my belly. I couldn't imagine how my baby-nest could stretch any further, though no doubt it would. Pregnant Chinese women seem to develop a tidy bump the size of a soccer ball; mine looked like a prize pumpkin at the fall fair. Since my arrival in Taman Damai, I had felt the subject of gawkers. Unfortunately, lately it had only increased. Nor did I want, ever again, to hear Tan talking about her grandSON. I was fed up with her monitoring my food. As for the soups and bird nests, she could stuff them! Worst of all, Chen still worked twelve hour days and often took emergency calls after that. I suffered from emotional weariness. The distress had grown in sync with by body, until my rubber bands were waiting to break.

I moped around, dredging up disappointments. Chen and I hadn't been out of Taman Damai since the weekend we spent in Kuala Lumpur. I wished I could go away for a break. *Why not? I'm going to do it! I don't have to stay in this little town, alone twelve hours a day! After all, fish gotta swim, birds gotta fly!*

My favourite resort was Awana Kijal—our honeymoon site,

and where Mom, Dad and I had stopped briefly on our way to Redang Island. At the most, it would be a five hour drive. Memories of the beach, pools, great food, foot massages and sun umbrellas flashed back to me. I would run it by Chen when he got home from work.

In the meantime, I would busy myself fabricating a bathing suit to accommodate me and my foetus. For me to buy an ordinary bathing suit in Taman Damai, was impossible; so I certainly wouldn't find one for a mother-to-be! The best I could hope for was to find some appropriate fabric. In my enthusiasm I walked too fast, arriving in town wet and red-faced. I searched through miles of silk, faux silks, and chiffons; not knowing what I wanted, but certain what I did *not* want. Inspiration was slow coming, but eventually I found some aquamarine crinkle cotton with small magenta and fuchsia daisies. I bought twice as much as I needed. From the experience with my wedding dress, I remembered that Malaysians don't sew with patterns. I would be flying on my own.

I waddled home at a more reasonable pace, all the time wondering just how to approach my new project. I didn't want to look like a torte in the midst of a batch of cupcakes.

With the fabric rolled out on the hall floor I pondered over a bikini, one-piece, or something never seen before. I remembered the elderly woman I saw on our honeymoon. With her shrivelled, draping skin, she looked totally at ease with her body in a two piece bathing suit. Would I be that confident?

Chen was late getting home. He dropped his briefcase and loosened his tie. My pent-up excitement burst like a balloon touching a firecracker.

"I'd like to go to Awana Kijal for a few days," I blurted.

"Why do you want to do that?" he asked.

His eyebrows were arched nearly up to his hairline and his body was poised in the shape of a question mark.

"I need to have a break, Chen."

"A break? A break from what?" He stood towering above me,

mystified. "I can't possibly take you to Awana Kijal. You know that."

"C'mon, Chen! I don't need to be taken. I'll drive myself."

"You're seven months pregnant! You can't drive yourself. I can't let you do that."

"You sound too much like your father. I am asking for your blessing to go, not your permission."

Chen knew the signal. He gave a defeated smile. We hugged briefly, and sat down to eat our rice, curried chicken and salad, followed by a cup of green tea in the living room. He seemed quiet and preoccupied. Then, out of the silence I heard, "What about if Ma goes with you? It would be a good break for her."

I felt selfish and unkind, but said firmly, "No, Chen. I need to go alone."

He looked more disappointed than surprised. "Couldn't you go somewhere closer to home?"

"Not really. Awana Kijal is sinfully beautiful. It's so easy to relax and dream. I'd only go for three days…"

"There's a certain degree of risk, you know. I don't feel good about it at all."

"Just what do you think could happen?"

"Anything from too much sun to premature labour."

"I'm perfectly healthy, Chen. Nothing will happen."

My oh-so-sensible husband picked up the newspaper. We sat there in silence—a silence long enough to read the paper from cover to cover six times. He had not turned a page. My impatience grew. It was almost ready to spew when Chen said, "I remember when we were there on our honeymoon, how happy you were and how refreshed you felt when we got home. If you think you can handle the drive, I guess you could go. I'll miss you a lot, you know."

"I'll miss you too, Chen, but this is something I really want to do."

Two days later, after promising Chen repeatedly that I would drive carefully, I thrust my small bag in the boot and left Taman Damai behind. The sun shone and the air was clear. I felt light as a pavlova—a feeling that was real, though not familiar to me lately. Excitement would keep me alert.

Morning traffic was heavy around the towns. People who could afford a car had one; the rest drove motorcycles skilfully in and out amongst the speeding vehicles. Usually the father donned a helmet but it disturbed me to see the mother sitting behind him, her only protection being her filmy tudung flying behind. Worst of all, the young children rode between the parents, bare-headed and clinging to each other. They seemed oblivious to the dangers. This would be against the law, in Canada. I wondered if people in this part of the world put less value on life. Surely not; perhaps it was a safety issue that hadn't been promoted, or wasn't affordable. On the positive side, I admired the fact that the whole family looked like an advertisement for Tide Ultra, in spite of the black exhaust issuing forth from the buses and other vehicles. Some men wore white shirts backward on top of their shirts, seemingly to prevent soiling their work clothes. I wondered how clothes that had been dried on lines hanging from small verandas in the polluted air, could look so bright.

Reaching the coast, I stopped at the Hyatt Resort for a glass of iced tea and a good stretch. The facilities were first rate. Maybe Chen had a point when he said I didn't need to go so far away. Oh well, I still felt my decision was right.

Heading north the traffic thinned. I drove through farm country, close to the sea but most often, not actually seeing it. Leaving one of the villages, I saw what looked like a flattened pipe curved along near the edge of the road—about eight or nine feet long. I privately chastised whoever had left it there, before realizing it was a snake! Even though it appeared to be very dead, I involuntarily shivered. I stopped the car on the side of the road. Although it initially repulsed me, I could not pass an opportunity to have a closer look. I watched for a few minutes to make sure the dead snake didn't plan to reactivate. Then quietly, with a feeling of privilege, I walked across the street. Most of the snake had been accidently flattened by cars or drivers perhaps wanting to drive over it, just to be sure it didn't squirm away. I estimated its circumference at eight inches. The skin reminded me of needlework done on fine linen—ecru with chocolate brown diamonds outlined with white dots. That there are many snakes of that ilk skulking around Malaysia, I couldn't believe. Then gazing around, I saw an Indian temple. *Aha! I bet the snake escaped from that temple! Yes, of course! The sacred snake. The Indians have worshipped snakes for eons. The loss of this amazing cold-blooded creature was probably very significant to the worshippers—a cultural icon.* I strode back to the car, thinking about the snake and our amazing world.

North of Chukai, I stopped at a hawker stall, and bought a paper plate of nasi lemack. Using chop sticks, I ate the rice and vegetables and followed it with a good slug from my water bottle. I felt refreshed by the stop, as much as the food.

Mid-afternoon found me sprawled flat out on a plump, blue and white striped mattress, gazing at the matching umbrella above me. I had to admit, though only to myself, that I arrived at the resort with a stiff and weary body. I briefly considered a nap, but couldn't wait to get to the beach. I could feel the tightness in my back and shoulders melting in the warmth. Everything was just as I remembered it; the air soft, and the breeze gentle. I cradled my unborn child with my hands. How I loved her. Sometimes I called my lump *he,* and other times *she;* the only certainty being that I dearly loved whichever it was. I took a book from my beach bag, and started to read. Soon the book felt heavy. I placed it, closed, on the sand, and lay peacefully listening to the waves lapping on the shore. I sensed, rather than heard, a vendor. I lifted my heavy head, and ordered some mango juice. He returned to find me asleep.

When I awoke, the ice had melted in my drink and the tab lay beside it. With all the energy I could muster, I propped up the back of my chair and drank my de-iced juice. I listened to the risen pitch of the children at the pool, tired after a day of excitement.

My custom-made bathing suit seemed to be quite okay—certainly decent. I decided to give it the acid test in the sea. I walked slowly to the water, savouring the feeling of the fine sand massaging the soles of my feet and filtering between my toes. The sand firmed as I reached the edge. Walking into the warm water, I remembered how cold the ocean and lake waters were in Canada. Everyone shivered and groused about the temperature, but there was always some brave soul who would dive in and encourage the rest with remarks about how refreshing it was or how nice after you get in. The bravest of all—to the point of insanity, was the group of revellers who entered the Polar Bear Swim on New Year's Day at English Bay in Vancouver. Most Canadians don't know about swimming in warm water. Feeling very fortunate, I walked in, and dove into a respectably-sized wave.

Chapter 66

SOMEONE FROM ROOM SERVICE knocked on the door, delivering my simple meal of a BLT sandwich, fruit salad, and a glass of skim milk, on a large tray spread with white linen. I signed the bill and asked that the tray be taken to the little porch. I had decided to eat by myself; an anti-social move to be sure, but I was wrapped up in self-indulgence.

I read my parenting magazine as I munched on my three tiered sandwich. Even with the short nap I had at the beach, the calming repetition of the waves made me feel sleepy again. I put the tray outside the door so I wouldn't be disturbed and lay on my bed, appreciating that even in my room I could still feel the comfort of the breeze and smell the sea air. With the fat pillows arranged for maximum comfort, I drifted off to sleep.

The phone rang at nine-thirty. I didn't feel ready to wake up, but I knew it was Chen, so I rolled over and stretched for the phone. He was still at work, but wanted info about my trip. I excitedly told him how marvellous I found everything and how happy I felt returning to this place of wonder. He seemed astonished that I found the snake so fascinating, and was relieved to hear I had not touched it. I didn't bother to tell him how stiff and uncomfortable I felt when I arrived. I asked if he'd had a good day and predictably, he said, "Busy and long." *And still at it.* We wished each other a sound sleep and farewell.

After the short chat with Chen, I went out on the porch. Small lights glittered in the darkness along the paths, and various spot lights focussed on the beach. Clusters of guests congregated outside the dining-room. Music from the lounge vibrated over the whole scene. I wanted to go to the beach and watch the waves. I could hear a voice: Chen's voice, saying, *don't go down there in the dark!* But this adventure was not about what Chen wanted.

Carrying a shawl and a few peppermints, I opened my door and stood over-looking the beamed roof and railings around the walks surrounding each of the seven floors below. Lofty! Lovely! I got off the elevator on the lowest floor and walked out on the beach. I sat in a chaise, taking in the beauty. The vista was even more appealing from here, than it had been from my porch, much more surrounding. I had an urge to be even closer to the sand. After spreading a big towel on the beach, I knelt, pivoted around, and plunked my tonnage on the towel. Lying on my back, I rolled my second towel and stuffed it under my head and neck. Wiggling around, I forced the sand to accommodate my shape. Not even a therma-plasma mattress could feel better. Stars peppered the clear, dark sky. Most familiar to me were the Big and Little Dippers and the northern star. Try as I did, I couldn't see anything I recognized. Finally I remembered how close to the equator I now lived. I peered at the sky above—the Southern Hemisphere, I supposed. In that case I should see the Southern Cross. I recalled my dad telling me it looked like a kite. I *did* see it, much to my delight. How far away were the stars, I wondered. Thousands, no, millions of miles. Still, they shone brightly enough for me to see them. Leaning on my elbow, I gazed at the point where dark water seemed to meet the dark sky. I lay at the edge of the

South China Sea. Beyond that it would fade seamlessly into the Pacific Ocean. At this minute, my parents were likely having breakfast; sitting opposite each other in the kitchen nook, sharing the *Vancouver Sun*. Mom, wrapped in her soft green bathrobe and woolly slippers would be sitting at the table, across from Dad, doing the crossword puzzle, while he scanned the headlines, before donning a warmly lined raincoat and leaving for work.

Lying on the sand, bit by bit, the vastness and beauty of the universe overwhelmed me. My mind, (or was it my soul?) felt expanded. Thousands of miles of water faced me. Miles of atmosphere surrounded me, fading into light years of unfathomable space. Uncountable grains of sand formed the beautiful beach beneath me. I felt insignificant. What am I? I am an incredibly engineered structure of bone, muscle, blood, and guts—much like the six billion other humans on the earth—and yet unique. I'm a twenty-four year old Caucasian female: reasonably attractive, and reasonably intelligent. But so what? Who cares? Of what *importance* am I? I mulled that question around, and concluded that I am important to myself, to my husband, and certainly to the mass of cells magically developing into a child inside my body. By good fortune I am part of a network of family and friends. But what am I to the universe? In spite of my heavy, swollen body, I am merely a speck in the scheme of things: a speck in the universe; dependent on the universe. Part of it. Yes, part of the family of the universe. Surely, though my whole life is a mere flicker in time, I have a significant role to play, and some commitments to make.

Awe, had a new meaning to me. I didn't want to move, for fear of breaking the contact. I felt wide-eyed and alert. A tingling sensation traveled up and down my arms and the back of my neck.

I wondered at the mystical power that drives our spectacular world, and, indeed, the universe. I thought of the human race, and the uniqueness of nationalities, languages, cultures, beliefs, freedoms, appearance, health, education, opportunities... all part of the universe. Humanity, some living in peace, and some living in war and strife… all part of the universe. I recognized the richness of my circumstances. Why should that be so? Why should I be "me" when the odds against it were so unimaginably high? Why was I born to a loving family in a free country, when I might have been born to poverty and oppression? Surely, winning the lottery on so many accounts puts a great onus on me to contribute to the world. With this thought, I became weary. The tide was coming in. Actually, I could feel the water nibbling at my toes. Squinting at my watch in the moonlight, I realized it was after midnight. Still, I felt warm and comfortable. I had no desire to leave. The music from the lounge was quieter now. A few couples strolled along the water's edge carrying their sandals. A security guard stopped to ask me if I was all right. I assured him that I was just enjoying the beach. He told me to go closer to the hotel and walked away shaking his head. I wondered if he ever looks at the sky and thinks of the universe in awe. I fought an urge to stop the people walking on the sand and ask them if they are ever overcome by the wonder and vastness of our earth, or marvel at the beach they are walking on. Do they recognize that they are a part of this sensational universe? Have they ever stopped and got out of their car to marvel at the beauty of a snake's skin?

The night was timeless for me. As I came out of my reverie, I thought of Chen and hoped he had not phoned for an extra "good-night." He would be frantic if I didn't answer the phone. He cares deeply for me. I am certain of that. I rolled over, and balancing on my knees, pushed myself up, shook the sand out of my towels, and strolled slowly to my room. I felt rubbery. I looked in the mirror, as if checking to be sure I hadn't physically changed. I skipped the teeth brushing and flossing, and flopped into bed.

I awoke to hear children already playing in the pools, and the smell of coffee and bacon wafting from the dining room. I was in no hurry to move. The repercussions from my sojourn on the beach into the wonder of humanity and the universe were very much alive. Simply, I had experienced a new awareness. Why did it happen? Why at that moment? Was I driven to come to Awana for this reason? Were the thoughts lurking in my subconscious mind while I was still in Taman Damai... or earlier? Did the feelings of awe somehow trigger what was already there —dormant, but waiting for the right moment?

What should I do next? Where do I go from here? With that thought, a favourite song, "Changes", written and sung by Vancouver artist Rachel Landrecht, drifted into my consciousness—*I feel a change coming on today, coming on the wind; where do we go from here. I feel a change coming on today, coming on the wind, let us now begin...* I felt both overwhelmed, and strangely comforted. I have a role. But, what is my role, my contribution? Would this be revealed in a *package* as my new awareness had—or would I have to slug it out? My foetus bunched up and kicked, as if to say, *Let's go for breakfast!*

The outside dining room was buzzing. I found a table for two (*almost* appropriate), with a view of the sea. Birds were having a picnic; some under tables and a few nibbling crumbs on top of vacated tables. I made three trips to the buffet table, each time coming back with a food not readily available to me in Taman Damai—orange juice, whole-wheat buns, ham, salmon and croissants. I enjoyed every morsel, and further treated myself to half a cup of coffee.

Back in my room, I felt duty-bound to exercise. I was in good physical shape when I became pregnant, and was anxious not to lose more of that than necessary. When I was in Vancouver last spring, Robin gave me information on exercises for mothers-to-be. Exercise was encouraged largely because a stronger body helps the mother to retain strength and hopefully have an easier labour. I could buy into that! Being in the third trimester, I had modified some exercises and eliminated others. After ten minutes of a mild work-out and breathing exercises, I lathered on sun screen and went for a stroll on the beach. The sand stretched as far as I could see in both directions. Amazing as that was, the fact that there were so few people continued to astonish me. I was one of probably a dozen strollers and there were scatterings of children playing in the sand. I sat on a rock, caked with small white shells, and watched the waves roar in with vigour, then lazily retreat. The sand was warm on my feet and I could feel the occasional light spray of salt water on my skin. I felt pampered and happy—but not calm. My mind churned. I thought of Chen. I wanted to talk to him; to *really* talk to him. In fact, I wondered if I should hit the road that afternoon. I would stay until check-out at three, and be home in the early evening. Yes, that's what I would do.

Chen was still at work when I pulled into the driveway. I phoned to alert him that I was home and assure him I was okay. He said he would come home as soon as possible. After showering and washing my hair to remove the salty, sandy film from my day at the beach, I put on a vermillion sarong. I felt clean and invigorated.

"Did you have a good time?" my sweetie asked.

"I had a sensational time!"

"Why did you come home a day early? Was it not what you expected?"

"No. Better! I feel totally renewed. I wanted to tell you about my experience. I wanted to be with you, talk with you, share with you—tonight, not tomorrow."

Chen looked puzzled. "You were so excited about going. I can't imagine what was important enough for you to come home early. Tell me what happened."

Sitting on the sofa with cushions at my back and my feet in Chen's lap, I hoped I could find the right words to explain the effect of the beauty, brilliance, and vastness of the night, and how it had grabbed onto me, filling my eyes and mind with awe and wonder. How questions led to more questions—until I thought I would burst.

I need not have wondered if I would find the right words—it

was all so recent and poignant that the words tumbled out. Chen seemed serious and struggling to keep up. Perhaps I should make myself slow down.

"Do you understand what I'm saying, Chen? Have you ever felt completely in awe of something?"

There was a pause. I thought I might be talking about things out of his realm. Then he said, "Yes. I have. When I was a medical student, I can truthfully say I was in awe of the human body. The more I learned, the more awed I became. I still feel that way at times. I hope that will never change. I still wonder at the complexity of the physical and mental and spiritual human being and how it can heal itself."

"Give yourself some credit, Dr. Wong"

"Yes, I can take some credit, but, really, I just help the body to heal itself. No matter how sophisticated medical machines and procedures become, the body will always be healing itself. That is the wonder for me. No matter how big or wonderful a thing I do for a patient, I always feel humbled by what the body can do for itself."

I felt my eyes sting and dampen. I had never loved him so much. "You *do* understand," I choked. He lifted my feet from his lap, and put his arms around me. "You're the one that knew how to express our feelings."

"Ha! You didn't do so badly, yourself!"

Chapter 67

Hi Mom and Dad!

I am just back from Awana Kijal where I spent a couple of days pondering how lucky (and thankful!) I am to have been born into this world. This all leads to more pondering about my purpose in life—how I can pay back. I'm very consumed with this challenge. So far I can't see it.

Love to you both,

Lauren

Half an hour later I had this reply:

My dear Lauren!

We are so proud of you. Each of us should search for ways to make the world a better place. But don't try to conquer the world. Your answers may not be far away. Search around you.

Love,

Dad

I read my dad's message carefully, three times. I knew Dad was right. My thoughts had been cosmic. There's nothing wrong with that, but my efforts must start in my locale. "Bloom where you are planted" darted into my mind; a common adage, but how wise and how apt for me right now. What could I change for the better? Today.

I thought of Tan. She had been my main challenge, even before I came to Malaysia. I strove to have a good relationship with her. She was the maypole of the family and I felt it was essential that I be one of the dancers around the pole. Had I been fair to her? Maybe fair, but certainly not tolerant. I had marked her narrow, snippy, critical, and obsessed with tradition, superstitions and taboos. She had introduced me to many delights and experiences and often I had reacted with doubt, disbelief, discourteous retorts and, usually, frustration. The worst times were when she critically analysed my grandmother's funeral and scoffed at the treasured armoire wedding gift from that same grandmother, the disinterest and disrespect for my art and the I-told-you-so-what-did-you-expect attitude when my dream to have an art school fizzled. Of course the night she called me a kwai loh was the worst. Things like telling me what to eat and do during my pregnancy, and the expectation of gifts yet never acknowledging them, although secondary, battered me as well. Was the hurt intentional? Did Tan really want to hurt me? Tan, who within minutes of my arrival, took my hand gently in hers, looked into my eyes and said, "You are welcome, Lauren." Tan, who bought me a ball of jasmine flowers to make my bedroom smell nice. Tan, who came quickly when I needed her. I could not believe she ever wanted to hurt me.

The more I thought about Tan's actions, the more I realized she was operating from what she knew—what her culture, developed by Chinese people for thousands of years, had taught and reinforced for her. I resolved to keep that in mind. At least I would not *blame* her. I was conscious of a new acceptance of Tan, my ma.

I felt a sense of growth… and accomplishment. I thought of Shanthi, the first time I met her, saying, "Buddhists call frangipani the emblem of immortality, because even after they are uprooted, they show signs of growth and new blooms." What a charming, strong visual that produced for me. That piece of lore paralleled my life. For the first time in weeks, I had a powerful urge to paint.

Chapter 68

THE CALENDAR INDICATED NOVEMBER; the thermometer, indicated the usual thirty-two degrees Celsius. I was hot. By nine a.m. I lumbered into the house and slowly climbed the stairs. I shed my clothes and plopped down on the bed. My bare belly was round and warm as rising dough. Wistfully I watched the fan above me, willing it to blow me a breeze from the Arctic.

I thought of my mother taking her daily walk in the woods at the end of our street in Vancouver. She would be strutting along, wearing wool slacks and a warm jacket against the frosty air. In preparation for winter, the trees would have shed most of last year's yellowed leaves. She would be walking briskly through them making a crackling noise, her cheeks rosy and her nose drippy. Then I imagined her home from her walk, plugging in the tea kettle and reaching for an Earl Grey tea bag. The air was heavy with the aroma of apple pies laced with cinnamon and nutmeg. Maybe I should make an apple pie. No, not a good idea. No apples. Don't know how to make pastry. The oven would make the house even hotter. *Can not, lah,* I sighed. Then Malaysian reality entered the scene, and I imagined my Tuscan yellow bowl, filled with jambu madu, rambutans, pineapples, melons, mangosteens and star fruit; all treats in their own right.

Surely my baby would be born soon...

That night I still felt blah. I lay on the couch with pillows under my head and knees, and one arm draped protectively across the taut drum of my belly. My feet were in my sweetie's lap.

"Would you like to do me a favour, Chen?"

"Definitely! I'd like to do you half a dozen favours. What would you like?"

"I'd like you to put nail polish on my toe nails."

"*What*? I've never done that before. You'll have to tell me what to do. By the way, one thing I won't do, is clip your nails, because you might be visited by a ghost."

"Good grief! You can start by getting my pink cosmetic case. It's in the top drawer of my dresser."

Obviously, he was naive about pedicures. Naughtily, I made the process as demanding as I could—removal of old polish, foot soak, cuticle treatment, under coat, and finally, two coats of *Pink Peony*.

I certainly couldn't find fault with the finished product. His surgeon's nimble fingers had produced a perfect job.

"Well done, sweetie. If you ever need a second career, you could give pedicures at Ma's Hair Saloon." He scrunched up his nose before giving me a wide smile.

"Now, your mother is telling me what to do *after* the baby is born. She seems to think that it's her duty to tell me because I won't have a *confinement lady*. The funniest stipulation is not to go out, or have visitors for a month in case they might bring bad luck with them. Of course she goes on about foods—more broth, red dates, fresh ginger...."

Chapter 69

MARIE WONG MEI LI was born on December twenty-first at 8:02 a.m. She weighed eight pounds, six ounces, and she screamed with every bit of it as she breathed her first air. When she lay sprawled against my belly, I was overcome with the love I felt for her. Tears of joy flowed across my cheeks and into my ears. Chen had not delivered her, but he had cut and tied the cord and was grinning proudly. "She's beautiful, Lauren. Her hair's curly, like yours."

"And she's got skin like yours and your dark eyes. She's a beauty! I want to phone Mom and Dad, Chen. I want them to be the first to know."

"They'll be the first to know, but try to hang on for five minutes, if you can," he laughed. I'll email Shanthi when I get home.

Ma would be disappointed that we had a girl. Just a month ago, I was so fed-up with her for constantly hoping for a boy that I secretly hoped we'd have a girl— just to make Tan upset. But today, I felt self-reproachful and ashamed of those feelings. Surely Tan will love

Marie Wong Mei Li with the rest of us. We will rejoice in our lovely daughter together.

When I'd been home from the hospital for a week, my body was large and slack. I still looked pregnant in a baggy, softened way. The chaos of adjusting to a wee person who demanded feeding every two hours and diminished our sleep to the equivalent of a few naps, was inching its way toward normalcy. Chen was deemed to need more sleep than I, since he had to be at the clinic at seven a.m. whereas I could nap during the day. Ha!

One day, I was excited because little Marie Wong Mei Li had missed a feeding completely and slept contentedly through four hours. I felt my boobs filling to the point of feeling uncomfortable. Incredibly quickly I was in pain. Marie was awake and howling. My breasts were huge and hard (*engorged*, I later learned). Marie could not latch on—nor could I stand the thought of her doing so. I phoned Chen. As usual, Padma said he was with a patient. I felt deserted and desperate. Marie continued to wail. I couldn't help her—or even comfort her. Tears ran down my cheeks, too. In utter desperation, I phoned Tan.

"You need cabbage leaves," she pronounced when she heard my predicament. "I'll come fast. You put ice on." She hung up.

I felt almost as desperate as before. *Cabbage leaves*? What could cabbage leaves possibly do? It would be just another of Tan's snake medicine ideas—like coriander seeds for a belly ache and cumin for wounds. I felt like calling Chen again. Surely, I was more important than his damned patient!

Tan arrived quickly, just as she had promised. Ordinarily, I could never have exposed my boobs to my mother-in-law. In fact, I remembered the day when I first arrived in Malaysia, and was even self- conscious to have Tan wash my *hair*. Today, I easily tossed propriety to the gods. I tore open my shirt, and wailed, "Look at this!" Quickly, Tan separated the hard, crisp, cool, cabbage leaves and cupped them around my swollen boobs. Almost instantly I could feel heat leaving my breasts. Soon the leaves that had been so firm, crisp and cool, became warm and limp. All of a sudden the pain subsided. It was a miracle! Whether the idea of cabbage leaves came from the east or the west was not of any significance. It worked! Marie had her lunch and Tan put the kettle on for Lapsang Souchong tea.

Chapter 70

MY PARENTS' JOY AND delight at their granddaughter's arrival was apparent. We plied them with photos on-line and they phoned at least once a day. Although I looked forward to the phone ringing, at the end of the conversations I always felt so sad—sad because they were so far away, sad because they couldn't cradle their grandchild and watch her develop, and sad because they were alone. However, a whirlwind, in the form of an email, was going to deliver overwhelming excitement.

> Dear Lauren and Chen,
>   You'll never guess the topic of the conversation Dad and I had this morning!!
>   I was whining about missing you—told him I miss you more every day—said I wanted to hold baby Marie—said I wish we lived nearer to you and Chen He said indignantly, that I wasn't the only one who wanted to live closer to you. We gawked at each other wondering what was holding us back.

Of course, I said he was the guilty one because he had to work. After a few moments, Dad's answer was, "What about if I *retire*? Or maybe I could work summers in Vancouver, and we could spend the winters in sunny Malaysia!"

I couldn't believe what I was hearing. By the time it sunk in, I had tears of joy running down my cheeks. Dad donned his raincoat and stood tall, looking proud of his brilliance. Isn't that a wonderful idea? We'll both have a lot to think about today!

We'll talk about it further after work tonight, and call you.

Lots of love,

Mom

Stunned, I stared at the computer. How could this be happening? I read the unbelievable news again. Sure, it could be possible! Why not? My mind spun with possibilities—all of them good. Marie Wong Mei Li was howling. I let her exercise her lungs while I phoned Chen. Predictably, he couldn't come to the phone, but I left him a message asking him to come home for lunch. I had to share this news with someone, or I would burst. I ran into Marie's room and picked her up. Her tears stopped. I said, "Grandma and Grandpa are coming to see you." I could swear she smiled.

At 2:48, Chen came in the door. I might have given him the cold shoulder for being so late, but not that day! I spit out the news. Chen was silent.

Finally he said, "I'm flabbergasted. Why would they *do* that? Did they just decide on a whim?"

"Listen, Chen. They're alone. Their family is here. They're

grandparents. They want the joy of watching Marie Wong Mei Li grow up. Surely you can understand that?"

"Yes, I guess so. But… can they stand the heat? And all the other things about Taman Damai that have been such a trial for you?"

"Don't forget that they spent two weeks with us and thoroughly loved it. I think being near us will override any problems."

"Will they *live* with us?"

Now I started seeing the news from Chen's point of view. He'd watched me struggle to live with his family, and we had both been relieved to move out and have our own place and privacy. No wonder he questioned whether or not they would live with us!

"I don't know where they'd live. Obviously, there's room for them here, but they might have something else in mind. They're phoning tonight, so we'll know more then." My bubbles were still rising; Chen was still quiet. Since he wasn't going to talk, nor go back to work, I had to guess what spun in his brain. Then I used *my* brain, and realized that, of course, Chen was wondering how *his* family would fare. His role was to do his best for his parents, and as his wife, mine was to comply. Ma and Pa were our parents and certainly wouldn't want interference from my family. Their red-headed daughter-in-law had challenged them plenty already.

"Chen, I think it would work. If my parents had come to live here soon after I did, it would have been a disaster. I would have clung to them. It could well have destroyed our marriage."

"Maybe it still will."

For a minute I froze. Obviously, Chen did not think my dream-come-true would work. Shaking but determined, I said, "No, Chen. I've grown up a lot since I've been here—especially in the last few months. You *know* that. I have more respect, understanding and love, not only for your mother and your whole family, but for Malaysian life as well."

Chen's face softened. "Have you ever wondered what the words in the name of our town—*Taman Damai,* mean?"

"No, I can't say that I have. Tell me."

"*Taman* means forest and *Damai* means peaceful, calm, and bringing about good understanding."

He stood up and gave me a long, velcro hug. He wiped his eyes with the back of his hand, and said, "Now, my love, I must go back to work."

Chapter 71

THE AWAITED CALL FROM my parents came before Chen was home from the office. I talked with Dad. He wanted to know if I thought there was any merit in them spending half the year in Malaysia. I told him there was a *lot* of merit in it and he couldn't renege now. Dad chuckled. Then he said, Mom thinks you still have the cottage, and if you do, could we buy it?

"*Buy* it? Are you sure you *want* it?"

"Yes, we're sure. We know you're fond of it and figured you'd like keeping it in the family, so to speak. What's Chen thinking of us dumping all this on him?"

"Well, he was stunned that you wanted to come, and he'll be even more stunned—but pleased, that you want to buy the cottage."

"Good. There'll be the odd little bit of planning to do, like what to do with my practice," he admitted, "but I'll get right on to it. We'll be in touch soon. You know, your mother and I think that subconsciously we both longed for this—the idea just hadn't made its way upstairs. Your mother and I are at the age when a reality check is in order. That's what we've had, and it feels good."

"It feels good all around. I'm thrilled!"

"And Chen's okay with it?"

"As I said, he's shocked. But he hasn't had much time to digest the idea. I think it will be great for all of us, Chen included."

I talked to Mom. Neither of us thought we'd be able to sleep. She asked me to give baby Marie an extra hug from her, and we promised to keep in close touch as plans evolved.

After I hung up the phone, I tip-toed into Marie's room. I watched her squirming and stretching, marvelling at every move she made. "Come, dear little one," I said, picking her up for no specific reason except that I wanted her close to me. "You are well loved."

I topped up the news when Chen came home about eight thirty.

"I'm surprised they want to live in the cottage—but won't it be a relief to be rid of it?" I nodded in agreement.

"Do you think they'd be happy there?"

"I'm sure of it! Mom will fix it up with originality and good taste... and she won't be worrying about the chi coming down the river and not being able to get in the house because the doors are in the wrong place!"

Chen ignored my jibe. "When do you think they will come?"

"There'll be lots of arrangements for Dad to sort out. I suppose it's realistic to plan for next fall. But you know, they should come soon—to see little Marie. That would make Mom feel better, and give us wonderful planning opportunities. They may even be able to have some work done on the house before they come to stay. Hey, lah, have you had anything to eat?" Chen shook his head. "I'll make some tea and chase up some grub."

Fifteen minutes later we were sitting in the garden, with some re-heated curried chicken, boc choy and fresh mango. The lights were soft and the air fragrant, but I can't say that we were relaxed. We had known about this big change in our lives for only matter of hours. Possibilities crept around in our minds until mine spilled out— "Mom will be a willing babysitter for Marie… maybe I can finally get my act together and take my paintings to Kuala Lumpur… maybe your dad will invest in Pa's oil palm dream. Wouldn't *that* be astonishing! I think our dads could have a great time renovating the cottage. If they don't want to do it themselves, Pa is always going to *know a man*. My dad might even have a role in your office. Maybe you could work more reasonable hours—that's going to be even more important now that we have Marie. "

"Okay, Lauren. That's fine. But what about Ma? As usual, it's Ma who has the most to lose. She's the one who'll expect to babysit. She'll feel your mother is taking over."

I was realistic enough to know that wonderful as my epiphany had been, in the future my resolve may wane and need rekindling. But not today. Bravely I said, "That's nonsense, Chen. There'll be plenty of opportunities for both of them. They can share. Maybe Ma can teach my mom how to cook Chinese food…or play Mahjong. There are so many possibilities! I feel our life is opening up."

"I see your point, but I still think Ma will feel that you spend all your time with your mother."

"Hey, Chen, that might have happened a few months ago, but I won't let it happen again. I'm in a different level of consciousness with your mother. You know that. I'll have one arm around each of them… my *mom* and my *ma*. And Chen, the next time I need a tune-up, just remind me we've already navigated from feuds to floods… and we're just beginning."

Acknowledgements

Great appreciation goes to my Malaysian friends, especially Jackie Ong, Lau Mei Chin, Wong Siew Choo, Ken Chong and Mun Meng Moy who were so kind and generous in sharing their culture with me.

Sincere thanks to my dear friends Elaine James, Katie Elliott and Alexandra Amor—all skilled and devoted readers and writers, who combed my manuscript as if it were a pleasure, providing me with help and cheer.

Appreciation goes to my accommodating editor, Patsy Alford.

Thanks to my marvellous children, Heather, Bruce, Megan and Sharon, for their on-going enthusiasm and tireless support.

Special thanks to Sharon Clarke Haugli who did the painting for the cover of the book and Megan Ollinger who did the Author's Photo.

Last, but first, thanks to my husband, Bill, the love of my life, and the champion of all my endeavours.